Triump[...]
Shipyard Girls

Nancy Revell is the author of the Shipyard Girls series, which is set in the north-east of England during World War Two.

She is a former journalist who worked for all the national newspapers, providing them with hard-hitting news stories and in-depth features. Nancy also wrote amazing and inspirational true life stories for just about every woman's magazine in the country.

When she first started writing the Shipyard Girls series, Nancy relocated back to her hometown of Sunderland, Tyne and Wear, along with her husband, Paul, and their English bull mastiff, Rosie. They now live just a short walk away from the beautiful award-winning beaches of Roker and Seaburn, within a mile of where the books are set.

The subject is particularly close to Nancy's heart as she comes from a long line of shipbuilders, who were well known in the area.

Why YOU love Nancy Revell

'How wonderful to read about everyday women, young, middle-aged, married or single all coming to work in a man's world. The pride and courage they all showed in taking over from the men who had gone to war. A debt of gratitude is very much owed'

'It's a gripping, heart breaking and poignant storyline. I couldn't put it down and yet didn't want it to end'

'I felt I was there in those streets I know so well. This series of books just get better and better; a fantastic group of girls who could be any one of us if we were alive in the war. Could only give 5 STARS but worth many more'

'What a brilliant read – the story is so good it keeps you wanting more . . . I fell in love with the girls; their stories, laughter, tears and so much more'

'I absolutely loved this book. I come from Sunderland and knew every street, cafe, road and dock'

'This is a book that lets the reader know the way our ancestors behaved during the two world wars. With strength, honour and downright bravery . . . I for one salute them all and give thanks to the author Nancy Revell, for letting us as readers know mostly as it was'

'Marvellous read, couldn't put down. Exciting, heart rending, hope it will not be long before another one. Nancy Revell is an excellent author'

'Oh my word, the Shipyard Girls series is truly amazing. Each book grips you and you come to the end immediately looking for the next in the series'

'I have now read all of the Shipyard Girls books – I was absolutely enthralled. I laughed, cried and rejoiced with each and every character'

'Each book, at some point, has had me lying wide-eyed in my bed wondering, and caring, questioning what's going to happen next? Thank you Nancy, as if I could be any more proud of my hometown'

'I love these books. The courage of all the girls at such a horrendous time is unbelievable. Bring on the next instalment!'

Triumph of the
Shipyard Girls
Nancy Revell

arrow books

1 3 5 7 9 10 8 6 4 2

Arrow Books
20 Vauxhall Bridge Road
London SW1V 2SA

Arrow Books is part of the Penguin Random House group
of companies whose addresses can be found at
global.penguinrandomhouse.com

Penguin
Random House
UK

First published in Great Britain by Arrow Books in 2020

www.penguin.co.uk

A CIP catalogue record for this book is available from
the British Library.

ISBN 9781787464261

Typeset in 10.75/13.5 pt Palatino
by Integra Software Services Pvt. Ltd, Pondicherry

Printed and bound in Great Britain by Clays Ltd, Elcograf S.p.A.

To the Hendon Community Library in Sunderland,
which exists thanks to the *Back on the Map* charity,
community support worker Pat Johnston,
and the volunteer library workers.

Acknowledgements

A huge thank-you to: artist Rosanne Robertson, Suzanne Brown, Kathleen Tuddenham, Megan Blacklock, Hilary Clavering, the Soroptimist International Sunderland, Kevin Johnson, Principal Landscape Architect at Sunderland City Council, and Louise Bradford, owner and director of Creo Communications, for all your determination and enthusiasm to make the commemoration to the real shipyard women a reality.

To the Sunderland Antiquarian Society, especially Linda King, Norm Kirtlan and Philip Curtis, for their help with research and for the use of the wonderful photograph on the cover of *Triumph of the Shipyard Girls*.

To Ian Mole for bringing the series to life with his Shipyard Girls Walking Tour.

Thank you also to all the lovely staff at Fulwell Post Office, postmaster John Wilson, Liz Skelton, Richard Jewitt and Olivia Blyth, who have supported the Shipyard Girls from the off, to the wonderful booksellers at Waterstones in Sunderland, researcher Meg Hartford, Jackie Caffrey, of Nostalgic Memories of Sunderland in Writing, Beverley Ann Hopper, of The Book Lovers, journalist Katy Wheeler at the *Sunderland Echo*, Simon Grundy and all the team at Sun FM, and Lisa Shaw and her fantastic producer Jane Downs at BBC Newcastle.

A heartfelt thank you to deputy publisher Emily Griffin, editor Cassandra Di Bello, and the whole of 'Team Nancy' at Arrow who have worked so hard to make the Shipyard Girls series a *Sunday Times* bestseller.

To my wonderful literary agent Diana Beaumont, and TV agent Leah Middleton, for all your hard work, experience and expertise.

And, of course, to my mum Audrey, dad Syd, hubby Paul, and my 'little' girl, Rosie.

Thank you all.

We are troubled on every side, yet not distressed; we are perplexed, but not in despair; Persecuted, but not forsaken; cast down, but not destroyed;

2 Corinthians 4 v8-9

Prologue

The Fishermen's Cottages, Whitburn, Sunderland

1936

'If yer make one sound . . . If yer make one move,' Raymond hissed into Rosie's ear.

His left hand was over her mouth.

Suffocating her.

His right hand gripped her neck.

'If yer try 'n get away, or shout fer help – '

Rosie could feel the full weight of his body pressing down on her. He wasn't big, but he was strong.

' – I swear t'God, I'll get straight off yer 'n go 'n do what I'm about to do to you to that little sister of yers next door.'

Raymond saw the fear in Rosie's eyes and his excitement increased.

'And dinnit think you'll be able to stop me, 'cos . . .' he breathed heavily and deliberately into her ear ' . . . I'll punch yer so hard in the head, you'll be out fer the count fer as long as it takes me to have my fill with young Charlotte there.' He cocked his head towards the wall.

Rosie could feel his growing fervour and gagged involuntarily.

'Understand?'

She inhaled his rancid breath laced with whisky.

'Understand?' His grip around her neck tightened.

Rosie nodded.

For the next twenty minutes Rosie lay there, eyes fixed on the ceiling of her bedroom, not daring to move. Hardly daring to breathe.

The only way to keep the screams at bay and the bile from rising up was to cut off her mind from what was happening to her body.

To make herself numb.

Totally numb.

When Raymond had finally satisfied his perversions, he lifted himself off Rosie.

A single bead of sweat dropped from his forehead onto Rosie's face and she flinched, instinctively trying to shake it off but failing. Instead, it merged with the tears that were rolling silently down her cheeks.

Rosie watched, her body trembling though still immobile, as her uncle pulled up his trousers and fastened his belt.

She took short, shallow breaths, her eyes following him as he turned to leave.

He reached the bedroom door, then turned his head sharply. His dark eyes fixed on her as he slowly raised his hand to the corner of his mouth and pulled an imaginary zip across his thin, dry lips.

And then he was gone.

Rosie sat up, her senses on high alert, straining to hear the sound of his footsteps going down the stairs – and not to her sister's room.

Clambering out of bed, she grabbed a jagged piece of rock she'd found on the beach and had kept because she liked the way the crystals embedded in it glinted in the sunlight. Every sinew of her body wanted to run after him and smash him on the back of the head – pummel him to death.

But she dare not take the risk. If she didn't succeed, she knew he would kill her.

But worse still, she knew he would carry out his threat and do to Charlotte what he had just done to her.

And that was something Rosie was never going to let happen.

Ever.

Chapter One

Boxing Day 1942

'Thank goodness you've come!'

Helen heaved a dramatic sigh of relief.

Manoeuvring herself around her desk, she strode across the office and gave Dr Parker a hug.

'I was worried you might be called into theatre on some kind of emergency at the last moment, leaving me to deal with my dear mama and all her old cronies on my lonesome.'

Dr Parker wrapped his arms around Helen, returning her embrace. She smelled of expensive perfume. As always, he had to force himself to let her go.

'I wouldn't have missed one of your mother's infamous soirées for all the tea in China,' he said, a smile playing on his lips.

'Come in and take your coat off.' Helen walked over to the tray that had been left on top of one of the filing cabinets.

'Talking of tea?' She took hold of the ceramic pot.

Dr Parker hung his jacket up on the coat stand by the door and rubbed his hands.

'Yes, please, I'm parched.'

He watched as Helen poured carefully, adding a touch of milk, the way he liked it.

'How are you feeling after yesterday?' He scrutinised Helen's face as she turned and handed him his cup.

'Still in shock,' she admitted, exhaling. 'The thing is, John, I'm at a loss as to what to do. I can't forget it, and I'm not the type of person who can just shove it under the carpet.'

'That's true,' he agreed, eyeing her.

'I have to know,' she said, picking up a pile of papers, shuffling them together and tapping them on the desk. 'Otherwise, I'll always be wondering.'

She paused, papers still in hand.

'Either way. Even if it *is* simply a fluke that my mother and Bel look alike . . . God, if it wasn't for the age gap, I'd say they were twins.'

She put the papers in the top drawer and slammed it shut.

'*Either way*, I need to know.'

She walked over to the large windows that divided her office from the open-plan work area that made up the rest of the administration department and yanked the wooden venetian blinds free, lowering them ready for Monday morning when everyone would be back from their three-day Christmas break. As she did so, her gaze was naturally drawn to Bel's desk, which had, as always, been left neat and tidy.

'I mean, it's not as if I can ask Bel, can I?' She turned back to look at Dr Parker drinking his tea. 'I can't just casually ask her when she gets in tomorrow, "Lovely wedding, Bel, wasn't it? Oh, and by the way, I couldn't help but notice that you are the absolute spit of my mother. You wouldn't know if you're related by any chance, would you?"'

Dr Parker allowed himself the slightest of smiles. Helen's dry sense of humour always amused him.

He looked across at her; her sparkling emerald eyes never failed to captivate him. 'The thing is, Bel's probably totally unaware of the fact that she has a doppelgänger. She didn't seem particularly shocked when she was introduced to your mother at the wedding yesterday.'

'Mmm.' Helen took a sip of her tea and put the cup and saucer back on the tray. 'That's true. But then again, that could be because she *is* well aware.'

Helen was quiet for a moment.

'Really, John, when Bel was introduced to my mum at the Grand, it must have been like looking into a mirror – a mirror that shows you an image of your future self.'

Still feeling the need to play devil's advocate, Dr Parker argued, 'Bel was run ragged yesterday organising Polly and Tommy's wedding. She probably barely even *registered* Miriam.'

'Possibly,' Helen said.

She put her hands on her hips and stared down at her desk, lost in thought.

'It could also be that she didn't react to seeing my mother because . . .' she looked up at Dr Parker with wide eyes '. . . she *knows* that they are *kin*.'

Dr Parker took a final slurp of his tea and stood up.

'I think you had one too many gin and tonics yesterday and your imagination has gone into overdrive. This is simply a case of two women who look alike.'

He went over to the stand and slipped his coat back on.

'Now, come on, get yourself ready. I feel like you're procrastinating because you don't want to go to your mother's Boxing Day extravaganza.'

Helen let out an exasperated sigh.

'Oh, John, *don't*. It's going to be hideous. And even more of an "extravaganza" as Mother has made it quite plain that she feels she was deprived of a proper Christmas Day celebration because I deserted her to go to "some welder's wedding".'

As John helped Helen into her winter coat, he had to force himself not to wrap his arms around her, hold her tightly, then turn her around and kiss her.

God! Perhaps *he* was the one with the overactive imagination.

As they walked out into the stillness of the shipyard, Helen looked around and took in the metal and concrete landscape she loved so much. It was a love that had grown greater since the start of the war, as the importance of what they did had increased tenfold. For the ships they built and repaired were crucial to the war effort. Without the cargo vessels and warships that this yard produced, along with dozens of other shipyards across the length and breadth of the country, the war would quite simply be lost.

'I don't think I've ever been here when it's so quiet,' Dr Parker said as he buttoned up his overcoat against the icy-cold air.

As if in defiance of the peace, the clanking of steel suddenly sounded out from the platers' shed.

Dr Parker looked askance at Helen.

'We've still got a skeleton staff keeping things ticking over,' she explained.

Five minutes later they had left the confines of the yard and were scrunching through thick snow along the promenade. Daylight was starting to fade, although there was still enough light to see the grey waters of the North Sea and the outline of the lighthouse on the North pier.

'So . . .' Dr Parker looked up at the darkening skies. The clouds looked heavy with yet more snow. 'I'm guessing that Tommy will be somewhere over the Atlantic by now?'

He tried to sound casual, but he was desperate to know how Helen was feeling about the departure of the man he knew she had loved all her life.

The man who had just married another woman.

'I'd say so,' Helen said, pulling up the cuff of her coat sleeve and looking at her watch. 'It's gone half four. I know his flight was at one – so, allowing for delays, and the time difference, I'd say he'd be there by now.' A worried look fell across her face. 'God willing.'

They walked for a while in silence. The snow glinting with a sparkling topcoat – the result of the morning's fall.

Eventually it was Dr Parker who spoke.

'So, how are you feeling about everything?' he ventured, his mind still on Tommy.

Helen sighed. 'Well, a little confused, to be honest.'

Dr Parker's heart sank. They had not talked openly about Tommy since the day Helen had declared her love for him at the hospital. That had been over two months ago, and Helen had barely mentioned it since.

'Well,' Helen said, 'I was thinking last night when I was trying, *unsuccessfully*, to sleep . . .'

Dr Parker felt an ache in his chest. His heart.

' . . . I was thinking,' she said, 'trying to work out that *if* Bel is related to my mother – and to me for that matter – then what are the possible options?'

Dr Parker was momentarily confused. Had Helen deliberately avoided talking about Tommy and her feelings for him? Or was she genuinely obsessing about Bel?

Sometimes he thought he could read Helen like a book; at other times she was a complete and utter mystery.

'Options?'

'Well . . .' Helen said as they crossed the road. There was no need to check for any traffic. The roads were empty.

9

'There's the possibility that Bel could be my mother's ille-gitimate love child, before she met Dad. I mean, they *do* look like mother and daughter. And the age gap is about right. I've worked it out. Mum would have been about six-teen. Possibly seventeen.'

'True,' Dr Parker conceded.

They continued walking.

'Actually, I wouldn't mind having another sister.' Helen laughed. 'I always wanted one when I was growing up. I might now have an *older* sister – as well as a *little* sister.'

Helen smiled as she thought of Hope. She'd looked particularly gorgeous in her ivory flower-girl dress yes-terday. She couldn't believe she was now nearly one and a half years old. She had fought with herself when Hope was just a baby; had tried her hardest not to have any-thing to do with her father's illegitimate child, but it had been hopeless. As soon as she'd clapped eyes on her in her pram the day she'd bumped into Gloria in town, she'd fallen in love.

'What about your aunty?' Dr Parker knew that Miriam had a sister who was very similar in looks, but the com-plete opposite in nature.

'Mmm,' Helen mused. 'I did think about Aunty Marga-ret – that Bel could possibly be her child – but I can't see her having a child out of wedlock. Besides, she was never able to have children with Uncle Angus – could never carry them to full term . . .' Her voice trailed off.

Dr Parker knew Helen would be thinking of her own miscarriage earlier on in the year.

Stepping aside, he let Helen pass through the wrought-iron gate and walk into the park. The place had been turned into a winter wonderland. Bushes and trees were draped in thick white shrouds. The model boating lake was a sheet of ice. The bowling green no longer green.

'The other spanner in the works,' Dr Parker said, 'is, even if your mother or your aunty Margaret had an illegitimate child, why would Bel's mother – what's her name again?'

'Pearl.'

'Why would Pearl claim that Bel was *her* daughter? From what I've seen, she doesn't strike me as your typical adoptive parent.'

'That's putting it politely,' Helen said. 'The only reason someone like Pearl would take on a child would be if she was being paid handsomely for it. And the woman clearly hasn't got two pennies to rub together.'

By now they had reached the other side of the park.

'Which,' Helen continued, 'brings us to the men in the family.'

'Your grandfather?' Dr Parker said, pulling open the gate.

Helen burst out laughing.

'Hardly, John!' She walked out and onto Roker Park Road. 'Do the maths. Bel's roughly the same age as me. She's more likely to be his granddaughter.'

Helen's face suddenly lit up.

'Unless it was my grandmother's secret love child? She was much younger than Grandfather. And I get the impression she was a bit of a dark horse.'

They crossed the road and started walking the short distance to the corner of Park Avenue.

Helen looked at Dr Parker.

Her excitement waned.

'But that still brings us back to the problem of Pearl, doesn't it?'

Dr Parker nodded.

Helen could feel herself getting exasperated.

'There's far too many ifs and buts and maybes and maybe nots. It'll end up driving me mad.'

She took Dr Parker's arm as they crossed Side Cliff Road to her front gate. It was the only house in the vicinity that had managed to keep its Arts and Crafts ironwork.

'To be continued,' Helen said.

Dr Parker smiled and shook his head.

'I still think that imagination of yours is running riot.'

He wondered, though, if Helen's current obsession with Bel was her way of avoiding thinking about Tommy.

They walked along the short pathway and up the stone steps. Putting her key into the front door, Helen turned to Dr Parker.

'I'm thanking you in advance,' she said with a grimace. 'I'm sure this is probably the last place you fancy being today. On Boxing Day of all days. And one of your rare afternoons off.'

Dr Parker dismissed her words with a shake of his head.

If only Helen knew. He didn't give two hoots where he was right now – as long as he was with the woman he loved.

When Helen opened the front door, they saw Miriam walking into the lounge, her hand clutching a glass of what could only be a large gin and tonic.

Their arrival caught her eye and she turned to welcome them with outstretched arms.

'Darling!' she said, air-kissing her daughter and then Dr Parker. 'I thought you'd deserted your dear mama – again.'

Neither Helen nor Dr Parker said anything.

Miriam inspected her daughter.

'Go and get yourself spruced up.' Miriam tilted her head towards the landing. 'I've put out a lovely dress for you to wear.

'And John,' Miriam purred, 'come and meet the rest of the guests. They're all *dying* to meet you.'

She suddenly burst out laughing.

'*Dying*. Well, I hope not.'

She leant towards Dr Parker.

'But at least if they are, we've got our very own doctor on hand to save the day!'

She chuckled again at her own joke.

Not for the first time, Dr Parker was reminded of his own mother.

As Miriam took Dr Parker's arm, more to steady herself than in affection, Helen shook off her coat and hung it up. She didn't go upstairs, though, but instead headed through to the back kitchen.

Dr Parker knew she was on her way to see the cook, Mrs Westley.

As he walked into the lounge with Miriam by his side, he stole a sidelong glance at Helen's mother.

There was no doubting it, she really was the double of Bel.

Chapter Two

The Grand Hotel, Bridge Street, Sunderland

'Thank you. Thank you so much,' Polly said, shaking the hand of Mr Pollard, the manager of the Grand Hotel – the most exclusive hotel in Sunderland, if not the whole of the north-east. 'I don't think I could have wished for a more perfect wedding. Or honeymoon. I really don't.'

Tears had started to well in her eyes. She blinked them back.

Mr Pollard squeezed Polly's hand and did something he would not normally have done – he raised the young woman's hand to his mouth and kissed it.

'It has been our pleasure, Mrs Watts,' he said.

Polly smiled her goodbye before walking down the stone steps and joining the swell of festive shoppers as they headed into town. Not only was it Boxing Day, it was also Saturday afternoon. She turned left into High Street West, where the shoppers were replaced by those heading to one of the many pubs and taverns that lined the long, wide road that led to the east end.

By the time Polly had reached the corner of Norfolk Street it was much quieter. She slowed her pace. She needed a little time to think before she got home, where she knew her sister-in-law Bel would be waiting with a barrage of questions; where her niece Lucille would demand she play with the toys Santa had brought her; and where her ma would be cooking a special Boxing Day dinner.

Her brother Joe would probably be out with Major Black and the Home Guard. A former Desert Rat with the Eighth Army in North Africa, Joe had been left lame with shrapnel injuries, but was still determined to be of some use to the war and spent every spare minute he had teaching more able men how to defend their country.

And Arthur, *dear Arthur*, would be sitting in his favourite armchair next to the warmth of the range, half reading the day's newspaper, half dozing, the dogs curled up at his feet. She couldn't wait to see him. She'd give him a big hug and tell him that Tommy had said not to worry, he'd be back before Arthur knew it.

Thank God she had Arthur. He had become a surrogate father to her these past few years. Always there with a few quietly spoken words of wisdom. A pillar she could lean on, shoring her up.

As Polly crossed over the Borough Road, she looked over to where Gloria and Hope lived. Hope had looked as sweet as pie yesterday. It was such a shame Jack hadn't been there to see her.

So much had happened in such a short space of time. She and Tommy had fallen out, but they'd made up. *Thank goodness.* The image of Tommy riding his motorbike across the yard would never leave her. Nor the feel of his arms as he'd pulled her close and told her he loved her.

Nor their making love for the first time after arriving back at the Major's flat.

Polly felt the wedding and engagement rings on her finger.

'Mrs Watts,' she muttered to herself. It had felt strange hearing the manager call her by her new name.

As she walked down Tatham Street, the place that had been her home her entire life, she didn't think it possible to feel so happy and yet so sad. Tommy had made her

15

promise, though, just before she'd waved him off, that she would not allow any sadness to infiltrate their joy.

A few tears had managed to escape on the way back to the Grand when she'd been sitting in the back of the RAF staff car. But when they'd driven up Fawcett Street and she'd spotted the latest newspaper headlines telling of a British submarine sunk by Italian torpedo boats, she'd brushed those tears away. If she needed a reminder of why Tommy was going back to Gibraltar, then this was it.

Continuing down Tatham Street, Polly felt an overwhelming sense of gratitude. She'd had the most magical of weddings. The most magical *Christmas* wedding. She was a lucky woman.

Almost home, Polly dodged a couple of the neighbours' children playing tag.

And that was when she noticed the curtains were drawn.
Odd.

She felt her heart skip a beat.

Followed by a sense of dread.

She hurried to the front door and let herself in.

'Ma! Ma!' Polly shouted out as soon as she stepped through the doorway.

She had only made it halfway down the tiled hall when Agnes came hurrying out of the kitchen, her arms open, ready to embrace. The two dogs, Tramp and Pup, scrambling to catch up on the tiled flooring.

'Ahh, Pol! Come here.' Agnes put her arms around her daughter. 'I'm so sorry, my love, but I've got some sad news.'

She took a step back, but still held her daughter by the shoulders.

'I'm afraid it's Arthur . . . He died . . . last night.'

Polly stood, shocked, and she stared at her mother.

16

'Arthur's dead?'

Agnes looked at her daughter and nodded sadly.

'He is, pet. I'm afraid he is. Poor soul.'

Polly still didn't move; she could not comprehend the news. She felt something push against her leg and looked down, seeing the dogs fussing around her feet.

'Come here,' Agnes said, giving her daughter another hug before guiding her into the kitchen. She knew Arthur's death would hit Polly the most. Apart from Tommy, of course.

'But he seemed so well yesterday . . .' Polly sat down at the kitchen table. 'And so happy.' A vision of his face as he walked her down the aisle suddenly sprang to mind.

Agnes poured out a cup of tea from the pot she'd made. She added milk and two teaspoons of sugar, stirred it and put it in front of Polly. The dogs settled in their basket by the range, their eyes trained on the two women. Tears slowly began to trickle down Polly's face as the reality of what her ma had told her started to sink in. Agnes pulled her chair up close and put her arms around her daughter. She could feel her body juddering as grief began and then gradually gained momentum.

They sat like that for a little while.

Finally, Polly looked up at her ma, her face wet with tears.

'Why, Ma? Why now?'

'It was his time, pet.' Agnes looked at her daughter's distraught face. 'It was his time.'

The house was quiet. Agnes had asked Bel to take Lucille into town so she could be alone with her daughter when she told her the news. For Polly, having Arthur in the house had been like having a part of Tommy close by. Now that comfort had been taken from her.

'He went to bed last night and he was so happy.' Agnes held her daughter's wet face in her hands and looked into her pretty green-blue eyes. She wiped away tears with the corner of her pinny, as she'd done when Polly was a child.

'When he didn't get up this morning,' Agnes said, 'I went into his room and he was lying there in his bed.' She took her daughter's hand. 'He looked contented, Pol. He was lying on his back, holding a photograph of Flo. I think he missed her every day. He'll be happy now. Trust me. He will. He won't want you to be sad.'

Polly nodded but still didn't trust herself to speak as more tears rolled down her face.

Chapter Three

Brookside Gardens, Sunderland

Sunday 27 December

'Night, Mrs Jenkins . . . Mr Jenkins.' Rosie smiled at both her neighbours, although she had to tilt her head to one side to see Mr Jenkins since his wife was commandeering the doorway.

'And thank you for the gorgeous meal. That was the best Sunday roast I've had for as long as I can remember,' she said, putting her hand on Charlotte's back and gently pushing her down the short pathway.

'Me too!' Charlotte said, opening the little wooden gate and adding cheekily, 'Rosie never does a roast. It's either pie and peas . . . or pie and peas.'

'Well, it's clearly not done you any harm!' Mrs Jenkins said.

She turned her attention to Rosie, who was giving her sister the daggers.

'Eee, pet, you've got your hands full with that one, haven't you?'

Rosie laughed.

'Just a tad!'

Charlotte was now making a show of opening their own little wooden gate and allowing her big sister to go first.

'And thank you so much for inviting us to the wedding. It was wonderful, wasn't it?' Mrs Jenkins said, looking behind her at her husband, who nodded enthusiastically. 'The whole day was marvellous . . . the church . . . the Grand.' Mrs Jenkins looked up into the starry sky. 'It was so Christmassy. So romantic.'

Rosie hurried up the path. She needed to get into the house before Mrs Jenkins went off – again – about Tommy and Polly's wedding.

Reading her sister's thoughts, Charlotte opened the front door and dodged straight in.

'Night, night!' she shouted out as she disappeared from view.

'Thanks again, Mrs Jenkins,' Rosie said.

'If you can't push the boat out at Christmas, when can you, eh? Well, as much as you *can* push the boat out with all this rationing . . . Anyway, it's nice to have someone else to cook for other than *the master of the house*.' Mrs Jenkins jerked her head back and pulled a funny face.

Rosie laughed, gave a little wave and shut the front door. After dropping the latch, she leant against it and sighed heavily.

'I don't think I've ever known anyone talk so much,' she said as she slipped out of her heels and put them next to her work boots. She then reached out and took Charlotte's shoes off her and put them neatly next to her own.

'Poor Mr Jenkins,' Charlotte said, turning and jogging up the stairs, 'he barely gets a word in edgeways.'

Rosie smiled and walked down the hallway and into the kitchen. It was true. Since moving in less than a year ago, she'd hardly heard the man speak. Mind you, she reckoned, most people would struggle to get a word in with Mrs Jenkins.

'Hot chocolate before bed?' Rosie shouted up at the ceiling. She could hear Charlotte banging about in her bedroom.

'Is the Pope a Catholic?' Charlotte shouted back.

Rosie sighed for the second time in as many minutes. Mrs Jenkins was not joking when she'd said that Rosie had her work cut out with Charlotte. It was more than two months since she'd turned up on her doorstep, and she'd not had a minute's peace since.

Having poured milk into the pan, Rosie lit the gas and put it on the hob before filling the kettle.

Not that she minded, if she was honest. She just had to keep Charlotte focused on her new school – and on making new friends – rather than obsessing about Lily and thereby finding out that Lily was actually a madam, her home was a bordello, and that Rosie used to be one of her 'girls'.

'What do you think?' Charlotte appeared in the kitchen wearing her Christmas present, a royal blue quilted dressing gown. 'It's so snug.' She pulled the lapels up around her neck to demonstrate. 'And so soft.'

Rosie inspected her sister. She was fourteen years old and shooting up. There was no denying that she was at that crossroads: no longer a child but not yet a woman.

'So,' Rosie said, quickly taking the pan off the hob as the milk threatened to spill over, 'what have you got planned for tomorrow, with me being back at work?' She poured the hot milk into a mug, added cocoa powder and sugar, and stirred vigorously.

'I think I'll go to the library in town,' Charlotte said, taking the hot chocolate off her sister. 'I'm going to swot up on my French. I want to be top of the class.'

Rosie threw a tea bag into a mug and added boiling water from the kettle, which was beginning to whistle.

Charlotte had always liked her French lessons; her love for the language, though, seemed to have grown since she'd been back home. Something Rosie put down to Lily being a self-confessed Francophile – rather than to Charlotte having a burning desire to be an A-grade student.

'Well, if you get bored, or want a break, you can always come in and see everyone at lunchtime. With the weather the way it is, we'll all be in the canteen. Bel and Marie-Anne will no doubt be there too – dying to hear all the gossip from the wedding . . . And you can pop in and say hello to your favourite person.' Rosie threw Charlotte a sidelong glance and suppressed a smile. Charlotte, despite trying to hide it, was more than a little intimidated by Helen.

Charlotte ignored her sister's teasing. 'That sounds like a great plan. I'll work in the library all morning and come and have lunch with everyone in the canteen. Then if Bel – or anyone else – wants me to do any chores in town, I can do that.'

'That's nice of you,' Rosie said. 'Bel really appreciated you running errands for her on Christmas Eve. She kept saying how she couldn't have done without you.' Rosie added milk to her tea. 'And Lucille was over the moon with what "Santa" had picked out for her.'

Charlotte smiled. 'It was fun . . . Shopping for Christmas presents – I've never really done that before.'

'Not even in Harrogate with Mr and Mrs Rainer?' It was at times like this that Rosie realised how little she really knew about her sister's life over these past six years.

Charlotte shook her head. 'Not really. They'd go to the Christmas market but that was mainly for food. And last year they didn't even do that. I think they were getting too old to go traipsing around the shops.'

They were both quiet for a moment as they sipped their hot drinks.

Suddenly Charlotte perked up.

'When I was shopping for Bel, trying to find the place that sold confetti, I spotted Maisie and Vivian in town.'

Rosie felt herself tense.

'Oh yes? Which shops were they in?'

'They weren't.' Charlotte blew on her hot chocolate. 'They were going into the Grand.'

'Really?' Rosie forced herself to sound casual.

'They looked like they were on a date,' Charlotte said.

'What gave you that impression?' Rosie wasn't sure she wanted to hear the answer.

'They were with two blokes and one of them kissed Maisie. *On the mouth.*' Charlotte's eyes widened. 'And the other put his arm around Vivian.'

'Were they Admiralty?' Rosie asked.

Charlotte nodded. 'The thing is, I'm sure I saw the same two officers in the Grand the next day at the wedding. Well, not *at* the wedding. They came in and were going up the stairs to where they're all billeted. And I'm pretty sure they saw Maisie and Vivian – and that Maisie and Vivian saw them . . .'

'And?' Rosie asked.

'*And* . . . they all ignored each other. Like they'd never set eyes on each other before,' Charlotte said, genuinely perplexed.

Rosie thought for a moment.

'Were they wearing their white uniforms?'

Charlotte nodded.

'Well, then, they probably weren't the same officers. They all look the same when they're in their uniforms.' Rosie eyed her sister. '*And* coupled with that glass of champagne I saw you guzzle back when you didn't think I was watching, I would guess your vision might well have been a little hazy.'

Charlotte pursed her lips. She hadn't realised Rosie had seen her sneaking a drink.

'Come on then. Time for bed,' Rosie said, making sure she'd turned off the gas.

She followed Charlotte out of the kitchen and switched off the light.

She would have to have a word with Maisie and Vivian tomorrow when she was at Lily's. Tell them to be more discreet.

Thank goodness Charlotte was still very young and very naïve.

After getting into bed, Rosie pulled open the top drawer of her bedside cabinet and took out Peter's letter. Putting it on her quilt, she straightened it out. Not that she needed to read it. She could probably have recited it by heart, she'd read it so many times.

God willing, my love, I will see you soon. Rosie ran her finger along the words. *But never forget how much I love you. And know that I will never forget the love you have for me. Nor its strength.*

Rosie knew these words could only have come from Peter. For only Peter would reassure her that he knew her love for him was steadfast and always would be.

Only he understood that she needed him to know what she was unable to tell him herself.

'Oh, Peter,' Rosie whispered to her husband, imagining he was there, lying next to her. 'Come back home soon.' She missed him desperately. So much had happened since his brief overnight visit in August. She'd love to tell him that having Charlotte back home to live was actually working out.

Switching off her side light, Rosie put the letter back into the top drawer and pulled the blankets around her, thinking of when Peter's arms would be keeping her warm.

As sleep edged closer, her mind wandered to the future. A possible future. To a time when Peter was back living here – with her and Charlotte.

They would be a family of sorts.

Something she had never dreamed she'd have.

Chapter Four

The Fishermen's Cottages, Whitburn, Sunderland

1936

Rosie stood in the middle of her bedroom, her hand clutching the jagged piece of crystal rock. Her head was pounding in time with the beat of her heart and her ears strained to hear the exact whereabouts of her uncle Raymond. She kept her breathing shallow for fear of obscuring any noise.

Hearing the front door shut and the sound of footsteps crunching along the gravelled pathway that led to the main road, she sucked in air, finally allowing herself to breathe properly.

Hurrying across to her bedroom window, she squinted through the crack of her curtains. She could see the darkened outline of Raymond's figure walking along the main road.

Away from the village.

Away from the house.

Rosie stood rooted to the spot, her eyes straining into the darkness.

She stayed like that for an hour, still clutching her crystal rock.

Having convinced herself that he was not coming back, at least not within the next few hours, Rosie got to work, consciously blotting out the horror she'd just had inflicted upon her.

There was no time.

No time for tears or self-pity.

All that mattered now was her sister's safety.

As she hauled her mam and dad's suitcase out of the top of their wardrobe, she imagined them next to her. Guiding her and keeping her strong. It didn't take her long to pack Charlotte's belongings: her clothes, her favourite cuddly toy, a framed photograph of their parents and, of course, her favourite book, *The Walrus and the Carpenter*. Their mam had told them how the story had been inspired by the author's walks along Whitburn beach. It would remind Charlotte of home.

Rosie closed the suitcase, snapped the clasps shut and put it down on the floor. It wasn't too heavy. She'd be able to carry it without too much of a struggle.

Bumping it down the stairs, she placed it by the front door.

Putting a huge pot of water on the hob, she waited for it to boil, poured it into the copper bath, and did the same again. After stripping off her nightgown, she scrunched it up and shoved it into the stove. The hot embers soon caught the cotton material. Rosie watched the flames flickering as she sat in the bath and scrubbed every inch of her body until it was red raw.

Afterwards she put on the black dress she had worn for the funeral, as well as her mother's gold watch. She took the cash she knew had been stashed away, then sat at the kitchen table to drink her tea and think.

She read and reread her parents' will, which she'd found crumpled up and discarded on the floor by the side of the range. It seemed quite straightforward. Everything had been left to her and Charlotte. As Rosie was now fifteen, soon to be sixteen, their savings, which she knew to be her parents' 'rainy-day money', were hers to do with as she wished.

When dawn began to creep over the horizon, Rosie took a deep breath and stood up. Tying her long blonde hair, now almost dry, into a tight bun, she walked out of the kitchen and up the stairs.

It was time to wake her little sister and take her to her new life.

A new and – most of all – *safer* life.

Chapter Five

J.L. Thompson & Sons, North Sands, Sunderland

Monday 28 December

'Morning,' Rosie said, reaching up to the counter of the timekeeper's cabin and taking her card from Alfie. 'Good Christmas?'

'Aye, it was that!' Alfie was beaming from ear to ear. 'What a wedding eh?'

Rosie smiled her agreement. Polly and Tommy's nuptials had given a lot of people a lot of pleasure, for a variety of reasons. Alfie, she knew, had been cock-a-hoop at being able to spend so much time with Kate, despite the fact that everyone had wanted to congratulate her on creating the most fabulous wedding dress, as well as ask her where she had learnt her trade – a question Kate had become adept at avoiding. No one was to know that the woman they were calling the town's 'very own Coco Chanel' had once been a beggar and worn nothing but rags.

Walking into the yard, Rosie could see that there were still patches of snow here and there, on the cranes that had been resting these past few days, and on the decks of the cargo vessels docked by the quayside.

'Rosie!'

Turning round, she saw Hannah, the squad's little bird, and Olly hurrying towards her.

'You two are in early?' she said.

'Yes, we wanted to get in before Basil. Give the place a tidy up,' said Olly.

'It was left in a bit of a mess on Christmas Eve,' added Hannah.

'Drawing-office Christmas party,' Olly explained, brushing his blond mop of hair back with one hand.

'Ahh,' Rosie said, not that she could imagine the team of draughtsmen Hannah and Olly worked with having a knees-up, let alone one raucous enough to leave a mess; they were all incredibly studious and rather strait-laced. Probably why Hannah and Olly fitted in so well.

'Did you both enjoy the wedding?' Rosie asked, although she already knew the answer. *Who hadn't?*

Hannah and Olly nodded and gave each other a shy look. They'd been inseparable all evening. Rosie didn't think Olly had let go of Hannah's hand once. She wondered how long it would be before the two got engaged.

When they reached the drawing office, Rosie looked at Hannah.

'I'm guessing you've not heard any more news?' Rosie didn't have to say about what – or whom. Ever since Hannah had told them about the concentration camp her parents had been taken to, they'd been expecting the worst. Not that anyone would admit it. At least not to Hannah. They'd agreed it was important she kept her hopes up.

'No.' Hannah's face clouded over. 'Aunty Rina says it's much harder to find out anything about the Auschwitz camp. I never thought I'd hear myself say it, but I wish they were still at the Theresienstadt ghetto. At least the Red Cross and the odd journalist were being allowed in there occasionally. Not like at Auschwitz.'

Rosie's heart really did go out to Hannah. It was a good job she had her aunty Rina and her work at the yard.

'See you all in the canteen at lunchtime?' Hannah asked.

'Definitely,' Rosie said, turning and making her way across the yard.

She'd always loved her work here at Thompson's, from her very first day as an apprentice, but she'd been a loner then, her gender making her the odd one out. Over the past two and a half years, since she had been tasked with training up her squad of women welders, she had grown to love her work for different reasons – for the friendship it afforded her and, though none of them would admit it outright, because of the love they had for each other.

Approaching their workstation, she was surprised to see that Martha was already there and had got the five-gallon barrel fire going.

'What a luxury – first day back and greeted by a red-hot fire,' Rosie said, dumping her haversack on the ground.

Martha poked the coals with a pair of metal tongs normally used to heat up rivets.

'Thought I'd come in early. Get a nice fire going. It's brass monkeys, as Angie would say.'

'*Cooee!*'

Martha and Rosie turned to see Angie and Dorothy marching across the yard, arm in arm.

'Talk of the devil,' Martha said. She stuck her hand up by way of a greeting.

'I'm surprised to see you two in so early,' Rosie said, splaying her hands in front of the fire.

'Yeah,' Martha chipped in, 'thought you'd both still be hungover.'

'No, Martha, dear,' Dorothy said. 'We had all day yesterday to recover from our festive overindulgences. Didn't we, Ange?'

Angie rolled her eyes heavenward.

'We did, indeed, Dor.' She swung her boxed-up gas mask and holdall off her shoulder and put them on the long wooden workbench. 'It's just my ears that need to recover.'

'From?' Martha asked.

'From Miss *Oh my God I'm so in love*.' Angie nodded over at Dorothy, who was pulling her flask out of her canvas duffle bag.

'Toby?' Rosie guessed.

Angie nodded, her face pure weariness. 'I think I might go mad if I hear his name one more time.'

Dorothy had met Toby on Christmas Eve, when she and Angie had gone to Lily's to drop off George's uniform. Toby had turned up at the same time to give Peter's letter to Rosie.

Dorothy looked at Angie, Martha and Rosie.

'I was really going to try and be very demure about it all.'

She took a deep breath and clasped her hands.

'But I can't.'

Another deep inhalation, then she declared, 'Oh. My. God. I am *soooo* in love!'

They all burst out laughing.

Dorothy looked totally affronted.

'What's so funny?' she asked.

'You!' Martha said. 'You've only known him five minutes.'

'That doesn't matter,' Dorothy said. 'When you know, you *know*.' She looked at Rosie for backup. 'Don't you?'

Rosie frowned and nodded at the same time. She *had* fallen in love with Peter straight away, only it had taken her several months to admit it.

'Am I right in thinking Toby had to go back up north on Boxing Day?'

Dorothy's face immediately dropped. She pulled a glum expression and nodded.

'Scotland?' Martha asked.

Dorothy nodded again.

'Whereabouts in Scotland?' Rosie was curious. She knew Toby had had something to do with Peter's recruitment by a part of the British army that apparently didn't exist.

'No idea,' Dorothy said, deadpan. 'He said he'd have to kill me if he told me.'

Martha looked horrified.

'She's only kidding yer, dafty.' Angie nudged Martha. 'He didn't tell Dor 'cos what he's doing is all very hush-hush 'n he knars it's a physical impossibility for Dor to keep her trap shut. Even if she wants to, she can't.'

Dorothy put her hands on her hips. She opened her mouth and shut it again.

'I'm speechless,' she said eventually.

''Cos what I just said is one hundred per cent right,' Angie declared.

Dorothy scowled at her flatmate. 'Well, at least I talk to my best mate.' She looked at Rosie and Martha. 'And I don't keep everything to myself, like *some* people.' She glared at Angie. 'Even the Gestapo would have a job getting any information out of Angie here about a certain someone.'

'Quentin?' Martha asked. They had all been surprised to see both Dorothy and Angie turn up at the wedding with dates. They'd gone on and on about how they were going to be 'young, free and single' at Polly and Tommy's wedding, only, to everyone's surprise, for Dorothy to turn up with Toby, and Angie with Quentin.

'Yes, *Quentin*,' Dorothy said. 'Angie had the audacity to leave me on my lonesome last night to go out on a date.'

'It wasn't a date!' Angie shouted. A group of riveters walking past automatically looked over.

'It wasn't a date,' she repeated, dropping her voice, but not the outraged tone. 'He's teaching me how to be posh.'

Rosie had to force back a smile. Bel had told her that Angie had only agreed to let Quentin accompany her to the wedding if, in exchange, he gave her what amounted to lessons in 'being posh'.

'But why do you want to be posh?' Martha asked.

'Because I do,' Angie said simply.

'I think it's more a case that she wants to better herself,' Dorothy explained.

'When did you decide that?' Martha was still confused.

'It started when we moved into the flat,' Dorothy answered for her friend. 'She fell in love with the towels George left for us in the bathroom.'

'The *indoor* bathroom,' Angie butted in. She had never had the luxury of *using* an indoor bathroom before, never mind living in a flat with one.

'Then I think she fell in love with George,' said Dorothy.

Angie opened her mouth to object.

'Not in love with George himself,' Dorothy explained, 'but in love with everything he stands for. You know, good manners, class . . . He's very much the old-school gentleman. Very kind . . . courteous.'

This time Rosie allowed herself a smile. George was certainly all those things.

Martha looked at Angie. She was not objecting.

'Oh, I see,' Martha said, although she still seemed a little perplexed.

'Look!' Dorothy pointed over at two women dressed in blue denim overalls, their hair wrapped up in turbans, their gas masks and haversacks slung across their chests.

It was Polly and Gloria.

34

'*Here comes the bride!*' Dorothy's voice sang out across the yard.

She was about to carry on singing the Bridal Chorus when she saw the looks on both women's faces.

'It can't be Tommy, he's only just left,' Angie said.

'Could be one of Gloria's boys,' Rosie said.

'Doubt it,' Dorothy said. 'Gordon sent a letter the other day saying they were both fine.'

'Well, something's happened,' Martha said, scrutinising her workmates' faces as they came nearer.

The canteen was full to bursting. The air was thick with smoke and the smell of stewed meat and cabbage.

Gloria got served first. On seeing that Hannah and Olly were already sitting at the women's designated table, she hurried over so that Polly didn't have to break the news for the third time that day.

'Arthur's passed away.' She kept her voice low.

'Oh, no . . . When?' Hannah said.

'Boxing Day.' Gloria looked round to see the rest of the women coming over.

Hannah stood up and went to give Polly a hug.

'Oh, Polly, I'm so sorry. I know how close you were to Arthur.'

'Thanks, Hannah.' Polly forced back tears. They still seemed to spring from nowhere.

The women took their places around the table.

'It's so strange,' Polly said, sitting down, 'him not being there. The house seems so empty without him. Even yesterday when everyone was about.'

They were all quiet for a moment.

'Tramp and Pup keep going to his room and lying by his bed. Ma's giving them loads of titbits, but they're not bothered. It's like they're keeping a vigil for him. Waiting for him to come back.'

'*Is* he coming back home before you bury him?' Angie asked.

Polly nodded.

'What do you mean?' Hannah asked.

'When someone dies,' Angie explained, 'yer have the body back overnight. Before the funeral. Everyone does it round here.'

'What about Tommy?' Rosie asked.

'I've sent him a letter. Told him Arthur died peacefully in his sleep. Which he did, thank goodness. Ma said he looked happy. Content. Holding a photo of Flo.'

Tears were now pooling in Hannah's eyes.

'Oh, that's so sad. Yet so beautiful.'

'Do you think . . .' Rosie hesitated ' . . . that Tommy'll be all right?'

They all knew that Tommy had suffered from 'dark moods' in the past. Like his mam. Only she'd succumbed to the darkness, taking her own life, unable to get over the loss of Tommy's father in the First War.

'Funnily enough,' Polly said, 'we chatted about it before he left.' She stopped. 'Gosh, that sounds awful.'

Gloria took her hand and squeezed it. 'That doesn't sound awful. More like yer both had yer feet planted firmly on the ground. Arthur was an old man. Yer could see his health was failing him.'

'That's what Tommy said. I guess it was more obvious to him than it was to me. I think he was quite shocked to see how much he'd aged while he'd been gone. He said in a roundabout way that he knew Arthur mightn't be here when he got back.'

Polly took a deep breath. Tommy never said 'if' he came back – it was always 'when'.

'Before he left, he said I mustn't worry about him if anything did happen to Arthur, that he'd be fine. That he'd been lucky to have his grandda in his life – and for so long.'

Polly looked around the table at the women.

'So now,' she said, forcing a smile, 'I just need to make sure Arthur's given a good send-off.'

Everyone murmured their agreement.

'When's the funeral?' Dorothy said.

'We've got him booked in at St Ignatius on Thursday.'

'New Year's Eve,' Martha said.

'I know. But I guess it's sort of fitting.' Polly gave a sad smile.

'The end of a year. The end of a life,' Olly said, pushing his heavy, black-rimmed glasses back up his nose.

'And the start of a new one,' Hannah said thoughtfully.

Bel knocked tentatively on the office door.

'Bel, come in, come in!' Helen had to stop herself sounding overly enthusiastic. She had been looking forward to seeing Bel after the short Christmas break. Her obsession was getting out of hand.

'I have to say well done for organising such a wonderful wedding. And at such short notice. Everything went off like a dream, didn't it? Talk about juggling a load of balls and not letting any of them drop. I think we need to put your skills to use here.' Helen flung out an arm towards the admin department, which was now empty. The last of the staff had gone to lunch.

'Thank you,' Bel said, taken aback.

'Come in, sit down!' Helen was waving a manicured hand at the seat in front of her desk. 'Now I'm thinking about it, perhaps we can get you trained in shorthand. Your typing's up to speed now, isn't it?'

Bel nodded. She felt a jolt of excitement. Adding short-hand to her skills meant she might get a promotion. She'd initially wanted this job so she'd get to know more about the Havelocks – her *other family*. Lately, though, she'd been keener to climb the administrative ladder.

'Leave it with me,' Helen said. 'I'll see what I can do about getting you on a course. It'll mean you having to go to night classes, though. Do you think that's something you'd be up for?'

'Oh, yes, I would. Most definitely,' Bel said.

'I know you've got family. Would they object?' Helen tried not to show how much she was scrutinising Bel's face. Those eyes. That mouth. Nose. Even her cheekbones. There was no getting away from it. She was a younger version of her mother.

'Oh, they'd be fine about me doing night classes,' Bel lied. She knew Lucille would lament loudly about her ma not being there on an evening, and although Joe wouldn't say anything, he'd miss her. They didn't get to spend that much time with each other as it was – not with her working full-time and Joe out so much with his Home Guard unit.

'Good! Leave it with me,' Helen said, scribbling herself a memo. When she stopped writing she looked up at Bel. 'Sorry, Bel, I'm guessing you came to see me for a reason?'

Bel felt a fluttering of nerves. She'd been dreading telling Helen all morning. She'd got to know her a little during the preparations for the wedding as Helen had provided the floral arrangements for the church – *and* a Christmas tree. Even so, she still didn't know her that well.

'Actually, I'm afraid I've come to tell you some sad news.'

'Oh, God,' Helen said. 'Someone's died.' A moment's panic. 'It's not Tommy?'

Bel shook her head.

'No, no, Tommy's fine. Well, as far as we know. Touch wood.'

She looked at Helen in her dark, military-style green dress and wondered randomly if it was one of Kate's.

'No, I'm afraid it's Arthur,' she said. 'He passed away in the early hours of Boxing Day.'

Bel paused, trying to gauge Helen's reaction.

'I'm so sorry. I know you and Arthur were close.'

Helen bent down and picked up her handbag from the floor, then took out her cigarettes and lighter.

'We weren't that close,' she said. Her voice was clipped. *Why did death make her angry?* 'But I have known Arthur all my life.' She lit her cigarette.

Bel noticed her hands were shaking.

'Polly would have told you herself, but . . .' Bel let her voice trail off.

'I'm guessing she's probably got a long list to get through. Arthur was a popular man.' Helen blew out smoke. She looked a million miles away. 'I'll never forget my father taking me to see him doing a dive when I was little. I'd never seen anything like it. That huge helmet. The metal boots. If I'm honest, he scared me.'

Helen stopped.

A thought had just occurred to her. She'd have to tell her father. He'd be devastated. Now, he *was* close to Arthur. Loved the old man to bits.

Helen looked at Bel.

'When's the funeral?'

'Thursday. New Year's Eve.'

Helen laughed sadly. 'Fitting.' She crushed her cigarette out and stood up. Bel followed suit. She was being dismissed.

'Tell Polly just to ask if she needs anything and to take off any time necessary to sort everything out. It's not as if Tommy's here to help. And Arthur's got no other family.'

Bel turned to leave.

'Oh, and Bel . . . Tell Polly not to spare any expense. Arthur gave his life to the Wear. To the town. To the ship-yards. Mr Havelock will foot the bill. There's to be no argument.'

The mention of the man who had fathered her gave Bel an involuntary jolt.

She nodded.

Forced a smile.

And left.

Chapter Six

Park Avenue, Roker, Sunderland

'Can I have a word, Mother?' Helen shouted up the stairs. She knew her mum would be getting herself ready for an evening at the Grand; she didn't know why she didn't just move in there permanently.

'Darling, I'm in a rush.'

'It's important, Mother!'

Helen heard her mother sigh impatiently and loudly enough so that she knew her daughter would hear. There was a moment's silence, followed by the jingle of ice against glass.

'Coming, *your Highness*!' Judging by Miriam's sing-song voice, she was in the early stages of inebriation.

A few minutes later she walked into the front reception room. Helen was standing by the fire, which had yet to be lit. There was no point, really, as there wouldn't be anyone there to benefit from it this evening.

'I'm afraid I'm the bearer of bad news.' Helen watched her mother as she headed over to the drinks cabinet.

'Nothing new there, then.' Miriam sloshed gin into her glass. It was on the tip of her tongue to elaborate, but she forced herself to hold back any incendiary comments. She was in too good a mood to ruin it by having another argument with her daughter.

'I'm sure you'll be devastated to hear that Arthur Watts has passed away.' Helen observed her mother. Since the scales had fallen from her eyes and she now saw her mother for the person she was, there was a part of her that found her fascinating; it was like watching some rare animal in a zoo.

'Oh,' Miriam added a touch of tonic to her gin, 'that's a shame – but I'd hardly class it as "bad news".' She took a sip of her drink. 'You *are* one for exaggerating, aren't you, my dear?' She looked deep in thought for a moment before adding more gin to her glass. 'I mean, it's hardly unexpected, is it? How old was he? Seventy? Eighty?'

Helen stared at her mother. She really was quite vile. 'About the same age as Grandfather, I believe.' Helen caught a look in her mother's eyes. She wouldn't be surprised if she was imagining the day *he* died. Calculating how much she would inherit. 'Isabelle Elliot told me. You know, Polly's sister-in-law? I introduced you to her at the wedding.' Helen's eyes remained fixed on her mother.

'Oh, yes, vaguely,' Miriam said, squinting. 'It was rather late in the day, but yes, I remember her. Blonde hair. Pretty little thing. I didn't realise she was the sister-in-law of that Polly woman. She must have married beneath herself.'

Helen didn't say anything. It was interesting that her mother thought that Bel came from a higher class. And even more interesting that she didn't seem to recognise Bel. Or know anything about her, for that matter. If Bel *was* related to the family, her mother clearly had no idea.

'So, when's the funeral? I suppose they'll be wanting us to pay for it?'

'It's on Thursday. And they've not asked us to pay. I've *told* them we're covering all the expenses.'

'I suppose,' Miriam said, 'we've not much choice, seeing as the old man worked for the Wear Commissioner. And, of course, everyone knows how close your father was to him. Wouldn't look good if he had a pauper's funeral, would it?'

'Anyway,' Helen said, walking over and taking a peek out of the blackout blinds. The snow was now a dirty sludge. 'On the subject of Father, he'll have to come back from the Clyde. He'll want to go to the funeral.'

Miriam spluttered on her drink. 'He might *want* to go to the funeral, darling, but he most certainly won't be attending.'

Helen turned round sharply.

'I think he *will*. Dad loved Arthur. They worked together for years. Decades. If anyone needs to be there, it's Dad. You can't stop him.'

Miriam looked at her daughter. A smile slowly spread across her face. 'Oh, but darling, I *can* stop him. And I *will*.'

Helen stared at her mother. She had presumed he'd be 'allowed' back for the funeral. She'd felt terribly sad about Arthur's passing, but had been cheered up no end by the thought of her father's return. Even if it would only be a fleeting visit.

'My dear girl,' Miriam continued, 'if your father so much as puts a foot across the Scottish border – never mind turns up at the old man's funeral – the first thing I will do is spill the beans about all those wretched women welders your dear papa and his bit on the side think so much of.'

Miriam took a drink of her gin.

'As I'm sure you'll recall that afternoon we were all having our private little tête-à-tête and you had your ear glued to that door listening in –' Miriam cast a look at the large living-room door that was slightly ajar ' – if it ever came out about your father's sordid affair, or his little bastard – ' Helen felt herself stiffen at the mention of Hope ' – then I, in turn, would decimate the lives of those my husband and his hussy seem to care so much about.'

Miriam inspected Helen for her reaction.

43

'I'm sure you'll remember that I made it quite clear I'd make it my sole mission to make sure every Tom, Dick and Harry got to know exactly who was the real mother of that giant man-woman, Martha.' Miriam sipped her drink. '*Manly Martha*.' Miriam smiled sweetly at her daughter. 'I'll make sure that everyone hears the gossip – that it spreads like wildfire – so that every person in this town knows Martha's mother was not only a *convicted* murderer, but a *child* murderer.'

Miriam walked over to Helen.

The pair were standing just inches apart.

'Then I will get the Chief Constable of Sunderland Borough Police round here and tell him that the town has a bigamist in its midst.' Helen could smell the alcohol on her mother's breath she was so close. 'So that airhead girl who works in the yard – what's her name? Makes me think of that terrible film everyone's always raving on about. That's it. *Dorothy*. So that, in future, if Dorothy wants to see her mother, she'll be following the yellow brick road all the way to HMP Durham – which is where, I believe, they put all the women convicts.'

Miriam's face lit up as though she'd just had an idea.

'Oh, she might even share a cell with Martha's dear mama.' She tutted. 'No, silly me. Martha's monster of a mother got the rope, didn't she? How could anyone forget? She's almost folklore in these parts.'

Miriam turned and sat down on the sofa, then took another sip from her crystal tumbler. She was obviously enjoying herself.

'And let's not forget the common one. The coalminer's daughter. *Angela*. Well, I would like to see the state of her "mam" after her father finds out she's been enjoying a bit on the side. By the time he's finished with her she'll look as though she's been down the mine herself.'

Helen clenched her fists. The desire to smack the look of self-satisfaction off her mother's face was all-consuming. Gloria had told her how relieved they all were when Angie had moved in with Dorothy as she'd be out of the firing line of her dad's bad temper and frequent backhanders.

'You finished?' Helen said.

Miriam smiled and nodded.

'Old age must be kicking in, Mother dearest,' Helen said. 'I do believe, when I had my ear "glued" to the door that insightful day, you were actually in possession of *six* bartering chips with which to silence Father and Gloria.'

'Meaning?' Miriam said. The self-satisfied smile had vanished.

'Meaning you've only mentioned three. You seem to have forgotten about Rosie, Polly and Hannah. Remember, you were going to "tell the world" Rosie was seeing a man "almost twice her age" and that the two had been practically "living in sin" . . .

'And how unfortunate it would be if rumours about Polly playing away were to find their way over to Tommy in Gibraltar. How it might *turn his mind*. Never a good thing when he was *playing around with explosives*.'

Helen was trying her hardest to hide her growing anger.

'And Hannah and her aunty, who was giving out credit and not collecting her dues. How the "little refugee" and her aunt might well find themselves homeless and knocking on the door of the local workhouse. How did you put it again? "From a palace in Prague to the slums of Sunderland."'

Miriam laughed.

'Well, there's nothing wrong with your memory, is there?'

Helen ignored her mother's comment.

'There's no more swinging the axe over *their* heads, is there? For starters, as you well know, Polly's married

45

Tommy, so it's highly unlikely that he'll give any credence to nasty rumours that might unbalance his mind.

'And as for Rosie, she's also married her *older* man, so it's not as if you can shame her – not that I think you would have done anyway. You clearly don't know the woman.'

Helen could feel her heart hammering in her chest.

'And you can't touch Hannah. Because, quite simply, *I* won't let you. As long as I'm drawing breath, she'll *always* have a job in the yard. She and her aunty Rina will *always* have food on their table and a roof over their heads.'

Miriam burst out laughing.

'Goodness gracious me, Helen, you have changed your tune this past year, haven't you?' Miriam allowed herself another short burst of laughter. 'Perhaps you are having problems with *your* memory? Have you forgotten that it was *you* who once wanted to rip that gaggle of women welders to shreds? And if my "old" memory serves me right, I distinctly recall being in this very room and you telling me, your *dearest mother* here, how you were going to split up Polly and Tommy so that you could have the boy all to yourself . . . And yes . . . I'm sure I'm right in my rec-ollection: you didn't just threaten to spread malicious and totally false rumours about Tommy, but you went ahead and did it. You might even have succeeded in breaking up the pair if you'd done the job properly and made out Polly was stepping out with someone who wasn't actually mar-ried – *and* had a child on the way.'

Helen felt herself cringe inwardly. She had worked hard at pushing to the far recesses of her mind that painfully embarrassing memory of when Ned the plater's heavily pregnant wife had stomped into the yard and shown her up in front of the whole workforce.

'And when that plan didn't work out, you decided to take it out on Polly's friends. Remember? Remember how it was *you* who was trying to get the little refugee sacked – how *you* worked the poor "little bird" to the bone? Gave her all the worst jobs in the hope she'd walk – or you'd have enough ammunition to sack her.'

Helen felt awash with self-loathing. A self-loathing she hadn't felt for a good while. Her mother's words had brought the feeling back with a vengeance.

Miriam stood up, sensing it was time to go for the jugular.

'You might like to think you're whiter than white these days.' Miriam walked over to Helen. 'You might like to think you're little Miss Perfect, with your new doctor friend, but the thing is, Helen, you're *my* daughter. You've got *my* blood coursing through your veins. We're the same, me and you. Whether you like it or not.'

She paused.

'And it doesn't matter how hard you try, there's no running away from it.'

'I'm so sorry, Jack.'

Gloria had just told Jack that Arthur had died. She had her ear pressed against the receiver. She would have given anything to be with him now. To have told him face to face instead of down some crackly phone line.

'I'm glad it's *you* that's told me, and not *her*.' Jack didn't have to say who he was referring to. Gloria knew that Jack hated Miriam so much he could barely bring himself to say her name.

'Fingers crossed, you'll be able to come to the funeral?' Gloria tried not to feel too excited about the prospect; it felt wrong to gain any kind of pleasure from someone's death.

'No chance,' Jack said, his tone flat. The anger he felt whenever he thought, never mind *talked*, about his estranged wife was pushing at the surface, trying to break through.

'Really?' Gloria was genuinely surprised. 'Yer don't think she'll allow it?' It hurt her to admit that Miriam had such a hold over them both; that they had to seek her permission.

'That woman won't miss the opportunity of driving the knife in even further,' Jack said. 'She knows how much it'll hurt me not being there.'

'But you 'n Arthur were so close.'

'My point exactly.'

'But everyone knows how close you were,' Gloria argued. 'People will wonder why you've not come back to say yer goodbyes.' Her hand was gripping the black Bakelite handset. She forced herself to relax.

'A few might think it's strange, but most people will just think it's the war. Too busy trying to save the living to wave farewell to the dead.'

Gloria realised that Jack was right.

Miriam controlled them.

And there was nothing they could do to stop it.

'Did Helen seem all right when you spoke to her?' Jack asked. 'She's known Arthur all of her life. Probably saw more of Arthur than she did her own grandfather when she was little.'

'Yes, I think so,' Gloria reassured. 'She's pretty level-headed about these things.'

She thought for a moment.

'Although she did seem to think that you'd definitely be coming to the funeral. She told me she was going to see Miriam to tell her this evening.'

There was a snort of derision down the phone.

'Well, she'll be in for a disappointment . . . Tell her not to worry when yer see her tomorrow. Tell her she'll be paying her respects for the both of us.'

'I will, love.'

There was a pause.

'Do yer think Helen's all right about Tommy going back? I know how fond she was of the lad,' Jack said, not needing to elaborate.

'She seems fine. I think her fondness for Tommy really is just that these days. I think her attention's been focused more on her doctor "friend" of late.'

Gloria heard someone shouting in the background.

'Listen, pet,' Jack said. 'I've got to go now, but don't worry about me not coming back for the funeral. And tell Helen the same. It's not as if Arthur's gonna mind, is it? I'll visit his grave when I'm back.'

He was quiet for a second.

'She can't keep us apart for ever, yer know.'

Gloria didn't say so, but she wasn't so sure.

'And give the bab a cuddle from me,' Jack said. 'Tell her that her da loves her to bits.'

Gloria told him she would.

Hope needed as many reminders as possible that she did, in fact, have a father. Having not seen him for a year, it was unlikely that she would recognise him when she did eventually get to see him.

If she ever got to see him.

That dream seemed to be fading rapidly.

Chapter Seven

J.L. Thompson & Sons, North Sands, Sunderland

The following day
Tuesday 29 December

'I'm so angry!'

Helen ushered Gloria into her office.

Winston the ginger cat managed to shoot through before Helen closed the door.

Marching over to the blinds, Helen pulled them shut. She didn't care if her staff started gossiping about why Gloria had been summoned to her office. They could say what they damn well wanted.

Helen stomped over to her desk and grabbed her Pall Malls.

'Mother won't let Dad come to the funeral!' She pulled out a cigarette and lit it. 'Honestly, Gloria, I think I can say – hand on heart – that I *hate* her. I actually hate my own mother.'

'Come on, sit down and tell me what happened,' Gloria said, throwing the cat a look of disdain as it rubbed itself against Helen's legs, purring loudly.

'You don't think I'm like my mum, do you?' Helen said out of the blue.

Gloria sat down on the chair in front of the desk.

'Of course I don't. I'm always saying how much yer take after yer dad. In looks *and* in personality.'

Helen gave Gloria a sad smile. 'You always try and make me feel better.' She blew out smoke. 'It worries me, though, that I *am* like her. That I *have been* like her.'

'Don't be daft, yer nothing like her,' Gloria reassured. 'For starters, you've got a conscience.'

Helen looked at Gloria and they both laughed.

'It fights its way through occasionally.' Helen smiled and stubbed out her cigarette. She knew Gloria hated smoking. Made her think of her ex.

'I do worry, though,' Helen admitted, 'that we're blood, you know? That I'll be like her, even if I don't want to be.'

'I've never heard anything so ridiculous,' Gloria said. 'You choose the person yer want to be. And if yer don't want to be like your mother, yer won't be. It's your choice.' Gloria looked at Helen. If she was honest, there had been a time when she would have said Miriam and Helen were similar. Very similar. But not any more.

'Let me guess,' Gloria said. 'Miriam said point-blank that Jack's not allowed back for Arthur's send-off – and if he dares come within a mile of the place, she'll make sure everyone's secrets aren't secrets any more.'

Helen let out a bitter laugh. 'That's about the nub of it.'

'Well, don't worry,' Gloria said. 'Yer dad guessed there was no way he'd be allowed back. Out of spite, if nothing else. He said to tell yer not to mind or get yerself all irate. He's just going to be glad you'll be there on his behalf . . . Everything will work itself out eventually.' Gloria sounded much more optimistic than she really felt. 'You'll see.'

Helen didn't look convinced.

'I was awake all last night. Thinking and thinking. Going over in my mind what I can do to get Dad back here. How to break the hold my mother has over everyone.'

She looked at Gloria, the beginnings of hope on her face.

'What if Martha actually *knows* about her real mother and doesn't care one jot if the whole world also knows?'

She paused.

'What if Angie's mam runs off with her young lover? Or her dad knows about her mam already, but doesn't let on – or care?

'And let's say . . . And I know this is a long shot . . . But what happens if Dorothy's mother decides she wants to come clean and admits to her bigamy? Sorts it all out legally?'

Helen took a deep breath. 'Then my mother will have no axe to wield over all our heads and it'll be *her* that's worried about being exposed – a spurned wife whose husband has left her for another woman. It'll be *her* that's worried about feeding the town's gossipmongers, knowing it'll keep them going for weeks – months.'

Gloria sighed.

'That's a long list of ifs.' She pushed herself out of her chair. 'Why don't we make the most of what we've got now? Why don't yer arrange to go 'n see yer dad in Glasgow for a few days? Yer can combine it with work. Chat to the manager at Lithgows about the things you high-ups chat about. Yer mam can't stop yer from seeing yer dad. And before yer go up there, I can get a photograph of Hope done 'n you can take it to him. He'll love that.'

Helen gave a resigned sigh and nodded.

Gloria, as always, spoke sense. She was the voice of reason. The mother she'd never really had.

Seeing Gloria out, Helen picked up Winston, who immediately started to nuzzle her neck.

'One day, Mother, I promise you,' she spoke her words aloud to the empty office, 'I'll get Father back here. And there'll be nothing you can do to stop me.'

Chapter Eight

New Year's Eve

Thursday 31 December

Polly watched as the coffin, carried by Ralph and three other divers, along with the two linesmen, slowly made its way down the aisle of the grand, Gothic-style St Ignatius Church.

Had it really been just six days since she'd walked down this very aisle with Arthur by her side, proud as punch to be giving her away?

Now it was Arthur who was the centre of attention. Something, Polly knew, he would have hated.

'You all right?' Bel whispered in Polly's ear, taking her hand at the same time.

'Yes, yes, I'm fine, honestly,' Polly said, squeezing Bel's hand to reassure her.

Bel looked at her sister-in-law and believed her. She seemed in control of her emotions and she looked well. The black dress she was wearing had not dulled her complexion. Married life suited her, Bel mused. Even if her new husband was thousands of miles away.

Sensing movement next to her, Bel looked down at her daughter, who was happily sandwiched between her mammy and her daddy, and then at Joe, who gave her a wink and a smile that was a little sad. They'd talked about Teddy while they'd been getting changed into their smart clothes. They'd never had a funeral for Joe's twin – Bel's first husband – because they'd never had a body to bury. One day, they'd agreed, they would visit the place called Sidi Barrani where he'd been laid to rest.

Bel glanced back down at Lucille, whose cherub-like face was beaming up at her. She looked as bright as the yellow dress she was wearing. Her joy at being able to wear her favourite dress twice within the space of a week was more than evident. The disapproving looks at Lucille's splash of colour amidst all the black had not gone unnoticed, though. Not that it bothered Bel. She knew Arthur wouldn't mind. Not one bit.

Hearing the reverend loudly clear his throat, she looked up to see him surveying the faces of his expectant congregation, his service book open in upturned palms.

'We are gathered here today to pay our last respects to Arthur Thomas Watts.' He spoke with great solemnity. 'Let us now pray.'

Bel lowered herself down onto the embroidered kneeler and clasped her hands in prayer, leaning forward a little to afford herself a sidelong glance at Mr Havelock.

This was the first time she had seen him since the day that was indelibly imprinted on her memory – when her ma had taken her to Glen Path.

That afternoon she'd been so full of expectation – excitement, even – knowing she was finally going to find out who her real father was; after all, she'd had a lifetime of wondering.

Now she wished she'd just kept on wondering.

She had never agreed with the philosophy that ignorance is bliss.

Until now.

Now she had to live with the knowledge she'd gained that day back in June when she'd learnt the true horror of her parentage.

Afterwards, she'd felt a strange kind of bereavement, as though she had somehow lost her father – which, in a way, she had, for she could not call any man who sired a child through rape a father. Such a man had no right to a claim of parenthood.

Bel took a look at the old man's profile. It was hard to view him with any kind of objectivity. All she could see was a parasite of a man who had sucked any joy that life could have offered out of a poor fifteen-year-old girl.

A vulnerable fifteen-year-old girl who was her ma.

Bel clenched her fists tightly and looked away for fear of what the violence stirring in her own heart might make her do.

She thought of her ma and part of her wanted to weep for everything she had been forced to endure because of the sadistic needs of one man.

'*Amen.*' The voices of the congregation were loud and enthusiastic, carried by the church's acoustics. There was a sense of importance in the air. Bel knew it was because the parish – one of the poorest in the borough – had been graced with the celebrity of the Havelock family.

If only they knew.

As the mourners all sat back on their hard oak seats, Bel looked at Miriam. She was the spit of her father.

As was Bel.

This was the first occasion they had all attended together. For the briefest of moments, Bel had a flash of anxiety that the similarities in their looks might be noticed, but she dismissed the thought as soon as it had registered.

She was being paranoid.

*

55

There was a mass rustling as everyone got to their feet and fussed about with their hymn books and Order of Service pamphlets. The huge pipes of the church organ droned into life and sounded out the first vibrating chords of 'The Lord is My Shepherd'.

Polly was standing, her hymn book closed. She knew the words. She looked about her, forcing herself to be observant, to remember as much about this day as she could so she could put it all down in her letter to Tommy. She wanted him to feel as though he had been here, saying goodbye to his beloved grandda.

She turned slightly and caught sight of Gloria with Hope in her arms. Dorothy and Angie were standing next to her.

Polly knew Gloria would be doing the same. Memorising every detail of the service and the day in its entirety so she could relay everything back to Jack. They'd all been a little surprised when Gloria had told them that he hadn't been given leave to attend the funeral. Everyone knew how close Jack and Arthur had always been.

It was only Rosie who hadn't seemed particularly surprised or incensed. She'd said Clydeside was under enormous pressure to get the ships out, and it really was a case of 'all hands on deck' for the next few months.

> The Lord's my Shepherd, I'll not want;
> He makes me down to lie
> In pastures green; He leadeth me . . .

Gloria sang the words of the 23rd Psalm, but it was a half-hearted effort. Her mind was wandering. She looked down at Hope, who seemed happy to mimic what the others around her were doing and was standing with an upside-down copy of the New Testament in her hands, opening and shutting her mouth.

Looking at Arthur's casket at the front of the altar, she thought back to Hope's christening. That had been some day. It had been thanks to Arthur that Jack had ended up at the church, dripping wet, having battled through a storm to get there, not only to see his daughter christened, but to meet her for the first time.

And it was because of Arthur that Jack had slowly started to get his memory back, for the old man had taken him to the quayside every lunch break and they had sat and looked out across the Wear, as they had done as younger men. Arthur, not normally the most loquacious, had chatted to Jack about his past and about the present, and in doing so had given Jack his future.

These past few days Gloria had felt so resentful about not seeing Jack – about him not being allowed to come to the funeral to say his final goodbyes to a man he loved. But thinking about Arthur, and how he had helped to bring Jack back into her life, she realised she had much to be thankful for.

For now, she just had to be patient.

The vicar allowed a few moments' silence after the hymn had been sung and the reverberation of the organ had diminished, before gesturing to show his congregation that they could sit down.

'And now,' Reverend Winsey said, 'a short reading from Ecclesiastes, chapter three, verses one to four.'

Rosie froze. It was the same Old Testament passage that had been read out at her mam and dad's funeral.

'To every thing there is a season, and a time to every purpose under the heaven: A time to be born, and a time to die.'

Rosie looked at Charlotte out of the corner of her eye. Would she remember?

'A time to plant, and a time to pluck up that which is planted.'

57

It was hard to tell.

'*A time to kill, and a time to heal; a time to break down, and a time to build up. A time to weep, and a time to laugh; a time to mourn, and a time to dance.*'

Rosie stewed over the words that had been engraved in her memory. *But it hadn't been time for her mam and dad to die, had it?* Rosie felt bitterness rise up inside her. Anger. God had got the timing of their demise terribly wrong. What had happened had been unjust and what had happened to her afterwards, unholy.

Rosie leant towards her sister and whispered, 'You all right?'

Charlotte nodded, but her eyes looked wet.

Rosie put her arm around her and gave her a quick squeeze as the organ started up for the next hymn.

They stood.

As the sound of the choir rose above the voices of the congregation, Rosie mouthed the words of hymn 552.

'*Lead us, heavenly Father, lead us . . .*'

She didn't feel like asking the Good Lord for guidance. She'd managed this far on her own, hadn't she?

A short sermon followed the hymn. The vicar said some kind words about Arthur, how he had worked hard his whole life and had been a loving family man who had recently seen his grandson married.

'I have also been told – ' he singled out Mr Havelock and smiled ' – that Arthur Watts was not only the town's most revered deep-sea diver. What is not so well known, for Arthur was a humble man and not one for boasting, is that he also saved many a person from drowning – both in the murky waters of the Wear and in our unforgiving North Sea.'

Rosie looked towards the front of the church and could just about see Polly. She appeared to be holding up. She'd been incredibly strong, despite having to say goodbye to the two men she loved so much within the space of a week.

Following the Lord's Prayer, the service came to an end with a blessing.

Agnes, who had been seated at the end of the front pew on the left side of the church, nearest to the aisle, stood up. She looked along the row at her daughter, her daughter-in-law, her granddaughter and her son.

She'd had a word with 'Him upstairs' during both sets of prayers and had told him in no uncertain terms that he had already laid claim to her husband, Harry, and son Teddy, and that was to be enough. No more. The rest of her family stayed intact. And that included Tommy.

She did not want to see history repeating itself, as it seemed to have a habit of doing. Polly was not going to follow in her own footsteps and be left a widow for longer than she'd been a wife.

Standing up, they all waited for the pallbearers to carefully manoeuvre the coffin onto their shoulders so that Arthur left the church, as was tradition, feet first.

After the coffin had passed, Agnes, knowing her place, allowed Mr Havelock, Miriam and then Helen to leave their seats so as to be the first to follow the casket up the aisle. She was surprised when Helen let her mother and grandfather go ahead before putting out a gloved hand to politely show Agnes that she would like them to walk up the aisle together.

Behind them, the rest of the mourners followed.

'Your ma not want to come?' Polly spoke out of the corner of her mouth as they made the slow walk up the aisle to a rather beautiful rendition of Ave Maria.

59

'Too much to do at the pub,' Bel said. It was a plausible excuse as the wake was to be held at the Tatham, but Bel knew that wasn't the real reason for her ma's no-show. She'd seen her face as soon as Polly had told them over tea the other night that the funeral was to be paid for by Mr Havelock. Her ma never looked particularly healthy at the best of times, but she'd turned as white as a sheet on hearing the 'good news'. It was the same look Bel had seen on her ma's face that fateful afternoon when they'd both turned to see Mr Havelock's glossy black Jaguar pull into the driveway of the house where an act of violence had spawned a life – and ruined another.

When Agnes had commented that the 'man himself' would no doubt be attending, Bel knew wild horses wouldn't drag her ma to Arthur's funeral.

'Is she all right?' Polly asked as they finally reached the top of the nave. She saw the doors open and was glad to see the rain had stopped.

Bel nodded. 'Why do you ask?'

'Dunno. She hasn't seemed her usual self these past few days. A bit quiet. Not as argumentative as usual,' Polly said.

'I guess we should be counting our blessings.' Bel felt uncomfortable lying to Polly. They had been inseparable since they were children and she couldn't remember a time when they had ever kept secrets from each other. For some reason, when her ma had told her the truth about the man who had fathered her, a barrier had gone up and she had not told Polly. She had only told two people: Joe and Maisie.

It had now been six months since that day and she still hadn't confided in Polly.

But what confused her the most was that she wasn't sure why.

Was it perhaps because she herself was still trying to come to terms with the horror of her conception? Or was it because she hadn't quite decided what to do about it?

As they walked out of the church and onto the pavement, Bel took a deep breath. The air was laced with the distinctive muggy smell that always seemed to linger after a rainstorm. They stood and watched as the coffin was carefully placed in the hearse.

'*Polly!*'

It was Helen.

'Would you and your mum like to come with us in the funeral cortège?'

Polly smiled. 'Well, yes, that would be nice. If there's room. Thank you.'

Helen's attention turned to Bel.

'Actually, it can take six if you would like to come with us as well?'

Bel's heart suddenly started to pound. The thought of being within touching distance of Mr Havelock caused panic.

'No, no!' Bel was aware of the alarm in her voice; she forced herself to be calm. 'Thank you anyway, Helen, but I'd best go with Joe and Lucille.'

'Of course,' Helen said, 'you'll want to go with your family.' She turned to leave. 'We'll see you at the cemetery.'

Bel watched as Polly and Agnes walked with Helen to the funeral car that was parked up behind the hearse. The chauffeur was holding the door open. She could just about make out Mr Havelock and Miriam sitting in the back seat.

Chapter Nine

Everyone was quiet as the coffin was lowered into the ground.

It seemed fitting that it was Ralph and his diving team who were in charge of the task. Walter and Kenneth, the two linesmen, had probably lowered Arthur down into the Wear a fair few times over the years. This time, however, they wouldn't be bringing him back up.

'In the sweat of thy face shalt thou eat bread, till thou return unto the ground; for out of it wast thou taken: for dust thou art, and unto dust shalt thou return.'

Reverend Winsey spoke the words of Genesis 3, verse 19. He then picked up a small handful of freshly dug soil and threw it onto the coffin.

Mr Havelock, who had clearly taken on the mantle of chief mourner, took his cue to do the same. He picked up a mound of dirt, walked over to the open grave and let the slightly damp earth filter through his fingers onto the solid oak casket.

Helen watched, knowing her grandfather would be inspecting the craftsmanship, making sure it was up to scratch; he had paid for it, after all. She looked at her mother, who was next in line. For some reason, she had a handkerchief over her mouth.

Helen watched as Miriam daintily picked up the smallest amount of dirt in her gloved hand. She threw it into the grave as if she was throwing a penny at a group of beggars she wanted shot of.

Since she was next, Helen took the few steps necessary to reach the small pile of soil. Bending down, she purposely took a generous handful before dropping half of it onto the coffin. She paused, then let the rest fall.

She turned and stared at her mother.

She didn't need to tell Miriam that she had just done her father's bidding.

As the rest of the mourners made their way over to the graveside, Mr Havelock and Miriam turned away and started back to the funeral car. They had fulfilled their obligation. As they walked carefully across the wet grass, Helen's immediate boss, Harold, and a few other shipyard bigwigs hurried across to shake Mr Havelock's hand. A few, she knew, would be asking him for favours. Or for money. Or both.

A photographer from the *Sunderland Echo* seemed to appear out of nowhere. There was a flash of a light bulb as he took a photograph of her grandfather and her mother. Then another with the Wear Commissioner in the shot. Helen thought her mother would be cheered up no end. Seeing herself in the local paper would make the whole laborious day worthwhile.

Helen moved back to allow the other mourners to say their final goodbyes. She recognised quite a few faces from Thompson's – from the past and the present. A little further away from the grave were Joe and Major Black, as well as some of their Home Guard unit looking smart in their khaki uniforms.

She watched as Polly, who had been chatting to Hannah's aunty and the old woman she knew to be called Vera, stepped forward and added to the earth now building up on top of the coffin.

Agnes came next.

Then Bel.

Helen subtly scrutinised the woman she was now convinced was a Havelock, squinting as the sun made a sudden appearance from behind pewter-grey clouds. Bel was holding Lucille's hand as the little girl crouched down to take her offering of earth, the hem of her pretty yellow dress just touching the wet grass. She sprinkled soil onto the casket as though it were icing on a cake.

Rosie followed, but her sister held back. As they walked away from the grave, Helen caught Charlotte taking hold of Rosie's hand. The gesture gave her a lump in her throat, although she was unsure why.

Last in the line of mourners were Gloria and Hope.

Taking a scoop of soil, Gloria held her palm out so that Hope could copy what she had seen the adults do.

Hope was still too young to grasp the meaning of death, but Helen knew she would be aware that the old man, whom she had seen almost every day of her short life, was no longer a part of it.

As Gloria turned to leave the graveside, she jigged Hope up onto her hip.

'Let me take her off you.' Helen stepped forward and stretched out her arms to relieve Gloria.

Gloria hesitated, her eyes flicking across to Miriam and then back to Helen.

Helen clocked her reticence.

'Come here, Hope, darling,' Helen said, beckoning.

''Elen!' Hope's little face creased up into a joyful expression. She, too, stretched out her pudgy little arms, mirroring her big sister's show of love.

Helen saw her mother and grandfather turn and look as Hope's voice sounded out over the muted chatter of those still milling around. It suddenly occurred to Helen that this was the first time they had been within spitting distance of Jack's mistress – and the child they only ever referred to as 'the bastard'.

Helen hoisted Hope onto her hip, and she in turn wrapped her legs round her big sister's waist.

'Are you sure this is wise?' Gloria spoke quietly so only Helen could hear.

'I'm not doing anything wrong, am I?' Helen turned her back on her mother and her grandfather but could still feel their steely glares. Providing she never let on that Hope was her sister, or Gloria her father's mistress, she could do what she liked.

'I'm simply being sociable with my workers – and their families.' She brushed a thick strand of Hope's black hair to the side. 'I think this little girl needs a haircut.'

Then Helen turned her attention back to Gloria, who was now looking very worried and very uncomfortable. 'All right, I give up,' she said, handing Hope over.

'I'll see you later,' Gloria said, her eyes darting to Miriam. To the woman who had changed the course of her life all those years ago when she had conned Jack into marriage. To the woman who was still controlling her life now, all these years later.

Stop it! Gloria reprimanded herself. *Stop being a bloody victim.*

Defiantly, Gloria looked Miriam straight in the eye for a brief moment, before turning and walking over to Dorothy and Angie, who were chatting away to Beryl and her daughters, Iris and Audrey.

Helen watched the unspoken exchange. She looked over at her mother and grandfather. They were putting on a good show, but she knew that underneath their veneer of calm cordiality, they'd be spitting feathers.

Looking at the women welders and then over to her mother and grandfather, Helen felt a sudden, overwhelming feeling of isolation. She didn't belong in either camp.

'Are you coming to the wake?' Polly suddenly appeared at her side.

Helen knew there was to be a bit of a knees-up at the Tatham. A celebration of Arthur's life, which would inevitably turn into a party to see in the New Year.

'Bill's managed to get an extended licence,' Polly explained. 'Thanks to your grandfather.' The two women looked over to Mr Havelock, now being helped into the back of the funeral car by the chauffeur. Miriam was already settled in the back and was glaring out of the window, her face as dark as the clouds gathering overhead.

'And thanks to everyone chipping in with their rations, Ma's made enough sandwiches and sausage rolls to feed the five thousand, so there'll be plenty to eat,' Polly said, bringing her attention back to Helen.

'Yes, I'll be there,' Helen said. She saw that the chauffeur was standing by the car door, waiting for her. 'I'm nipping back to work to make sure everything's all right. While the cat's away and all that. Plus, Crown's launched *Empire Demon* today, so I just wanted to check that went off all right.'

Polly nodded. They all knew the owners of Thompson's were planning to buy Crown's sometime in the not too distant future.

Helen looked at Polly. 'How are you feeling? I know how close you and Arthur were.'

'Sad,' Polly admitted. 'I'm going to miss him terribly.' She looked at the grave, which had been positioned right next to Flo's. 'I wish I'd had a chance to thank him for everything he did.' She felt the tears welling up and swallowed them down. 'It was really thanks to Arthur that Tommy and I got back together.'

'How so?' Helen said. She was curious.

'Apparently, they were both here.' Polly looked round at the cemetery. 'Tommy was saying to Arthur that he didn't

66

know what to do – whether it was better to let me go and be free of him.' Polly shook her head. 'As if that's what would have made me happy.' She rolled her eyes, glistening with the beginnings of tears. 'And Arthur suddenly said that he had this image of Flo standing, hands on her hips, telling Tommy that if he wanted something, he had to go and get it. That no one else was going to get it for him.'

Helen thought that it was good advice.

'And that's when Tommy came to the yard and got me,' Polly said.

Helen remembered the scene well. Had watched them kiss and make up from the office window, along with Bel and Marie-Anne and the rest of the admin staff. The women had all *ahhed*. Some had said how jealous they were of Polly and Tommy's romance, and Helen had been surprised that she hadn't felt even the faintest stirrings of the green-eyed monster. She'd seen it as proof that she had finally let go of Tommy. That she was no longer in love with him. She doubted whether she ever really had been.

'I'm guessing Tommy knows about Arthur?' Helen asked.

'Yes, I wrote him a letter,' Polly said.

Helen saw the main bulk of mourners start to disperse. 'Do you want a lift back?'

Polly shook her head. 'No, thanks anyway. I'll go back with my lot.'

Helen looked over to the funeral car.

The engine was running.

Time to face the music.

'What the hell do you think you're playing at?'

Miriam's voice was a hissed whisper.

She turned and checked that the glass partition dividing the driver from the passengers was properly closed.

'What do you mean, Mother?' Helen made a good show of looking genuinely puzzled.

'Now, now, my dear.' Mr Havelock kept his voice low. 'I think you know what your mother is referring to. Do you think it's wise to be seen to be so friendly with Gloria and your father's bastard?'

Helen looked at her grandfather. 'That "bastard", Grandfather, is called Hope. And Hope is my sister. She might not be a Havelock, but she is a Crawford. As am I, don't forget.'

'Yes, my dear.' Mr Havelock's voice was placatory. 'That's exactly the point. You clearly take after your father in looks. As does the bastard.'

Helen looked at her grandfather. It was obvious by his tone that he wasn't trying to be offensive by calling Hope a bastard. He simply saw her as just that – an illegitimate child, and therefore totally insignificant. If not a hindrance. And that was what Helen found most perturbing.

They were quiet for a short while.

'As your grandfather is saying, *Helen*.' Again, Miriam was speaking in a half hiss, half whisper. 'You and the brat look alike. You're both the bloody spit of your father. People might well put two and two together.'

No one spoke. You could have cut the atmosphere with a knife.

Miriam finally broke the stand-off with an almighty sigh. 'For the life of me, I really can't understand how it is you've gone from hating Gloria and her motley crew of women welders to being the best of buddies.'

'And why,' Mr Havelock raised an eyebrow, 'you risked your own life a few months back getting Gloria and the bastard out of that bombed house in Tatham Street.'

'I didn't know anything about that.' Miriam's tone was sharp. She looked from her father to Helen.

'Perhaps, Mother, if you didn't spend so much time swilling gin at the Grand with that lush Amelia, you might know more of what's happening in the real world.'

Mr Havelock extracted a cigar from his top pocket. 'Your daughter has a point there, my dear.'

'Perhaps if my daughter actually talked to her poor mama occasionally, I might know what's happening "in the real world",' Miriam jibed back.

Helen looked out the window. *Thank God, they were nearly at Thompson's.* She felt as though she would explode if she didn't get out of this car.

Leaning forward, she yanked open the glass partition.

'Can you pull over here, please?' she said to the driver, before turning to her grandfather. 'I can walk down to the yard. The fresh air will do me good.'

The chauffeur looked to Mr Havelock for permission. The old man nodded his assent and the car pulled over.

Helen climbed out.

Before shutting the door, she leant back in.

'On the way back home, Mother, you might want to tell Grandfather about the lovely little postbox you had put up. And about all those letters that were sent to the house but mysteriously went missing. It might go some way to explaining why your daughter doesn't talk to her "poor mama" much these days.'

And with that she slammed the door and walked off down the embankment to work.

Chapter Ten

'Oh, John, thank goodness you've come!' Helen stopped for a moment. 'God, I must stop saying that!' She had welcomed John with those same words on Boxing Day. 'It sounds like I'm incapable of doing anything on my own.'

Dr Parker smiled. He knew Helen was more than capable of being her own woman, standing on her own two feet and going places unaccompanied, but he also knew she lacked confidence at times, and going to Arthur's wake at the Tatham was one such time. It was on occasions like this, he knew, that Helen needed a friend. It was clear to him now, more than ever, that Helen saw him purely as a friend – and nothing more. It wouldn't have been a problem *if* he hadn't been so in love with the woman.

'Come on, I've managed to nab Grandfather's chauffeur to take us over there,' Helen said. 'Not that I'm in his or my dear mother's good books today.'

Dr Parker gave Helen a questioning look.

'I'll tell you in the car.'

Ten minutes later they were making their way over the Wearmouth Bridge. The chauffeur was driving carefully as the temperature had dipped, causing the wet roads to turn icy. Helen looked out of the window. She couldn't see much – the vague outline of the barrage balloons, and the dark shadows of the dozens of frigates, warships and colliers docked along the hem of the river.

'So, your mother now knows about your heroics during the Tatham Street bombing?' Dr Parker asked.

Helen nodded. 'Not that I think Mother will see it as being particularly heroic. More than likely she'll be worried that people will be asking why I did what I did. She'll be terrified they'll "put two and two together", as she puts it.'

Dr Parker thought for a moment.

'I'm surprised your grandfather knew about it.'

'What? My "heroics"?'

Dr Parker nodded.

'He might be ancient,' Helen mused, 'but he's still got his ear to the ground. Besides, there's not a lot he doesn't know when it comes to what happens in the town. He's got moles everywhere.'

Dr Parker thought about the time he had met Mr Havelock when Helen was in the hospital after her miscarriage. He'd never forget the way her grandfather had written out a cheque, saying he hoped it was enough for helping Helen and, moreover, for keeping shtum about what he had described as the 'dire predicament' his granddaughter had got herself into. He had been 'eternally thankful' that the situation had ended up 'resolving itself'. Dr Parker had wanted to say that the resolving of the 'predicament' had nearly claimed his granddaughter's life, and perhaps it was her recovery for which he should have been 'eternally thankful'.

'Anyway, I told him about her keeping back Father's letters,' Helen said.

'And what was his reaction?'

'No idea. I left them to it.'

Somehow Dr Parker didn't think Helen's grandfather would have been morally aggrieved by what Miriam had done.

Helen suddenly turned her attention back to John. 'You don't think I'm like her, do you?'

'What, your mother?' Dr Parker's brow furrowed.

Helen's eyes searched his face, wanting to know what he really thought.

'Well, put it this way.' His face was deadly serious. 'I wouldn't be sat here now if you were in any way like your mother.'

Helen's face lit up with sheer relief. His words had been spoken with total candour.

'That's why I love you so much,' she said.

As soon as the words were out, Helen felt herself flush bright red.

'Oh, gosh, how embarrassing. I meant to say, "That's *what I love* about you so much." You know? Because you know me. You know what I'm really like.'

Dr Parker looked at Helen. He could see her obvious embarrassment at her faux pas. He knew that in a way she did love him. Like a brother. A friend.

'I know exactly what you meant,' he said. 'And I do know exactly what you're like.' He smiled to ease her still evident mortification. 'Warts and all!'

Helen slapped his arm playfully, relieved the awkward moment was over.

When Helen and Dr Parker walked into the main bar, it was heaving. The air was heavy with smoke and the smell of spilled beer.

'Gosh, I think half the east end's in here tonight,' Helen turned and shouted back at Dr Parker.

When they got to the bar, they saw a picture of Arthur in his canvas diving suit, holding his twelve-bolt copper helmet under his arm. Next to him there was a rather faded sepia photo of Arthur and Flo on their wedding day. The third photograph was of Arthur holding a baby in his arms.

'Is that Arthur's daughter?' Dr Parker asked.

'No, that's Tommy,' Helen said.

'Ah.' Dr Parker pretended to inspect the photograph, all the while fighting the now familiar rush of jealousy, quickly followed by despondency.

'Can I have your attention, please!' Bill's voice boomed out. The pub fell quiet.

Pearl spotted Helen at the bar and quickly turned away, pretending not to notice them. Her pretence did not go unnoticed, though. Dr Parker had seen Pearl's slightly panicked reaction; seen something in her face that he couldn't quite read. Strange. He watched as Pearl made herself busy, clearing empty pint glasses off the far end of the bar.

'As this is Arthur Watts's wake, I'd like to say a few words to honour a man who I'm sure you will all agree was the epitome of a true gentleman and a true friend to all those he encountered.'

The barmaid, Geraldine, who had been drafted in for the evening, saw Pearl's reluctance to serve the posh-looking couple and went over to see what they wanted.

'Not many of you might know this, but it is thanks to Arthur we now have our North pier—'

'What yer after?' The young barmaid half spoke, half mouthed to Dr Parker.

Helen leant over the bar and asked for a pint of bitter and a vodka and lemon.

The girl looked at Dr Parker as though needing his acquiescence.

Helen rolled her eyes to show her annoyance and leant over the bar again.

'This year, if you don't mind.'

'—He was also the longest-serving deep-sea diver the Wear Commissioner has had to this day. And probably the most highly regarded.'

73

Bill's words were met with a mumbling of assent.

'Vodka and lemon?' Dr Parker quizzed.

'Yes,' Helen said. 'Time for a change.'

Dr Parker thought it might be more to do with her wanting to be as different from her mother as possible.

Helen glanced around as she waited for their drinks. She looked over a sea of flat caps, searching the pub for Bel.

When the surly young barmaid put the drinks on the bar, Helen got out her purse and paid. Dr Parker didn't object. He'd given up objecting; had come to believe that it was Helen's way of saying this wasn't a date. They were simply friends.

Dr Parker looked at Pearl as she turned around.

Seeing that Helen had been looked after, she moved back to the middle of the bar to serve a group of elderly men in their best suits. Pearl started to chat loudly to one of the men, called Albert, saying that even though Arthur 'had gone to meet his maker', Albert should still drop by with any spare veg from his allotment.

Dr Parker looked at Pearl's profile. She was definitely Bel's mother. You could see the similarities in their looks, if nothing else. But who was it that *Pearl* reminded him of?

'Thank you.' Dr Parker smiled at Helen as he took his pint from her.

As they made their way over to the women welders, who had congregated at the far side of the pub, it suddenly came to him. He would have slapped his forehead with the palm of his hand if he'd been able to.

It wasn't just Bel who looked the spit of Miriam – *Pearl did too*.

Miriam and Pearl looked uncannily similar, only Pearl's looks were camouflaged by the ravages caused by a harsh, impoverished life.

With that realisation, other thoughts followed.

And not particularly nice ones either.

By the time he and Helen had squeezed and man-oeuvred their way across to the other side of the pub, Bill had finished his speech and a toast had been made.

'Hi, everyone!' Helen's greeting rang out as they reached the women welders.

Dr Parker knew Helen was making a good show of being completely relaxed in her environment when inwardly she felt anything but.

'Helen! I'm so glad you made it!' Polly said. 'We were just going to make our own little toast to Arthur.'

Polly made room so that Helen and Dr Parker could be a part of their circle.

Polly raised her glass of port in the air.

'A toast on behalf of those who couldn't be here: Tommy and Jack, who both loved Arthur to bits.' Polly looked at the circle of faces. 'Who will, I'm sure, be saying their own goodbyes to Arthur in their own way in Gibraltar and in Glasgow.'

There was a brief pause as everyone raised their glasses in the air.

'To Arthur,' Polly declared.

'To Arthur!' the women's voices rang out in unison.

They each took a sip of their drink.

Helen was about to edge her way towards Gloria and Hope, the only people she really felt at ease with, when she was stopped in her tracks by Dorothy and Angie.

'Do you think your dad'll be back any time soon?' Dorothy said.

Helen was taken aback by the question and by the fact that Dorothy and Angie were staring at her expectantly.

She looked around for John, but he had turned round and was talking to Joe.

'Well . . .' Helen hesitated. 'I hope so.'

'It's just that Gloria's not seen him for ages.' Dorothy dropped her voice, even though it was totally unnecessary as the noise levels in the pub were now high and everyone was engrossed in their own chatter. 'And if he doesn't come back soon, Hope's not going to know who her dad is. I swear she thinks Joe's her father.'

Angie was nodding her agreement.

Helen looked at Dorothy and at Angie. They might act the fools – the jokers of the pack – but they were far from stupid.

'I know.' Helen said it in a way that she hoped conveyed empathy. 'But it's madness on the Clyde at the moment. They really are up against it. It's all hands on deck.'

'Funny – those were the exact words Rosie used,' Dorothy said.

'Yeah, exactly,' Angie agreed.

Helen looked at the two young women.

'That's because it's true,' she said, trying not to sound defensive. 'It really is a case of all hands on deck. Every man – and woman. You both know more than most how punishing our deadlines are – especially with all the overtime you've all done.'

'Ah, Helen!' Gloria had seen that Helen was cornered. 'Take this little monkey off me, will you?' She handed Hope over. 'She's getting heavier by the minute.'

'You could have always asked me, you know,' Dorothy said. 'I *am* her godmother, don't forget.'

'I know, Dor, but you and Angie have been playing with her all afternoon. You need a rest.'

'Why don't you . . .' Helen grappled around in her handbag with her free hand ' . . . go and get everyone a round in? My way of saying thank you for all your hard work – all the hours you've been notching up.'

Dorothy and Angie looked at the crisp ten-bob note.

Rosie suddenly appeared and tapped Dorothy on the shoulder. 'And Charlotte here can give you a hand.' She nodded her head towards her sister. 'But don't let her con you into getting her anything alcoholic.'

'Oh,' Helen chipped in, 'and buy the barmaid a drink as well. Show her it's not only the men that are able to tip.'

'Come on, then!' Dorothy said to Angie and Charlotte. 'Into the fray!'

Once the two inquisitors and their helper had been swallowed up in the throng and were out of earshot, Rosie gave Helen and Gloria a worried look. 'They're getting suspicious, aren't they?'

They nodded.

Helen jostled Hope to get a more secure hold of her. The toddler looked at her big sister, then at her mother and Rosie, scrutinising the serious looks on their faces.

'And the longer it is before Jack comes back, the more suspicious they're gonna be,' Gloria sighed.

'But Dorothy's right,' Helen said. 'This little one's growing up fast. She needs her daddy.' She looked at Gloria and Rosie. 'Needs to know *who* her daddy is.'

'I know,' Rosie said, 'especially as Jack could be doing equally important war work here.'

'You don't think either Dorothy or Angie know? About their mothers?' Helen said, looking at Rosie. 'I know Gloria thinks that Angie might know about *her* mam.'

'I wouldn't be surprised if Angie's got an inkling,' Rosie said. 'But I wouldn't have thought Dorothy has a clue about her mother's . . .' She paused, not wanting to say the word.

'Oversight?' Helen filled in the blank.

'That's one way of describing it,' Rosie said. As she spoke, she took hold of Hope's hand and gave it a kiss. The little girl was always fascinated by her scars, forever trying to touch them, even when she had them well covered with make-up.

'It's just, if they did,' Helen continued her train of thought, 'then you could tell them.'

'What?' Rosie said, surprised. 'About your mother's blackmail?'

Helen nodded. 'It would go a long way to lessening my mother's hold.'

'Which would mean,' Rosie added, 'we'd be nearer to getting Jack back.'

Gloria felt her heart lift at the very thought.

Dorothy and Angie were standing at the bar, waiting for the rest of the round they were buying on Helen's behalf.

Angie had given Charlotte a demonstration on how to carry three drinks in two hands. She had mastered the technique quickly and delivered two half-pints of shandy and a brandy and lemonade to Martha and her mam and dad. She was now coming back for Helen, Gloria and Rosie's drinks and was making haste as Dorothy had promised her a sip of her port for helping them out.

'Can yer imagine living somewhere like Lily's?' Angie said to Dorothy. It was their favourite conversation and had been since they'd been inside the bordello on Christmas Eve. It had given them hours of endless chatter and it always had them whooping with laughter that Toby had thought Dorothy was one of Lily's 'girls'.

'It was that chandelier that did it for me,' Angie said. 'Honestly, I thought my jaw was gonna hit the ground.'

'The *ground* being a rather gorgeous polished parquet floor,' Dorothy added.

'And that staircase,' Angie said, taking a sip of her gin and tonic; a drink, Dorothy noticed, her friend had started having since beginning her lessons in 'being posh'.

'I knar Lily's a bit o'er the top, but her house is really something else.'

Dorothy nodded. 'I know. I swear I felt like I'd walked onto the set of some Hollywood movie. Those plush velvet curtains, that chaise longue, the beautiful cherrywood desk . . .'

'And dinnit get me started on the wallpaper. I had to stop myself gannin over 'n touching it. It was gorgeous.'

'Oh, and that fireplace. It looked like it'd been hand-carved and shipped directly from Paris.'

'Here you are!' The barmaid put the rest of the drinks down in front of them. 'Is that yer lot?' She looked at Dorothy and Angie and then nodded over at someone behind them. 'Does yer little waitress want anything?'

Dorothy and Angie both spun round to see Charlotte.

'How long 'ave yer been there?' Angie demanded.

'Just got here,' Charlotte lied.

'That was very kind of you,' Dr Parker said to Helen.

Martha's parents, Mr and Mrs Perkins, had been over to thank Helen for the hamper she had sent to the house at Christmas.

'It was the least I could do,' Helen said, dismissively. 'Their daughter *did* put her life on the line to save me and, of course, Gloria and Hope.'

'Well, it obviously meant a lot to them.' Dr Parker watched as Martha and her parents said their goodbyes to everyone. They were going to see in the New Year at home.

Dr Parker looked around. He was glad they had done the rounds and chatted to those they had to and those they wanted to. Midnight was approaching and, remarkably, they'd found themselves a table in a relatively quiet corner.

'So, Sherlock, do you still think Bel's a Havelock?' Dr Parker said. Helen had been on about who Bel reminded her of for months, and now she knew; the annoying, hard-to-get-to itch had been scratched. He worried, though, that if Helen kept scratching, as it appeared she was wont to do, it might well lead to an open wound.

'Definitely. Even more so after seeing them together at the funeral.' Helen took a sip of her drink.

'So, what are you going to do?' Dr Parker asked.

'I'm going to find out if we're related,' Helen said. 'And I have a plan.' She tapped her nose playfully.

Dr Parker furrowed his brow. 'Mmm?'

'I'll tell you more when I have put my plan into action,' Helen teased. 'But enough about me. I want to hear all about life at the Ryhope. What's been happening since I saw you last?'

'Actually, there is some exciting news to impart,' Dr Parker said.

Helen's eyes widened in expectation.

'I just heard, before I left, that we're going to get a psychologist.'

'Really?' Helen was curious. 'That's very progressive. I thought all that "chatting-about-it-will-make-it-all-right" nonsense was deemed to be a bit of a trifle – especially at the moment, when you've got men barely out of short pants needing their limbs or their lives saving. Or both. Surely the hospital needs more brilliant surgeons like yourself – not "head doctors" who think they can talk you better?'

Dr Parker let out a loud guffaw. 'And that's what *I* love about you, my dear Helen,' he said, looking into her eyes. *God, he could lose himself in them.*

'And what's that, John?'

'Your bluntness. Your brutal honesty.' He smiled. 'And, of course, the fact that you think I'm a "brilliant" surgeon.'

'Well you are,' Helen said. 'It's not a compliment. Rather a statement of fact.' She took another sip of her vodka and lemon. 'So, tell me more about this *psychologist*? Why are you getting one?'

'Well, Dr Eris will mainly be based at the Borough Asylum, but it sounds like there'll be a bit of a crossover.'

'Really?' Helen said. The notorious mental hospital that backed onto the Ryhope had always intrigued her. As, she was sure, it did most people.

'Dr Parker!'

They looked round. Both catching sight of Bill at the same time. He was holding the handset of the pub phone close to his chest. Seeing he had caught their attention, he pointed to the receiver.

'It's the Ryhope!' he shouted out.

'Oh no.' Helen pulled a face. 'And there was me thinking I had you all to myself for the rest of the year.'

Dr Parker went off to take the call.

He was back a few minutes later.

'Bloody Clarkson,' he said. 'Hasn't turned up for his shift, so they need cover.'

'And they couldn't get anyone else?' Helen said.

'Sounds like they couldn't get hold of anyone else. It being New Year's Eve and all.'

'No surprise there,' Helen said. 'And clearly not everyone was as honest as you were about telling them exactly where they'd be.'

Dr Parker put his jacket back on.

'Come on.' Helen put down her drink. 'I'll see you out. Who's picking you up?'

'They're sending a car from the Infirmary. Should only be a few minutes.'

Dr Parker led the way through the crush.

Finally, they made it out onto the street.

'Gosh, that's nice. Fresh air,' Helen said.

They both looked around, aware that they were totally on their own. Tatham Street was deserted.

'Well, I guess I'd better wish you a Happy New Year – in advance,' Helen said, suddenly feeling awkward.

And nervous.

She stepped forward.

Looking into John's eyes, she felt an overwhelming urge to kiss him. Not an entirely new feeling, especially of late.

But she stopped and reprimanded herself. Reminded herself of the evening of the Tatham Street air raid. She'd had the same urge then – had closed her eyes, waiting to feel the touch of his lips on her own, only to receive a chaste kiss on the cheek.

'Happy New Year,' she said. She leant up to him, put her hands on his shoulders and kissed him on the cheek.

'Yes, yes, a very happy one,' Dr Parker said. He bent his head down and kissed Helen back gently on the cheek. *When all he wanted to do was take her in his arms and kiss her all the way into the New Year.*

The blare of a horn made them both jump.

'Looks like my lift's arrived,' Dr Parker said.

As the clock struck twelve, the whole pub erupted.

At the same time, the shipyard klaxons sounded out across the town, as though they themselves were calling out their own celebratory 'Happy New Year!'

Helen saw Bel and Joe kiss each other tenderly. They looked very much in love.

She looked around her to see people hugging and kissing. Some chastely, like she and John had just done – others more passionately, like she had wanted to do.

Earlier on today she had felt she didn't belong anywhere – that she was a misfit.

Thinking of John, and wishing he was here with her now, it suddenly struck her, like the chimes on the clock signalling the start of a new year, that she *did* actually feel as though there was somewhere she belonged – where she felt at home.

And that was with John.

Chapter Eleven

'Perhaps we should pop in and wish Lily and George a Happy New Year?' Charlotte suggested tentatively.

'I think perhaps not.' Rosie took a sidelong look at her sister. The light from the full moon enabled her to just about see her sister's expression.

'Why?' Charlotte said. 'I'm not at all tired.'

'Well, *you* mightn't be, but I jolly well am,' Rosie said. Her words were followed by a slightly exasperated laugh. 'Besides, I told you, Lily and George are having a party.'

It wasn't an outright lie. Lily *was* having a party. A very profitable one. Something to draw the punters in on New Year's Eve. Not that they needed much persuading. This was always the busiest night of the year and was why Lily and George had left so promptly after the church service.

'If they're having a big party, then that's exactly why we *should* pop in to see them,' Charlotte argued.

'No, that's exactly why we *shouldn't*. It's a grown-up party. Not for children.'

'But I'm not a child.'

'I'm afraid you are, Charlie. The last time I checked, a person is a child until their eighteenth birthday. You were very lucky that Bill allowed you in the pub this evening.'

'It's legal as long as I'm accompanied by an adult,' Charlotte informed.

'Only if the licensee says so.' *God, she could be hard work.* They walked on.

'Anyway, you saw Lily and George today at the church. It's not as if you haven't seen them.'

'I know, but I've been back for two and a half months now,' Charlotte moaned, 'and I've still not been round to theirs for tea. And Lily *did* invite me. Remember? The first time I met her at the Maison Nouvelle.'

'Well, Lily does work a lot, you know,' Rosie said. 'She might seem like a gadabout, but underneath that rather colourful exterior lies a serious, hard-working business-woman. She works pretty much round the clock. She's not got the time for having people round for tea.'

They walked on. The occasional burst of laughter and flash of light could be seen as revellers bade farewell to those with whom they'd welcomed in the New Year before now heading back to their own homes.

Charlotte looked up at the big Victorian houses they were passing. They were like Lily's – only she'd bet they weren't half as amazing. Dorothy and Angie's description of Lily's hallway alone had sounded incredible. If she had a New Year's resolution, then it was to see inside Lily's fantastic house – *and sooner rather than later*.

Rosie and Charlotte walked for a while without chatting.

Charlotte was thinking about Lily's. Her imagination running riot.

Rosie was thinking about the funeral. And their mam and dad. It was a topic she had avoided since Charlotte had been back. This was the perfect opportunity, especially after the day they'd had.

Walking down Tunstall Vale, Rosie took a deep breath.

'So, how are you feeling – after the funeral?'

'All right.' Charlotte's voice was defensive.

'Charlie, you can talk to me, you know. About how you feel.' Rosie paused. 'About Mam and Dad.'

Charlotte still didn't say anything, but Rosie persevered.

'Arthur's funeral made me think about Mam and Dad's funeral, and I think it did you too.' Rosie looked at Charlotte as she spoke.

Still, Charlotte didn't say anything.

'Can you remember much about it?'

'Not really.'

Rosie thought about Charlie taking her hand today at the burial. She had done the same when they were at their parents' open grave. *God, had it really been six years ago?* It felt like another lifetime.

They carried on walking in silence.

Finally, Charlotte said, 'I remember the vicar saying the same words as the vicar today.'

Rosie smiled and put her arm around her sister, but she could feel her unease and let her go again.

'I remember the bit about "A time to be born, and a time to die",' Charlotte said. 'Back then, I didn't understand how it could be Mam and Dad's time to die. Still can't.'

'No,' Rosie agreed. 'Neither can I.'

Charlotte looked deep in thought before suddenly perking up. 'I remember people had been going on about us not having any family.' She looked at Rosie. 'But just before the funeral a man turned up. He said he was our uncle. Can you remember?'

Rosie felt her skin prickle. Her heart started to thud loudly in her chest.

'Yes, I can remember. He was Mam's brother.'

'Uncle . . .' Charlotte dug deep in her memory. 'Raymond. Uncle Raymond. That was his name, wasn't it?'

'That's right.'

They reached the turning into Brookside Gardens.

'I remember being puzzled,' Charlotte continued, 'because he was meant to be staying overnight, but when you woke me up in the morning, he'd gone.'

'That's right.' Rosie hoped her voice sounded normal. 'He got up early and left.'

Charlotte opened up the little five-bar gate that led to their home. They walked through and Rosie let it clatter shut, for once hoping that it would alert Mrs Jenkins so that she would come out and chat to them, putting an end to this conversation, which was making her feel ill.

But of course Mrs Jenkins didn't make an appearance; nothing ever happened the way you wanted it to.

Why, oh why did Charlotte have to have such a bloody good memory?

Rosie opened the front door and went into the house.

'So, what happened to him?' Charlotte took off her coat and hung it up.

'I don't know, Charlie.' *One day perhaps she would tell her.* 'He left and never came back.' *If only.* Rosie's hand instinctively went to the scars on her face.

'Hot chocolate?'

Charlotte's face lit up. 'Yes, please . . . I'll do it!'

Rosie followed her sister into the small kitchen.

Raymond might have left his mark, but at least he'd never be back.

She thought once again about the words the vicar had spoken today – *a time to mourn, and a time to dance.*

Raymond's death had certainly given her cause to dance.

Chapter Twelve

The Fishermen's Cottages, Whitburn, Sunderland

1936

'Charlie, wake up.' Rosie gently shook her sister awake.

'Rosie,' Charlotte mumbled.

'Come on, wake up, sleepyhead.' Rosie forced a smile on her face. 'We're going on an adventure.'

Her little sister's blue eyes looked confused.

'An adventure,' Rosie repeated. 'But we need to be quick. We have to go now.'

Charlotte sat up and rubbed her eyes.

'An adventure?'

Rosie widened her eyes and nodded.

'Now, come on, wash your face and put on your best dress. The one you wore . . .' Rosie let her voice trail off. She didn't want to remind Charlotte of the funeral. It was too late, though; her sister's eyes were already pooling with tears.

'Come on.' Rosie forced her voice to sound bright. 'There's no time for tears. Mam and Dad wouldn't want you to cry.' Rosie swallowed back her own sadness. 'They'll be up there now, sitting on their cloud in heaven. Dad'll be trying to light his pipe, saying, "Come on, Charlie, gerra a move on. Do as yer big sister says!"'

Charlotte let out a short chuckle. Their dad always seemed to spend more time trying to light his pipe than he did smoking it.

'You sounded just like him!'

Rosie smiled. She'd been a real daddy's girl. *Me and my shadow*, he'd say.

Rosie got off the bed.

'See you downstairs in five minutes. And no dilly-dallying.'

Twenty minutes later they were walking along the main road towards the bus stop. It was still early. The air was cold, and there was a wind blowing in across the North Sea. The suitcase wasn't heavy, but it was banging against Rosie's legs as they walked.

'Where are we going?' Charlotte asked. She wasn't totally convinced that this was what could be classed as an adventure.

'First off, we're going into town,' Rosie said.

'Sunderland?'

Rosie nodded.

She looked behind her, hoping the bus would come soon. The sun was starting to come up. Her fear that Raymond would decide to return to the house now that daylight was breaking was growing by the second.

Forcing her voice to sound full of intrigue, Rosie said, '*Then* we're going on a train.'

'Really! I've never been on a train before!' Charlotte moved the bag she was carrying to her other shoulder. She was trying to be careful because it contained their packed lunch.

'Actually, you *have* been on a train once. When you were *real*ly little. Not just *little* little, like you are now.' Rosie nudged her sister in a show of playfulness.

Charlotte looked at Rosie suspiciously. She was being un-usually nice to her. She hadn't even asked her to help make the sandwiches, which she normally would have done.

'So, where are we going?' she asked.

Rosie heard an engine. Her head swung round. For the briefest moment she felt paralysed with terror that it would be her uncle in a car, coming to get them.

When she saw it was the South Shields to Sunderland service, she gasped with relief.

'I'll tell you on the bus. Now, go on, stick your hand out!'

Chapter Thirteen

Wednesday 13 January 1943

'How's Charlotte getting on at the High School?' Helen asked.

Rosie was just leaving the office. They'd been discussing what needed to be done on a frigate that had been pulled into the dry dock. It had a hole in its flank that you could drive a tank through.

'Oh, she's doing well,' Rosie said. 'Getting top marks in all her classes. She actually seems to enjoy doing homework.' She pulled a face. 'I personally can't think of anything worse than being hunched over a load of books indoors.'

Helen laughed. It was exactly what she spent her life doing here at the yard and, like Charlotte, she loved every moment. 'I take it you were never that keen on school?'

Rosie looked at Helen. It was the first time she'd asked something personal. About her past.

'I didn't mind it,' Rosie said. 'But I wasn't mad on it either.' She wasn't being entirely truthful. She had been intending to keep on with her studies, at least until she was sixteen, but that had been before her mam and dad's accident.

'Did *you* like it at the High School?' Rosie said, batting the conversation back into Helen's court.

'I think it was more a case of *enduring* it there, rather than liking it.' Helen sat down and pulled out a Pall Mall from the packet on her desk. 'Is she fitting in all right? With her classmates?' Helen lit her cigarette.

'Good question,' Rosie said. 'I'm really not sure. I keep telling her she can bring any friends back for tea, but so far she seems happy to do her after-school clubs, then come home and bother me.' *And*, Rosie felt like adding, *beg me to let her come to Lily's.*

'It might take her time to find her "set",' Helen said. 'She's not even been there a term yet, has she?'

Rosie nodded, although she couldn't ever foresee a time when Charlie would be part of a 'set'. At least she had one good friend – Marjorie. It was just a shame she lived in Newcastle.

Rosie made to leave.

'And Polly's keeping her chin up?' Helen said. Work had been so full on these past few weeks, she'd only managed to pop round and see Gloria and Hope twice since the New Year, so she wasn't up on all the gossip and goings-on.

'Yes, Polly seems fine, fingers crossed. She's had a few letters from Tommy. That's keeping her spirits up.'

It was on the tip of Helen's tongue to ask Rosie about her husband, who she knew had been a detective with the Borough Police, but she didn't. Their new-found friendship didn't extend that far.

'I better go,' Rosie said. 'Talking of classes, I've got one to go to now.'

Helen looked puzzled.

'Don't ask,' Rosie said.

'Right, who's got what papers?' Polly was sitting at the head of the women's table in the canteen. They'd all had their lunch and cleared it away.

'Are yer gonna tell us what we all have to dee?' Angie said, getting out her copy of the *Daily Telegraph*.

'Blimey, Ange. Where did you get that from?' Dorothy gave a gasp of disbelief as her friend smoothed out the newspaper on the table. 'No, let me guess.' She looked around at the rest of her squad, who were all pulling newspapers out of their haversacks. 'I'll bet Quentin gave it to you?'

'He might have done,' Angie said. 'Then again I could have bought it from the newsagent.'

'Mmm, I don't think so – someone has scrawled "7A" on the top corner.' Dorothy pointed a finger at the evidence. 'Which I do believe is the number of Quentin's flat.'

Angie looked around the table before explaining defensively, 'I was telling Quentin about Polly's idea of bringing in newspapers so we can "keep abreast of the news", 'n he said what a brilliant idea that was, especially with everyone having someone they loved away at war.'

The women were listening intently. Angie's burgeoning friendship with Quentin fascinated them all. It proved that opposites did indeed attract, even if Angie totally denied that there was *any* kind of attraction there.

'Do you want to start then?' Polly said, putting her copy of the *Daily Mirror* on the table.

'Yer dinnit think I've read it, do yer?' Angie's face showed her disbelief. 'Look at it! It's huge. And look at the writing – it's tiny.'

'The *print*,' Dorothy corrected.

'Well, I can't tell whether it's print or writing, can I, it's that small!'

The women all laughed.

'Sorry I'm late.' Rosie dumped her haversack on the ground and got out her sandwiches. 'Have I missed much?'

'Angie's brought the *Daily Telegraph*,' Martha said.

'Really?' Rosie took a bite of her lunch.

'But she's not read it because the "writing's" too small,' Dorothy said, rolling her eyes.

'What have you brought, Hannah?' Rosie asked, looking across at a newspaper she didn't recognise.

'The *Jewish News*,' Hannah said. She was sitting up straight, ready for what she was calling their 'current affairs class'. 'It's a "weekly review of Jewish events".' Hannah read the small headline under the paper's emboldened title. 'Aunty Rina gets it from the rabbi.'

'*Cooee!*' The women all looked up to see Marie-Anne approaching with Bel in tow.

'Sorry, *miss*, we're not late, are we?' She was waving a copy of the *Sunderland Echo* about. Bel was clutching a copy of the *Daily Mail* that Joe had pilfered off the Major.

'No, we've not exactly started yet,' Polly said.

'Just so I've got this right,' Gloria said. 'We've all got to bring a newspaper into work every day, so we know exactly what's happening in the world?'

'And in Great Britain,' Bel chipped in.

'And Sunderland,' Marie-Anne added, again waving the morning's edition of the *Echo*.

'That's about the sum of it,' Polly said.

'Glor, where's yours?' Dorothy demanded.

'I thought I'd share Angie's paper. It looks big enough for two.' Gloria looked to Angie, who was sitting next to her.

'Definitely,' Angie said, pushing the newspaper towards her. 'We can share.'

Gloria gave Angie a wink, then looked down at the newspaper, making a show of squinting hard.

'I think I need glasses.'

'So, to summarise today's news,' Dorothy said. She had, of course, taken on the role of head teacher during the lunchtime class. Polly, despite being the one to organise it, had been demoted to deputy.

'The call-up for women,' Dorothy said, 'has been lowered to nineteen for single women with no dependents. And there is now a total ban on civilians travelling to the Isle of Wight.'

Angie let out a bark of laughter. 'As if anyone would want to gan there anyway.'

'Actually, it's meant to be really nice,' Marie-Anne chirped up. 'My nan used to live in Portsmouth and apparently they've got lovely beaches – and the weather's loads warmer.'

'That can't be hard,' Gloria huffed.

Everyone murmured their agreement. December's snow had been replaced by a New Year of rain, rain and more rain. On top of which it was bitterly cold. Rosie had promised that she was going to try and get them working on the inside of the new ship once they'd patched up the frigate that had been brought in.

'And elsewhere in the world?' Dorothy asked.

Martha put her hand up.

'Yes, Martha.'

'The Soviets are going all out to get back Stalingrad. And in my opinion, they're going to succeed.'

'Well, let's hope so,' Rosie said, standing up and looking at the canteen clock. It was a few minutes before the end of the lunch break. 'Come on then, back to work we go.'

Everyone groaned and dragged themselves to their feet.

The canteen windows were rattling with the force of the wind and the rain. The women welders buttoned up their overalls and made sure their turbans were on tight. Bel and Marie-Anne used their newspapers as makeshift umbrellas and made a dash across the yard to the administration building. Hannah carefully folded the *Jewish News* in half and put it inside her jacket before hurrying back to the drawing office.

'Hopefully another air-raid-free night,' Gloria said to Rosie as they left the warmth of the canteen.

'Fingers crossed it keeps on like this,' Rosie said.

The town was having a respite from Hitler's bombs. There had been a few air raid warnings, but no more attacks since the Tatham Street bombing three months ago. Not that a day went by when the women didn't think of that night, or what might have been.

When the air raid sirens sounded out at eight that evening, Rosie silently cursed herself. If Angie had heard Gloria and her talking earlier on, she'd blame them, saying they'd jinxed it. Rosie put down her pen and closed her ledger. This was the first time she hadn't been with Charlotte when the sirens sounded out.

'Come on, *ma chère*.' Lily appeared in the doorway. 'George reckons this one's going to be real. He's been looking into that crystal ball of his.' Lily was fanning herself. She had apparently run out of her Chinese medicine and her hot and cold flushes had come back with a vengeance, as had her rather erratic mood swings.

Hearing that George thought this one was for real worried Rosie, for she knew he was privy to information not normally broadcast to the general public. She walked out of her office. Two of the girls were wrapping silk dressing gowns around themselves as they hurried down the wide staircase. Their 'dates' for the evening were on the landing, wearing white vests and pulling on their trousers.

Rosie looked at Lily herding everyone down to the cellar, telling them to be careful on the stone steps and to help themselves to a drink once they were down there to calm their nerves.

Rosie thought of Charlie.

She'd be grabbing her siren suit and getting herself settled in the Jenkins' shelter . . .

Wouldn't she?

'Charlotte! Where are you going?' Mrs Jenkins was standing at her front door, trying her hardest to make herself
heard over the blasted sirens.

'I'm going to Lily's,' Charlotte shouted back. She was
already on the gravel pathway, her gas mask slung over
her shoulder.

Mrs Jenkins opened her mouth to object, but Charlotte
had already turned her back and had started to run towards
the gate at the end of their street. Within minutes she was
crossing over the main road and jogging up Tunstall Vale.
She reckoned she could make it to Lily's in under five minutes. It was only about half a mile away, and although it
was mainly uphill, she was good at athletics; when she'd
last been timed for the 800 metres, she'd done it in under
four minutes.

Once she was halfway up the hill she had begun to slow
down. Her legs were tiring, but she still felt invigorated.
Her adrenaline was pumping. This was the first time she'd
been out in an air raid on her own. She felt free. More than
anything, though, she was excited. So very excited. *She was
going to see inside Lily's.* See the big chandelier, the polished
parquet flooring and the sweeping staircase. She was going
to fulfil her New Year's resolution.

She looked ahead.

It was dark but she could see the turning to West Lawn.

She was nearly there.

Lily wouldn't mind her turning up. It's not as if she'd
be working. Not during an air raid. Then, afterwards, they
could all have a cup of tea, or better still, a hot chocolate,
and Lily could show her around the house.

She'd see it with her own eyes.

She turned the corner.

Only a few hundred yards more and she'd be there.

Suddenly she slammed into something.

Another person.

'Charlie!'

Charlotte stood and stared at her sister.

She saw the look on her face.

'What the hell are you doing here?' Rosie was shouting not only because she was angry, but also because she had to if she wanted to be heard over the wailing of the sirens.

'I . . . I thought I'd come and see you,' Charlotte shouted back. Her heart had turned over, seeing how furious her sister was.

Rosie grabbed Charlotte's shoulder and practically dragged her back around the corner.

'Come on!' Rosie bellowed as she started running back down Tunstall Vale.

Charlotte followed, desperately wanting to ask why they were going back home when it would have been quicker and safer simply to go to Lily's.

But the mood Rosie was in, she knew better than to argue.

Having spent the last three-quarters of an hour with Mr and Mrs Jenkins in their Anderson shelter, Rosie and Charlotte were now back in their own kitchen.

'Why on earth did you take it upon yourself to go to Lily's?' Rosie demanded.

'I don't know,' Charlotte said. She had been dreading this. Knew Rosie wouldn't play holy war with her in front of their neighbours, but would be storing it all up for when they were on their own.

'There must have been a reason, Charlie?' Rosie was trying her hardest not to have a complete fit at her sister. 'Not only have I drummed it into your head that you are to go straight next door and get yourself safe as quickly as possible, but to go out – on your own – in the middle of a raid . . .' Rosie gasped. 'To be honest, words escape me . . . I really don't know why you would do something so stupid – and so dangerous.'

Rosie could feel the anger rising again.

'All I've ever wanted to do is keep you safe!'

Charlotte looked at her sister. She'd never seen her like this.

'I'm sorry, Rosie,' Charlotte said. She knew what she'd done was reckless. She'd just got it into her head that she had to see Lily's and all other logic had flown out the window.

'So, what on earth possessed you?' Rosie could see her sister's defences had dropped.

'I wanted to see the inside of Lily's.' *There, she'd said it.*

'You wanted to see Lily's?' Rosie repeated.

Charlotte nodded.

'It wasn't because you were frightened something might happen to me?' The thought had gone through her head – Charlotte would be left totally alone. No mam, no dad, and no sister.

Charlotte shook her head.

'So, this whole running about the streets in the middle of an air raid was really all about you wanting to see Lily's?'

Another nod.

'Why are you so desperate to see Lily's house?' Rosie asked.

'I heard Dorothy and Angie talking about it on New Year's Eve. When I was helping with the drinks.'

Rosie held her breath. *Had Charlie heard anything else?*

'And?' she asked.

'And they were saying how incredible it was. The chandelier. Curtains. Some magnificent French mantelpiece . . .'

'And that was all you heard them say?'

'And that the floor was polished parquet,' Charlotte added.

Rosie breathed a sigh of relief.

She knew her sister was telling the truth.

Chapter Fourteen

Thursday 14 January

The town had been hit, but not badly. Just a scratch here and there. A cluster of small fires in the south docks caused by incendiary bombs, but no real damage. And, mercifully, no lives lost.

Rosie was in her office, juggling the accounts and working out how much of Polly and Tommy's wedding could be put through the books. She thought a good portion could be palmed off on the Gentlemen's Club.

It was still early, but she was shattered. She felt well and truly wrung out, having hardly slept after her chat with Charlotte. Then all day at work she'd had to stop herself from having a go at Dorothy and Angie about letting their mouths run off with them. She'd said nothing, though. The cat was out of the bag and there was no shoving it back in.

'*Bonsoir, ma chère!*' Lily came bustling into the room, full of energy. 'Oh, *mon Dieu!*'

She stopped dramatically in her tracks and stared at Rosie.

'For heaven's sake, don't stand up, my dear, otherwise your face will trip you up. What's the matter?'

'I've got a problem,' Rosie said.

'Let me guess . . .' Lily started walking over to Rosie's desk.

Knowing what she was about to do, Rosie opened the top drawer, took out a packet of Gauloises and handed it to her.

'*Merci, ma chère*. You know me too well.' Taking the proffered packet, Lily pulled out a cigarette and lit it. 'I would wager a bet that your *problem* is something beginning with C. A capital C.' Lily blew out a plume of smoke.

Rosie sat back in her chair.

'This is not a joke or some game, Lily.'

'But I'm right, aren't I?' Lily took another deep drag. 'Your problem is Charlotte. Now that you've got over the problems with that awful fascist school in Harrogate and Charlotte is happily ensconced at the High School, you're back to your original concern – or should I say *obsession* – about this place.' Lily gestured dramatically around the room. 'About her finding out what happens within its four walls.'

Just then the door opened.

'George, *mon amour, entrez! Entrez!*'

'Are you two sure you want company? I'm not disturbing anything, am I?' George looked at Rosie for confirmation.

'No, George. Come in and sit down. I might get some sense out of you. I can see Lily is in one of her – how should I put it – *happy* moods.'

George grimaced. 'I would agree with you there, my dear.'

'Honestly.' Lily scowled at George and then at Rosie. 'You two can be such stick-in-the-muds.' She waltzed over to the fireplace and tapped her cigarette ash into the fire.

'Aren't you hot, *mon cher*?' Lily fanned herself and moved away from the fire. 'Rosie was about to tell me about a little problem she has. And I guessed correctly that her problem was Charlotte and that now she's settled here – *where she should have been all along* – Rosie's back to square one with her anxiety over Charlotte finding out about this place.'

She sat down next to George on the chaise longue.

'Well,' Lily sighed theatrically, 'I'm not going to waste my breath telling you what *I* think – as you know it already.'

'I think George and I know perfectly well that you consider Charlie old enough to know the truth,' Rosie said wearily. 'That she's not as naïve as I think she is, et cetera, et cetera . . . But that's *not* my immediate problem.'

Lily raised her eyebrows.

'The problem I have,' Rosie continued, 'is her safety. This has been ongoing, to be honest, but it came to a head last night . . . When I left here to check Charlie was all right, I literally bumped into her as she rounded the corner into West Lawn.'

Lily looked at George.

Both were surprised.

'But I thought she was meant to go to the Jenkins' Anderson shelter whenever there was a raid,' George said, getting up and pouring himself a brandy from the decanter on Rosie's desk. 'Regardless of whether or not you were at home.'

'That's exactly what I had drummed into her to do,' Rosie said. 'Only Charlie got it into her head that she had to see Lily's – has had it firmly stuck in her head since New Year's Eve, when she overheard Dorothy and Angie chatting about how absolutely wonderful this place is.'

'Oh dear,' George said. 'Did she overhear anything else they might have been chatting about?'

'Like the fact Peter's friend thought Dorothy was one of my girls?' Lily chuckled. She stopped when she saw Rosie's face. '*Ma chère*, it *was* funny – even *you* have to admit it.'

'No, thank goodness, Lily, she didn't overhear anything else. Which is about the only good thing I can take from all of this.'

Lily patted George on the knee and pushed herself up from the chaise longue. Walking over to the mantelpiece, she warmed her hands in front of the open fire.

'I thought you were hot?' Rosie looked at Lily.

'Hot one minute, cold the next.'

Lily turned her back to the fire.

'Right, this is what I think,' she declared.

Rosie looked at Lily.

Any port in a storm.

'Go on.'

'I think you should give Charlotte what she wants, but . . .' Lily paused to stress her point ' . . . in such a way that *you* get what *you* want.'

Rosie looked at Lily and then at George, who looked equally perplexed.

'Explain, darling,' George said.

'Well, Charlotte's obviously determined to find out more about this place.' She waved her jewelled hand around. 'Is intrigued by my good self and all those who live here. Is desperate to see where her big sister goes on an evening while *she's* stuck at home doing a mound of boring homework.'

Rosie held back from telling her that Charlotte actually enjoyed doing homework.

'For years, the poor girl's been cooped up in that odious school, picked on and bullied relentlessly by the offspring of those who would gladly have that mad-brained, moustached German dwarf run our country.' Lily drew in breath. 'She's been stuck in the middle of nowhere, with no excitement.'

Lily moved away from the fire.

'You know what they say, *variety is the spice of life* and all that . . . Well, your little sister has been eating bread and butter for too long. Now she's back in the real world, the girl's like a child let loose in a sweet shop.'

George took a sip of his brandy. Lily might enjoy playing the role of a rather frivolous and flamboyant madam, but when necessary she could be remarkably astute, and surprisingly sensible.

'She's meeting all these different characters,' Lily continued. 'Women who wear overalls and weld and do men's work. Women who look like Maisie or sound like Vivian. She wants to know everything about this new world she's suddenly been allowed to inhabit. Everything about those around her. And because she's got something between her two ears, she's curious.'

Rosie thought about the time in the Maison Nouvelle when Charlie had been asking about what business Lily was in – and then they'd bumped into Maisie and Vivian going into town and she'd started to ask about what they did for a living.

Lily struck a match dramatically against the mantelpiece and lit another cigarette to punctuate her point.

'So, let's show her.'

She blew out a billow of smoke.

Rosie and George were quiet.

'I suggest we shut up shop for the day. Possibly the Saturday after next. Give us time to tell all of our clients. The girls will be glad of it. They could all do with a day off. To say business has been booming is an understatement. That's something we have to thank the war for, if nothing else.'

She took a long drag on her cigarette, thinking the whole scenario through.

'We close for the day. And George and I invite you and Charlotte over for tea. Then Charlotte can have a good old nose around. Cure that curiosity of hers, and at the same time stop you worrying about her finding out that you work in a bordello.'

And that you didn't always just do the bookkeeping, Lily thought but didn't say.

'It will be a chance for us to chat about everything she's been champing at the bit to find out. I'll make her feel she can ask me any question she wants, without cottoning on that it has all been carefully orchestrated to satiate that inquisitive mind of hers.'

Rosie raised her eyebrows and again glanced over to George, who mirrored her look.

'That all sounds good so far,' Rosie said, trying to hide her surprise that Lily, of all people, might have found the solution to a problem that was becoming more pressing by the day.

'But what *are* you going to tell her?' George said, reading Rosie's thoughts and wondering the same himself.

'Well, for starters I'll tell her that I own properties here and in London, which isn't exactly a lie. I own La Lumière Bleue in Soho, and George, you own your flat in Foyle Street . . . And I can tell her all about playing the stock market—'

'But you don't play the stock market,' Rosie butted in. 'That was something that came into my head when she was quizzing me about what "business" you are in.'

'*Ma chérie*, just because I don't gamble my own hard-earned cash doesn't mean I don't know a thing or two about what's going on in the financial world.' Lily looked at George.

'I keep my ear to the ground,' George confessed. 'I was actually going to chat to you about investing some of your money as soon as the tide of war starts to turn in our favour.'

Rosie noted that George never wavered in his belief that they would win the war, no matter how dire the news.

'See?' Lily said. 'Charlotte's head will be so positively buzzing with thoughts of property ownership and playing the market that the last thing she'll be thinking is that this lovely abode is anything other than a home owned by a rich and financially savvy couple. And it'll also quell a very natural need to know where it is her sister goes off to on an evening. She can see it all with her own eyes.'

Rosie sat back in her chair.

'That actually sounds like it might be a good idea,' she conceded.

'Yes, a bloody good idea,' George agreed.

'*Mon Dieu*, don't sound so surprised!' Lily gasped. 'I have my moments, *n'est-ce pas*?'

She winked at George.

'We can even tell her about the Gentlemen's Club next door,' Rosie mused, 'and that Maisie and Vivian work there. It will explain *their* eccentricities.'

'Good idea,' Lily said. 'Keep to the truth as much as possible – but without giving the game away.'

Lily let out a hoot of laughter.

'Give the *game* away?'

Rosie raised her eyebrows at George.

They both suppressed a smile.

Chapter Fifteen

1936

'Where are we going?' Charlotte asked once they'd paid their fares and the bus was carrying on its route along the coast road.

'We're going to the same place you went the first time you travelled on a train.'

'When I was *really* little, not *little* little,' Charlotte chuckled. Now they were sitting on the bus her sister seemed happier. This felt more like an adventure.

'We're going to a wonderful place called Harrogate, which sells fudge and toffee and there's the best tea shop in the whole wide world called Betty's, where they sell the best cakes ever.'

'Even better than Mam's?'

Rosie felt a physical pain in her heart. No one would ever make cake that was as lovely as their mam's.

'Even better,' Rosie said. She was surprised how easy it was to lie – to smile when she felt like crying.

Half an hour later they were at the train station in the centre of Sunderland.

Rosie once again felt on high alert.

There was a good chance Raymond would have come into town after he'd left their house.

She just needed to get Charlie away.

She took hold of her sister's hand as they quickly made their way from the ticket office, down the two flights of stairs and onto the platform.

They sat down on one of the long wooden benches.

'Let's play I spy,' Rosie suggested, knowing that she'd have an excuse to keep looking about, checking every person who came onto the platform.

A few times she felt herself gripped by panic on seeing someone who looked similar to Raymond. It was amazing how many scrawny older men there were in worn three-piece suits and flat caps.

They didn't have to wait long for the train to arrive, but even when they were finally in their seats, Rosie couldn't let herself relax.

When she heard all the doors slam shut and the stationmaster's whistle sound out, she told Charlotte to stay put, keep an eye on the bags and not to talk to strangers. She then proceeded to walk the full length of the train, checking the toilets and even going into first class to double-check that Raymond wasn't following them. She knew she was being overly cautious, perhaps even paranoid, but she didn't care. She had to be sure that there was no way he would know where she was taking her sister.

When she returned she found Charlie fast asleep, her head resting against the window.

Rosie sat down next to her.

Only then did she finally relax.

And within minutes she too was fast asleep.

An hour and a half later they had pulled into York station and another half an hour later they were on the local service train to Harrogate.

'When we get to Harrogate, we're going to go and see some friends of Mam and Dad's,' Rosie said.

'But I thought we were going to eat fudge and cake at the best tea shop called Betty's?' Charlotte said, her expression crestfallen.

'Yes, yes, we will,' Rosie said. 'But first we need to go and see this couple. They're called Mr and Mrs Rainer. They're lovely people. They're the people you saw the last time you were here.'

'When I was *really* little?'

Rosie smiled and nodded.

'You might even remember them when you see them. They thought you were the best little girl they'd ever come across. "Totally adorable," I remember Mrs Rainer saying you were.'

'Really?'

Another nod.

'But we can go and have cakes and fudge afterwards?'

'Course we can.'

The train stopped for a few minutes in a place called Knaresborough and a group of schoolgirls boarded. They were chatting away nineteen to the dozen.

'Are these taken?' one of the older girls asked on seeing two empty seats opposite Rosie and Charlotte.

'They're free,' Rosie said, sitting up straight. The older girl and her friend sat down and carried on their conversation.

Pretending not to eavesdrop, Rosie looked out the window, inspecting their uniform in the glass reflection – grey with a red border. Rosie had only ever seen schoolgirls dressed like this on the covers of books and in comics. The emblem on the breast pocket of their blazers had 'Runcorn' embroidered on it.

As the train approached Harrogate, Rosie turned her attention away from the passing greenery and looked straight at the older girl, who had been doing most of the talking.

'Sorry to interrupt,' Rosie said, putting on her best voice. 'But can you tell me what school it is that you both go to?'

'The Runcorn School for Girls,' came the slightly brusque reply.

'And is the Runcorn School for Girls near Harrogate?' Rosie asked.

'Just about a mile or so out of town. On the outskirts.' This time the girl's tone was not quite so brusque.

'Forgive me for being so inquisitive,' Rosie continued, again in her best King's English, 'but I'm sure my aunty used to go there. Is it by chance a boarding school?'

'Yes, it is. What's your aunt's name? We might know her. The head's always going on about former alumni.' The older girl looked at her friend, who nodded her agreement.

'Oh really? What's the head's name?'

'Miss Tilley.' The girls both giggled. 'We call her "Silly Tilley".'

Rosie forced herself to chuckle.

'Really? And is she? Silly?'

'Oh, she's as mad as a March hare,' the girls said in unison and burst into more fits of giggles.

'But she's harmless,' the older girl said. 'It's the deputy head, Mrs Willoughby-Smith, who's a right old dragon.'

The carriage jerked forward and started to slow down.

The two girls jumped up.

'Nice to chat,' the older girl said.

She turned to leave the carriage.

'Oh, you didn't tell us the name of your aunt?'

'You wouldn't know her,' Rosie smiled. 'She's ancient. Gosh, she must have been at the school sometime in the last century.'

The girls let out another burst of giggles and left.

'I didn't know we had an aunt?' Charlotte said.

'We don't,' Rosie said.

Charlotte looked puzzled.

'She died years and years ago.'

As they got their bags and prepared for the next part of their 'adventure', Rosie realised she had lied more in the past few hours than she had in her entire life.

It would be a craft she would hone and refine as the days, weeks and months wore on.

'Mr and Mrs Rainer?' Rosie said.

'Oh, goodness me! Rosie! Charlotte! What a surprise!'

Mrs Rainer craned her neck to look over the two girls and down the street.

'Where's your mother and father?'

There was an awkward silence.

Mrs Rainer turned her attention back to the two girls standing on her doorstep. She realised for the first time that they had a suitcase with them.

And were dressed from head to toe in black.

'They're . . .' Rosie hesitated. She looked at Charlotte and back at Mrs Rainer. 'They're . . . not here.'

Mrs Rainer's hand went to her chest.

'Come in! Come in!' She ushered them in, touching Charlotte affectionately on the head as she walked past her.

'My, how you've grown . . . Go on into the lounge . . . Rosie, just leave the suitcase in the hallway. Dear me, it looks like it weighs a ton.' She stepped towards the kitchen door and shouted through: 'Thomas! We've got company. Eloise's two girls.'

When Rosie explained that their mam and dad weren't here because they were dead, Mr and Mrs Rainer didn't move.

Rosie remembered doing the same when the teacher at school had taken her out of the class and told her.

Watching Mrs Rainer now, Rosie expected tears to follow. Shock followed by an unstoppable grief.

She was surprised when they didn't, and found herself liking her mother's friend all the more for it.

'Oh, my poor dears.' Mrs Rainer got up and sat down next to Charlotte to give her a hug. She reached over, took hold of Rosie's hand and squeezed it. 'I'm so sorry. So, so sorry.'

Mrs Rainer looked up at her husband, who was still in shock.

'Why don't you go and put the kettle on, love?' she said.

She watched her husband get up and leave, before focusing her attention back on Charlotte, who was keeping her feelings in check.

'Well, it looks like you're both being very brave about it all.'

She gave Charlotte another hug before releasing her.

'Charlotte, why don't you get Mr Rainer to take you into the back garden to show you our new chickens?'

'Chickens?' Charlotte's face lit up. 'You've got chickens?'

'We have indeed, my dear. And I do believe it's feeding time. Ask Mr Rainer to show you how it's done.'

Charlotte was already standing up.

'And have a look to see if there's any eggs. We had two yesterday,' Mrs Rainer said.

Within seconds Charlotte had gone in search of Mr Rainer.

'This is terrible news.' Mrs Rainer turned to Rosie. 'I can't say how sorry I am for you both.' She looked at Rosie. 'To be honest, I can't quite take it on board myself, so heaven knows how you're feeling . . . And Charlotte . . .' She paused. 'I didn't like to ask with Charlotte sat there, but how did it happen? I'm guessing it must have been some kind of accident, if they're both dead?'

Rosie was glad Mrs Rainer had no qualms about using the word 'dead'. So many people since her mam and dad had died seemed unable to say it.

'It was a car accident,' Rosie explained.

Mrs Rainer looked puzzled.

'But I didn't think Eloise or William drove – never mind had a car.'

'No, they didn't. It was a car that hit them.' Rosie said. 'Then drove off.'

'Drove off?' Mrs Rainer was incredulous. 'Why would they drive off?'

'I'm guessing because whoever was driving the car would have been done for it,' Rosie said. 'That's what the police said, anyway.'

'Really . . .' Mrs Rainer shook her head in disbelief.

'The police explained to me that they were looking into it,' Rosie said, 'but it was unlikely they'd find the person because no one saw the accident.' She stopped. 'No, I tell a lie, there was one witness, but they were so shocked at seeing Mam and Dad knocked over, they couldn't even tell the police what kind of car it was.'

'Oh my goodness. This is truly appalling.' Mrs Rainer inspected Rosie. 'Are you all right? I mean *really* all right? You must be traumatised.'

'I'm fine,' Rosie lied. It felt better than telling the truth. 'I really am. Honestly. I know Mam and Dad wouldn't want me to sit around wringing my hands and sobbing into a hanky.'

Rosie took a deep breath.

'I know Mam and Dad would also have wanted me to make sure Charlotte was all right too . . . Which is why I'm here.' She looked at Mrs Rainer to gauge her reaction, but couldn't tell. '*I'm* all right because I'm nearly sixteen. I can get a job and look after myself, but Charlotte's still too young.'

'How old is she now?' Mrs Rainer asked.

'Eight,' Rosie said. 'And that's the problem. They won't let me become her guardian, which means she'll have to go into a children's home. I heard them talking the day before the funeral, saying that as Mam was Catholic, even though she wasn't practising, they'd be able to get Charlie into a place called Nazareth House.'

'Run by the Poor Sisters of Nazareth?'

'That's right.' Rosie was surprised Mrs Rainer had heard of them.

'They've got them all over the country,' Mrs Rainer explained, seeing Rosie's surprise.

'Well, they might seem all righteous and godly, but I know they're not.' Rosie started to talk quickly. She had to convince Mrs Rainer that the nuns weren't good people like everyone thought. 'I don't want Charlie to go there and I know Mam wouldn't either. We saw my friend Kate after the nuns had taken her in. Her legs were covered in bruises – black as the nuns' habits, they were. She was trailing behind, looking like she'd had the life beaten out of her. It was awful.' Rosie shivered. 'I said to Mam I thought nuns were meant to be kind, like Jesus, and she said that sometimes people aren't what they appear.'

'That's true. Very true,' Mrs Rainer said.

'So, I was hoping, as we don't have any more family—' Rosie said tentatively.

'I know your mam had a brother,' Mrs Rainer interrupted.

Rosie felt herself freeze.

'He came to the funeral.' She knew she had to be honest about this. Mrs Rainer might hear he was there. If she lied, she'd wonder why. Might even try and contact him so he could look after Charlotte.

'But he left right after,' Rosie said. 'Made it clear he didn't want anything to do with Charlie or me.'

'That sounds about right,' Mrs Rainer mused. 'I remember your mam mentioning him. Said they didn't get on. That he was a nasty piece of work. I'm surprised he turned up for the funeral.'

Rosie knew then and there that if by any remote chance Raymond found out Charlie was here, he wouldn't get over the threshold.

Mrs Rainer stood up.

'Come on, let's get you a cup of tea. You must be parched.'

Rosie stood up too.

'And don't worry,' Mrs Rainer reassured. 'It's fine. I can have Charlotte for as long as you want. She'll be in good hands. And she'll be well looked after.'

'Thank you. Thank you so much. This means so much,' Rosie said. *You have no idea just how much.*

Rosie felt as though a colossal weight had been lifted from her shoulders.

Her sister would be safe.

Chapter Sixteen

Monday 25 January 1943

'So where's this "Iraq" place?' Angie said.

They had all been reading that Iraq had finally declared war on the Axis powers.

Angie sighed. 'I didn't knar there was so many places in the world I've never heard of.'

'You'll have to get Quentin to teach you,' Dorothy goaded.

'He's teaching me how to be posh, Dor. He's not teaching me lessons like I'm back at bleedin' school, yer knar.'

Everyone looked at Angie with slightly puzzled expressions.

'So, what kinds of things *has* he been teaching you?' Marie-Anne asked.

'Well, he's not been teaching me anything lately, 'cos he's not been here.'

'Really?' Bel said. 'Where's he gone?'

'He's at the War Office in a place called Whitehall in London.'

'And what does he do there?' This time it was Rosie.

'Says he's a "pen-pusher".'

'What does a pen-pusher do?' Bel said. 'I've heard the expression, but I've never really understood what it means.'

'I think it's like what you and Marie-Anne dee,' Angie said. 'Work in an office, shuffle paper about, type letters . . . all that sort of thing.'

Bel suddenly looked up at the canteen clock.

'Talking of which, I said I'd get some letters typed up for the afternoon post . . . Said I'd make up time with leaving early today.'

'Bel's learning shorthand,' Marie-Anne declared.

'Really?' Hannah said. 'That's exciting.'

'Yes, Bel's turning into a right old teacher's pet,' Marie-Anne huffed.

'How's that?' Gloria was curious.

'Well, *I* had to practically beg Helen to send *me* to shorthand classes, whereas Bel's been here all of two minutes and Helen's got her onto a course – *and* is letting her leave work early so she's got time to see Lucille and have some tea.'

'I think it's more a case of her needing someone else apart from you who can do shorthand,' Bel said, fighting back a wave of irritation.

God, she'd never known anyone get so much gyp for trying to educate themselves. Her ma had been openly hostile about her night classes, demanding to know who was paying for them. When she'd told her that work was picking up the tab, she'd presumed that meant Helen – or, rather, the Havelocks – and had gone off for a fag in the yard, mumbling to herself. Joe hadn't exactly been cock-a-hoop about it either. He'd also gone off muttering about being 'ships passing in the night', and Lucille, as expected, had been in uproar.

'See you later,' Polly said, 'and don't worry about LuLu. I'll keep her entertained.'

'Thank you,' Bel mouthed.

As Polly pulled out the slightly crumpled map from her haversack, Hannah and Olly cleared the table of plates and trays and cutlery.

Muriel came over with a dishcloth and gave the top a wipe-down.

'If it's not newspapers, it's world maps. Yer all having a geography lesson now?'

'We just wanna see where these places are that we've never heard of,' Angie said.

'But which are very important,' Martha added.

'Is that so?' Muriel said, pulling out her tea towel and making sure the table was dry. 'There yer are,' she said. 'You dinnit want that map getting any marks on it, do yer?'

'Thanks, Muriel.' Polly unfolded the map and spread it out.

'That's a grand one.' Muriel stood, the dirty dishcloth in one hand, tea towel in the other.

'It was Arthur's,' Polly said.

'Oh, God bless.' Muriel gave Polly a sad look and headed back over to the canteen.

'So, where's this Iraq place?' Angie said, leaning over the map.

'There it is, right next to Saudi Arabia.' Olly stretched an arm across the table. 'You know – *Arabian Nights* . . . Sinbad the Sailor.'

Angie's eyes widened. 'Cor, it's big, isn't it?'

'And where's Warsaw?' Martha said.

Hannah had been telling them what her aunty had heard from the rabbi about the stirrings of a rebellion in the Warsaw ghetto; how the normally passive Jewish community had fought back when German troops had tried to round up another group of men, women and children for deportation. After two days the troops had retreated, giving the Jews living in the ghetto the hope that, in the face of resistance and armed confrontation, the Germans would think twice before embarking upon more mass deportations

'Yer ma all right?' Gloria asked Polly as everyone scrutinised the atlas. 'Only she's seemed a little on edge the past week or so?'

'I think she's worried about Lucille getting the measles – or a bout of influenza,' she said. Everyone with a child under the age of ten knew there'd been an outbreak of both. The *Echo* was calling it an epidemic.

Gloria looked at Polly. She looked well. Very well.

'Yer all had the measles when yer were young, I take it?'

'I know Joe and Teddy had it. They always got everything the other one had – and always at the same time. Used to drive Ma up the wall. And I know Bel had it.' Polly laughed. 'Covered from head to toe, she was.'

'Can *you* remember having it?' Gloria said.

Polly thought about it.

'I remember having chickenpox.' She shivered involuntarily. 'Makes me want to itch just thinking about it.'

Twenty minutes later, Polly was folding up the map and the women were heading back out for the afternoon shift.

'So, have you set a date yet?' Gloria asked Rosie.

'For the dreaded tea party?' Rosie said.

Gloria nodded.

'This Saturday,' Rosie sighed.

'What's this Saturday?' Dorothy appeared from behind.

'Nothing wrong with your hearing, is there?' Gloria said.

'Gloria was asking if we'd set a date for Charlotte to go to tea at Lily's'

Dorothy's face fell.

Just then, Angie bounded up. 'What's wrong? Yer got a face like a slapped backside.'

Dorothy threw Angie a look like the summons. 'Rosie was saying that they've set a date for Charlotte's visit to Lily's.'

'Eee, we're so sorry, miss,' Angie said. 'I can't believe we dobbed yer in it like that.'

'Don't be daft, Angie. It would have come to a head anyway. Charlotte's obsessed with Lily and everything about her, so it would just have been a matter of time before she started mithering me about going there.'

'I know, but we should still've been more discreet,' Dorothy said.

Gloria guffawed. 'Surprised you know the meaning of the word!'

As they neared their workstation, Rosie told them all to grab their gear and head over to *Denewood*, a screw steamer that was taking shape on the ways at the top end of the yard. The platers' foreman had told her they were 'hanging up' this afternoon, which meant they were needed to tack-weld the metal plates onto the ship's ribs before the final welding was done.

'And remember,' Rosie told them, 'speed is of the essence. We've been asked because we're fast.'

'The fastest welders in the West,' Dorothy said in a mock-American accent, hooking her welding lead over her shoulder as though it was a lasso and she a cowgirl.

'The speediest in Sunderland,' Angie chipped in.

As they walked across the yard, Rosie shot a look at Gloria before turning her attention back to the squad's terrible two. 'Your mam keeping all right, Angie?'

'Aye,' Angie said. 'Why?'

'She must be missing you at home, helping her look after the bairns. Especially with Liz being away,' Gloria chipped in.

'Yeah, she's had to do less overtime, hasn't she, Ange?' Dorothy gave her friend a loaded look.

A look that wasn't missed by either Rosie or Gloria.

Chapter Seventeen

Helen's heart lifted as she spotted her mother.

Not only had she found her in the lounge bar – as opposed to the one on the first floor where the latest Admiralty were billeted – but she'd also caught her on her own.

'Well, this *is* a surprise!' Miriam said, looking her daughter up and down but finding nothing to criticise. 'To what do I owe this pleasure?' She sat up straight on the tall stool.

'Amelia not here?' Helen asked, giving her mother a quick kiss on both cheeks. She could smell Yardley and gin.

'She's gone to powder her nose.' Miriam looked over in the direction of the Ladies.

'Why don't you sit over there, Mother,' Helen suggested, pointing to the Chesterfield, 'and I'll get some more drinks sent over.'

'Well, my dear, I shan't argue,' said Miriam, looking at her daughter a little suspiciously. 'Everything all right? You've not come to tell me anything ghastly, have you?'

Helen felt her hackles rise, knowing her mother was referring to the time she'd come to the Grand in a right state, having found out that not only was she pregnant, but the father of the baby was already married, with two children and his wife expecting a third. Foolishly, she had thought her mother would help her. Or at least offer comfort. She'd done neither – and had been quite horrible, into the bargain.

'No, Mother,' Helen said. It took all her willpower not to simply walk out. 'I'm meant to be meeting John. We both fancied getting out. All work and no play and all that. And there's no better place for a decent gin and tonic, is there?'

Miriam got off the bar stool and Helen watched as she carefully made her way over to the lounge area. She was walking slowly and self-consciously, which meant she was already half-cut. Helen congratulated herself on her timing. This was going to take less time than she'd anticipated, which was just as well. She didn't know how easily it would be for her to hold her tongue in the face of any more venomous comments.

She turned to the barman.

'I'll have a tonic please, and a double gin and tonic for my mother. She's had the day from hell, poor thing.'

Seeing the look of surprise on the barman's face, she added, 'She hides it well.'

Helen walked over to Miriam, now settling herself in one of the soft leather armchairs.

'I won't be a moment, Mother. It's blowing a gale out there. I just want to check my hair.'

Miriam scrutinised her daughter.

'Good idea. You could do with a little more lipstick too. Remember, "Beauty is a Duty."'

Helen took a deep breath and headed over to the women's toilets. She preferred the saying 'Knowledge is Power'; it was what had motivated her to come here this evening.

Walking into the powder room, she saw Amelia drying her hands and checking herself in the mirror.

'Amelia, so lovely to see you!' Helen said.

'Helen, darling, what a surprise!' Amelia kissed Helen lightly on both cheeks. 'What are you doing here? Your mother says you're working round the clock these days. Hardly have a minute to breathe.'

'Which is exactly why I'm out this evening,' Helen said, looking at Amelia's heavily made-up face. She was certainly taking the whole 'Beauty is a Duty' ethos to heart, although it was questionable as to whether she had succeeded.

'You with your chap this evening?'

'John?'

'Yes, that rather gorgeous doctor of yours.'

'Well, he's not really *my* doctor,' Helen said. 'He's just a friend.'

'Of course he is, my dear,' Amelia winked. 'Just like the Admiral is *my* friend.'

Amelia turned to reapply her lipstick. She looked at Helen in the mirror.

'Oh, the joys of youth,' she lamented. 'You're looking stunning as always, Helen.'

'Thanks, Amelia. As are you,' Helen lied.

Amelia batted the compliment away with a well-manicured hand. 'I do the best of a bad job.'

'Rubbish,' Helen said, forcing a smile onto her face. 'And Harvey? How's Harvey doing?' she said, keeping her eyes on Amelia, who was now fluffing up her hair. 'He looks well, I have to say. Very well,' she added.

'He's fine,' Amelia said, her voice flat and disinterested. 'You know Harvey.' She turned back towards the mirror. 'Never changes.'

Helen counted to five in her head.

Suddenly there was a look of panic on Amelia's face.

Bingo!

'When did you *see* Harvey?' Amelia said, putting the lipstick lid back on and throwing it in her handbag.

'Just now. On my way here,' Helen said, all wide-eyed innocence. 'As I say, he looked very well.'

'Bugger! He's not meant to be back until the weekend.'

She hurried to the door.

'Sorry to be rude, my dear, but must dash.'

She heaved open the door.

'And tell your mother I'm sorry too. I'll call her tomorrow – and huge apologies I couldn't stick around and have a good old catch-up, my dear. It's been an age.'

And with that she was gone.

Helen knew that by the time it took Amelia to get home, wait for Harvey, then ring his base and find out he was exactly where he should be, Helen would have done what she had come here to do.

If Amelia made it back to the Grand before she'd gone, well, it was clearly a case of mistaken identity, wasn't it?

So easily done in these wretched blackouts.

'Well, darling, it looks like you've been stood up?' Miriam looked at her watch. 'It's gone nine.' She gave Helen a side-long glance.

'It's always a bit hit and miss with John,' Helen said, making herself sound suitably disappointed. 'He never knows when he's going to get called into theatre. Or there's some sort of emergency.'

Miriam thought back to the time she had first met Dr Parker at the Royal. He'd been one of the junior doctors looking after Jack when he was in a coma. Helen's new squeeze had certainly climbed the ladder since then.

'You know, darling, I've been meaning to have a quiet word with you for a while now.' Miriam took a sip of her gin and tonic. 'You're not serious about your doctor "friend", are you?'

'Mother, he *is* just a friend. Nothing more.'

'*Of course* he is, darling.' Miriam's words belied their meaning. It was quite clear by her tone that she did not for one minute think they were 'just friends'.

'Don't get too serious with him, will you?' Miriam advised. 'Men like that enjoy playing the field . . . I hate to

125

even mention his name, but . . . like that frightful Theodore fellow.'

'John's nothing like Theo,' Helen snapped.

'Well, you mightn't think so now, darling, but I'm sure you thought Theodore was the best thing since sliced bread and look what happened there.'

'That was a totally different scenario, Mother, and as I keep telling everyone, not that anyone seems to be listening to me, John and I are *merely* friends.'

'Fine, have it your way, Helen, but – and I'm saying this to save you any more heartache – surgeons are like gold dust. Any single woman in her right mind will leap at the chance to bag one for a husband. And these doctors and surgeons know it.' She paused. 'And Dr Parker, my dear, *knows* all about you. He might enjoy your company, but trust me, darling, when it comes to marriage, he will want someone . . .'

She stopped in mid-sentence.

'Oh dear, how do I say this nicely?'

A pause.

'He'll want someone . . . *unsullied.*'

Helen looked at her mother.

God, she hated this woman.

'Mother, I have no intention of getting married any time soon, so let's drop the subject. Let me get us another drink and then you can tell me all about your day. We might as well enjoy the evening since we're both here.'

Helen walked to the bar. She could feel her cheeks burning. Her mother's words had cut deep.

Was that really how John viewed her? *Sullied*? But it didn't matter if he did, did it? They were only friends, after all.

Returning with their drinks, Helen sat down and lit up a cigarette. It helped calm her, and she needed to be in control if she was going to get what she wanted.

126

'So, tell me, Mother, what's been happening? I hear you were at the Doxford launch the other day?'

For the next hour Helen boxed clever. Being careful not to be too nice as it would make her mother suspicious, but at the same time she wanted it to seem as if she was amenable to a truce.

Neither of them mentioned the strong words they had exchanged in the car on the way back from Arthur's funeral. Or the real reason for Miriam putting up a postbox.

'This feels like old times,' Miriam said, looking at her daughter. 'The way we used to be. Just you and me. Chatting. Getting on.'

'At the end of the day, Mother, *we're family*,' Helen said. She signalled over to the barman for another round of drinks. 'It's a true saying. Blood *is* thicker than water.'

'It certainly is, darling, and to hear you say that – well, it really is music to my ears.' There was only the slightest slur to Miriam's speech. Helen knew if *she'd* had a gin in every tonic she'd drunk this evening, she'd be on the floor. She certainly wouldn't have been able to put on the kind of performance she'd managed thus far – one that would have got her a standing ovation had she been performing at the Empire.

'I know we've had our differences, Mother, but I have to say that you really are a force to be reckoned with.'

Miriam smiled. 'Why, thank you, darling. What makes you say that?'

Her mother was angling for a compliment and Helen was more than willing to give her what she wanted, knowing that in return she was also going to get what *she* wanted.

'Well, I was thinking the other day about how you found out all those – ' Helen dropped her voice and leant towards her mother conspiratorially ' – *secrets*.'

Miriam recrossed her legs and sat up in her chair. She reminded Helen of a bird shaking its tail feathers, revelling in the attention and admiration being foisted upon her.

'The women's *secrets*.' Miriam copied her daughter's conspiratorial tone.

The barman arrived with their drinks and placed them on clean coasters.

They were both quiet until he had gone.

'I'm intrigued,' Helen said, raising her glass and chinking it with her mother's. 'How on earth did you manage to find out all that information?'

She had a sip of her cold tonic water, pretending to grimace at the strength of the non-existent gin.

'It can't have been easy.' Helen looked at her mother. 'I mean . . . honestly, Mum, Hercule Poirot has nothing on you.'

Miriam's face lit up. She had felt exceedingly pleased with herself at the time, but had always felt so frustrated that she hadn't been able to boast about her antics to anyone. She hadn't even confided in Amelia. She might be her best friend, but Amelia was hardly the best keeper of secrets. Now, finally, it looked as though she could make good on that missed chance to brag.

'You wouldn't believe it – even if I told you,' Miriam said.

'Go on, try me,' Helen said. 'There's nothing that shocks me these days.'

'Well, your dear mother here . . .' Miriam said, looking about to make sure no one could overhear their conversation, ' . . . did a little bit of subtle prodding and poking around, and managed to find out the name of someone who, well, let's just say someone who is, in real life, a bit of a Poirot.'

'A proper private eye,' Helen whispered.

128

Miriam chuckled at the memory.

'He was that. A proper private eye. As old as Poirot but without a shred of his grace and charm – or impeccable dress.' Miriam took a sip of her gin. 'God, you could tell the man was a widower. During my first visit there I couldn't concentrate for looking at the gravy stain on his tie.'

'Really? Sounds like some character in a film,' Helen gently cajoled.

'Exactly! And his office wasn't must better. Very run-down.'

'I hope you didn't put yourself at risk going somewhere too rough and ready.'

Helen had learnt over the years never to ask her mother a direct question if she wanted to know the answer. If her mother sensed you wanted to know something, she'd hold back, enjoying the power of having something she knew you wanted.

'No, no, my dear, I was careful. It wasn't exactly in the best part of town, but not the worst either. On the cusp.'

Helen furrowed her brow.

'It was on the corner of High Street West. Very discreet. No brass plaque on the main entrance, just a small one on the first floor.'

'Fascinating.'

Helen looked at her watch. It had taken a little over an hour.

And three large G & Ts.

'Funny set-up,' Miriam mused, her mind now back in time. 'He had this plain-Jane secretary working for him. A bit younger than you, but dressed like she was some old maid. Not a touch of make-up on, and believe you me, she could have done with some.'

Miriam took another sip of her drink.

'And the old man with the gravy stain,' Helen said. 'Did he do all the digging around?'

'Mmm, I believe so.' Miriam put her hand up and drummed her forehead with her fingers. 'God, I can't think of the name.'

Helen didn't speak.

'That's it!' Miriam said. 'Mr Pickering . . . Pickering & Sons. That was the firm. Never met the sons, though.'

Another look of deep concentration.

'And the young girl. Now what was her name . . .' Another pause. '*Georgina*. The plain Jane was called Georgina. She was the one who put together the report I was given.'

Miriam looked pleased with herself.

'See.' She smiled at her daughter. 'There's nothing wrong with your dear old mama's memory.'

'Nothing at all,' Helen agreed.

At last! Time for a celebratory drink.

'I'll get us a nightcap,' she said.

She walked over to the bar.

'Make that two gin and tonics this time, please,' she told the barman.

She went back and sat down.

'It just shows you, doesn't it?' Helen said. 'Scratch the surface and you're bound to find something. Everyone's got a skeleton shut away in their closet.'

Miriam let out a tinkle of laughter. 'That was exactly my thinking at the time.'

Helen looked at her mother. 'Makes you wonder about *our* family, doesn't it?'

She had got what she came for, but what the hell, it was worth trying for the bonus ball.

Miriam let out a loud laugh.

'God, darling . . .'

She waited for the barman to put down their fresh drinks and leave.

' . . . I don't know about your father's side, but I think the Havelock skeletons would take up a whole dressing room.'

Chapter Eighteen

Saturday 30 January

'Go and see yer aunty Aggie.' Gloria let go of her daughter's hand and watched her toddle down the hallway. Agnes had, as usual, left the front door ajar. It would have been wide open had they not been in the depths of winter and therefore freezing cold.

'Ah, 'tis me favourite little girl.' Agnes's voice sang out as she appeared from the kitchen. Hope already had her arms in the air in anticipation of a hug. Agnes picked her up, giving her the once-over.

'Don't worry,' Gloria said. 'She seems fine. No spots.'

'That's what I like to hear,' Agnes said, giving Hope a kiss on her rosy, unblemished cheeks. 'Yer boys keeping themselves safe?'

Gloria nodded and crossed her fingers. 'God willing.' She looked over Agnes's shoulder. Normally Polly would have been there, bustling down the hallway, pulling on her coat and hoicking her haversack and gas mask over her shoulders.

'She's not exactly tip-top this morning,' Agnes explained, putting Hope down. 'Said the milk smelled off – or odd. She couldn't quite decide.' Agnes raised her eyebrows at Gloria. 'Said it was making her feel a bit queasy.' She hung Hope's little woollen coat up on the stand. 'She's in the lavvy.'

The two women exchanged looks but didn't say anything.

'*I'm ready!*' Polly's voice sounded out as she clattered through from the kitchen. Tramp and Pup roused themselves from their basket and pottered after her.

'You feeling all right?' Agnes scrutinised her daughter. 'You look as white as a sheet.'

'Yes, Ma, honestly, I'm fine. I'll see you later.'

Agnes, Hope and the two dogs watched as Polly and Gloria stepped out onto Tatham Street and were immediately swept away in a swell of flat caps, all bobbing in the direction of the docks.

Within a few minutes, Polly and Gloria were crossing the Borough Road and making their way down Norfolk Street. It was still dark and the pavements, as usual, were jammed with overall-clad bodies making their way to work.

'You all right?' Gloria said.

'I think so.' Polly gave Gloria a fleeting look as they circumvented two old men who had stopped to light their hand-rolled cigarettes.

'Yer look a little pale, 'n yer ma said you'd been feeling a bit sickly?'

Polly looked at Gloria but didn't say anything.

They turned right onto High Street West and carried on walking as the long stretch of road became High Street East.

Polly gave Gloria a sidelong glance.

'I think I might be pregnant.'

Gloria turned her head to get a good look at her workmate.

'How long since yer last monthly?'

'A couple of weeks before the wedding.'

They slowed their pace as they turned the corner onto West Wear Street.

'I remember because I was glad I didn't have to worry about it when we were staying at the Major's flat.' Where she and Tommy had enjoyed their week's honeymoon *before* their wedding. 'And I was even more relieved I didn't have to worry about anything like that on our actual wedding day.'

'So,' Gloria said, as they slowed their pace, 'I'm guessing, if yer *have* fallen, it would have been the period from when you 'n Tommy made up – a week before yer got married?'

Polly nodded.

'In my reckoning that'll make yer around six weeks gone – give or take,' Gloria said.

As they turned left and started down Bodlewell Lane, they slowed their pace as they hit the crowd of workers bunching up by the ferry landing.

'That was my calculation too,' Polly said.

Gloria looked as the workers paid their penny fares and made their way onto the ferry.

'And yer've started to feel a bit bilious?' Gloria asked.

Polly nodded.

'Anything else?'

Polly blushed a little and lowered her voice.

'My boobs seem to have got bigger.' She paused. 'Well, they *feel* bigger. And they're a bit . . . well . . . a bit *sore*.'

'Sounds about right,' Gloria said. She'd had the same with all three of her children. 'If yer *are* expecting,' she dropped her voice, 'would yer be glad about it?'

'Oh, yes! Over the moon,' Polly said. A big smile spread across her pale face.

Gloria squeezed her arm. 'Well, that's great. Really great to hear.'

'But I don't want to say anything to anyone,' Polly said. 'Not at the moment. Just in case I'm wrong. I remember Beryl saying ages ago that some woman had what she called a "fake" pregnancy 'cos she wanted to have a baby that much.'

Gloria laughed. 'Trust Beryl.'

They paid their fares and stepped onto the ferry. The river looked dark grey and choppy.

'What about Agnes? Do yer think yer should say something to yer ma? I think she might have her suspicions.'

'I don't think she'll exactly be clicking her heels in the air if I am,' Polly said. She grabbed the rail as the ferry churned up water and started its short journey across the river.

'Why's that? I'd have thought she'd be chuffed to pieces. Another grandchild 'n all that.'

'Mmm,' Polly sighed. 'I think she's worried that I'll end up like her. Widowed. Left on my own to bring up a baby without its da.'

'Does that worry you?' Gloria looked at Polly's face. She was getting paler with each bob of the boat.

Polly looked out towards the mouth of the river – out at the darkness she knew to be the North Sea. She shook her head.

'If Tommy doesn't come back, at least I'll still have a part of him with me. A part of him will live on.' She was quiet for a moment.

'Besides,' she said, looking over at Thompson's, 'Ma didn't really have anyone around her to help when she had me and the twins – whereas I've got Ma, and Bel and Joe, and all you lot.'

Gloria suddenly chuckled at the thought of the women welders clucking around Polly and the baby she might have.

'You'll be sick of everyone fussing,' she laughed. 'You'll be wishing fer a bit of peace 'n quiet.'

The ferry hit a particularly large wave as it passed a tug.

Polly's smile dropped. Her pallor turned ashen.

She leant over the iron railing on the side of the ferry and threw up.

'So, we'll keep this just between me and you for now?' Polly said as they walked up the embankment to the time-keeper's cabin. 'I don't want everyone getting all excited, only to find out it's a false alarm.'

'Mum's the word,' Gloria promised, reaching up to take her time board off Alfie. 'Have yer said anything to Bel?' she asked.

'I haven't,' Polly said. 'I feel awful, actually.'

'Why's that?'

'Well, normally I'd have told her at the first inkling I had, but I haven't said anything because I know she's gutted that she's not fallen herself. It's been well over a year since she married Joe – and nothing.'

'I keep forgetting they're trying,' Gloria said.

They walked across the yard.

'Probably because she seems so happy in her new job,' Gloria mused. 'Especially now she's learning shorthand.'

They slowed down as they spotted the women by their workstation, drinking tea and chatting.

'Well, I think yer doing the best thing,' Gloria said. 'Wait till yer know fer definite . . . Try 'n take it a bit easy, though, eh? Yer don't want to make yerself ill or wear yerself out. Yer gonna need all the strength yer've got.'

They both saw that Dorothy had spotted them and was waving a letter in the air.

'Yeah! They're here!'

Another celebratory wave.

'Look what I got!'

Polly laughed and reached into her top pocket.

'Snap!' she laughed.

Dorothy jumped up and down on the spot.

'Letters from our lovers!'

Within minutes the women were gathered around the five-gallon barrel fire that Martha had stoked up, listening to Dorothy read out her letter from Toby, then Polly hers.

Both caused an uproar when they left out the odd sentence here and there because it was either too risqué (in Dorothy's case) or too lovey-dovey (in Polly's), before the klaxon put a stop to any more questions and cheeky banter.

As Polly went down on her haunches in order to get into the right position to do a particularly awkward overhead weld on the flank of the *Chinese Prince*, she wondered how she would feel doing this in a few months' time. She had to be realistic; there were some things she quite simply wouldn't be able to do. The changes that being pregnant would inevitably bring about were going to be huge – in many ways. If she was honest, it frightened her as much as it excited her.

When they all stopped for their mid-morning break, Polly went off to the toilets, accompanied by Dorothy.

Angie and Martha tucked into some flapjacks that Mrs Perkins had made.

'Polly all right?' Rosie asked, giving Gloria a loaded look.

'You guessed?' Gloria said, glancing over at Angie and Martha and looking around to check that no one could hear.

Rosie nodded. 'That's the second time she's been to the lav this morning. Plus, she looks as white as a ghost. And let's face it, it wouldn't be totally unexpected – especially as her and Tommy had that week together before the wedding.'

Gloria nodded. 'She brought up her breakfast on the ferry on the way over here, poor thing. But she's sworn me to secrecy. Wants to be totally sure.'

'That's understandable,' Rosie said.

For a short while, they both drank their tea in silence.

Gloria looked at Rosie. She and Polly were the only married women in the squad.

'Do yer think you 'n Peter might want a family?' It was something Gloria had wondered about a few times. She'd been surprised that Rosie had not fallen after her wedding and honeymoon in Guildford last New Year. Or after Peter's visit during the summer.

Rosie shook her head.

'No,' she said simply.

Gloria was surprised by the lack of emotion.

'Besides,' Rosie said, 'I've got my hands full with Charlie, haven't I?'

'I forgot,' Gloria said. 'Today's the big day, isn't it? The day she finally gets her own way 'n sees inside Lily's "home".'

Rosie nodded solemnly. 'At least when it's done, it's done. Curiosity cured and all that.'

Gloria threw the dregs of her tea on the ground and screwed the top back onto her flask.

She couldn't help but wonder, though, if, rather than extinguished, Charlotte's curiosity might actually be intensified after a visit to Lily's.

Chapter Nineteen

'Ma chérie!' Lily took Charlotte's face in her hands and planted a kiss on both cheeks.

'Bienvenue! Bienvenue!' Lily welcomed her guest.

'Merci,' Charlotte answered automatically.

'Let me take your coats.' George came hobbling down the hallway.

Charlotte and Rosie shrugged off their grey mackintoshes and George hung them up on the coat stand.

Lily pulled a handkerchief from her bosom and wiped off two red lipstick marks she'd left on Charlotte's already flushed cheeks. Standing back, she inspected her young guest, a slight frown appearing on her brow as she surveyed the sensible A-line skirt and light blue V-neck jumper that Charlotte was wearing.

'I thought you'd be wearing your lovely red dress. The one Kate made you for the wedding?'

Charlotte swung round and glared at her sister.

'Rosie wouldn't let me. She said it was too *over the top*. That I had to save it for special occasions.'

Lily pursed her lips. She had been warned about being on her best behaviour, which was hard.

'Well, that makes sense. You don't want to wear the dress out, do you?' She looked over at Rosie and forced a smile.

'Now, let me give you the grand tour, *ma chérie*.' She threw out her arm in the direction of a huge oak-panelled door that had been wedged open. 'Come, let me show you where your sister spends hours hunched over her ledgers.

'This,' she said, walking into the room, 'used to be the front reception room, but I decided I needed an office to do all the boring paperwork and correspondence that has to be done when one is a businesswoman.'

Lily stood in the middle of the room and watched as Charlotte walked in and stared about her in wonder. There was the cherrywood desk – *much bigger than she had expected* – the floor-to-ceiling velvet curtains – *gorgeous* – a chaise longue that looked too beautiful to sit on, and the French marble mantelpiece. *Amazing.* It was just as Dorothy and Angie had described, only better.

'Your big sister might have her nose to the grindstone most evenings,' Lily winked at Charlotte, 'but at least she is doing so in very plush – and, I hasten to add, very warm – surroundings.'

Charlotte looked at the fire blazing away, then around at the magnificent room.

Wait until she told Marjorie about this place! It was wonderful. So extravagant. So like Lily.

Coming out of the office and back into the hallway, Charlotte looked up and couldn't believe she hadn't noticed the incredible fourteen-armed chandelier hanging from the ceiling.

'Beautiful, isn't it?' Lily said, seeing Charlotte's head tilt back and the look of amazement on her face. 'Shipped over from Paris before the war, like so much of what you see.' She sighed. 'A reminder of a previous life.'

Charlotte continued to gawp as she was shown into the kitchen. Even this was so unlike any kitchen she had ever seen before, with its long oak table, French armoire and huge pillar-box-red Aga.

'Typically,' Lily said, 'it's the kitchen where we all tend to gather.'

She guided Charlotte back out into the hallway.

'Although, this afternoon . . .' she stopped outside a door at the end of the hallway ' . . . we are all in here.'

She pushed the door open to reveal a room that made Charlotte feel as though she had stepped back in time. To the era of Louis XIV. It was all so *French*. Bow-legged, hand-carved furniture, vibrant gilt wallpaper, another chaise longue, another roaring fire.

'Hi Charlie!' Maisie and Vivian spoke in unison. They were standing next to a beautiful black baby grand, both smoking. Maisie's cigarette was in a long ebony cigarette holder. She reminded Charlotte of a photograph she had once seen of a flapper looking incredibly sophisticated and glamorous. She just needed a feather boa and the image would be complete.

The pair came over to give Charlotte a dainty kiss on both cheeks.

'Welcome to our modest abode, hon,' Vivian said in her best Mae West accent. She smiled and pinched Charlotte's cheek affectionately.

'But this is the best bit,' Maisie said, taking Charlotte's hand and walking her over to a three-tier cake stand taking centre stage on the coffee table, along with a china teapot and cups and saucers.

'Wow!' Charlotte's eyes were out on stalks. 'I've never seen such lovely cakes! Not even at Betty's.' She looked over at Rosie.

'I know,' Rosie said, smiling. 'Come and sit down and I'll pour the tea.'

Charlotte did as she was told and sat down on one of the cushioned high-backed chairs, her eyes still darting about, enraptured by the whole decadent beauty of the place.

Just then Kate came flying into the room.

'Charlie!' She flung her arms out, marched over to Charlotte and gave her a hug. 'How lovely to see you! You've not been to the Maison Nouvelle for ages.'

She gave Charlotte a quick once-over.

'You'll have to pop in when you get a minute. I'm sure we can get you fixed up with something a bit more . . .' she looked guiltily over at Rosie ' . . . well, a bit more stylish.'

'And where have you been?' Lily had produced a fan and was cooling herself. She sat down in the chair furthest away from the fire and glared at Kate. 'You're always late,' she admonished. 'I hope that Alfie boy hasn't been taking up your time.'

Rosie looked at Kate, who had completely ignored Lily's jibe. She still couldn't work out if Kate was actually aware of Alfie's infatuation with her, and if so, whether she was happy about it.

'Well, it wouldn't matter if he *was* taking up Kate's time, would it?' Rosie glared at Lily.

George coughed and, with the aid of his walking stick, eased himself down into the chair next to Lily's.

'This is amazing,' Charlotte said, looking at Lily before continuing to stare around the room.

'*Merci, ma chère*, one does one's best.' Lily looked like the cat that had just got the cream.

'Oh, chocolate cake!' Kate said, looking at the selection of cakes on the porcelain stand.

'Apparently, it's eggless,' Lily said, 'but I was reassured it tastes just as nice. Rosie told me it was our guest's favourite.'

'It is! Thank you,' Charlotte said.

'Vivian, would you do the honours, please?' Lily snapped her fan shut and pointed it at the tea and cakes. '*Merci beaucoup.*'

'*De rien,*' Vivian replied, although she still made the words sound American rather than French. She got up and started putting slices of cake onto plates and handing them out.

'So, Charlotte,' Lily said, settling herself into her chair, 'tell us all about the Sunderland Church High School. Rosie tells me there's no boys there?'

Rosie glowered at Lily. 'You know fullwell no boys go there. You were, after all, the one to tell Charlie all about the school, remember?'

Lily took a sip of tea and waved away a plate with a slice of Victoria sponge on it.

'I love it there,' Charlotte said. 'Much better than Runcorn. And I get to go home every night.'

'No more beastly dormitories and bullies,' Lily said.

Charlotte nodded as she took a big bite of cake, savouring the taste of the chocolate.

Lily looked at Charlotte. She had been allowed to visit her home – at long last. Lily had wanted to meet Charlotte the moment Rosie had told her about her little sister who was, to all intents and purposes, hidden away at some stuffy school in the middle of nowhere.

That seemed a long time ago.

Finally, everything had come right.

'I've waited so long,' Lily mused.

Everyone looked at her.

'Waited so long for what?' Charlotte asked.

'Dearie me, did I say that aloud?' Lily looked around. '*So long* for you to come to visit me here – I was most definitely last on the list.'

'Well, you know what they say, darling,' George said, taking a puff of his cigar, 'better late than not at all.'

'And leave the best till last,' Charlotte chipped in, taking another big bite of her cake.

143

For the next hour everyone chatted away. Lily told Charlotte about her various business interests and George explained how they dabbled in the stock market, as well as about their decision to take a gamble investing in property. Charlotte listened, fascinated, asking lots of questions and declaring that she wanted to study economics when she went to university.

Rosie saw Charlotte drinking up every word Lily uttered. If Lily suggested she study Swahili, she'd probably demand the school give her lessons. And, likewise, Lily's attention was focused solely on Charlotte. Rosie had always been able to see through Lily's brash exterior – the care and compassion she felt for her girls was transparent – but this was the first time she had glimpsed Lily's maternal side.

Maisie put on a record called 'Stormy Weather' and informed Charlotte that the singer was Lena Horne, adding that, in her opinion, she would have much more fun if she studied music and the arts.

Charlotte's fascination with Lily was almost rivalled by the intense curiosity she had for Maisie and Vivian. She had never met two women who were so glamorous and so beautiful. She'd certainly never met a woman who was mixed race. She still found it hard to believe that Pearl was Maisie's mother – and Bel her sister. They were all so completely different.

By the time a second pot of tea had been made and consumed, Charlotte plucked up the courage to ask Vivian where in America she came from.

Everyone had a good chuckle.

'Oh, sweet pea, I hate to disappoint,' Vivian drawled. 'But my origins are closer to home. A hundred and seventy miles closer to home.'

'She's from Liverpool,' Maisie informed.

'The Wirral, to be exact.' Vivian gave Maisie a mock scowl. 'You southerners have no geographical knowledge of anywhere outside of Greater London.'

Knowing that Charlotte was curious as to what they both did for a living, Maisie managed to weave into the conversation that she and Vivian ran the Gentlemen's Club next door. When Charlotte asked exactly what a gentlemen's club was, Vivian laughed loudly and explained it was where old men with lots of money went to escape their nagging wives.

'Well, I don't know about you all,' George declared. 'But I've drunk enough tea to sink a ship.' He got up and went over to the drinks cabinet. 'Anyone fancy joining me in a little tipple?'

Maisie and Vivian declined.

'We've got our dates this evening,' Vivian drawled.

Charlotte had a brief image of seeing them on Christmas Eve when they had been with two Admiralty officers.

'Actually,' Charlotte said. 'I've also drunk enough tea to sink a ship. Do you mind if I use your toilet, please?'

'Of course, *ma chère*, when nature calls . . . It's upstairs. Second on the left.' Lily waved her hand up towards the ceiling.

'Go with her, Kate, *s'il vous plaît*.' Lily looked over to Kate, who was flicking through a copy of *Vogue*. 'We don't want our guest getting lost.'

Lily looked over at George, now taking the top from the decanter.

'And yes please, my dear, I shall partake in a "little tipple" too.' Lily sparked up a Gauloise, feeling celebratory. Her high tea had been a resounding success. Charlotte had seen the bordello, her curiosity was now satiated, and all her unasked questions had been answered.

'Be back in a jiffy,' Charlotte said, as she and Kate left the smoky warmth of the parlour.

As they walked up the first flight of stairs, Kate looked at Charlotte in her drab daywear. The girl needed a little help in the wardrobe department and she was the one to give it.

'I've got a pattern for a skirt that I think might suit you,' she said. 'Let me get a picture of it and see if you like it.' Kate hurried up to her attic room, which was now more dressmaker's studio than bedroom.

Charlotte used the bathroom, washed her hands with lavender soap and gawped at the bidet and the huge roll-top bath.

When she came out, though, Kate had still not come back down.

She stood looking at the long landing.

There seemed to be a lot of rooms.

She did a quick count.

Six.

Presumably all bedrooms.

She wondered why Lily didn't have more lodgers.

She certainly had the room.

I wonder what they're like inside. Bet you they're as magnificent as the rest of the house.

Charlotte took two steps along the landing and stood outside the door to the nearest bedroom.

She looked down at the round brass doorknob.

It was so shiny she could see a distorted reflection of herself in it.

She put her hand on it – obliterating her image.

She knew she shouldn't. *It was rude to snoop around someone's house, wasn't it?*

But still.

Turning it gently, she opened the door just enough so that she could pop her head through the gap.

Just a little peek.

It wasn't really being nosy, was it?

'Found it!' Kate's voice sounded out as she hurried back down the stairs.

Charlotte jumped and quickly pulled the door shut.

'I knew I had it somewhere!' Kate said, waving the paper packaging of the pattern, which had a picture of a woman posing in a chic-looking skirt.

Two minutes later the pair were back downstairs and had rejoined the tea party.

Chapter Twenty

'So, what I plan to do,' Rosie explained, 'is get Charlotte a place at the Runcorn School for Girls.'

Rosie and Mrs Rainer were standing in the kitchen watching Charlotte and Mr Rainer in the chicken coop at the bottom of the garden.

'That sounds like an excellent idea,' Mrs Rainer said.

She hesitated.

'I've heard it's meant to have a good name for itself. And from what I've seen with my own eyes, its pupils always appear very well behaved whenever I see them out in town.'

She put her teacup back on the saucer.

'And it's apparently had some quite famous alumni.'

There was that word again.

Seeing Rosie's blank look, Mrs Rainer explained, 'Former pupils.'

'Really?' Rosie was curious.

Mrs Rainer rattled off a few names, none of which Rosie recognised.

'Although,' Mrs Rainer looked at Rosie, 'I would assume, because of its high standing, it would be quite costly to send Charlotte there.'

'Mam and Dad had a little bit put away,' Rosie explained. 'I think it was money Mam's parents left her when they died. I don't think they spent much of it. Mam always said it was our "rainy day" money. And, well, I guess, that rainy day has come.'

'Well, like I said, I think it's an excellent idea.'

Rosie could tell that, as she'd expected, Mrs Rainer was relieved she would not have to look after Charlotte full-time, but she understood. She didn't blame her. She was getting on. Mrs Rainer had always been her mam's 'old' friend. She wouldn't want to be running about after an energetic eight-year-old day in, day out. On top of which, Charlotte could be a handful. As the younger child, she'd been given much more leeway than Rosie growing up and had used it to her full advantage.

'So, if Charlotte can just come and stay with you during the holidays?' Rosie asked.

'Of course she can, my dear. We'd love to have her.'

'Obviously I'll come and visit her as much as I can,' Rosie said.

Their attention was caught by Charlotte charging down the garden path.

She burst into the kitchen, her face full of wonder.

In her cupped hands there was a single white egg.

Charlotte's excitement about the freshly laid egg and the chickens scratching around in Mr and Mrs Rainer's back garden waned somewhat when Rosie sat her down and explained that she was going to remain with the Rainers for a little while, until she was able to start at the Runcorn School for Girls.

Charlotte cried and cried when Rosie told her that she had to go back to Sunderland but would come and visit as much as she could. As Charlotte continued crying, Rosie told her that she had to be brave.

'I don't want you to be a crybaby when I've gone, do you hear?' Rosie said. She felt cruel saying it, but she knew Charlotte had to harden up if she was to survive on her own.

'I'll visit you as much as I can,' she said, trying to re-assure her. 'And we can write to each other all the time. Every day if you want to.'

Rosie took hold of her sister's hand.

'I'll always be here for you. Always. You remember that, all right?'

Rosie pulled her close and gave her a cuddle.

'You still up for a trip to Betty's before I go back?'

Charlotte nodded through the tears.

Thankfully, the trip into Harrogate town centre distracted Charlotte and cheered her up a little. As did their arrival at Betty's Café. Neither of them had seen the like. Their mam had taken them to the tea rooms in Binns, but even that didn't compare to this Aladdin's cave of all things scrumptious. But, despite the splendour, and the delicious cake, it was Rosie who had to fight the overwhelming urge to cry like a baby as she felt her heart breaking, knowing she had to leave her little sister behind.

Chapter Twenty-One

'Georgina, please come in!'

Helen stood up and strode across her office, hand stretched out.

'Sorry for sounding so informal, but I'm afraid I don't know your surname?' Helen took her visitor's hand and shook it. It was cold and felt fragile.

'It's Pickering,' Georgina said. There was nothing fragile about her voice, though. 'But, please, call me Georgina. I'm rather averse to being called *Miss*.'

Helen guessed Georgina Pickering could have been no more than twenty, although she dressed like someone much older.

'Oh,' Helen said, pulling out the chair in front of her desk for Georgina to sit in. 'I didn't realise you are related to Mr Pickering?'

'Yes, I'm his daughter,' Georgina said, sitting on the proffered chair and putting her handbag on the floor. As she did so, she noticed a marmalade-coloured tomcat eyeing her from its basket next to the heater.

'Well, that's a surprise.' Helen went over to the tea tray that had, as usual, been placed on top of one of the tall steel cabinets. She poured them each a cup. 'My mother just presumed you were Mr Pickering's secretary.' Helen handed Georgina her tea.

'Don't worry, it's a common assumption,' Georgina said, taking a sip, then putting the cup and saucer down.

'Forgive me if I sound like I'm in any way doubting your abilities,' Helen said, 'but I assumed, as the firm is called Pickering & Sons, that I would be dealing with either your father or your brothers?'

Georgina gave a smile that in no way reached her eyes.

'Don't worry,' she said. 'I've become quite used to people casting aspersions about my "abilities" to do the job because of my gender. One becomes used to it after a while.' Georgina looked about the office. 'I'm sure it's something you yourself have had to endure – and probably still have to – being a woman in what is intrinsically a man's world?' Georgina knew she was being a little precocious, possibly bordering on a tad out of turn, but she didn't care. She hadn't liked Mrs Crawford and was doubtful she would like her daughter much more.

Helen didn't know whether to be annoyed or to agree. She eventually decided to laugh. 'Well, you certainly don't mince your words, Georgina . . . But you're right. It has been, and probably always will be, a constant battle for us women – having to prove our worth just because we're female – and made so much worse by the knowledge that we're actually so much better than the men.' *If Georgina could be a little outrageous, then so could she.* She took a sip of her tea and put it down on top of some invoices that needed filing.

Georgina smiled. This time it did reach her eyes.

'Well,' she said, delving into her handbag and retrieving a small spiral notebook, 'now that we have established the superiority of the downtrodden sex, let's do business.'

Helen looked at Georgina in her brown schoolmarmish skirt and a jacket that looked a little too big for her. She was certainly a peculiar one.

'Yes, let's,' she said.

Helen pulled out her pack of Pall Malls and offered one to Georgina, who refused with a shake of her head.

'First of all,' Helen said, lighting up a cigarette, 'I have to say that my mother was very pleased with the work you did for her, and that she was particularly pleased with the level of discretion with which you conducted your . . . what shall we call it? . . . *research*.'

Georgina showed no emotion and simply listened.

'And it goes without saying that I would expect the same.'

Georgina gave a curt nod. 'And it goes without saying that I would give it.'

'The job I have in mind, however,' Helen said, blowing out a plume of smoke, 'is probably even more delicate than that commissioned by my mother.'

Georgina had her fingers crossed that this job would not entail any more digging up dirt on the women who worked in this very yard. She had often wondered to what ends Mrs Crawford had used the information she had given her.

'You see,' Helen tapped her cigarette in the ashtray, 'the *research* I want you to conduct is very personal.'

She looked at Georgina.

'Personal as in it concerns my family. The Havelock family.'

Now Georgina's interest was piqued.

'You might want to take notes.'

'So, just to reiterate what you've told me so far.' Georgina flicked back the pages in her wire-bound notebook. 'The primary aim of this investigation is to find out who the biological parents of a woman called Mrs Isabelle Elliot are. And moreover, to find out if she is in any way connected or related to the Havelock family. Obviously, to prove or disprove any connection or relationship to the Havelock family, I will have to ascertain who Mrs Elliot's mother and father are.' She paused while she turned over a page and looked at her notes. 'At the moment it appears to be mainly conjecture and speculation on your behalf that Mrs Elliot is somehow connected to your maternal family.' Another flick of the notebook. 'You have no suspicions that Mrs Elliot is anything to do with your paternal side. Your biological father being Jack Crawford.'

Helen sat and listened, played around with another cigarette but didn't light it.

'The reason you believe Mrs Elliot to be somehow related to the maternal side of your family, the Havelocks, is due to Mrs Elliot's striking resemblance to your mother, Miriam Crawford, née Havelock.' Georgina turned over a page. 'You believe it is likely that Mrs Elliot is, in fact, the biological daughter of a woman called Pearl. You don't know the woman's surname. The reason you believe this is because she does resemble her daughter.'

Another glance down at her notepad.

'Your theory is strengthened by your belief that you think it is unlikely that Pearl is,' she quoted from her notes, '"the kind of woman who would adopt a child, unless it was for money, which she clearly has very little of". Despite this, you still want me to check that this is, in fact, the case, and that Mrs Isabelle Elliot – whom you refer to as *Bel* – is not actually the daughter of your mother, Mrs Miriam Crawford, or her sister – your aunty Margaret.' Georgina took another look at her notebook. 'Or your grandmother – Mrs Catherine Henrietta Havelock. Who, you have told me, is no longer with us.'

She closed her notebook and looked up at Helen.

'At this stage, all we have is the fact that Mrs Elliot resembles your mother.'

'Hearing it put like that, it sounds rather fanciful,' Helen said. 'Like I'm seeing something that might not be there.'

Realising she had somehow made Helen doubt herself, Georgina silently cursed. The last thing she needed was to talk Miss Crawford out of giving her this commission. They needed the money and she knew the Crawfords, or rather the Havelocks, had the money to spend.

'No, don't take my slightly clinical approach as demeaning this in any way. It's just that I like to make sure I have all my facts right before I start. That is, if you are sure that you want to go ahead with this investigation?'

'Yes,' Helen said. 'And if I am being silly and I have got a slightly overactive imagination – as a good friend of mine has accused me of having – then so be it. I can put a line through it and move on.'

'And if that's not the case? If Mrs Elliot is in some way connected – related – to your family?'

Helen looked puzzled.

'I mean, if it's not a case of you having an overactive imagination – which, by the way, I think is something to be lauded rather than lambasted – then I suppose what I'm saying is that you need to be prepared for the possible consequences.'

Helen waved off Georgina's concerns with her hand.

'I'll worry about that if and when the times comes,' she said.

Georgina breathed a sigh of relief. Time to go before she put her foot in it any further.

'For the moment I just need two things from you, Miss Crawford.' Georgina looked at Helen. 'Although, as the investigation progresses, I may well have to ask for more.'

'And what would they be?' Helen asked.

'If it is at all possible, it would help me in my research if you could provide me with any photographs of your mother and your aunty – and of your grandparents, too, if there are any.'

'I'm sure there are,' Helen said. Both her mother and her grandfather were lovers of the camera.

'And regarding payment . . .' Georgina said. This was always the part she hated the most. Normally, it was something her father would deal with. But as he was now practically housebound, and Miss Crawford had, rather unusually, asked to meet her at her place of work, she had no choice. 'It would be the same terms and daily rate negotiated with your mother,' Georgina finished.

'Ah, that's something I forgot to mention,' Helen said. 'This job might be about my family, but there's absolutely no way I want anyone from the family knowing anything about what I have asked you to find out.'

Georgina nodded. 'Understood.'

After Georgina explained how the payment worked, including the daily rate and any extras, Helen agreed without batting an eyelid. Georgina wished she'd upped the money a little. Still, this wasn't going to be the most straightforward of jobs. Paternity cases – which she was sure this was – were notoriously hard to prove. Which meant more hours, and therefore more money.

'This mightn't be what we in the trade call a quick turnaround,' Georgina warned.

'That's fine,' Helen said. 'I'm not in a huge rush. Just as long as you get there in the end.'

Georgina looked at Helen. Money was clearly no object – but results were expected. She had her work cut out, but at least she didn't have to rush the job, worrying that the client was watching every click of the money meter. It meant she could concentrate on the job at hand.

Helen stood up and walked around the desk. 'So, shall we rendezvous again in two weeks? Same time, same place?'

Georgina had got to her feet and was picking up the brown leather handbag that had once belonged to her mother. The cat, she noticed, was now out of its basket and rubbing itself against Helen's leg.

'That sounds perfect,' she said.

The two women shook hands and Helen went to open her office door.

'And if anyone asks what you were doing here,' Helen said, 'you were applying for a job as a clerk.'

'I'm sure they won't,' Georgina said. 'I don't think I know a single person who works in any of the shipyards. Clerical or manual.'

As they both stepped out of the office and into the main admin department, Helen saw Rosie waiting to speak to her.

'Sorry, Helen.' Rosie started to walk towards her.

Seeing Georgina, she slowed her pace.

'*Georgie Pickering!*' Rosie said, her face breaking into a surprised smile. 'Dear me, what a blast from the past!'

Helen watched, intrigued.

'Rosie Thornton!' Georgina said. She looked down to Rosie's hand and spotted her gold wedding ring. 'Or perhaps it's not Thornton any more?'

Rosie laughed.

'No, I got married.' She raised her hand. 'I'm now Rosie Miller.'

So, she had married her older man.

'What a surprise to see you here?' Rosie said, looking towards Helen for an answer.

'Oh,' Helen said, 'I'm looking for another clerical assistant. Bel's climbing the ladder at a rapid rate and I'm going to need someone to replace her when she "graduates".'

Everyone turned to look at Bel, who was typing away as though she'd been doing the job for years.

'But, alas,' Helen said, 'I think your friend here is more than a little overqualified for the job. As much as I would love to snatch her up, I fear she will reject my offer for something more challenging – and better paid.'

'I will be in touch,' Georgina said, turning to Helen. 'I do appreciate your time and offer of employment.'

'I'll walk you out,' Rosie said, turning and pointing towards the main doors. 'How long's it been? '

Helen watched as the two women walked off, chatting animatedly as they made their way out of the admin department.

Interesting. Was that why no real dirt had ever been dug up on Rosie?

As soon as she was back in her office, Helen picked up the phone.

She couldn't wait to tell John all her news.

'The Ryhope,' Helen said into the receiver.

Unusually, she got put through straight away.

'Can you find Dr Parker for me, please?' Helen had learnt it paid to be polite to the receptionist at the hospital.

'Ah, is that Miss Crawford?'

'It is, Denise. How are you today?'

'I'm well, thank you. But I'm afraid Dr Parker's over at the asylum this afternoon.'

Helen knew it would be to do with the new psychologist he'd mentioned.

'That's all right. Would you mind passing on a message, please? Tell him that I'll see him as planned this evening, and just to call if he gets held up.'

'So, how are you and your family?' Rosie asked Georgina as they left the office. She let out a short laugh, adding, 'It was always the highlight of Mam's week when she went for her "coffee and catch-up" with your mother in town. And, I have to say, you're her absolute double.'

'Mam died,' Georgina said matter-of-factly.

'Oh, I'm sorry to hear that,' Rosie said, her face serious.

'As I was to hear both your mother and father had been killed in that terrible car accident,' Georgina said as they walked down the stairs. 'It must have been devastating for you – and your sister.'

Rosie didn't know what to say. Instead she asked, 'I'm guessing you read about it in the paper?'

'Yes, Dad showed me. I thought *I'd* been cheated, losing my mother when I did – but to lose both parents, and at the same time . . .' Her voice trailed off.

They were quiet for a moment, before a smile suddenly appeared on Rosie's face. 'Can you remember when I came to your house that day?'

Georgina nodded, remembering how she had peeked a look at the pretty blonde girl from behind her mother's skirt. 'Strange how some things really stick in your mind, isn't it?'

'I think that was the only time I met you,' Rosie said, 'but I felt I knew you because Mam would always talk about your mam and dad, and you and your two brothers. Are they all well?'

'Father's got bad arthritis. Can't get around much these days. Both my brothers are in the navy.'

When they walked through the main doors and out into the yard, Georgina was hit by the clanging and clashing of metal, the deafening sound of men and machinery at work. It was like another world. She might have lived within ear-shot of the town's shipbuilding industry most of her life, but never before had she ventured into any of the nine yards that lined the river.

As they walked over to the main gates, she spotted an overall-clad man sitting on a plank suspended in mid-air. He was partially hidden behind scaffolding that had been erected by the side of a half-built ship, his pneumatic rivet gun ready in his gloved hand, his face upturned, watching a huge sheet of steel swinging into place. She felt a shot of nerves for the man's safety.

'Why don't we meet up sometime?' Rosie shouted into Georgina's ear as they reached the timekeeper's cabin.

Georgina nodded.

'I'd love that,' she shouted back. 'Like our mams used to.'

Chapter Twenty-Two

1936

When Rosie arrived back in Sunderland, she felt a sharp stab of depression – a stab of depression that might have morphed into something bigger had she not had so much to do.

After catching the tram to Seaburn, she walked the rest of the way back home.

Once there, she didn't allow herself to sit down, even for a cup of tea.

Instead, she packed her bags.

When it was late, unable to face lying in the bed in which she had been so violently abused – and still fearful that Raymond might return – she slept on the beach. The night was cold, even though it was now summer, but she had the benefit of thick blankets to keep her warm. More than anything, though, she felt safe. If Raymond did come back, he wouldn't think to look out on the beach to find her. If by chance he did, she'd made her makeshift bed behind some rocks and was shielded from view.

The next day she went to see the landlord and gave up the tenancy on the little cottage that had been her home since birth. Mr Gantry, the owner of the property, was a decent man and gave her a fair amount for the furniture, rugs and other bits and pieces that her mam and dad had bought over the years. Money that would pay for a month's lodgings in a small bedsit in town. When Mr Gantry asked about Charlotte, Rosie told him she had gone to stay with friends of the family in London. She would tell the same story to anyone else who might ask. She also said that she would be going to join Charlotte. If Mr Gantry or anyone saw her in Sunderland, she would simply say she was staying on for a while longer. If Raymond tried to find either herself or Charlotte, he'd be thrown off the scent. Trying to track anyone down in London would be like trying to find a needle in a haystack.

As soon as Rosie dumped her bags in her new lodgings, she went straight back out to the GPO and rang the Runcorn School for Girls. She explained to them that as Charlotte's parents had both been killed in an automobile accident, it had been decided she would be best off at boarding school. 'And, of course, Runcorn is known to be one of the best. If not *the* best,' Rosie buttered up the deputy head. 'Especially with its impressive list of past alumni.'

Mrs Willoughby-Smith seemed convinced by Rosie's posh telephone voice, as well as the lie that she was working as a secretary at one of the largest shipyards in Sunderland. Suitably impressed, she'd offered Charlotte a place there and then, providing, of course, she was in receipt of funds within the week.

Rosie had a cheque in the post half an hour after hanging up.

The amount covered the first lot of fees, which Rosie had been overjoyed to hear were not as steep as she had imagined. The school was what was known as a 'state-funded boarding school'. This meant the government paid the actual teaching fees, and the parents or guardians the fees for board and lodgings. There were extra costs, of course, which ate into the money Rosie thought she was saving, but she didn't care. Charlotte would have a roof over her head, food in her belly and she'd be getting a proper schooling – which, in turn, would give her the chance to make a decent life for herself. But, most of all, she would be out of harm's way. No one would know where she was, and the school had the added benefit of being located in a very remote part of North Yorkshire.

Now all Rosie had to do was find herself a job so that she, too, could keep a roof over her head and food in her belly. She'd worry later about how she was going to keep Charlotte at the school, once the 'rainy-day money' was gone.

For now, she had to find work.

Her lie about being a secretary in one of the town's ship-yards had got her thinking.

Chapter Twenty-Three

'So, tell me all about it.' Dr Parker took a sip of his pint.

He looked at Helen sitting opposite him on the stool at 'their' corner table in the Railway Inn. She looked stunning. He didn't think he'd ever seen her looking so well. Or so happy. If he didn't know better, he'd say she had a man in her life.

'Oh, John, I feel like I'm in an Agatha Christie novel,' she said.

Dr Parker nearly spluttered on his bitter.

'As long as no one gets murdered,' he chuckled.

Helen nudged him playfully and proceeded to tell him how she had set up her accidental meeting with her mother at the Grand, gleaned the necessary information, then gone home and written a letter to Mr Pickering, asking for his assistance in a 'most delicate matter', suggesting a date and time. Mr Pickering had sent a brief but courteous reply saying that it would indeed be possible and that he – or someone from the firm – would be there at the yard at the designated time. He had ended the letter by thanking her for considering Pickering & Sons and hoped that they would be able to be of assistance.

'So,' Helen widened her eyes, 'you can imagine my surprise when a *young woman* stepped into my office?'

'Interesting,' Dr Parker said. Only Helen could find herself a private investigator – and a woman private eye at that.

'We had a slight locking of verbal horns, but once we'd each established where the other stood, it was fine.'

Dr Parker smiled to himself. He wondered what the verbal 'locking of horns' was about, but didn't want to interrupt Helen's flow. He sat back and took a sip of his beer, content to simply sit and listen. And yes, to enjoy losing himself in those emerald eyes of hers.

As Helen told him about her meeting with the mousy-looking young girl called Georgina, who was 'anything but mousy in character', he realised that he had now accepted that Helen could never be his. Like some pathetic medieval knight he was doomed to love from afar.

'I'm seeing her again in two weeks' time,' Helen said.

'Well, it will certainly be interesting to see what she finds out, although I have to ask, will you be prepared for what might be unearthed?'

'You sound like my Miss Marple,' Helen said. 'She asked me the same question.'

She looked at John and smiled.

'*Of course* I'll be all right. Besides, I have to know now, either way. It's imperative for my mental health.' She laughed and took a sip of her vodka and lemon. 'Talking of which, how's your psychologist getting along at the asylum?'

'Yes, yes,' Dr Parker said, 'it's all working out very well. Very advantageous for me, to be honest.'

'Because?' Helen asked.

'Because I've got one patient in particular – a young lad called Jacob – who is just about physically well enough to be discharged, but far from well up here.' Dr Parker tapped his head. 'He's adamant that he won't go to the asylum – even for a short spell. So, Dr Eris has kindly agreed to see him at the Ryhope.'

They carried on chatting, trying to fit in all their news, aware that John might be called back at any time.

'So, there wasn't too much damage from the air raid?' John asked. He'd been relieved that the bombs and incendiaries that had landed the other night had done so on the south docks, well away from Helen on the north side.

'It was one of those delayed-action bombs,' Helen said. 'Exploded just before five in the morning – eight hours after it landed. Caused quite a lot of damage to the gas main and to one of the main coal staithes. But no one was hurt, which was the main thing.'

They chatted as they always did about the latest war updates. The papers had been full of news that the RAF had started a major bombing campaign on the Ruhr in an effort to bring Germany's industry to its knees, and that Jerry had lost the Battle of Stalingrad. The Allies had finally taken control of Libya, and they both agreed that for once it felt as though the war was going in their favour.

'Oh, that's what I meant to tell you,' Helen said, glancing up at the clock and knowing she would have to catch the last train back into town very soon. 'I knew there was something else . . . Guess who my Miss Marple knows?'

Dr Parker smiled. Helen's private investigator, he knew, would now forever be referred to as 'my Miss Marple'.

'I really have no idea,' he said, looking at his watch. 'Why don't you tell me on the way to the station? We don't want you missing your train and having to rough it by staying at my humble abode.'

It was on the tip of Helen's tongue to say that it really wouldn't be the end of the world if she had to, but she didn't. The words of her mother resounded loudly in her head. She was fine as a friend, but there was no getting away from it – she was 'soiled goods'.

Chapter Twenty-Four

Sunday 14 February

Dear Tommy,
     I wanted you to be the first to know –
     I have just seen Dr Murphy (he kindly agreed to see me today because we've been doing so much overtime at the yard) and he has confirmed –
     I am pregnant!
     I didn't want to tell you that I had my suspicions in case it turned out to be a false alarm.
     But I am!
     Dr Murphy reckons I'm about two months gone – well, eight weeks here or there.
     Our first child! I'm so excited!
     And so happy!
     I know you will be too.
     I am writing this on Valentine's Day and couldn't think of a better Valentine's surprise to give you.
     I'm sending you so much love.
     No. Let me rephrase that – we're sending you so much love.
     Stay safe.
     I miss you.
     I love you,
     Polly x

     PS I will write to you again tomorrow! And the next day. And the next . . .

*PPS I know it's still early (and Dr Murphy said noth-
ing is ever certain when it comes to having babies), but
what about Arthur if it's a boy?*

Polly sealed the letter, kissed it and hurried out to the GPO.

'Get there quickly,' she muttered as she pushed it into
the postbox. 'Actually, just get there,' she added.

She then turned and walked back to Tatham Street.

This time her pace wasn't quite so fast. She needed a little time to think about how she was going to tell everyone.

Bel in particular.

'Where have you been?' Bel asked. She was setting the
table for a later than usual Sunday dinner.

Polly looked around.

'Blimey, I've never known it to be this quiet on a Sunday
afternoon. Where is everyone?'

'Your ma's just popped the dumplings in the stew and
has gone next door to Beryl's for a cuppa, and Joe's where
Joe always is.'

'Home Guard?' Polly asked.

Bel nodded. 'And *my* ma's where she always is—'

'The Tatham?' Polly said.

Another nod.

'And little Miss Muffet is in Arthur's old room with
Tramp and Pup, playing with her toys. She's a little sub-
dued because we went to see Pat in the Winter Gardens
yesterday.' Pat was a blue macaw and Lucille's most
favourite bird in the whole world. 'And Pat wasn't there.'
Bel pulled a glum face. 'LuLu's been desperate to know
where the bloody bird is, and we just heard from Beryl that
Pat is dead.'

Bel sat down at the kitchen table and poured herself a cup of tea. 'Pat managed to survive the Winter

Gardens getting bombed, but there's been no soft fruit available, so the poor thing's dropped off its perch. Literally. Beryl said most of the exotic birds have now died off because the kind of fruit they need to survive is non-existent.'

Polly suddenly felt tearful, which was ridiculous. Crying over a dead bird when there were men being killed every day – probably every hour of every day.

'Oh, Pol, you look as devastated as LuLu. Sit down and have a cuppa.'

'I'm just being ridiculous,' Polly said.

'Maybe you're just feeling a bit emotional at the moment,' Bel said, pouring the tea and adding milk.

Polly smiled at Bel. This was the perfect opportunity. *Just do it.*

'Actually, I've got something to tell you.'

'Oh yes?' Bel said, her attention focused on her best friend.

'Well . . .'

Polly hesitated.

'I'm pregnant.'

Bel's face lit up and a huge smile spread across her face. She jumped out of her chair.

'Come here,' she said, putting her arms out. 'I thought you might be.'

Polly stood up and the pair hugged.

'This is the best news ever,' Bel said. 'I'm so happy for you.' She stepped back. 'And for me too.'

Polly looked at her. 'Really?'

'Yes, *really!*' Bel said. 'I'm going to have a little niece or nephew to coo over. LuLu is finally going to get another little playmate. She keeps complaining that all her friends have brothers and sisters to play with and demanding to know *why hasn't she?*'

Polly gave Bel a hug. 'That's why I thought this might be – I don't know – a bit difficult for you. And Joe.' Polly looked at her sister-in-law. 'I know how much you both want to have a child together.'

'Oh, Polly,' said Bel, sitting back down, 'that's completely different. I'm gutted I haven't fallen pregnant, but that in no way spoils how excited I am about you expecting. Honestly, you must believe me . . . I *will* fall, I'm sure of it. It's just, for whatever reason, Him up there has decided it's not the right time.' She smiled. 'Whereas this is the perfect time for you. And, most important of all, *I'm* going to be an aunty for the first time!'

Just then, hearing her mother's excited voice, Lucille came hurrying into the room, closely followed by the two dogs. She looked at her mammy and then at her aunty.

'Come here, LuLu.' Bel stretched out her arms and picked up her daughter, putting her on her lap. 'Aunty Polly has some good news. She's going to have a baby, which means you're going to have a cousin.'

Lucille looked again at her mammy and across the table at her aunty.

'When?' she demanded.

The two women chuckled.

'It takes a while,' Bel explained. 'It has to grow in Aunty Polly's tummy first.'

Lucille shuffled off her mother's lap and went over to her aunty. She looked at Polly's stomach.

'There?' She pointed at Polly's tummy. 'It grows in there?' Her little face was full of wonder.

Suddenly the front door slammed shut. It was windy outside. A short blast of cold air made its way down the hallway and into the kitchen, followed by Agnes.

'Nana, Nana!' Lucille ran to greet her grandmother.

'Well, this is better . . .' Agnes groaned with the exertion of picking up her granddaughter. 'No more tears over poor Pat, eh?'

Lucille shook her head and declared, 'Aunty Polly's having a baby in her tummy!'

'Is she now?' Agnes did not look surprised.

Polly felt herself flush. 'I am, Ma. I'm expecting. Dr Murphy's confirmed it.' She stood up and took Lucille off her mother. 'I wanted to tell you myself. I was just telling Bel . . .' Polly let her voice trail off.

'And are yer happy about it?' Agnes asked, looking at her daughter's serious face.

'Oh, yes, Ma, I'm thrilled to bits,' Polly said, her face lighting up.

'Well then,' Agnes said, 'if you're happy, that's all that matters.'

She walked over to the range and opened the door to check on the stew, letting out a waft of hot air. 'I'm guessing yer about two months gone? Give or take?'

Polly nodded.

'Let's get yer through the next month without any hiccups, eh?' Agnes said, bending over to pat Tramp and Pup, now curled up in their basket. She stood up straight and stretched her back.

'I don't know, yer auld mother's always the last to know,' she said, shaking her head and walking into the scullery.

Neither Polly nor Bel could see the smile that had just spread across Agnes's face.

Nor the tears that had started to well up in her eyes.

When Polly heard Joe come in late from his Home Guard duties, she tiptoed out of her bedroom and into the kitchen where she knew he would be having a cuppa – perhaps even a little Scotch – before he went to bed. His leg still pained him and the whisky helped him sleep.

'Hey, Joe,' Polly whispered as she crept into the still-warm kitchen. Her ma kept the fire in the range going for as long as she could, knowing that Joe would need a little warmth when he got back in.

'Aye, aye, little sis. What you doing up so late?'

'Trouble sleeping,' Polly said, watching him pour a small measure of single malt into a glass.

He looked at the bottle before he put it back in the sideboard.

'Feels wrong having a nightcap without Arthur.' He smiled sadly. 'He used to do what you've just done. Come out in his nightgown and slippers, have a drink and a little chat.'

'Really?' Polly never knew that.

Polly went to pour herself a glass of water and sat down at the kitchen table.

'I miss him,' she said. 'Still feels odd him not being in the house.'

'I know, like he's just nipped out and is due back in any moment.'

Polly smiled.

'I think Lucille's still a bit teary about him "going to heaven". Bel said she got upset today when she heard Pat the blue macaw had died. She said LuLu mentioned Arthur a few times in between the tears. I think she blames heaven.'

'Depriving her of all the things she loves,' Joe mused. 'Anyway, here's to you, old man.' He lifted his glass. 'I miss our chats.'

Polly raised her glass of water.

'Me too.'

They both sipped their drinks in silence for a moment.

'I've some good news,' Polly said finally. 'I think Arthur would be pleased.'

'Oh, aye?' Joe said. 'What's that?'

'Well,' she said, taking a deep breath. She kept getting slight palpitations every time she thought about the reality of becoming a mother.

'You're going to be an uncle.'

Joe jumped up. Polly saw a flash of pain in his face that was immediately replaced by a wide smile. 'That's brilliant news! I'm so chuffed fer yer, Pol!' He put his arms out and gave his younger sister a big bear hug. 'Does Tommy know?'

'I've just put a letter in the post to him.'

'He'll be on cloud nine, he will. As Arthur would be.' Joe grabbed his stick, which had been hooked on the back of his chair, and eased himself back down.

'Yer gonna take it easy at work, though?'

'Of course,' Polly said. 'You sound like Ma. She's been giving me all the dos and don'ts over dinner. I don't think she wants to properly celebrate until I get to three months, when she says "the bab'll be nicely settled in".' Polly put on a mock-Irish accent, making Joe laugh.

'Ah, she'll be chuffed 'n all. At long last, another grandchild.'

They looked at each other. Both thinking the same thought.

'Do yer think Bel will be all right?' Polly asked. 'I told her first, and she seemed fine. Genuinely happy.'

'She will've been,' Joe said, his face serious now, 'but I know she's gutted she's not fallen herself. She doesn't show it much, but I've caught her crying a few times when it comes to, yer know, that time of the month.'

Polly took a sip of her water.

She looked at Joe, who suddenly started to smile.

'I know someone else who'd be over the moon,' he said.

Polly knew who Joe was talking about; he was never far from her brother's thoughts.

Tears stung her eyes.

'Teddy,' she said simply.

Another one that heaven had taken.

Chapter Twenty-Five

Monday 15 February

'Time to put the earplugs in,' Gloria joked as she and Polly walked across the yard towards their squad.

It was ten minutes before the start of the day's shift. Time for a quick chat before the noise of building ships overwhelmed and blotted out any chance of a normal conversation.

'Morning, everyone!' Polly felt bursting with energy. She'd slept like a log last night after her midnight chat with Joe. She'd had the most wonderful dreams that she was with Tommy and was still carrying that lovely feeling with her now.

'Someone looks perky,' Martha said, adding a few more bits of coal to their five-gallon barrel fire.

'Actually,' Polly looked at Martha, and then at Rosie, Dorothy and Angie, 'I've some good news.'

'Yer've not found another newspaper for us to study, have yer?' Angie said. She had been amazed at how many different types of daily papers there were.

Polly chuckled. 'No, I've got my own breaking news today.'

Dorothy took a deep breath in anticipation.

'I'm pregnant!' Polly said, her eyes sweeping the women's faces.

Gloria immediately put her fingers in her ears, just in time to block out what could only be described as a full-on, high-pitched scream coming out of Dorothy's mouth. All the workers within a hundred-yard radius automatically looked to see if help was needed. When they saw it was Dorothy, they turned back and continued smoking and chatting.

'Congratulations!' Rosie gave Polly a hug. 'Although I'm gutted. What am I going to do without you?'

'I'm going to work for as long as possible,' Polly said, looking as optimistic as she sounded.

Dorothy practically pushed Rosie out of the way and flung her arms around her workmate.

'I'm ecstatic!' she said. 'This is the best news ever!'

'Aye,' Angie said, 'but just dinnit gan into labour in the middle of a bloody air raid like Glor did.'

Everyone laughed.

'I've still not gor over having to cut the cord. Put me off childbirth fer life,' Angie said.

Dorothy nodded her agreement. 'Yes, I'll second that. Having babies is for everyone else.'

'Just as well,' Martha said, waiting patiently in line to give Polly a congratulatory hug. ''Cos for starters, you're not married, and secondly, we can't lose another one of our squad, otherwise we won't be a squad.'

Polly hugged Martha. 'Honestly, you're not going to lose me. I'll be off for a few weeks after the baby's born and then I'll be back again.'

Everyone looked sceptical, but they didn't have time to argue the point as the klaxon sounded out.

At the lunchtime break the women dropped their tools and were among the first to make it to the canteen, all eager to talk more about Polly's pregnancy. As soon as Hannah and Olly arrived, Dorothy blurted out the good news before the pair even had time to sit down.

'Oh, Polly, I am so happy for you!' Hannah said, dumping her satchel and hugging Polly.

'Me too,' Olly said, sticking out his hand. 'Congratulations.'

'We all knew, you know,' Dorothy declared, unwrapping her home-made sandwiches.

'I thought you might be getting suspicious,' Polly said, unbuttoning the top of her overalls, which seemed to be getting tight around the chest.

'The bog-trotting might have given it away,' Angie said, taking the top slice off her sandwich and looking inside; it had been Dorothy's turn to make their packed lunches today. 'My mam spends half her life on the lav when she's up the duff. Either weeing or puking.'

'Charming.' Dorothy rolled her eyes. 'It's good to see Quentin's lessons are making such a difference.'

Everyone suppressed their chuckles.

'And you have been looking a bit peaky,' Dorothy said, throwing Angie a look and making a show of biting into her sandwich with relish.

'I noticed you weren't eating as much as you usually do,' Hannah chipped in.

'Eating's been a bit of a challenge,' Polly agreed, looking down at her bacon bap with little enthusiasm. 'I'm not going to broadcast it, though. Not until I'm through the first three months.'

'You all right about me telling Helen?' Gloria asked quietly, taking a sup of her tea. She could see Muriel loitering by the counter, making a big deal of cleaning and restacking the trays.

'Of course,' Polly said, pouring herself a cuppa from the pot. 'Is she all right? Bel keeps saying how busy she is. Looks like she's thinking of taking on more staff.'

'I saw an old friend there the other day, being interviewed,' Rosie chipped in. 'Sounds like Helen's after another clerk.'

'I think she's like everyone at the moment, working flat out,' Gloria said.

'She's not got it together with that doctor friend of hers, then?' Dorothy asked, brushing crumbs off her overalls.

Gloria shook her head and put down her teacup. 'She claims they're "just friends".'

'They looked more than friends at Arthur's wake,' Martha said, polishing off her meat pie.

'People *can* just be friends, yer knar,' Angie argued.

'What? Like you and Quentin?' Dorothy said, raising her eyebrows.

'Exactly,' Angie said, her face dead serious.

Gloria sighed. 'I don't understand you young 'uns. It seemed a lot more straightforward in my day.'

Later that evening Helen was sitting on Gloria's sofa with Hope, flicking through a children's picture book she'd brought round, one of her own favourites as a child. When Gloria told her that Polly was pregnant, she looked up.

'That's brilliant news,' she said. 'Tell Polly "Congratulations" from me. I'll tell her myself when I see her next. And, obviously, say to her that if she needs anything, anything at all, she just needs to say. Any time off. That kind of thing. I'll have a think about what we'll do when she's further along. If she's still only a couple of months gone, we've got time to play with.'

Gloria started pouring out the tea she'd just made.

'How do you feel?' She looked up to gauge Helen's reaction.

'What do you mean?' Helen looked genuinely puzzled.

'About Polly being pregnant,' Gloria said, adding a drop of milk to Helen's cup.

'I feel pleased for her . . . You say it as if I mightn't be?'

'I suppose,' Gloria said, adding milk and sugar to her own tea, 'I was thinking it might make you feel . . . I don't know . . . a little *sad*, perhaps. After what you went through.'

'Oh, Gloria, that's in the past now.'

'Is it? Is it all in the past now? Five months isn't that long ago,' Gloria probed.

'It is and it isn't,' Helen said, looking at Hope pointing at a picture of a rabbit dressed in a waistcoat. She pulled a surprised face and Hope giggled.

'I asked John if it was a girl or a boy.' She glanced across at Gloria.

'Really? When was this?'

'At Polly and Tommy's wedding.' Helen looked back down at the book and turned another page.

'And what did he say?' Gloria stared at her.

Helen looked up and smiled sadly.

'A girl,' she sighed. 'Like you said. Like we both thought.'

'I'm sorry.' Gloria reached over the coffee table and squeezed Helen's hand.

'At least I know,' Helen said. 'I can move on now, can't I?'

Gloria nodded, although she wondered if anyone ever truly moved on after going through what Helen had experienced. Perhaps it was more a case of getting used to it. An unwelcome companion on life's journey. She guessed everyone gained a few of those as time went by. She certainly had.

'And,' she asked tentatively, 'it doesn't bother you that Polly's pregnant with *Tommy's* baby?'

Helen laughed.

'Well, I'd hope that it *is* Tommy's baby!'

Gloria didn't laugh.

'You know what I mean. It wasn't so long ago that you really did feel Tommy was the one for you.'

Helen cringed. Again, thinking of her actions of old. The actions of the old Helen. She wished she hadn't been a total cow to Polly and the rest of the women, with her desperate need to gain revenge on those she thought had taken what was hers. Tommy had never been hers and never would have been, regardless of Polly. But it had only been these past few months – since she'd seen Tommy lying semi-conscious in his hospital bed – that she had come to that realisation.

She just wished she'd wised up sooner.

'Oh, Gloria, that really does seem like another lifetime. I look back now and see it would have been a total disaster if I *had* managed to bag Tommy for myself.'

Gloria took a sip of tea and sat back in her chair. She felt shattered. She'd been doing flat welds and had spent most of the day squatting down on her haunches.

'Why's that?' she said.

'God, where do I start?' Helen said, sighing a little and putting her arm around Hope, who was clearly tired. She was snuggling up and sucking her thumb.

'For starters, any fool could see we were totally mismatched. On top of which, Tommy never loved me – and I think it helps if someone actually loves you back.' Helen smiled and kissed the top of Hope's head. 'Seeing Polly and Tommy together at the wedding, you could tell that they were made for each other, and how much they love each other. I never had anything even close to that with him. But, you know, the saddest thing is, it wasn't until I saw them together at the wedding that I realised I'd never really *loved* him. I think it was more a case of being in love with the idea of being in love. Putting it bluntly, I had a girlish crush on Tommy. A crush which went on for ages and made me think it was love, when really it was just infatuation.'

Gloria thought Helen's take on her and Tommy was spot on. She was glad she had realised it and wasn't secretly harbouring any 'What if . . . ?' feelings.

'And as we're on the topic of love 'n the like,' Gloria said, taking a deep breath, 'what about John?' *There. She had taken the plunge.*

'Oh, God, *John.*' Helen exhaled. 'Well, that's the weird thing. Seeing Tommy and Polly together made me realise that John and I are similar in a funny kind of way. I mean, I know we're completely different, but what Polly and Tommy have – that natural kind of meshing . . .'

Helen paused.

'Well, I think that's what I've got with John.'

Gloria felt like shouting 'Halleluja!' but didn't. Instead, she said, 'Perhaps, you should let John know that you feel this way.'

'Really?'

'Yes, definitely,' Gloria encouraged. 'I think you'll find he feels exactly the same way you do.'

'You really think so?'

'Yes,' Gloria said. 'I *do* think so.' *A blind man could see that.*

'It's just . . .' Helen waited until Hope had shuffled herself around so that her head was now on her big sister's lap. 'It's just something my mother said.'

Gloria groaned. 'What's she been saying now?'

'You know, the usual . . . That because of everything that's happened I'm "soiled goods" . . . That kind of thing.'

Gloria felt a rush of anger. *That bloody woman. She brought upset and misery wherever she went.*

'Her new word,' Helen continued, 'is "sullied". She reckons that John might well like me, want to be with me, but he wouldn't want to get serious because of what he knows about me. That he would want someone "unsullied".'

Before Gloria had a chance to say anything, Helen changed the subject. 'But enough about that,' she said, stroking Hope's thick mop of black hair. 'I keep meaning to ask about Charlotte. How is she getting on? I haven't had a chance to ask Rosie. She came to see me about something, but she got waylaid.'

'I know, she said you were interviewing an old friend of hers,' Gloria said.

Helen looked at Gloria. She was about to tell her about Georgina, but something stopped her. She'd tell her when she knew more. Besides, Gloria was already having to keep enough secrets.

'When I last asked Rosie,' Helen said, 'she said Charlotte was settling in at the High School, but didn't seem to be making that many new friends.'

'I think you're right. She's not got many friends. Other than her little friend Marjorie. But she seems happy enough. And she seems to be doing really well in her classes.'

As Gloria went to make some more tea, she thought about Rosie and the relief she'd seen on her face when she'd told them all about Charlotte's visit to Lily's.

It had clearly been a success.

Her secret was safe.

For now, at least.

Chapter Twenty-Six

'Here's another letter from school,' Charlotte said, handing over an envelope that had clearly been opened and resealed.

'Why don't you tell me what it says, as you've obviously already read it?' Rosie sighed. It was hard work being a sister-cum-mam-and-dad all wrapped into one. 'If I had the energy, you would now be getting an earbashing from me about why it is totally unacceptable to read someone else's post. If you are given a letter which clearly states it's for me, that means it's for *me*. How would you feel if I read Marjorie's letters to you? Or your diary?'

Charlotte blanched.

'See? It's not nice having your privacy invaded, is it?'

'Sorry.'

'Some things are private for a reason,' Rosie laboured the point. 'Sometimes you're not meant to see – or know – things for your own good.'

Charlotte shuffled about uncomfortably on the kitchen chair and mumbled another 'Sorry.' She waited a beat. 'It's about the new summer uniform.' Her eyes went to the letter in Rosie's hand. 'When I have to start wearing it, where to get it from, how much it is – that kind of thing.'

Rosie opened the letter out and quickly scanned it.

'It's a lot of money,' Charlotte ventured. 'Marjorie was telling me how much her uniform costs, and all the other stuff – you know, art overalls, science overalls, gym kit. She says her mam and dad are always complaining how ridiculous it is that there's only the one school outfitter they're allowed to go to. Something about it being a monopoly on trade.'

Charlotte didn't say that Marjorie had also commented that Rosie must have to work all hours to afford the school fees.

Rosie looked at Charlotte. She had been conscious the last time they were in the snotty outfitters in town buying her new winter uniform that Charlotte would see how much it all cost and start to wonder how she was able to afford it. She'd tried to settle the bill discreetly and had told Charlotte to have a browse around the shop, but Charlotte being Charlotte, she hadn't ventured far. Rosie was sure she'd been near enough to hear the sales assistant itemising everything on the bill.

'I personally don't think you or Marjorie should be worrying your heads about how much your school uniform costs. I think you've got enough to concern yourselves with.' Rosie looked at the pile of textbooks Charlotte had just dumped on the table. 'Come on, take all your books into the dining room and let's get the tea ready. I don't know about you, but I'm starving.'

'What are we having?' Charlotte asked, gathering up her books.

'Toad in the hole,' Rosie said, getting out the frying pan and turning on the oven.

After setting out the homework she had to get done for the next day, Charlotte pushed a small blue book into the pocket of her skirt and went back into the kitchen. Every now and again, while helping Rosie to make the gravy and set the table, she kept touching the corner of the slightly battered notebook.

'How long have you worked at Lily's for?' Charlotte tried to make the question sound casual.

Rosie felt herself bristle. 'Why you asking?'

Charlotte laughed. 'You always do that!'

'What?'

'When you don't want to answer a question, you ask a question,' Charlotte said.

Rosie forked a sausage. 'Mmm, interesting observation . . . So, how long do you think I've worked there?'

'Ahh,' Charlotte laughed, 'you're winding me up now.'

Rosie smiled.

'I've worked for Lily for years,' Rosie conceded.

Charlotte knew not to probe further, but she thought it was weird her sister had never mentioned working there before when she'd been at boarding school in Harrogate.

It wasn't until they had eaten their supper and were tidying up that Charlotte finally took out the notebook.

'I think you dropped this the other day.'

Rosie's heart dropped. It was Gloria's rent book. It must have fallen out of the side pocket of her haversack.

'I couldn't help but look inside,' Charlotte said tentatively. 'It's a rent book. For Gloria's flat.'

Rosie took the book from Charlotte but didn't say anything.

'If Gloria's paying you rent, that means you own the flat. Doesn't it?'

'Well,' Rosie said, 'that's true to a certain extent . . . I do sort of own the flat.'

'Sort of?'

'Well, obviously, you know that I used to rent that flat.'

'From the old man upstairs,' Charlotte said.

'That's right.' Rosie took her time in answering. 'Well, I'd heard he was interested in selling the house – or rather, the flats that make up the house – and I thought it would be a good investment. You know, like George was talking about at Lily's. And he suggested that, as I'd be saving money on rent, with me moving here and not paying anything—'

'Because it's Peter's,' Charlotte said.

'Yes. And he owns it outright, so there's no mortgage or anything to pay on it – you know what a mortgage is?'

Charlotte tutted.

'Well, because I wasn't paying out anything on accommodation, George advised me to buy the flat and pay back the money in instalments.'

'But I didn't think women could get mortgages or any kind of loan from a bank without a husband or father's say-so,' Charlotte said. 'Peter's away and not contactable – and we haven't got a father, so I would have thought you'd be stumped?'

'That's right.' Rosie looked at her little sister. She was savvier than she'd thought. 'I'm impressed. Where did you learn that?'

'Some woman came in to school one day and talked to us about women in society. Their rights. That kind of thing.' Charlotte snorted. 'Or rather their lack of them. She was talking about women getting the vote and how it's important to use it when we're old enough.'

Charlotte started to fill the bowl in the sink to wash up.

'It was really interesting. That's when I learnt what a mortgage is and how women can't get one without a man's permission. Honestly, it's treating women like they're thick.'

It was at moments like this that Rosie was glad Charlotte was back at home and not still at the Runcorn School for Girls. She couldn't imagine Mrs Willoughby-Smith letting someone like that come to the school to give a talk.

'So, if you couldn't get a mortgage, how were you able to get a loan?' Charlotte asked.

'Well, it was actually a man who lent me the money I needed,' Rosie admitted.

'Who?'

'George,' said Rosie.

'That was kind of him,' Charlotte said. 'He's nice, George, isn't he?'

'He is,' Rosie said. 'He's one of the good ones.'

Chapter Twenty-Seven

***Thompson & Sons Shipyard, North Sands,
Sunderland***

1936

'So, Rosie, let's strike while the iron's hot and get you started on Monday, eh?'

'Yes, please, that would be great, Mr Crawford.'

'Jack . . . Get used to calling me Jack. Everyone does. And in return, I get to call everyone else by their first names. Deal?'

Rosie smiled and nodded.

Jack was, as her mam would say, 'one of the good ones'.

Rosie knew she had fallen on her feet when she'd walked into Thompson's and asked to speak to the yard manager. She'd had to deal with the expected catcalls and wolf whistles when she'd been let into the yard by the old timekeeper, but she hadn't cared, for she knew half the battle had been won simply by making it through the gates. Once inside, she'd marched up to one of the would-be Lotharios, who looked old enough to be her father, and asked him where she could find the manager. The aged Romeo had laughed and, speaking through a half-smoked cigarette hanging on his lower lip, told her that 'the gaffer' was all of fifty yards away, chatting to the head plater.

Rosie was glad she'd had the sense to go there after the lunchtime klaxon had sounded out, as the noise of the yard had died down enough for speech to be possible.

Tapping Jack on the shoulder, she'd explained that she was here to apply for the position of apprentice welder. Jack had laughed good-naturedly, saying he didn't realise that there was such a position available at present.

Rosie had persevered, spoken quickly and confidently, knowing she'd only get the one shot, and told him that she wouldn't need much training as she already knew how to weld, but they'd only have to pay her an apprentice's wage.

Jack had taken her up to the administration building and Rosie had noticed that none of the men in the yard heckled her. Walking into the main office, she'd immediately spotted a stunning-looking woman with long, perfectly coiffured black hair sitting at one of the desks. She had felt the hostility as soon as the young woman clapped eyes on her. Not that Rosie gave two hoots. She wasn't here to be liked. She wanted – *needed* – a job.

Jack had left the door of his office open, as well as all the blinds, making Rosie feel more at ease as she explained why she would be a good asset to the yard in spite of her gender. Her father, who had worked at Whitburn colliery, had taught her how to weld.

Later, it occurred to her that she hadn't once lied to Jack. There hadn't been any need. She had been honest about her mam and dad, how they had died in a car accident, and Jack said he had read about it in the *Echo* and offered her his condolences.

He'd left the office for about five minutes, telling her he needed to discuss it with his boss – a man called Harold.

Rosie felt like hugging him when he'd returned and offered her an apprenticeship.

It wasn't until Rosie had been at the yard for a little while and had begun to be accepted that she'd learnt that Jack was married to the daughter of one of the town's most important businessmen and revered philanthropists, Mr

Havelock. And that the glamorous woman with the steely glare was, in fact, Jack's daughter.

Rosie loved her new place of work. She loved the discipline, the exact timing of the shifts signalled by the blaring of the horn, and the way, despite the apparent chaos of the yard, there was an order and logic to everything that happened. She was fascinated by the whole process of how a ship was built, from the ceremony of the laying of the keel all the way through to the actual launch.

She would often talk to her mam and dad in her head, or sometimes out loud if she was on her own, and she would regale them with what had happened that day at work.

She explained how a ship gradually rose up from the dark depths of the dry basin and morphed into a huge Moby Dick, how its skeleton of enormous, rib-like iron girders was fleshed out with giant sheets of metal.

'It's incredible,' she'd tell them both, lying in her bed, her whole body aching with the physical demand of her job.

The love for her new job was a bonus – one she hadn't expected – but most of all, she was just relieved she had found work and was able to survive.

Now she just had to work out how she was going to keep Charlotte at Runcorn.

Judging by the letters she was getting from her sister, Charlie was settling in. The school seemed to keep its pupils busy morning, noon and night, with back-to-back lessons, sport and homework.

Rosie, in turn, wrote letters that were full of encouragement, telling her how proud their mam and dad would be if they could see her now, which, Rosie made a point of stressing, she was sure they could. She hoped that Charlotte would feel as though they were still about, keeping an eye on her.

Knowing that it was important to Charlie to still feel connected to her sister and where she came from, she would tell her about her work in the shipyard and anything else of interest.

As time wore on, Rosie continued to rack her brains about how she was going to find the money for Charlotte's fees once the 'rainy day' money was all used up. The answer, ironically, came when Rosie started to suffer terrible pain around the time of her monthlies. After what Raymond had done to her, she'd been relieved to get her period, but when the months wore on and the pain and bleeding became worse, she'd started to worry, especially when she had to take a few days off sick. Fearful it would cause her to lose her job, she sought the aid of a medical practitioner, who, thankfully, was able to give her the help she needed. The final bill, however, was far more than she could afford and it was agreed that Rosie could pay the doctor back in weekly instalments.

Just as she was leaving, the doctor called her back and scribbled the name and address of a woman who, he said, might be able to provide Rosie with some part-time work that was surprisingly well paid.

'If you do go,' the GP said, 'make sure you use the back entrance.'

A mix of curiosity and desperation led Rosie to the three-storey Victorian house on West Lawn.

She had faltered on seeing a red light peeking out from the curtain drawn across a large sash window overlooking the backyard, but something propelled her on.

Something made her knock on the door.

She'd nearly turned and walked off when no one answered straight away. But she didn't.

When the door finally opened, she was hit by a waft of perfume and cigar smoke, mixed with the sound of laughter and a gramophone record playing something that Rosie thought sounded rather beautiful.

Her vision, however, was monopolised by an eccentric-looking woman with an unruly bird's nest of orange hair piled high, a bosom barely concealed by a corset dress that looked as though it came from a different era, and an accent Rosie guessed to be French.

The woman ushered her in.

'Ah, *ma chère, entrez, entrez!* Come in out of the cold!'

Within the month Rosie had paid her doctor's bill in full.

She often saw the GP at the place Lily liked to refer to as her 'bordello'. He was always polite and tipped his hat whenever he saw Rosie, but he never requested her services. Lily, who she now knew to be pure-bred cockney, explained that he never saw the girls he treated.

It didn't take long for Rosie to adapt to her new existence and learn how to divide her life in two. There was her life at Thompson's and her life at Lily's. The two were as different as black and white. As night and day. But somehow her transition from one to the other felt seamless.

When she went up to one of the rooms on the first floor with a new client, she told herself that she was in control. She was agreeing to what they were about to do. Most importantly, she was being paid handsomely for it. It was a business transaction. A trade.

It helped enormously that Lily had a set of stringent house rules that she made no bones about enforcing. None of her 'girls' did anything they didn't want to – and if they felt threatened or at risk, there was a bell they could pull that would sound out in the kitchen downstairs and within minutes help would be at hand.

Rosie, though, knew she would never have been able to do this kind of work had her uncle not done what he'd done. But that cursed night, she'd learnt how to flick a switch in her head – and it was that switch she would flick whenever she was doing what she called her 'second job'.

And after a while, that is exactly what it became. A job. A way of earning money to keep Charlotte at Runcorn.

But most of all, enough money to keep her sister safe.

Chapter Twenty-Eight

Friday 19 February

'Come in, Georgina.' Helen waved her in. 'I can't believe it's been two weeks already.' She shut the office door, took Georgina's coat and hung it up on the coat stand.

'Did you go to see the launch today at Short's?'

'The *Empire Friendship*?' Georgina said, going to take her seat.

'That's the one, although why they've named a cargo vessel *Friendship* in the middle of a war is beyond me.'

'No, I didn't get to see it,' Georgina replied.

'Of course you didn't. Too busy working.' Helen waved her hand at the chair in front of her desk.

'Before I forget,' she said, pulling out a Pall Mall, 'if Rosie asks why you're here again, I think it would be best to say that we have come to a compromise and that although you are clearly overqualified for a simple clerical job, you are going to do some part-time work for me, which you're doing at home. Agreed?'

'Perhaps, if it comes up in conversation,' Georgina said, taking her seat, 'I can say that I'm helping with the annual audit and can work faster and more efficiently at home.'

'Yes, good idea,' Helen said, settling herself in her chair behind the desk.

She lit a cigarette.

'I didn't realise you and Rosie knew each other?'

Georgina nodded.

'Our mothers used to be friends.'

Helen waited for more details, but none were forthcoming. She knew not to push. It wouldn't have been professional. Still, the fact that Rosie's and Georgina's mothers had been close cemented Helen's belief that Georgina had kept something back about Rosie's private life. One day she'd find out what it was. For the moment, though, she had enough secrets of her own to uncover.

'So,' Helen said, reaching into her handbag, 'I've done as you asked and brought some family photos.'

Georgina shifted forward in her chair and craned her neck to look.

'That's my grandfather, Mr Charles Havelock, whom I'm sure you know,' Helen informed her. 'He must have been about fifty in this shot . . . and this is my grandmother, Henrietta.'

Georgina stared at the photograph.

'Did you know your grandmother at all?' Georgina asked, as she pulled out her notebook and took the top off her pen.

'No, not really. I was only a baby when she died. To be honest, no one really talked about her all that much when I was growing up. I always got the impression that she was a little odd. Peculiar. I remember Mother telling me once how she would call her staff "the cavalry" and gave them all nicknames. Usually characters from her favourite books.'

They both looked at the photograph.

'She does certainly look quite unusual,' Georgina commented, staring at the bird-like woman wearing a huge taffetta skirt with a tiny waist. A knot of hair was piled up on her head, thick strands hanging loose around her narrow neck. 'Very pretty, though.'

They looked back down at the sepia photograph and scrutinised the woman's heart-shaped face. There was something quite captivating about her, despite the garish make-up she was wearing.

'What did she die of?' Georgina asked, genuinely curious.

'Good question,' Helen said. 'I'm not sure.'

Georgina focused her attention back on the stern-looking Mr Havelock. She reckoned the photograph must have been taken about twenty-five, possibly thirty, years ago. You could just about see the man he would become. He still had his blond hair, although it was now more grey than blond and thinning. The eyes were the same, though.

'And here's one of my mother, Miriam, and her sister, my aunty Margaret, when they were about sixteen and seventeen. I think at the time they were at some finishing school over in Switzerland, so this must have been taken when they were back home for the holidays.'

'Mmm, I see what you mean about the resemblance,' Georgina said.

Over the past two weeks, she had spent a few days watching Bel and had managed to get a photograph of her with her little Brownie. Bel had been walking around Mowbray Park with her daughter and Georgina had got a shot of her while pretending to take pictures of the bomb damage.

'Well,' Helen said, 'I thought it would be a good idea to get photos from around the time Bel would have been conceived.'

Georgina looked at two pretty but unsmiling blonde girls staring at the camera. If she put her photo of Bel next to them, the three of them could easily have been mistaken for sisters.

'Is it all right for me to take them?' Georgina said.

'Yes, of course,' Helen said, handing over the photos.

Georgina put them in her handbag and sat up straight.

'To recap, then . . . From what I've found out so far, I don't think that your mother, your aunty Margaret or your grandmother could be Bel's mother.'

'That's not surprising, but how can you be so sure?' Helen asked.

'Because I have managed to get hold of a copy of Bel's birth certificate and it clearly states that Pearl Hardwick is her biological mother.'

Georgina looked at her notes.

'The date of birth being the sixth of January 1915. There is no name under the "Name and Surname of Father". That space was left blank.'

Helen took a drag on her cigarette, listening with rapt attention.

'Is there any way she could have been handed over at birth?' she asked. 'The certificate forged?'

'Highly improbable,' Georgina said. 'Anyone falsifying part of a birth certificate is liable for prosecution. Also, my father knew the superintendent who signed the certificate, and in his words, he was "whiter than white". On top of which, it just doesn't make sense that someone like Pearl would pretend a baby was hers, especially as she clearly did not benefit financially from it.'

Helen stubbed out her cigarette.

Georgina could see that she was disappointed, but not surprised.

'So, what I now have to find out is who Isabelle Elliot's father is.' Georgina closed her notebook.

'That's going to be the hard part. Paternity is always hard to prove. Even when you have everyone's cooperation. I'm going to concentrate on the men in the Havelock family, but I will still keep an open mind and look at other

197

possibilities. I might find that her father is totally uncon-
nected to your family and is some sailor boy from foreign
lands—'

'Like Bel's sister,' Helen mused.

'Exactly,' Georgina agreed.

After seeing the photographs she now had in her bag,
though, Georgina thought that would be unlikely. *Very*
unlikely.

Chapter Twenty-Nine

When Bel walked into the Tatham, she was glad to see it wasn't busy. There were just a few locals having a quiet pint. Two elderly gents were playing dominoes. Another was sitting on his own, a half-drunk pint of bitter in front of him, his flat cap partially hiding his eyes. Bel knew the old man had a habit of falling asleep sitting up straight as a rod.

'Well, it's the daughter I hardly ever get to see these days.' Pearl's coarse voice sounded out across the pub. Her words were, as usual, purposely antagonistic, but they were also true. With Bel now working full-time at Thompson's and Pearl pulling pints most nights, their paths barely crossed.

'Hello, Bel. Lovely to see yer. What yer having?' Bill asked, a smile, as always, on his face.

'I'll just have a lemonade, please, Bill,' Bel said, looking up at the clock. 'It's a bit early for me to have anything stronger. And I've got my night class in an hour. Don't want to go there stinking of booze, do I?'

'No, definitely not,' Bill agreed in earnest. 'You've got learning to do. Need a clear head to remember what all them squiggles and lines mean.'

'I do,' Bel laughed. 'It's like learning another language. Thank goodness I'm only having to write it and not speak it.'

Bel looked at Pearl, who was getting herself a shot of whisky from one of the optics lining the mirrored wall of the bar.

'So,' Pearl turned back to face Bel, 'I'm no mind-reader, but I'm guessing this is not just a social call.' She walked towards the end of the bar and lifted the hatch. 'I've a feeling you want something. Come on, the snug's empty at the moment. None of the auld grannies are in there yet.'

Bill poured out Bel's lemonade and handed it to her.

'Thanks, Bill. You all right being left on your own for a little while?'

'Course,' Bill said. 'I'm not exactly run off my feet, am I?'

Bel smiled, knowing that her ma would have happily left Bill to it even if he had been.

When Bel walked into the snug, Pearl was already sitting down on one of the stools positioned by the fire. For the briefest moment Bel had an image of being here on her wedding day, after Maisie had dropped her bombshell that she was the daughter Pearl had given up as a baby, and her ma had done something Bel had never known her do before – faint. She'd gone down like a tree being felled and smashed her head on the floorboards. Some young lad from Joe's Home Guard unit, she couldn't remember his name, had picked her up and brought her in here.

'Come on, spit it out.' Pearl picked up the poker and stabbed the fire. 'Yer've that look on yer face. Makes me feel uneasy.'

Bel sat down on the stool next to her ma and took a sip of her lemonade, savouring it. Even now the cold fizzy drink still felt like a treat. She'd never tasted any kind of pop until she was about ten, when one of her ma's blokes had bought her a small bottle with a straw in it and told her to stay on the front doorstep while he went inside with her mam. She'd sat there, slowly sipping the sugary nectar, with the sun on her face and feeling heavenly.

'I wanted to ask you something,' Bel said, looking at her ma. She'd never had any trouble pulling the men. She had been a good-looking woman. There was still a hint of attractiveness about her now – well, Bill and Ronald clearly thought so.

'Go on then, out with it,' Pearl said.

Bel hesitated, suddenly unsure how to word her question.

'I was just wondering . . . after you had Maisie, and then me, if you ever wanted to have more children?'

Pearl looked at her daughter. So pretty. *She only wished she didn't look so much like him.*

'Is this 'cos yer can't fall?'

Bel took another sip of lemonade, wanting to feel that heavenly feeling of innocence from when she was ten years old.

'It is, Ma. I don't understand why it's not happening . . . You fell straight away with Maisie.' Bel hesitated, knowing she was heading into uncharted waters. 'And obviously . . . well, clearly, you fell straight away with me.'

Bel watched as Pearl lit up a cigarette.

'So, I was wondering, what happened after me? Did you want to start a family with anyone?' Bel was sugar-coating her words. Her mother had never been with anyone long enough to settle down.

Pearl looked at Bel and blew out smoke.

'I wish yer wouldn't fanny around so much, Isabelle. What yer really wanting to know is why didn't I get pregnant again?'

Bel nodded.

'I couldn't – even if I'd wanted to,' Pearl said. Her tone was blunt. Unemotional. 'Not that I think I'd have wanted to.'

'Why couldn't you?' Bel felt herself leaning towards her ma, wondering if perhaps she held the answer as to why she and Joe were not able to have the family they both so desperately desired.

'When I had you,' Pearl said, smoke billowing from her mouth, 'there were problems.' She had a sudden flash of the old woman who had brought Isabelle into the world. And blood. Whenever images of her daughter's birth forced their way back into her mind, there was always blood. Lots of it.

'Afterwards, the old witch told me that I was lucky to be alive 'n that there'd be no more babs ... "Mightn't be a bad thing," she said. She was probably right.'

Bel knew that her conception had been a dark and terrible violation, but she hadn't realised that her ma had nearly died giving her life.

Bel took another sip of her lemonade. It tasted bitter.

Her conception, her birth – her very existence – had decimated her ma's entire life.

Why did she have to keep prodding the hornets' nest? She should know by now that nothing good ever came of it.

Half an hour later, Bel was walking to her night class.

She had her little electric torch switched on, although she knew every street and back lane in this part of town. So much of her childhood had been spent wandering around on her own. Once, she must have been only three or four, she'd climbed on board a tram, unnoticed, and ended up at a place where the air smelled of salt. She knew now it must have been either Roker or Seaburn. Luckily, the conductor had realised she was on her own and brought her home.

'Evening.' A middle-aged man doffed his cap and moved aside to allow Bel to commandeer the pavement.

'Thank you,' Bel smiled.

Why was it she wasn't falling pregnant? It had been over a year since she had married Joe. And nothing. *Why?*

She had admitted to Joe one evening, when he'd caught her crying, that she worried it was her punishment for marrying her dead husband's brother. Joe had surprised her by roaring with laughter and telling her he'd never heard anything so ridiculous.

'How can anyone be punished for loving another person?' he'd said, kissing her tears. 'Perhaps for hating another being – but never for loving.'

He'd taken her in his arms and they'd shown each other the love they felt for one another. Afterwards, she had thought how wonderful it would be if their making love had also made a baby. But it hadn't.

It had hit her hard when Polly told her she was pregnant – not that she would ever show it. The jealousy she felt had to stay buried deep. Or at least very well hidden.

Passing the Golden Lion, Bel thought of her ma. The spit-and-sawdust pub had been one of her most frequented drinking holes when Bel was young. She wished she had known then what she knew now. If she had, she wouldn't have hated her ma so much.

As she crossed the road, it suddenly occurred to her that it was more than likely that her ma wouldn't have been the only one to have suffered at the hands of Mr Havelock. She suddenly felt overwhelmed with a terrible sorrow for those he had abused and the lives he had ruined. And then she felt an even greater anger, outraged at how during all that time this awful man had led a gilded life.

It was wrong.

So very wrong.

And for the first time Bel felt the need for retribution.

Chapter Thirty

Saturday 20 February

As Polly finished off a particularly long flat weld, she pushed up her metal mask and inspected her workmanship. Her long line of beading was just about perfect. She'd always remembered Rosie telling them when they were trainees that their welds should look like a miniature twisted rope. At the time it had felt like an impossible task; now it was second nature. Feeling cramp starting to creep down her right calf, she stood up and stretched her leg. Laying her welding rod and stinger down on the ground, she put her hands on her hips and straightened her back. This was the first time in her life that she had felt as though she'd put on weight. It was barely discernible when she looked in the mirror, but she could feel it. Her waist had expanded ever so slightly and her bump seemed to be getting a little bigger with each passing day.

She looked at the rest of the women. They were all engrossed in their welds. They were on *Denewood*'s upper deck, welding together the steel flooring that circumvented the ship's bridge. Squatting back down on her haunches to start on one of the corner joints, Polly let her thoughts wander to Tommy, as they invariably did when her world became a blur of molten metal.

Please, please keep yourself safe. She breathed heavily into her mask, causing the tinted protective glass to mist up momentarily. A small explosion of sparks flared up along with her own anger. *Who was she kidding?* She'd once heard someone say that the job of a mine-clearance diver was like playing Russian roulette over and over again. She'd tried to forget those words, but the more she tried to push them back, the more they seemed to come to the fore.

She would change her mantra.

Instead of begging Tommy to keep safe, she would implore God, or whoever it was that ruled their destiny, to end this war soon. Very soon.

Over the next few hours Polly tried to force her mind to focus on something other than Tommy, but it was a mental tug of war she repeatedly lost. When she finally felt Rosie's hand on her back, telling her that it was time to down tools, she felt relieved, physically and emotionally.

'So, what's everyone doing this afternoon?' Dorothy asked as soon as she'd taken off her mask.

'This job must be extra hard for you, Dor,' Gloria said, her expression deadpan.

'Why's that?' Dorothy asked, puzzled.

'Because yer have to keep yer gob shut for hours on end.'

Martha guffawed. 'Yeah, must be purgatory.'

Dorothy opened her mouth to speak, but was beaten to it by Angie.

'Actually, she *doesn't* keep her cakehole closed. She talks to herself when she's welding. Or makes up imaginary conversations. She's told me.'

Dorothy gave a dramatic huff.

'I get bored,' she explained.

'But never bored of hearing the sound of yer own voice!' Gloria hooted with laughter as she walked round checking that all their welding machines were switched off.

'So, what's everyone doing with the rest of their day?' Rosie asked, piling their rods into a cardboard box and pushing it under some tarpaulin. As the Saturday shift finished at three o'clock, she knew they'd all have something planned.

'I think Ma and I are going up the cemetery,' Polly said, tying the drawstring on her haversack.

'To visit Arthur's grave?' Dorothy asked.

Polly nodded. 'I think they might have put his headstone up. It'll be lovely to see it if they have. I know Mr Havelock was going to sort it. I'm guessing it'll be a nice one.'

'And if they have, then *I'm* guessing you'll be going straight home and writing a letter to your husband,' Gloria said, smiling. She was the same with Jack, as well as with her two boys. If there was anything new to report, she'd put pen to paper straight away. Mind you, she wrote to Gordon and Bobby every week regardless, even if it was just a few lines to say she loved them.

'You know me too well,' Polly said, smiling.

'You not heard from Tommy yet?' Martha said.

'I think Pol would have told us if she had.' Dorothy's words were accompanied by an exaggerated rolling of the eyes.

Polly shook her head. 'Not yet, Martha.'

'I'm surprised yer mam isn't nagging yer to pack in work,' Angie said.

Polly let out a hollow laugh. 'Oh, I'm sure that's not far off. I think she's holding out until I'm a few weeks further on.'

'The three-month marker,' Gloria said. She had spoken to Agnes when they'd been on their own. Gloria had reassured Polly's ma that she'd keep an eye on her daughter, and that it went without saying that Rosie would be watching her like a hawk too, making sure she didn't do anything that might put Polly or her pregnancy at risk.

'So, when will yer be three months gone?' Angie said.

'About the middle of March,' Polly said, undoing her turban and letting her curly chestnut hair break free.

'Cor, that's just over three weeks' time.' Angie's eyes widened.

'You feeling any different?' Dorothy said.

Everyone looked at Polly.

'Not really,' she said, a slight blush showing through her dirt-smeared face.

'Still sicky?' Gloria asked.

Polly nodded. She constantly felt nauseous, but was thankful she was only being physically sick early in the morning.

'My boobs feel huge,' she said, looking down at her chest.

Everyone laughed. They'd all noticed the change in Polly's figure, certainly her bosom, despite the camouflage of her overalls.

They all started to make their way along the makeshift wooden bridge that led from the deck to the yard.

'You up to anything later, Glor?' Polly looked at the group's mother hen.

'I'll be picking up Hope from Beryl's, frying us up a nice bit of fish, and then I'll be putting my feet up 'n having a date with the Home Service.'

'Is Helen popping round?' Dorothy said, trying to sound casual but failing, as they all walked across the yard.

'I think she might well be dropping by later on. Early evening probably,' Gloria said. 'Yer can still come around, yer know. Just 'cos Helen's there doesn't mean you 'n Angie can't also visit.'

'Mmm.' Dorothy didn't sound convinced.

'Nah, it's all reet, Glor, me'n Dor are gannin to the Ritz.'

Martha guffawed. 'No surprise there then.'

'Well, it's a sad state of affairs if you're not out on a Saturday night,' Dorothy said. 'Isn't it, Ange?'

They all stopped to let a crane pass. Martha, Gloria and Rosie looked at Angie, then back to Dorothy. There was something in the air.

'Dor, I can't help it if Quentin wanted to take me to that posh place on the corner of St Thomas Street. Especially as he's only here fer the one night.'

'The Continental Hotel?' Rosie asked. It was Lily's favourite place, but even she admitted it was expensive and very well-to-do.

'Aye, that's the place,' Angie said, as they all carried on walking. 'He said if I want to see what posh is all about, then I had to gan there.' She looked at Dorothy. 'But of course I told him there was no way I could go. I couldn't *not* go to the Ritz with Dor on a Saturday night.'

'I think Quentin would tell you that you can't use a double negative in a sentence,' Dorothy huffed. 'Bad grammar.'

Angie looked at Dorothy as though she were speaking gobbledegook.

'So, you're not going?' Gloria asked, failing to hide her incredulity at Angie passing up a date at a lovely restaurant.

'Nah,' Angie said. 'I told him it'd have to be any night but a Saturday.'

'Well,' Rosie said, 'I hope a certain someone would do the same for you if Toby came a-calling.'

'Of course I would!' Dor defended herself. 'I'd never leave Angie in on her own on a Saturday night.'

Her words were met by a collective look of scepticism.

'You doing your ARP duties, Martha?' Gloria said.

'Yes, although my mam is still on at me to give it up. Says I'm doing enough here to help the war effort.'

Everyone knew Mrs Perkins had been far from happy about Martha's work with the Civil Defence since she had nearly died in the Tatham Street air raid.

'Yer could always come out with us to the Ritz?' Angie piped up.

Martha let out another loud guffaw. 'I don't know which my mam would think is worse.'

Everyone chuckled as they approached the main gates.

'What about you, Rosie?' Martha said.

'Well, if you all look up to the admin office window, that'll give you a clue,' Rosie said with a mock-weary sigh.

Everyone looked up to see Charlotte standing at the window. She had her red dress on and was waving at them all with a big smile on her face.

Everyone waved back.

'So, you two getting on all right?' Gloria asked.

Everyone looked at Rosie.

'It's actually going really well,' Rosie said. 'I mean, Charlie's a handful and all that, but I think things are settling down now. Although I have to say I'm so glad this half-term is almost over and she's back to school on Monday. It's a job keeping her busy and out of mischief.'

'Where yer both gannin now, miss?' Angie said.

'Yeah, Charlie looks all togged up and very excited,' Martha observed.

'The Holme Café,' Rosie said.

They all looked at Charlotte as she came bursting out the main doors of the admin building.

'Is that lipstick she's wearing?' Angie said, frowning.

'So, *ma chère*, has Kate sorted you out with some decent clothes to wear?'

Lily, George, Rosie and Charlotte were all in the café next door to the Maison Nouvelle.

Charlotte nodded and sat up straight in her chair. She'd been to see Kate this morning and had been measured up for a new skirt. She'd also tried on some second-hand clothes, which Kate was going to alter for her.

'What can I get you all?' The waitress was standing with her little notebook to hand.

'Tea for five, my dear,' Lily said. She caught the young blonde girl looking a little perplexed. 'We've got another coming to join us. The seamstress from next door.' The girl smiled. She knew Kate. Everyone knew Kate. Or rather, everyone wanted to get their clothes designed and made by Kate.

'And I think we shall have a selection of sandwiches to start with, please.'

When the waitress had gone, Lily turned her attention to Charlotte.

'Well, *ma chérie*, you look positively radiant – doesn't she, George?'

It was obvious to everyone that Lily adored Charlotte – and Charlotte, Lily. And that Lily was fast becoming a mother figure to Charlotte.

Rosie had come to realise that her sister had existed on very little love and attention after their mam and dad had died. Having been stuck out in the desert for so long, she was now drinking up her new life with those who wanted nothing more than to lavish her with all that she had missed out on.

'She does indeed look radiant, my dear,' George said, getting out a cigar and preparing to light it. 'Charming. Just like her older sister.' He looked at Rosie and gave her a wink.

'I hear Kate's doing home visits now?' Rosie asked Lily. 'Charlie said she's off to some big house up Barnes way to do a fitting after she's been here?'

'Yes, she's been braving it further afield since she ventured over to that yard of yours to sort out Polly's wedding dress.'

'A visit she made thanks to Alfie escorting her there and back,' Rosie said, raising an eyebrow.

'Mmm,' Lily said, her lips pursed.

'I don't know why you are so set against Alfie?' Rosie said, a hint of exasperation in her voice.

'It's not that I'm against him as such,' Lily said. 'More that I'm against any young man who might have desires on our Kate. She's not ready for any of that nonsense yet. It was very kind of him to take the time, especially as Kate now feels able to see clients at home, but I believe it shouldn't go any further than friendship.'

Just then the bell over the door tinkled and Kate slipped into the shop.

'Talk of the devil . . . *Bonjour, ma petite!*'

Kate smiled and slid into the empty chair next to Lily.

'Now,' Lily said, with a big smile on her face, 'I can hear exactly what our very own Coco Chanel is going to have Charlotte wearing next time we all go out . . . Ah. Perfectly timed!' she declared, seeing that the skinny blonde waitress was wheeling a rather rickety tea trolley towards them.

Rosie sat back and glanced at Charlotte. Her sister's smile stretched from ear to ear. She was in her element.

Lily also looked as happy as Larry.

Rosie looked around the table. She could never have envisioned such a scene. She wished she could tell Peter about it. Lately she'd found herself chatting to him in her head, rather like she had with her mam and dad.

If she could speak to him now, she would tell him that he had been right and – loath though she was to admit it – so had Lily.

It really had been the best thing for Charlotte to come and live back home.

'But remember, Charlie,' Kate said, 'you must never wear anything simply because it is in fashion. You must wear what suits you. What *is* you.'

'Just as you must always be true to yourself, *ma chère*,' Lily added, looking at Charlotte. 'Never be ashamed of what you are – or of those who love and care for you.'

Rosie would have kicked Lily under the table had she been able to reach.

'Interesting piece in the *Telegraph* today,' George said, changing the subject. 'Well, actually in all the papers today.'

Rosie was immediately attentive. Whenever George mentioned anything to do with the war, she knew it invariably concerned France, which, in turn, concerned Peter.

George had told her what Peter had not been able to: that he had been enlisted into 'Churchill's secret army', the Special Operations Executive. Peter's ability to speak French like a native, thanks to his mother's refusal to speak English, had led to him being tasked with carrying out covert missions behind enemy lines.

'Pray, tell us more, darling.' Lily looked at Charlotte and gave her a sly wink. 'I'm sure if it was in the *Telegraph* it'll be scintillating.' She made a show of yawning and tapping her mouth gently with the palm of her hand – a hand, Charlotte noticed, that had even more jewellery on it than normal.

'Well, as you are so eager to hear,' George said, 'I shall continue.' He focused his gaze on Rosie. 'It would seem that the prime minister of Vichy France, Pierre Laval, and the Minister of Justice, Joseph Barthélemy, have formally created something called the STO – the *Service du travail obligatoire*.'

'Compulsory Work Service,' Charlotte translated through a mouthful of ham sandwich.

'Now that, my dear, is the reward for working every hour God sends.'

Rosie shot Lily a warning look.

'If I were you,' Lily continued regardless, 'I'd feel very proud of myself for producing such an educated *enfant*.'

Charlotte caught the look between the two women, but couldn't interpret it.

'The Compulsory Work Service,' George continued, 'is a way of conscripting and deporting thousands – probably tens of thousands – of French workers to Nazi Germany to help its war effort.'

'That's terrible,' Rosie said.

'I suppose it is, my dear,' George said. 'But it could be viewed from various perspectives. Of course, any kind of forced labour is despicable, but it also shows that Hitler is short of manpower at home. And as the *Telegraph* pointed out today in one of its commentaries, the increase in forced labour is because Hitler has had to enlist more soldiers for the war on the Eastern Front.'

Knowing that Rosie would be wondering how all this affected Peter, he added, 'The knock-on effect will undoubtedly be that more and more Frenchmen will be going into hiding to evade service and many of those will join ranks with the French Resistance.'

Rosie felt a surge of hope. *So, this was good news for operatives like Peter.*

'Dear me, George, we've come here for a little frivolity, not to be depressed with the state of my adopted homeland.' Lily got out her fan from her handbag and snapped it open like a professional flamenco dancer.

'So,' Kate said, looking at George puffing away on his cigar, 'when do I get to design a new wedding dress for your future wife?'

George coughed. 'Kate, my dear, when have I *ever* been the one to make such decisions? I would get married tomorrow if I had my own way, but my future wife here has her own ideas, which, I'm sure, will come as no surprise to you.' He put his teacup back on the saucer. 'I've just put myself on standby. When I get the signal I'll be there, at the registry office, spick and span, with a thick rose-gold band to hand.'

'I'll know when the time is right,' Lily said, pushing her plate to the side and pulling out her packet of Gauloises. 'I'm still very partial to a winter wedding, although I don't think we could ever match Tommy and Polly's rather magical day.'

She paused.

Then her face lit up.

'I've just had an idea! Perhaps we could get married on New Year's Eve? Now that really would be a rather huge and spectacular wedding, wouldn't it?'

Everyone laughed when George groaned.

Chapter Thirty-One

Ashbrooke, Sunderland

1938

'She'll be all right, won't she?' Rosie looked up at the huge, overhanging elm trees as she strolled through Ashbrooke on her way to Lily's. This part of town was so affluent, so different to where she worked during the day.

'You'll make sure she doesn't get too lonely, won't you?' Rosie walked slowly, breathing in the clear air. 'I don't know what it is, I just feel she needs you to keep an extra-special eye on her at the moment.'

Before she'd left her bedsit this evening, the landlord had given her a letter from Charlotte. She'd read it quickly while getting ready for Lily's and had immediately picked up on something. Was it an underlying sadness? Was she lonely?

Rosie always asked Charlie if she was all right, trying to put it in such a way that her sister could be honest and tell her if there was anything wrong, but it was hard. Especially as they were so far apart.

'I know, I worry too much.' Rosie continued her imaginary conversation, second-guessing what her mam and dad would say. 'It sounds like she's got a nice friend called Marjorie . . . Mind you, the poor thing doesn't sound in the best health. Charlie says she's got something called asthma. A problem with her breathing.' Rosie looked at a robin perched in the bushes of one of the perfectly manicured front gardens she was walking past.

'I'd let her come back here,' Rosie said, turning down the back lane that ran parallel to West Lawn, 'I know it'd be good for her to come back occasionally, perhaps even have a trip to Whitburn, but it doesn't feel safe.' Rosie knew her mam and dad would understand. She just wished Charlie could too. She had gone on and on when she'd first started at Runcorn, asking, no, *begging* Rosie to let her come home – just for a few days. She'd given in the once but had spent the whole time on tenterhooks, waiting, fearful that Raymond would suddenly appear out of nowhere.

Clicking open the latch on the back gate and walking down the narrow path to the back door, Rosie knocked the required three times. She waited a moment while the shutter to the spyhole opened and closed.

'*Ma chère!*' Lily's welcome put an end to Rosie's one-sided conversation. 'A word, *ma chérie*, before the *travaille*.' She waved Rosie into the kitchen.

'Come, come, sit down. There's a pot of tea stewing.' Lily went over to the armoire and poured herself a glass of cognac. She knew Rosie rarely drank and if she ever did it would be at the end of the evening.

'I want to offer you the role of "head girl",' Lily said, getting out her cigarettes and lighting one. 'You know that Lucinda has nabbed herself a man and has this week run off into the sunset to get married – and have copious amounts of children, no doubt.'

Rosie smiled. Lily loved to dramatise. Lucinda had got engaged months ago and had given Lily plenty of notice.

'Well, now that my lovely Lucinda has jumped ship, I need another captain – or captainness, if there is such a thing.'

'I think it's simply captain,' Rosie said.

'Well, I'd like you to take the reins – or the steering wheel – or whatever it is that drives a ship.'

'The helm. You want me to take the helm – to steer the ship,' Rosie said, suppressing a smile; for someone who lived in 'the biggest shipbuilding town in the world', Lily knew next to nothing about ships.

'Exactly,' Lily said. 'I want you to take the helm of this most wondrous establishment.'

'I suppose,' Rosie said, 'it will depend on what kind of incentive I can expect.'

Lily clapped her hands in glee.

'That's what I love about you, Rosie, you're a born businesswoman. I was only saying so to George the other day.'

Rosie knew George had been a patron of the bordello for a good few years, though she hadn't known him to go with any of the girls. He seemed to spend his time playing the piano and chatting with Lily and the rest of the clients.

'Anyway, I digress,' Lily said, waving her hand. 'You will indeed be given a twenty-five per cent rise on all your earnings.' It was a smart move. One that would be mutually beneficial: Rosie would be inclined to take on more clients, which, in turn, would bolster the bordello's coffers.

'Do we have a deal?' Lily stretched out her hand.

'We do,' Rosie said as the two women shook on it.

'Now,' Lily said, 'your first task will be to welcome a new girl to the flock. She's just tipped up from Liverpool – somewhere called the Wirral. Anyway, she's going to need the benefit of your expertise and advice.

'And I want you to encourage her to give herself a little bit of a makeover. I'll stump up the money. Tell her not to worry about that.'

Rosie finished her tea and stood up.

'What's the girl's name?'

'Vivian,' Lily said. 'Go easy on her, though.' She again waved her arm around. 'She's not accustomed to all this.'

Just like I wasn't, Rosie thought.

How life can change in such a short time.

Rosie's musing proved spot on when, six months later, Vivian had transformed herself from Minnie Mouse to a full-blown Mae West. She had taken Lily's advice – and money – and given herself one hell of a makeover.

Thanks to her own increased wages, Rosie was now easily earning enough to keep Charlotte at Runcorn.

She had also been given a promotion at Thompson's and been made head welder on the proviso that she trained newcomers and apprentices. There had been murmurings that any kind of educational role was a woman's job. Not that Rosie minded. It was a step up the ladder and more money.

When war was declared ten months later, it made Rosie even more steadfast in her refusal to allow Charlotte to come home. Instead, she tried to increase the amount of times she visited Charlotte at the Rainers', but it didn't matter how often she went there, the goodbyes were still just as heartbreaking.

Nothing much happened during the first few months of the war, but all that changed when in the summer of 1940 the first bombs were dropped and the Battle of Britain began. Everyone knew the town would be top of Hitler's hit list because of the world-renowned shipyards lining the Wear, and, of course, the area's thriving coal-mining industry. Rosie congratulated herself that was she keeping her sister safe not only from her uncle's clutches, but also from the bombs that had started to rain down on the town.

It was ironic that the first houses to be hit were the fishermen's cottages.

Reading about the attack and seeing the photographs of the damage they had caused to her old house left Rosie feeling as though her previous life had also been obliterated.

She just wished that the same fate had befallen her uncle. She was sure, however, that he was very much alive and kicking. She had no proof as such; it was more a sense. A sense that told her it was just a matter of time before he'd be back.

It was the reason she only ever stayed in her rented accommodation for six-month stretches.

There'd be less chance he'd be able to track her down.

Or so she hoped.

Chapter Thirty-Two

Sunday 14 March

'Georgina, come in, come in. I wasn't sure if you'd be here with all these wretched air raids we've been getting. I hope no one you know has been affected?'

'No, no one. Thank goodness,' Georgina said, taking her pew in front of Helen's desk. She looked to her right and was glad to see the tea tray in its usual place. She could do with a pick-me-up; like most people in the town these past couple of nights, she'd had little sleep.

'I heard an AA shell fell in the grounds of the Children's Hospital, and another in some poor woman's front garden. Both exploded,' she said as she watched Helen pouring their tea.

'I know, a friend of mine works at the Ryhope.' Helen handed Georgina her cup and saucer. 'He said it was pandemonium there.'

'Your friend a doctor?' Georgina asked.

Helen nodded.

'They get the overspill. Only one dead. Thank God.' She sighed heavily. 'What times to live in when you're actually thankful that there was only the one casualty.'

Helen went to sit down at her desk with her own cup of tea, reaching down to her handbag for her cigarettes. 'I don't know, it makes my concerns about Bel's parentage seem so insignificant.' She lit a Pall Mall. 'Maybe even a bit pathetic. I wonder if I should just forget it and put my time into something more constructive.'

Georgina sat up and put her cup and saucer down. 'Well, I think that's the good thing about employing someone like me. *You're* not having to waste any valuable time whatsoever . . . I do the time, as it were, and you can get on with what's really important.'

Georgina looked out the window at the empty office. It was Sunday. There were no office workers, and only a skeleton staff out in the yard, by the looks of it.

'You can concentrate on running this place, getting the ships built,' she continued to stress her point. 'I hear you're launching the *Chinese Prince* in the next week or so?'

Helen's face lit up with pride.

'Yes, on the twenty-third. On schedule. She's going to be taking troops as well as cargo across the Atlantic. Let's hope Lady Luck's on her side.'

'Yes, she'll need all the luck she can get, the rate Jerry is sinking ships . . .' Georgina was relieved she'd steered Helen away from any thoughts of ending the investigation. She and her father were living on a shoestring – a very thin and frayed shoestring at that. 'So, let me fill you in,' she said, pulling out her notepad.

'Well, first of all, I didn't realise that your grandfather, Mr Havelock, had a younger brother?'

'Gosh, yes, of course, I completely forgot about him! Dear me, memory like a sieve . . . I do believe he died before the start of the First War. Tuberculosis, I think. Grandfather's not one for talking much about family. Never has been. It's always work, work, work.'

Helen tapped her cigarette on the steel ashtray on her desk.

'Neither is my mother, come to think of it, although she's more play, play, play.'

Georgina looked at Helen to discern whether her comments were meant to be humorous. They weren't.

'And we've never been one of those families that has a hoard of photographs cluttering up the place, gathering dust,' Helen added, although she had not thought it unusual until now.

She took a sip of her tea.

'So, that would make this brother my great-uncle . . . God, you know I can't even remember his name. Isn't that terrible?'

Georgina didn't think it terrible, but she did think it odd. She knew all her relatives – alive and dead.

'Alexander,' Georgina said. 'Master Alexander William Havelock.'

'How interesting,' Helen said, blowing out a stream of swirling grey smoke and patting back her victory rolls with her free hand.

Georgina thought Helen looked a tad distracted.

'Do you think it could be him?' Helen turned to Georgina. 'That Pearl and my great-uncle Alex had some great love affair – you know, from different sides of the track but hopelessly in love. Then he died and Bel was born?'

Georgina tilted her head and nodded as though she was seriously considering what Helen had said could be a possibility. She had her own theories, however. Ones she'd keep to herself for now. 'Perhaps,' she said. 'But I've still got a heck of a lot more research to do to see if I can connect Pearl to your great-uncle. Or anyone else in the family.'

She waited for Helen to suggest the obvious – that the only other possible male person in the family was her grandfather.

But she didn't, and Georgina wasn't going to offer up his name either. It was far easier to defame the dead than the living.

'Well, that all sounds like great progress,' Helen said.

Georgina caught her looking at her watch.

'So, if you're happy for me to keep ploughing on?' she asked.

'Yes, yes, of course,' Helen said, standing up.

Georgina stood up but didn't make to leave. *God, those with money were always the same.*

Helen looked at Georgina before exclaiming, 'Oh, I'm so sorry, Georgina – your retainer. Dear me, I'd forget my head today if it was loose.'

She pulled out her top drawer and got out her cheque-book, scrawling out the agreed amount and handing it over.

'Thank you.' Georgina put the part payment in her hand-bag, along with her notebook, and turned to leave.

As she walked out of the office, she saw a rather hand-some fair-haired man sitting in one of the chairs by the window. He was stroking the ginger cat, which was wrapping itself around his legs.

As soon as he saw the two women he stood up.

'*John!*'

Georgina turned to see Helen's face light up. Had the anticipation of this man's arrival been the cause of Helen's slightly distracted demeanour?

'You should have said you were here,' Helen repri-manded. 'Rather than sitting out here on your tod.'

'I managed to arrive a little earlier than expected,' John said. 'It's actually nice to have a moment's peace and quiet.'

Helen laughed. 'And to think you ended up getting it at a shipyard. Lucky it's Sunday . . . Georgina, meet my friend John – Dr John Parker – a surgeon at the Ryhope Emergency Hospital.'

Georgina put out her hand.

'Pleased to meet you,' she said. His hand felt warm and gentle. She could see why Helen might be distracted.

'And you too,' Dr Parker said, putting his other hand on top of hers and giving it a rub. 'My, you've got cold hands.'

Georgina blushed before agreeing to meet with Helen again in a fortnight's time.

Dr Parker watched her leave.

Helen's Miss Marple was exactly as described.

Half an hour later, Helen and John were sitting in the Victor Hotel public house, just a ten-minute walk up from the yard.

'So, what's the update?' Dr Parker asked. He'd been amazed Helen had let him get the drinks in without any objection.

'Well, I can't believe I'm admitting this, you'll think I'm such a scatterbrain, but I totally forgot my grandfather had a brother. Honestly, I felt a little bit embarrassed. I didn't even know his name.'

Dr Parker took a sip of his bitter. 'Which was?'

Helen starting fishing about in her bag. Because John had turned up earlier than expected, she'd not had a chance to put on her lipstick. It looked as though she might have left it at work.

'Which was what?' Helen said.

'His name.' Dr Parker laughed. Helen was certainly not with it this evening.

'Oh, his name?' Helen said, standing up. 'Alexander something or other . . . Sorry, John, I just need to go and powder my nose.'

John watched as she made her way to the Ladies. His weren't the only pair of eyes on her. Helen drew admiring looks everywhere she went.

When she came back, Dr Parker noticed she had applied some lipstick.

'Everything all right?' he asked. 'You seem a bit preoccupied this evening?'

'Do I?' Helen sat down and took a rather large gulp of her vodka.

'So, no real update on a certain someone's lineage, then?' Dr Parker said, keeping his voice low, not that he really needed to. The pub was full. And full meant loud.

Helen smiled.

'Nothing definite, but my little Miss Marple is slowly but surely squirrelling away. She'll get there in the end, I'm sure of it. She's that kind of person.'

'What kind is that?'

'Determined. Like a dog with a bone. Won't let go until she's got what she wants.' Helen took a sip of the drink. 'Don't be fooled by that veneer of childlike vulnerability . . . Anyway, enough of my life. I want to hear what's been happening at the Ryhope and if you and your Dr Eris have managed to fix any more bodies and minds?'

'Well, yes, I hope so. There's been a definite improvement in young Jacob since he's been seeing Dr Eris. His amputation's healing up nicely as well, which is always good to see.'

Helen immediately felt sad. She had never met 'young Jacob', but her heart bled for him having to go through the rest of his life with such a disability. No wonder he needed help keeping his sanity.

'We'll need a lot more Dr Erises about when this war does finally come to an end,' Dr Parker prophesised. Helen could hear that John admired the new psychologist. They seemed to get on well.

'And how's Polly doing?' Dr Parker said, changing the subject.

'Yes, all's going well, from what I can gather,' replied Helen.

He watched Helen's reaction carefully. He still wasn't sure what her real feelings were about the news that Polly and Tommy were having a baby.

'And I'm guessing Tommy knows now?' Dr Parker probed. He'd thought about the impact of Polly's pregnancy quite a lot since Helen had told him the news. Was it a bit of a double blow? Not only was the man she loved about to have a family, but Helen was still recovering from the loss of her own baby.

'Oh, he sounds over the moon,' Helen said. 'Gloria was telling me he'd finally got Polly's letter – apparently it took ages to reach him. He wrote back straight away, telling Polly to be careful and take it easy.'

Helen took a sip of her drink and suddenly laughed.

'He even suggested she join Bel doing office work if she really felt the need to keep on working, which, according to Gloria, was met with complete hilarity.'

Dr Parker chuckled. He'd got to know Polly a little over the past six months and even he could tell she was not one to be working in an office.

'And how are *you* feeling about it?' he asked tentatively.

After learning more about the complexity of the mind from Dr Eris, he'd come to realise that Helen was still 'in recovery'. She probably didn't realise it herself, but the very fact that she had been obsessing about the gender of her baby was evidence she had not got over her loss.

'I'm fine . . . I *feel* fine about it,' Helen said, a slightly puzzled look on her face. 'Why do you ask?'

'I just wondered,' Dr Parker said, suddenly uncomfortable, 'because of what happened to you last year.'

Helen's face became sad.

'Oh, John, I think the chats with your "head doctor" might be making you overthink things. I'm fine. Honestly.' She looked at the people in the bar. 'I've not given it a lot of thought, to be truthful. I probably expected it. I mean, they were "living in sin" before they got married.'

Dr Parker looked at Helen. At those eyes. She was either a damn good actress, or she was in denial.

Helen took a deep breath. This was the perfect opening for her to chat about what she had wanted to talk about all evening.

'Listen to me – "living in sin". I sound like some preacher. I suppose in this day and age, with everything that's happening in the world, you wouldn't think people would care so much about that kind of thing, would you?'

Helen forced out a light-hearted laugh.

'You know, getting married in white and all that?'

Helen looked at John.

'What do you think?'

'Mmm, it's hard to tell, but my guess is that it's still important. I don't think the war has changed our views that much.'

Helen was just opening her mouth to ask if *he* thought it was important to be virtuous before marriage when the bell for last orders sounded out.

'Honestly, where does the time go?' Dr Parker stood up. 'I'm getting these in.'

Before Helen had time to object, he was on his feet and making his way to the bar.

A few minutes later he was back.

'Thank you,' Helen said as he put the drinks on the table.

'So, what were we saying?' he asked as he sat down.

'How the war has changed our views – or rather *if* it has,' she said, taking a sip of her drink. 'Do you think we're getting less puritanical? More liberal?'

'Good question,' Dr Parker said. 'I do think there's no denying women's role in society is changing. I mean, look at your women welders. That would have been unheard of before the war. That in itself must be making people – men *and* women – change the way they think and feel.'

Helen nodded her agreement, wondering how she could manipulate the conversation back to *women in white* as opposed to *women welders*.

She should just come out and say it: *John, would you consider courting a sullied woman?*

'Goodness me,' Dr Parker suddenly perked up. 'I completely forgot to ask you – how did your meeting with Mr Thompson go?'

'Oh, it went really well,' Helen said.

She took a sip of her drink, realising her window of opportunity had gone.

'He basically said, in a roundabout way, that he would be keen for me to take over from Harold when the time comes.'

'Well, that's brilliant,' Dr Parker said. 'That would be a promotion and a half, wouldn't it?'

'It would,' Helen mused, 'but, to be honest, I can't see Harold taking retirement voluntarily, and I also can't see Mr Thompson pushing him into early retirement. Still, it's good that I'm being considered as the person to step into his shoes eventually.'

'And what was it that gave you the push to see him?' Dr Parker asked. Helen had been keen to see the big boss since the launch of *Brutus*, which had coincided with the yard hitting a thirty-six-year production record.

'Actually, it was something Polly said at Arthur's funeral.'

'Oh, yes?' Dr Parker was intrigued.

'She was telling me how Tommy had been asking the old man for advice; he didn't know what to do about Polly – whether he should just let her go, so she'd be free.'

Helen looked at John's face and laughed. 'I know! As if that would have made her happy.'

Dr Parker wondered if it might, however, have made *Helen* happy.

'Anyway, Arthur said that if Flo, Tommy's grandmother, were still alive, she'd tell Tommy that if he wanted something, he should just go and get it.' Helen took a sip of her drink. 'And I thought, *she's right*.'

Dr Parker nodded. 'I suppose that's one way of looking at life.' He wanted to add that such advice was worth taking, but only if the object of the other person's desire was keen to be acquired. 'Come on, let me walk you home.'

Dr Parker expected to hear Helen's usual objection that she was perfectly capable of walking herself home, so he was surprised when she simply got up, grabbed her handbag and gas mask and said, 'All right, then.'

Perhaps she'd known he would insist.

'What a lovely evening.' Helen looked up at the inky-black sky as they left the pub and started walking along Victor Street.

Dr Parker was about to agree and comment on how remarkably quiet it was when the calm was interrupted by the familiar wailing of the air raid sirens.

'Oh, blast!' Helen shouted. 'You'll just have to come back to mine. Our basement's about as safe as it gets.'

'No, you get yourself home,' Dr Parker shouted back. 'I'm going back into town . . . If we get a pasting, I want to be at the Royal to help out.'

'It's not worth the risk,' Helen panicked. 'You might get hurt.'

Dr Parker let out a hollow laugh.

'Just like all our boys serving on the front line might get hurt . . . Get home. Get safe, you hear?' he said leaning in and giving her a quick kiss on the cheek.

'Be careful,' Helen said, nearly kissing him on the lips but stopping herself at the last moment.

'Go!' Dr Parker commanded.

Only when Helen had turned and started to hurry up Zetland Street and into the darkness did he run back down the road and into Dame Dorothy Street.

Seeing an army truck heading towards town, he waved it down.

'I'm a doctor,' he yelled at the driver.

Seconds later, the passenger door had slammed shut and the truck was heading towards the Wearmouth Bridge just as the first bombs dropped.

Chapter Thirty-Three

The following day
Monday 15 March

Georgina was sitting at the dining-room table with the morning edition of the *Sunderland Echo* laid out in front of her.

'Oh dear, Father, it looks as though this one's been the worst yet. Worse even than the Tatham Street bombing.'

'How many dead?' Mr Pickering asked as he shuffled his way across the large, high-ceilinged room to the table and eased himself into his chair. He was wearing what he always wore – his green and brown tweed three-piece suit that had seen better days, and a dicky bow which seemed to have a will of its own.

'Seventeen killed, thirty-one seriously injured and sixty-one with minor injuries.' Georgina quoted the figures from the article. 'It says here thousands of homes and businesses were damaged, some made totally uninhabitable. Well over a hundred have had to be demolished.'

Mr Pickering shook his head, his face a mixture of sadness and anger.

'Oh my goodness!' Georgina said, her eyes glued to the newspaper. 'A landmine hit Union Street and moved the Empress Hotel six inches!'

'Well, I'll be damned,' Mr Pickering said, pausing for a moment as he poured himself a cup of tea from the pot his daughter had made.

'Two Fire Guards died – a Mr Ernest Johnson of Peebles Road and Mr John William Simpson of Ward Street.' Georgina looked up at her father to see if he knew the men. Thankfully, he didn't. 'Honestly, there's going to be nothing left of the town if it carries on like this.'

She read on silently.

'I do wonder whether we should move out to the country,' Mr Pickering said. He looked around the room that had once been so full of life. Now, with his two sons at war and his wife long since passed away, the place was beginning to resemble a mausoleum.

'No, Father, Jerry isn't going to force us out of our own home. Have us scampering off like scared rabbits to hide in the hills.'

Mr Pickering looked at his daughter. He knew she wasn't being entirely truthful. Her resolution to stay put was just as much because she couldn't bear to leave the home where she had been brought up.

'I'm going to do us some toast.' Georgina stood up. Before she left the room, she went over to the sideboard, picked up a dog-eared blue file and took it over to her father.

'Here's what I've got so far on the Havelock case. See what you think. I won't be a minute.'

Mr Pickering pulled his wire-rimmed spectacles from his head, took a sip of his black tea and opened the file.

Five minutes later his daughter was back with a breakfast tray made up of a rack of toast, a small knob of butter and an almost empty jar of marmalade; they both spread it sparingly as they had nearly used up their monthly rations and still had a week to go.

They ate in silence. Mr Pickering went over his daughter's neatly handwritten notes, while Georgina continued to pour over the contents of the *Sunderland Echo*, nibbling occasionally on her toast.

'This job seems to be dragging on rather,' Mr Pickering finally said, looking up at Georgina over his half-moon spectacles. 'You're not perchance dragging this out longer than necessary, are you? Clocking up the hours and driving up the fee?' He gave his daughter a reprimanding look. 'Because if you are, I don't approve.'

'Honestly, Father, as if I'd do something so underhand.' She put her half-eaten toast back on her plate and brushed her hands together. She then got up, went over to the sideboard where she had left her handbag and rooted out the cheque Helen had given her.

'That family's got more money than sense,' she said, putting the retainer down in front of her father. 'That'll keep us going for a little while.'

Mr Pickering looked at the amount and then pushed it aside.

Georgina thought she'd glimpsed disdain on her father's face.

'Just watch that family,' he said, topping up his tea.

Georgina noticed his hands were shaking. She forced herself not to jump up and help him pour. Her father hated being fussed over.

'They're a strange lot,' he said, 'the Havelocks. Always have been. And always will be, in my opinion.'

Georgina looked at her father. It was unusual for him to deride others.

'Something tells me you know more about the Havelocks than you're letting on.' She stretched across the table and topped up her own cup.

Mr Pickering blew on his tea but didn't take a drink.

'Come on, Father. It's not like you to hold out. Especially on a job.'

Still, her father was quiet.

'I need to know everything and anything about this family,' Georgina said, 'if I'm to get to the bottom of this puzzle. And you know how difficult paternity cases are to prove. I don't need my own father holding out on me.'

Mr Pickering looked at Georgina.

He took a long sup of tea.

Georgina waited.

Finally, her father spoke.

'When I was a boy, Charles – Mr Havelock – was known as an expert horseman. It's probably hard to see that now he's so old.' Another short pause. 'I used to see him riding his horse around Backhouse Park.'

Mr Pickering put his teacup down.

'I'll never forget seeing him on his black steed – beautiful she was. A mare. Lovely white muzzle. Glossy black coat . . . I watched entranced from afar as horse and rider got nearer and nearer. I remember feeling awed at what I thought was a beautiful sight . . . Man and horse. In total unison. Galloping across the park.

'I thought the horse was sweating . . . The nearer they got, the more I could see. Charles's blond hair was swept back away from his face. I kept looking, my heart in my mouth, as they jumped a small mound of logs. They came closer and finally I saw . . .'

Georgina looked at her father and could see the glint of tears.

'I could still cry now at the sight,' he said. 'The mare's beautiful flank was ripped to ribbons of red – for one childish moment I thought they *were* ribbons, until I saw the blood.

'I looked into her beautiful black eyes and that's when my heart truly did break. They were full of fear and pain. I'd never seen such terror in an animal. Before or after.'

'Oh God.' Georgina had put her own cup back in its saucer. She could feel the prick of tears herself.

'But what shocked me even more,' Mr Pickering continued, 'was the look of sheer evil on Charles's face. His eyes were demonic, his face splattered with the spray of the mare's blood. I swear to God, that day I saw the devil himself.'

Mr Pickering pulled out his pipe from his top pocket.

Stuffing it with tobacco, he lit it and started puffing, as though to expunge the vision of true evil that had stayed with him his whole life.

He looked at his daughter. His only daughter. And worry crept to the fore.

'You'll find the answers to all your questions in that house, Georgina . . . Just be careful. And whatever you do – stay clear of that man. He might be old, but don't let that fool you.

'He mightn't be able to whip a horse half to death any more, but sadists like him will always find ways to hurt and torment.'

Chapter Thirty-Four

'Thank God you're all right,' Helen said. She had the phone pressed to her ear. 'I've been worried sick all night. Haven't slept a wink. You *are* all right, aren't you?'

Helen was sitting at her desk, stroking Winston, who was nuzzling her legs.

'Yes, yes, Helen, I'm fine. Honestly,' Dr Parker reassured her. 'You really shouldn't worry. No harm's going to come to me. Are *you* all right?'

'Of course. I stayed down in the cellar until the all-clear. I went to have a chat to some of the wardens afterwards – they said all the bombs had dropped over on the south side.'

Helen took a drag of the cigarette that she'd left burning in the ashtray.

'What happened after you left me? Did you get to the Royal in time?'

'Yes, just. Good job I went there. The Children's Hospital had to be evacuated. Thank God none of them were harmed. As if the poor mites haven't had enough to contend with. We got most of them settled down in the basement – managed to get the more seriously ill ones hooked up to drips and give them the pain relief they needed. The Royal took in about thirty. I think they managed to get another twenty over to Monkwearmouth.'

'Was there much damage to the actual hospital?' Helen asked, sitting back in her chair, her energy suddenly depleted. She hadn't slept a wink. Her mind had been working overtime.

'Mainly broken windows and loosened plaster,' Dr Parker said. 'They'll be moving most of the children back in there later today, I'd have thought.'

'You can't have been back long then?'

'I was just walking through the main door when Denise waved me over.'

'Thank goodness she caught you, otherwise she'd have had me ringing every couple of minutes.'

Helen heard some shouting in the distance.

'Looks like we're taking in casualties from town,' Dr Parker said, explaining the commotion.

'Go on, as long as you're all right. That's the main thing,' Helen said.

When she put the phone down, she breathed a sigh of relief.

After hearing of last night's devastation – and the lives lost – she realised how precious and precarious life was.

If anything had happened to John, she would have been devastated, but also full of regrets.

She'd made some huge mistakes in her life, but this wasn't going to be one of them.

'Oh my goodness, listen to this.'

It was lunchtime and the women were all sitting in the canteen. Polly was reading from the *Echo*.

'A couple were trapped in their indoor shelter, under *fifteen* feet of debris, but they were rescued unhurt!'

'Blimey,' Angie puffed out air. 'Fifteen feet!'

'How weird,' Polly continued. 'The bomb landed right next to a filled-in crater caused by another bomb that was dropped a couple of years back – and the house nearby that had to be rebuilt back then was totally demolished this time.'

'Talk about lightning striking twice,' Dorothy said, taking a bite of her sandwich. She always got hungry when she was tired.

'"The bomb fell in the garden of number three Seaforth Road where six people were sheltering in a Morrison shelter in the dining room,"' Polly continued reading. 'They were all right, but the house was totally destroyed around them.'

'That was like what we saw this morning coming into work, wasn't it?' Hannah looked at Olly and Martha.

'Yeah,' said Olly. 'The roof and all the walls of this building we passed had totally disappeared—'

'But the cupboard was still standing – in one piece. It even had all the clothes still hanging in it!' Martha said.

'I dinnit understand how that happens,' Angie said, drinking a glass of water in one go. She and Dorothy had walked around some of the ruins after the all-clear. She felt as though she had sucked in a bagful of dust.

'It says here,' Polly said, 'that the River Wear Commissioner's building was severely damaged and that a fire-watcher called Joseph Mutagh was killed.'

Everyone looked at Martha. She knew most of the wardens and fire-watchers.

She shook her head. 'No, I don't know him.' She, too, was tired, having been up half the night helping the Civil Defence.

'Oh no, St Thomas's was bombed,' Polly said. 'The vicar killed . . . He was on fire-watch duty by the sounds of it . . . His wife and family had to be rescued from the ruins of the vicarage.'

'I know,' Dorothy said, wiping her mouth with a napkin. 'We went to see what was left of the church, didn't we, Ange?'

238

Angie nodded solemnly.

'Was the Major all right?' Gloria looked at Polly, who nodded.

'He's in Scotland this week.'

'We had a walk up John Street,' Dorothy said, 'but none of the houses had been hit.'

The pair had also checked on Gloria's flat in Borough Road – it had been their first port of call, not that they'd tell Gloria.

'Where else was hit?' Olly asked.

Polly looked down at the *Echo* and read on. 'A third stack of firepots fell in Ashbrooke Cricket Grounds, Glen Path and The Cedars. But none caused any serious fires.'

Polly looked at Rosie.

'I know. Charlie and I had a quick run up to West Lawn to make sure Lily's was still standing. Which it was, thank goodness.' Rosie took a slug of tea. 'Of course, I had to practically drag Charlie back home.'

'She wanted to go and see Lily?' Gloria asked.

Rosie nodded.

'I told her they'd all be back in their beds and wouldn't appreciate being disturbed.' Rosie rolled her eyes towards the ceiling. 'And, of course, reminded her that she had school today.'

'What? They still have to gan to school even after half the town's been bombed?' Angie asked, amazed.

Rosie nodded again. 'They certainly do. As long as the building's standing.'

As they all started to clear away their dirty dishes, Rosie looked at Polly. She looked pale and tired. As they all did – but they weren't all three months gone.

'You feeling all right, Pol?' Rosie asked.

Everyone looked at their pregnant workmate. Her overalls, which had always been a little too big for her, were now quite snug.

'Yes, I'm fine,' she said. Seeing everyone's looks of concern, she stressed, 'Honestly, I am. Just tired, like everyone else.'

'Come on, then,' Rosie said, knowing the hooter would be sounding out the start of the shift in the next few minutes. 'Let's get the *Chinese Prince* ready for her big day.'

Chapter Thirty-Five

A week later

Monday 22 March

'To my granddaughter or grandson. Boy or girl, may the bairn be strong 'n healthy.'

Agnes raised her teacup.

'To the baby,' Polly said.

Mother and daughter chinked their china cups and took a sip of their tea.

'I'd feel a lot happier if you packed yer job in, though.' Agnes eyed her daughter. This was their main bone of contention. She didn't want to push the issue too much and make Polly even more resolute than she already was. But at the same time, she didn't want her to think it was fine to carry on doing what amounted to a man's job when she was expecting.

'You know, Ma, you worry too much. I promise you, if I start finding it hard or I'm feeling unwell, I'll stop. You've got to trust that I'll be sensible and do the right thing.'

She picked up her cuppa.

'I know this baby's going to be fine.' Polly threw a look at her mother and smiled mischievously. 'After all, yer not the only one who has the gift o' foresight,' she said, taking off her mother's subtle Irish brogue down to a T.

'Mmm,' Agnes said, pouring her tea into her saucer to cool it down and then taking a sup. 'At least the bab should be nicely settled now. God willing.' She took another sup. 'Not that anything's ever certain, but it's as certain as yer can get, I suppose.'

'I wish you'd told me you were so worked up about me catching the measles,' Polly said, stroking Tramp, who was curled up at her feet. 'Thank goodness for Beryl having a memory like an elephant.'

Agnes laughed. 'It's a bit worrying when yer neighbour can remember more about yer own bairns than yer can yerself.'

Polly looked at her ma, her face becoming serious. 'I know, but it was understandable. Beryl said it was just after Dad had been declared missing, presumed dead.'

'It's true,' Agnes said, 'shock can play games on the mind – and the memory.'

She pushed herself out of the chair.

'Anyway, no more morbid talk.' She went into the scullery and brought out a plate of custard tarts. 'It's not exactly the Grand, but it's a little something to mark the occasion. My daughter having her first bab, eh?'

'Thanks, Ma. My favourites.' Polly took one and put it on a side plate. 'I seem to have developed a real sweet tooth.' She took a bite. 'Gloria was the same when she was carrying Hope.'

'I remember being the same with you,' Agnes said. 'But not the twins. With them, I'd eat anything and everything. I was starving all the time.' She smiled, thinking of her own pregnancies, before her face became sombre.

'We might be allowing ourselves to have a little tea party of sorts, but yer must remember – there's to be no buying of any baby clothes. Not until the bab's born.'

'Honestly, Ma, you're so superstitious.' Polly laughed, but seeing the look of earnestness on her mother's face, she added, 'Don't worry, I won't.'

'And just so you know, this is not a celebration. There's to be no celebrating until the bab's arrived safe and sound. This is simply the marking of the bab's presence in our lives.'

They were quiet for a moment, both enjoying the rarity of a calm, quiet house. Everyone was out – Joe was with the Major, Pearl was at the Tatham and Bel had taken Lucille to the cinema. She had apologised no end, saying she had totally forgotten they were having a little tea party, but there would be another war on if she told Lucille their trip to see *Jungle Book* was cancelled.

'It's nice, just being us two,' Polly said. She had felt a little relieved when Bel had said she was taking Lucille to the flicks. She knew her pregnancy was difficult for Bel, even though she was doing a good job of not showing it.

'It is,' Agnes said. 'It's good that Bel's busy with LuLu. It's not easy – not with her so desperate for another little 'un.'

Polly looked at her mother. She had an uncanny knack of reading her mind sometimes.

'It's good yer being so thoughtful,' Agnes added, 'but yer must still enjoy this time. It's special, you know. Yer making a life . . . And it's even more special with all this warmongering and death going on.'

Polly nodded. 'Tommy said something similar in his last letter. "A bit of love to combat all the hatred" was how he put it.'

Agnes smiled. Polly had found a good man. He had a sensitive soul. This baby would be special in many ways.

'He'll make a good father,' Agnes mused.

'If he makes it back,' Polly said.

Agnes looked at her daughter. She had thought the same but would never have said it. It was important for Polly to be hopeful.

'We talked about it,' Polly said. 'If he doesn't make it back.'

Agnes sat back. 'And what did yer both say?'

'Tommy made me promise that I wouldn't give up on life if he lost his out there.' Polly topped up their cups.

'And did yer? Promise?'

Polly nodded solemnly. 'I did.'

Agnes felt a sense of relief.

'But knowing that I've got a part of Tommy growing inside of me now,' Polly added. 'That I'm going to have his child – well, that makes me feel like I could *really* keep on going if anything happened to him.'

As they continued to chat and enjoy their custard tarts, Agnes said a silent prayer that nothing – absolutely nothing – would threaten the life of this baby now growing in her daughter's belly.

Chapter Thirty-Six

Four days later
Thursday 25 March

'So, we're definitely on for this evening?' Helen was trying not to appear too pushy.

'Definitely.' Dr Parker's voice sounded tired, but certain. 'I'm going to make sure that Clarkson is on standby this evening should there be an emergency. He owes me one. Actually, he owes me more than one.'

Helen felt reassured.

'Right, so you'll come here around six, and we'll go straight there.'

It had been agreed they were to go to a little café-cum-restaurant on the promenade at Seaburn run by a woman called Mrs Hoggart who had decided to open the cafeteria every Thursday evening for pie 'n pea suppers. Helen had heard about it from Polly, who had worked there before she'd started at Thompson's. It wasn't the café – or the pie and peas – that had appealed to Helen when she had been planning this evening so much as the location. This time when John insisted on walking her home, *she* was going to insist he come in for a nightcap.

She was holding steadfast to her resolve to lead a life of no regrets.

'Yer boys all reet?' Angie asked.

They had all been going through the newspapers at lunchtime and had been reading about the devastating convoy losses in the Atlantic due to increased U-boat activity.

'I hope so,' Gloria said. 'I got a letter from them on Saturday. They'd written it on the Monday.' She paused. 'It's just hard not to worry, isn't it?'

She looked at Polly, who nodded.

'Whenever I get a letter from Tommy, I always look at the date . . .'

'And worry that something might have happened from the time they wrote the letter to when yer got it,' Gloria said.

The women's attention turned to Rosie, who they all knew would have given anything to receive a letter.

'I really don't know what's worse,' she said, knowing what they were all thinking, 'getting a letter or not. Either way, you can't help but be worried sick.'

'We'll be gibbering wrecks by the time this war does end.' Polly forced out a laugh. 'They'll be sending us all up to the local asylum by the busload.'

'I don't understand,' Martha said, looking down at the front page of the *Daily Express*. 'It says the middle of the Atlantic is not "sufficiently" covered by planes or ships.'

'But last month they were saying our anti U-boat campaign was doing well,' Dorothy said, looking puzzled.

'Aye, I knar, it doesn't make sense,' Angie agreed. 'We're knocking them out fast and furious. We just sent the *Chinese Prince* down the ways on Tuesday.'

'In spite of the air raid on Monday night,' Martha added.

'And Pickersgill's just launched *Stanridge*,' Marie-Anne chipped in.

'And Laing's launched *Empire Alliance* and Doxford's the *Empire Cheer* the other week,' Bel said.

'We can't build the buggers any quicker,' Angie lamented. 'It's not possible.'

'And it's not possible to do any more overtime,' Dorothy said wearily.

For once, she wasn't full of beans.

No one was.

'And it says here,' Martha continued to read the paper, 'that this is the worst it's been – even though we've got the Yanks on board.'

'And their production rates are pretty immense,' Rosie said.

'Only 'cos they're not having to worry about being bombed every minute of the day,' Angie said.

They were quiet for a moment.

The town was beginning to feel punch-drunk with the barrage of blows being meted out by the Luftwaffe of late.

'And just to depress everyone even more,' Bel said, 'I heard today from Helen that the mayor's son's been reported killed in action. His *only* son. Flight Lieutenant Michael Myers Wayman.'

Everyone was quiet. They had wondered why the mayor hadn't been at Tuesday's launch.

'You feeling all right?' Gloria asked Polly as they were walking back over to the dry basin.

'Yes, I'm fine,' Polly said, pushing loose strands of hair back into her turban.

'You look a little peaky, that's all,' Gloria said. She was keeping an extra-close eye on Polly after Agnes had expressed concerns.

'I think I'm just tired. After Monday's air raid I seem to be struggling to sleep.'

Everyone knew the hour-long raid shortly before midnight on Monday had resulted in the death of one person after two bombs had been dropped near the south dock. There had also been a load of homes damaged by incendiaries. It had been the fourth bombing in as many weeks, with the south of the river and the east end being the worst hit.

'Not that I've been sleeping brilliant anyway, but the past couple of nights I've been jerking awake every time I start to nod off. It's really annoying.'

'And very tiring,' Gloria said.

They walked on in silence for a little while.

'I don't want to sound like a nag,' Gloria said, 'but would yer not think about asking Helen to move you somewhere else in the yard that's not so labour-intensive?'

Polly looked at Gloria.

'You didn't go over to the cranes until you were out here . . .' Polly put her hand out in front of her stomach. 'And even then it was only because Angie wanted to do a job swap with you.'

Gloria laughed at the memory. 'I'm not sure she wanted to, more that she got bullied into it by Dorothy.'

Gloria slowed down.

'I know, but I'm different to you. For starters, Hope was my third child, and I didn't have all these air raids we seem to be having at the moment.'

'Only when you were giving birth!' Polly gasped.

'Well, that was really bad luck, but what I'm trying to say is that I wasn't spending most of my evenings in a shelter, getting next to no sleep, and I hadn't just waved my fiancé off to war.'

She took a deep breath. 'And before you say it, Jack was in America. He was safe. He wasn't doing what Tommy's doing.' Gloria could have slapped herself. She was meant to be trying to get Polly to take it easy, not making her even more worried than she already was.

'Honestly, Gloria, I'm fine. You're getting as bad as Ma. I think she's more worried about this baby than I am.' Polly put her hand on her stomach. It mightn't be showing too much with her overalls on, but when she'd tried to put her skirt on the other day she'd had to leave it half unzipped at the back.

'It's just—'

Gloria was about to continue her case, but was prevented by the klaxon sounding out the start of the afternoon shift.

'I'll see you all tomorrow,' Polly said, grabbing her holdall. 'I'm just nipping across to see Ralph and his lot. I said I'd say hi from Tommy and see what they've been up to.'

'See you tomorrow!' the women chorused back as they made their way over to the main gates.

Polly walked over to the quayside and for a while stood chatting to Ralph and the two other divers and the linesmen. Every time she saw them, they never failed to mention the wedding and how much they'd enjoyed it. 'The best Christmas ever,' they said every time, without fail.

Making her way back across the yard, Polly took off her turban and let her hair free. She always thought of Tommy when she let her hair down. He had told her he loved the feel of her hair brushing his face when they made love. Polly looked up to the sky. It was still light. The start of her second trimester had coincided with the beginning of spring, and today, for the first time, it *felt* like spring. The air was warmer and the winds had dropped.

Suddenly, Polly changed direction and instead of heading to the main gates, she veered off to the right.

She might have stopped feeling sick this past week or so, but when she needed to go, she needed to go.

*

Helen was applying her new Victory Red lipstick and carefully pinning back her hair into a neat French roll.

She had put on the blue dress she had worn for *Brutus*'s launch as well as the *Chinese Prince*'s. John hadn't seen her in it before. If he said she looked done up, she could say she'd had an important meeting. She didn't want it to be too obvious that she was viewing this evening as an actual date, but at the same time she also wanted to look her best.

Snapping her little mirror compact shut, she took a deep breath.

God, calm down!

She felt her heart beating like a drum.

Just be yourself!

She tried to remind herself of the advice Gloria had given her, but she'd forgotten it. Something about simply relaxing, enjoying herself.

Gloria seemed certain that John was keen on her – and not merely as a friend. When Helen had asked if she was sure, Gloria just shook her head and laughed.

Glancing up at the time, she saw it was nearly six o'clock.

He'd be here any moment.

Helen took out a cigarette. Perhaps she'd just have a quick one before he arrived. Scrabbling around for her lighter in the top drawer of her desk, she jumped when she heard the clash of the door downstairs.

Putting the lighter in her bag and straightening her dress, she brushed away non-existent bits of fluff before walking over to her office door. She would greet John with a warm hug and a kiss on the cheek, which somehow she would do in a way that wasn't completely chaste.

She heard the main door open and smiled to hide her nerves.

A few seconds later her face dropped as soon as she saw that it wasn't John walking through the door – but Polly.

Her face was ash-grey and her hand was holding her stomach protectively.

'Oh my God, Polly!' Helen rushed forward.

'I didn't know where else to go,' Polly mumbled.

She looked in shock.

'I thought Bel might be here . . . working late.'

'Come here,' Helen said, guiding Polly over to the nearest desk and sitting her down on the chair. 'What's wrong?' she demanded. 'You look terrible.'

'I've just been to the lav,' Polly began. There were tears in her eyes. But it was the fear Helen saw in them that gave her a shiver down her spine. She had a flash of her own miscarriage. The pain, the blood, then the darkness.

'What's happened? Are you bleeding?' she asked, staring at Polly's face, trying to read her thoughts.

Polly shook her head.

'No, water. Quite a bit of water,' she said.

'Water?' Helen asked, puzzled. 'I don't understand.'

And then the penny dropped.

Polly's waters were breaking.

She was going into an early labour.

A *very* early labour.

'Have you had any contractions?' Helen asked.

'No,' Polly said. She thought for a moment. 'I don't know. I might have had a few twinges. But I thought that was normal.'

'Yes, yes, of course, it probably is.' Helen forced herself to sound reassuring when inwardly she was filled with the most terrible dread.

No, not again!

They both turned on hearing the door swing open.

Dr Parker came striding into the main office door, heading towards Helen's office.

'John! Over here!' Helen shouted.

Dr Parker turned and saw Helen crouched down next to Polly. He didn't know who looked the most distressed.

'What's happened?' He bounded over to the two women and bobbed down so that he was facing Polly.

'She's just been to the toilet,' Helen said.

'Are you bleeding?' Dr Parker asked.

'No,' Polly said, her voice trembling. 'I don't know what's happening. I needed the loo and then all this water came out.' She looked down at her overalls. They looked wet.

Dr Parker's face was grave.

'We need to get you to the hospital.'

He looked at Helen.

'I'll call an ambulance,' she said, standing up. 'Don't worry, you're going to be fine.' Helen squeezed Polly's hand before hurrying to her office.

Stomping over to her desk, she snatched up the receiver and dialled the operator.

And waited.

For God's sake, answer the phone!

Still no answer.

Finally.

'Good evening. This is the operator speaking,' the sing-song voice sounded out down the receiver.

'Ambulance. I need an ambulance!' Helen barked down the phone.

'Ah, right.' The voice immediately became panicked. 'Yes . . . right . . . please, just hold on while I try to connect you—'

Then the line went dead.

The operator had unintentionally cut her off.

'*Nooo!*' Helen shouted into the receiver.

She looked up to see Dr Parker sitting next to Polly. He was taking her pulse and had his hand on her forehead, checking her temperature.

His face, though, said it all.

This was serious.

Helen dialled the operator again. This time it was engaged.

'Bloody hell!' Helen spat the words out.

Banging the phone down, she stomped out of the office and over to the main window. She flung it open and craned her neck.

'Thank God for small mercies,' she muttered.

The St John's ambulance was still here.

She looked at Dr Parker and then at Polly, whose face showed that the enormity of what might well be happening had hit home.

Helen saw Polly grab hold of Dr Parker's hand.

'Please tell me I'm not losing my baby?'

Helen stopped still.

Dr Parker avoided the question.

'For some reason it would appear that your waters have broken. We need to get you to hospital to see what's going on.'

Tears had started to drip down Polly's face.

'This is all my fault,' she said bitterly.

Helen could see anger starting to break through the fear.

'I should have taken it easier.' Polly looked at Dr Parker and then at Helen. 'Like everyone's been telling me.'

She stared at them both.

'I *can't* lose this baby. I just can't!'

'Don't you worry.' Helen hurried over, bent down and took hold of her hands.

'John and I aren't going to let you lose this baby, are we?' Helen said, looking at Dr Parker with pleading eyes.

'Of course we're not. Now, let's get going,' he said, easing Polly into a standing position. 'Are you all right to walk?'

Polly nodded as Dr Parker grabbed her arm and guided her to the door.

Helen hurried ahead and held the door wide before clomping down the stairs in her high heels and yanking open the main door.

As soon as Polly and Dr Parker had made it out into the yard, Helen ran as best she could, cursing the fact she had worn a dress that only allowed the shortest of strides. When she got to the ambulance, she flung the driver's door open. There was no one there.

Damn!

Her eyes darted to the ignition. They'd left the keys.

Thank God.

She tottered round to the back of the van.

Dr Parker was helping Polly into the back.

'I'll drive,' Dr Parker said.

'No, you stay with Polly. She needs you. I'll drive.'

'Can you drive?' Dr Parker asked, surprised.

Helen hurried off without answering.

'How hard can it be?' she muttered to herself as she jogged round to the driver's side. 'Been watching people drive me around my whole life . . .' She opened the driver's door. 'Nothing to it . . .'

She tried to climb up into the front seat but the tightness of her dress was restricting her movement.

'*Argh!*' She voiced her frustration, before bending over and ripping the bottom of her dress.

Hauling herself up, she got herself settled in the driver's seat. Looking at the footwell, she put her foot down on the clutch, looked up again and turned the ignition key. Putting her other foot on the accelerator, she revved the engine.

Taking a deep breath, she rammed the gearstick into first and lifted her foot off the clutch. A little too quickly.

The ambulance juddered forward, but didn't stall. She kept the revs high and drove through the main gates and up the embankment. Seeing there was no oncoming traffic, she pulled the steering wheel round and swung into Dame Dorothy Street.

She kept going, crunching through gears, muttering a silent prayer of thanks it was still relatively light and she could see where she was going.

Crossing the Wearmouth Bridge, she had a sudden flash of the day she had walked over this very bridge, heading to the same hospital, booked to have a termination. She had walked back over the bridge just hours later, having changed her mind at the last minute.

As she drove through the town centre, tears came into her eyes.

But she'd lost the baby anyway, hadn't she?

She felt a wave of sorrow and bitterness almost as strong as the day she'd woken up in the hospital to learn that her baby was dead.

John had saved her life that day, but not the life of her baby girl.

Please, God, don't let the same happen to Polly.

Chapter Thirty-Seven

The rest of the journey took another five minutes. Drawing up outside the Royal, Helen slammed on the brakes and stalled for the first time. Pulling on the handbrake, she jumped out of the driver's seat.

Dr Parker was already helping Polly out of the back.

Helen ran ahead, up the main steps, and marched straight over to the receptionist.

'Call Dr Billingham. Tell him it's an emergency.'

The young receptionist recognised Helen, although she had never seen her look so dishevelled. Her mascara was smudged. *And was that a huge rip up her dress?*

'Tell him it's Miss Crawford – Charles's daughter – and that I've a friend who needs urgent care.' Helen turned around to see Dr Parker and Polly making their way into the main foyer.

Helen looked at Polly. One hand was gripping John's arm, the other was splayed out on her stomach. She had what could only be described as a fierce look on her face.

'Where are you going to take her?' Helen shouted out to Dr Parker.

'Straight to theatre.' He nodded ahead.

'I'm getting Dr Billingham. I'll tell him to meet you down there,' Helen said before turning back to the receptionist, who was in the middle of relaying verbatim what she had been told to say.

Helen snatched the phone off her.

'Dr Billingham. Helen Crawford here. Listen, I need you to drop everything and get down to theatre. I've a friend there. She's about three months gone.'

She listened for a moment.

'No bleeding, but it sounds like her waters broke. John's with her.'

She gave the phone back to the receptionist.

'You all right, miss?' the receptionist asked.

'Course I'm all right,' Helen snapped.

She stood and thought for a moment.

'Get me an outside line,' she demanded.

The receptionist flicked a switch and handed her the receiver.

Helen leant over the counter and dialled.

'Hello, Eddy? Is Grandfather in? Good, good, so the car's there? Good. Listen, I need you to do me a favour. Is the driver still there? Can you tell him to go to 34 Tatham Street in the east end and pick up Mrs Agnes Elliot and her daughter-in-law Miss Isabelle Elliot. Tell them there's been a bit of an emergency and that Mrs Elliot's daughter, Polly, has been taken to the Royal. But please tell them not to panic. I'm sure everything's going to be OK.' Helen crossed her fingers. She was anything but sure.

Handing back the phone, Helen forced out a civil 'Thank you' to the receptionist and went to sit down on one of the chairs in the reception area.

Suddenly, she felt exhausted.

When Mr Havelock's black Jaguar pulled up outside the Elliot household, all the neighbours came to their doors to find out what the occasion was. Seeing the look on Agnes's face after opening the door and speaking to the smartly dressed chauffeur, they went back inside. This was not a celebratory visit from some bigwig.

Most watched from behind curtains as Agnes and Bel hurried out of the house.

Joe stood in the doorway with Lucille next to him. Both sombre.

The car was just pulling away when Pearl came hurrying out of the Tatham.

She spoke briefly to her daughter before stepping back and watching the car drive off.

Seeing the back of her daughter's head through the Jaguar's small rear window, Pearl felt sick to the pit of her stomach. If Isabelle hadn't been with Agnes, and there wasn't an emergency, she would have pulled her daughter out of the vehicle with her own bare hands.

Pearl shook her head, trying to rid herself of the sickening thought that by getting into the car belonging to *that* man, Isabelle was being taken away from her.

And for the first time, Pearl worried about the safety of her daughter should Charles Havelock ever find out about her. His illegitimate child. A child who was proof of the monster he really was.

'She's going to be all right, Agnes.' Bel held her mother-in-law's hand tightly. 'Trust me. I know Polly and she's a fighter. She's tougher than everyone thinks.'

Agnes looked at Bel. 'Do yer think so?' She shook her head. 'I think the girl puts on a good show, but underneath it all, she's as soft as clarts.'

She turned and stared out of the window. She recalled her daughter's words from the other day – that having Tommy's baby made her feel as if she could really keep on going if anything happened to him.

The words had jarred then; now they were clanging loud and clear in her head. The worry she had pushed under the carpet was leaping back up at her. If Polly lost

Tommy's baby – and he himself never made it back – would her daughter *really* have the will to carry on? Agnes knew her daughter inside out, but on this score, she was not so sure.

Agnes turned her attention to the driver.

'Miss Crawford didn't tell yer anything else?' she demanded.

'Sorry, ma'am, no, she didn't.' The chauffeur kept his eyes on the road.

'This is my fault,' Agnes mumbled. 'I should have made her stop working at that bloody yard. I knew it was too much. I should have put my foot down.'

Bel looked at Agnes. It was pointless reminding her mother-in-law that even if she had tried harder to get Polly to stop work, she wouldn't have succeeded. Polly was her own woman. She always had been.

'Can yer not go any faster?' Agnes leant forward so that she was practically cheek to cheek with the driver.

'Agnes.' Bel gently pulled her back onto the seat.

'I should never have had that bleedin' tea party,' Agnes said. 'It's brought bad luck.'

'Don't be ridiculous,' Bel said. 'Pol was saying how lovely it was, just you two, mother and daughter, chatting. Your tea together did good – not bad.'

Agnes didn't answer, just stared out of the car window. As they drove up Toward Road she saw yet another bombsite – it was as if the town was infested with giant molehills.

'Bloody madman!' Agnes suddenly spat out. 'It's his soddin' fault.'

Bel looked at Agnes. It was rare to hear her swear.

'The poor girl's been running to 'n from the shelter at all hours of the night . . . She's been worried sick about Tommy. Even if she doesn't show it . . .' Her face was pure fury. 'And as for the poor bab – scared stiff before it's even born.'

Bel took hold of Agnes's hand again, knowing she just needed to be allowed to rant, to get it all out as she always told them to do whenever they were angry or upset.

Afterwards, as they sat in a tense silence, Bel had to admit to herself that she too felt terribly guilty. She had been jealous of Polly for the first time in all the years they had known one another. Or rather, she'd been jealous of Polly's pregnancy. Now this had happened, she somehow felt culpable.

Logically, Bel knew she was being irrational. Being jealous couldn't cause Polly to miscarry. But, she wondered as the car trundled towards the hospital, if she hadn't been so wrapped up in her own selfish thoughts about her failure to fall pregnant, she might have seen the warning signs that something was amiss.

'Mrs Elliot . . . Bel.' Helen hurried over to meet them both as they ran into the main foyer.

'Is she all right?' Agnes demanded.

'Yes, yes, Polly's going to be all right,' Helen said.

'And the baby?' Bel asked. 'Is the baby all right?'

'That's something I'm not so sure about,' Helen admitted. 'It looks as though Polly's waters broke.'

'What do yer mean, her *waters broke*? That doesn't make sense. It's too early. Far too early,' Agnes said.

Helen looked from Agnes to Bel, her expression equally perplexed.

'I know. I've no idea. All I know is that Dr Parker was on hand as soon as she became unwell and we managed to get her to the hospital straight away and they took her down to theatre to see if they could see what's wrong.'

'She's having an operation?' Agnes said, panic-stricken.

'I'm not sure if they're actually operating on her,' Helen said. 'Or if they just need to have a look, as it were.' She looked at Bel for help.

'They'll be looking to see if they can work out why her waters broke, Agnes. Perhaps try and stop it.' Bel looked at her mother-in-law.

'But if her waters have broken, that means the bab's coming, doesn't it?' Agnes demanded.

No one said anything.

They didn't have to.

They were all thinking the same.

Agnes, Bel and Helen waited in a private room that would later be charged to Mr Havelock. As would all the medical costs. If he objected, Helen would pay out of her own pocket, but she had a feeling he wouldn't.

'Are you sure you won't let me get you both some sandwiches?' Helen asked.

'No, thank you, pet,' Agnes said, 'this tea's all I'm wanting. Thank you anyway.'

Helen looked at Bel, who shook her head and forced a smile.

'All right, but I'm going to go and get us a fresh pot and I'll see if there's an update while I'm out.' She looked at Agnes's and Bel's upturned faces. Their heartbreak was plain to see.

As Helen left the room and walked to the canteen, she thought how lovely it must be to have a family that was so normal. So caring. So loving.

'*Helen!*'

It was John.

She turned around.

'Oh John, thank God you're here.'

She took a deep breath.

'Please tell me the baby's all right?' Her eyes bore into John's.

Pleading.

Willing him to give her the answer she so desperately wanted – *needed* – to hear.

Chapter Thirty-Eight

When Polly came round from the anaesthetic, it took her a while to work out where she was and why she was lying in a hospital bed and not in her own. Her head felt foggy and her mouth dry.

Then, all of a sudden, everything came back to her like a bolt of lightning.

She craned her neck and saw a nurse dressed in a blue uniform and starched white apron at the bottom of her bed.

'My baby?' Her voice was croaky and full of fear; of her terror at what the answer might be.

Her hand automatically went to her stomach.

Please, God, please, let my baby be all right, she begged silently in her head.

Seeing her patient was waking up, the nurse quickly walked out of the room.

Seconds later Dr Parker appeared.

'Please . . . *please* tell me my baby's all right?' Polly asked. The desperation in her voice was heartbreaking. Tears were pooling in her eyes.

Dr Parker moved towards the bed and sat down on the chair next to her. His thoughts spun back momentarily to September when he had come to see Helen in this very room.

He took hold of Polly's hand, as he had done Helen's, and squeezed it.

Polly was staring at Dr Parker's face, not daring to breathe until she knew.

'Your baby's fine, Polly.' A reassuring smile appeared on his face. 'You're both going to be fine.'

Polly looked at Dr Parker.

He had saved the man she loved, and now he had saved her baby.

She wanted to grab him and hug him, but instead she simply burst out crying.

For the next few minutes, she sobbed from the very core of her being, all the while mouthing the words, 'Thank you . . . Thank you.'

'Much as I would love to take all the credit,' Dr Parker smiled at Polly, 'I have to tell you that it was another doctor who really saved your baby.'

Polly pushed herself up on the bed.

'The one I met before you took me into theatre?'

'That's the one.'

'I vaguely remember him telling me his name. It began with B . . .'

'Dr Billingham,' Dr Parker said. 'He's one of the best obstetricians in the area. Probably in the country, to be honest. He did all the work. I was just there to assist.'

Polly tried to digest what he was saying.

'But my baby is definitely all right?' Polly said.

'Yes, definitely . . . but I'm going to get Dr Billingham in to explain exactly what happened. Is that all right?'

Polly nodded.

Dr Parker stood up to leave and Polly grabbed his hand.

'Thank you. I really can't thank you enough . . . And Helen . . . I don't know what I would have done if you hadn't both been there.'

Dr Parker squeezed her hand, pushed himself out of the seat and left the room.

A few minutes later Dr Billingham bustled in.

'Well, young lady, you have been a very, very lucky woman.'

He went to check her charts at the bottom of the bed.

'Yes, you both had the gods on your side this evening. Without a doubt.'

He hooked the charts back and walked around to the side of the bed.

He remained standing.

'I'm guessing you're wondering exactly what happened?'

Polly nodded.

Dr Billingham took a deep breath.

'First of all, do you know what a cervix is?'

Polly shook her head.

Dr Billingham sighed.

Why was it women were so ignorant about their own bodies?

'The cervix is the neck of the uterus.' He looked at Polly and saw her confusion. 'The womb.'

He scratched his head, leaving a tuft of grey hair sticking up.

'The cervix joins the womb and the vagina.'

He put his hands into the pockets of his white overcoat.

'For some reason – and we don't know why this is the case for some women and not others – the cervix isn't as strong as it should be and when a woman's pregnant, and the baby is growing, it can start to soften and expand.'

Polly shuffled herself up even more in the bed until she was sitting upright. This was important.

'And *because* it's not as strong as it should be,' Dr Billingham continued, 'it can start to open. And when that happens, some of the fluids that are in the womb, helping to make your baby, start to leak through.'

Polly nodded.

'The water that came out?'

'That's right. Those waters are actually the fluids I'm talking about – they fill what is called the amniotic sac, and it is that sac which protects and cushions the baby in the womb. What you experienced was that amniotic fluid leaking out.'

Dr Billingham coughed to clear his throat.

'And this is the part where you had the gods on your side . . . There's never much warning with these things. Occasionally a little spot of blood, a few cramps, but by the sounds of it, you didn't have any of that?'

Polly shook her head.

'Just the water,' she said.

'If you hadn't managed to get to the hospital as quickly as you did,' Dr Billingham said, 'you would have, without a doubt, lost your baby.'

Polly inhaled sharply. She could feel herself starting to shake a little.

'What I managed to do before it was too late was something called a cervical cerclage,' Dr Billingham explained. 'This is really just a stitch in the cervix. "Cerclage" comes from the French word for the metal hoop around a cask. I suppose it conjures up an appropriate image. The hooped stitch closes the cervix and keeps your baby exactly where it should be until it's ready to come out. At the proper time, that is.

'I have to say that you were also doubly lucky that your waters didn't break properly – you have two layers of membranes and thankfully they didn't completely rupture. If they had, you'd have lost all your amniotic fluid, and if that had been the case, then there's no way your baby would have been able to survive.' Dr Billingham paused. 'I know this is a lot to take on board, but I'll be here tomorrow if you want to ask me any more questions.'

Polly nodded. 'Yes, please, that would be good. Thank you . . . Thank you very much, Dr Billingham. I really can't say how thankful I am. And I know my husband would be too if he knew what you've done.'

Dr Billingham smiled. John had told him the young girl was newly married and that her husband had worked for the Wear Commissioner and joined the navy as a mine-clearance diver. Brave man.

'Well, you'll be able to continue thanking me – and stroking my ego . . .' he chuckled ' . . . for the next six months or so, because I'll be keeping an eye on you. You'll need to take it easy, and I will be wanting to see you for regular check-ups.'

Charles's granddaughter had wanted Mrs Watts to have the full works. She had also stipulated that he was to be the one to deliver the baby. He had thought this was a little beneath him – what were midwives for, after all – but he'd been promised a handsome amount of money, which was not to be sniffed at.

'Righty-ho.' Dr Billingham brushed his hair back with one hand. 'You get some rest and I'll see you again in the morning. And all being well, you should be back in your own bed tomorrow night.'

Polly's face broke into a wide smile.

It was the first time Dr Billingham had noticed how pretty she was. Her husband was a lucky man.

Or he would be if he made it back in one piece.

Chapter Thirty-Nine

'Oh, my good Lord.' Agnes came bustling into the room, followed by Bel.

They both took it in turns to give Polly a hug and a kiss.

'How are yer feeling?' Agnes sank down in the chair that Dr Parker had been sitting in. She took hold of her daughter's hand, put it to her mouth and gave it a big kiss.

'I feel fine, Ma,' Polly said.

Seeing the sceptical look on both her mother's face as well as Bel's, she laughed.

'Honestly, I do. I really do feel fine.'

Polly patted her sheets, gesturing for Bel to come and sit on the bed.

When she sat down, Polly took her best friend's hand and kept hold of it as they all chatted away for the next half-hour.

Polly explained what the doctor had told her and Agnes and Bel listened intently, trying to make sense of it all. The only thing that mattered, though, was that Polly and her baby were both alive and well.

'I should never have let you keep on working at the yard,' Agnes said.

'Ma, it wouldn't have made any difference. What happened would have happened regardless, even if I'd been sat on my backside for the past three months,' Polly said.

Seeing her ma's mouth open and knowing exactly what she was going to say, Polly beat her to it.

'But don't worry, Ma, I won't be welding – not until after the baby's born,' she reassured. 'I might be stubborn but I'm not stupid.'

Agnes's relief was clear to see.

Buoyed up by Polly's well-being, Bel relayed how the curtains had been twitching along the length of Tatham Street when the chauffeur had turned up at the house, making Polly laugh as she hammed up the drama of their journey to the hospital, telling her how Agnes had verbally bullied the chauffeur, demanding to know why he couldn't drive any faster. 'I think she would have jumped into the front seat and taken the wheel if she could have,' Bel said.

They all chuckled.

Neither woman, though, told Polly how truly worried they had been . . .

When Helen walked through her front door it had just gone half-past nine.

She'd gone to Gloria's after leaving the hospital to tell her what had happened. Then, at Gloria's suggestion, she'd nipped round to see Dorothy and Angie too. Gloria had been right in guessing the pair would drop what they were doing and go straight up to the hospital.

Catching her reflection in the mirror, she stopped in her tracks. She looked dreadful. Her hair was all over the shop, her mascara smudged.

When John had told her that Polly and the baby were all right, she'd managed to keep a semblance of restraint and dignity about her – until she'd reached the Ladies, where she'd had no choice but to let the rush of tears out and run their course.

She knew, of course, that those tears weren't just for Polly and her baby, but also for her own.

Her baby girl, whom she still loved so much, and probably always would.

When she had finally managed to stop crying, she'd tried to spruce herself up, but it had been a losing battle and she'd only succeeded in making herself look worse.

Looking at her reflection again now, she had to laugh at the irony. She had been so meticulous about how she looked today in anticipation of her 'date' with John, and she'd ended up looking as if she had been dragged through a hedge backwards.

'Oh, John . . .' She spoke the words out loud. 'Would you really want to be with a woman who has not only been with another man – but got pregnant by him?'

She had been so sure of herself just four hours ago.

Now, after this evening, she wasn't so certain.

This evening had proved to her that she couldn't simply erase the past.

Walking into the lounge, Helen saw the fire was still going. She put on another shovel of coal and gave it a poke. She had the house to herself for the next hour and a half at least. Her mother never made it back from the Grand until eleven, if not later.

She looked down at her dress and felt the tear at the bottom. She'd give it to Kate – she'd put it to good use.

Walking over to the drinks cabinet, she poured herself a large gin and tonic and went to sit in the armchair nearest the fire. It wasn't particularly cold, but she felt she wanted the comfort of the heat. She also hoped the gin would slow down the rush of thoughts and feelings swirling around inside her.

Images of the day she had lost her baby kept flashing in her mind's eye.

Her baby girl would be about three months old now.

About the same age as Polly's unborn baby.

How strange.

Helen rose and put the fire guard up. The coal was spitting as the fire got going.

When John had come to find her, he'd said it'd been a close shave. If Polly hadn't found Helen when she did, if they hadn't got her to the hospital so quickly, if Dr Billingham hadn't been on hand to do the procedure . . . So many ifs.

Helen stared into the flickering flames.

The warmth and the gin began to do their work.

She sighed.

She mightn't have been able to save her own baby, but she had helped to save another.

And for that she would be eternally grateful.

Chapter Forty

Friday 26 March

It was just after a quarter-past seven in the morning. Gloria still had her overcoat buttoned up against the usual early-morning chill drifting in from the North Sea, but her face felt warm as the sun was up and ready to show off its full glory.

She had come into work a little earlier than usual to catch Rosie before the start of the shift to tell her about Polly. Last night Helen had offered to go to Brookside Gardens and tell Rosie about Polly's near miscarriage, but Gloria had put her off, knowing that Rosie was probably working at Lily's.

'And the baby's *definitely* going to be all right?' Rosie asked, her face showing concern, as well as guilt. They'd been working at full pelt yesterday on *Denewood*'s top deck – on their feet all day, either bent double or doing tricky vertical welds. She'd stopped herself moving Polly onto the lower deck to do some flat welds, where she would at least have been able to sit down while she worked. She'd been worried Polly would accuse her of fussing. She wished she had now. Wished she'd insisted Polly lay off welding altogether until after the baby was born.

'Yes, it sounds like the baby should be all right now, but I think Pol's gonna have to take it easy from here on in. They've put some kind of stitch in her to keep the baby in.'

'That sounds awful.' Rosie sat down on one of the pallets. 'Honestly, nothing goes the way it's supposed to, does it?'

Gloria let out a bitter laugh. 'God forbid!'

'So, she's still in hospital?'

Gloria nodded, sitting down next to Rosie and getting out her flask of tea.

'They'll probably discharge her today. Apparently, she's perfectly healthy. As is the baby as far as they can tell. She's just got a weak cervix.' She looked at Rosie. 'That's the neck of the womb.'

Rosie nodded. The cervix was something she unfortunately knew a lot about.

'I don't think she'll be able to do any welding work, though,' Gloria said. 'Doctor's orders. Nothing too physical or strenuous. Mind you, even if the doctor had said she could, I think Agnes would have had a complete fit. The way she was talking last night, she wants Polly bedbound for the rest of her pregnancy.'

'I can't see Polly agreeing to that,' Rosie said.

'Me neither.' Gloria looked up to see Dorothy and Angie chatting to Hannah, Olly and Martha. She guessed they were telling them about Polly.

'The doctor said she can do some kind of desk job, but nothing that's too physical,' Gloria relayed.

'I'll go and see Helen later on. See what we can work out,' Rosie said.

'I was just coming to see you.' Rosie had walked through the main doors of the admin building to see Helen hurrying down the stairs towards her. The lunchtime klaxon had just sounded out.

'I'm guessing it's about Polly?' Helen said.

Rosie nodded.

'I'm off to see her now. They're keeping her in until early evening. Just to be on the safe side.'

Rosie turned and opened the door and they both walked back out into the yard.

'But don't worry,' Helen said, 'I've got an idea. Not exactly a job swap, more of a reshuffle.'

'Brilliant,' Rosie said. 'Tell Polly I was asking about her – and that I'll pop round to Tatham Street tomorrow after work with Charlotte. That's if she's up to it.'

'Will do . . . Chat later,' Helen said, before hurrying off across the yard to the main gates.

It only took ten minutes to get to the Royal thanks to her grandfather's chauffeur and car, which she'd commandeered for the day.

Reaching Polly's room, she realised it was the same one she had been put in after her miscarriage. She forced herself to breathe normally and push away thoughts of that godforsaken day.

She knocked tentatively on the door.

'Come in.'

Helen opened the door just enough to poke her head through.

'You up for visitors?' she asked.

Polly pushed herself up in the bed.

'Come in, come in!' She waved her in and patted the chair next to her bed. 'I'm so glad you've come.'

Helen thought Polly looked well. She had roses in her cheeks and a smile on her face. She went and sat down on the chair.

'How're you feeling?'

'Well,' Polly said, 'very well.'

Helen saw that Polly was in the middle of writing a letter.

'Let me guess,' she said. 'Tommy?'

Polly nodded; tears started to wet her eyes.

'Actually, I was just telling him about you – well, you and Dr Parker.' She grabbed hold of Helen's hand. 'I was saying I didn't know how I was going to be able to thank you both for saving our baby's life.'

A tear slowly made its way down Polly's cheek.

'Still don't know.'

Helen desperately fought her own emotions. Being in the same room, seeing Polly in the same bed, had knocked her for six.

'You can thank me by making sure you look after yourself and that baby.' Helen looked down at Polly's slightly pronounced stomach.

'Oh, I fully intend to,' Polly said, her voice thick with tears. 'I don't think I could have forgiven myself if I'd lost this baby.'

'Not that it would have been your fault if you had,' Helen said, thinking of her own miscarriage. John had reassured her she was not to blame, although no one seemed to know why she'd lost her baby.

'That's what Dr Billingham told me,' Polly said, putting her letter to Tommy to the side and shuffling around so that she was facing Helen.

'I want you to know,' Polly said, looking at Helen, eyes sparkling with a mix of tears and gratitude, 'I will never forget what you and Dr Parker did for me. Never. And I don't think I will ever be able to thank you enough . . . And I know Tommy would want to thank you as well. This baby means the world to him. Especially now Arthur's gone.'

Helen nodded. Now the old man had died, Polly and their baby were his only family.

Polly sat back and sighed. Her face suddenly became sad.

'You know, I made a promise to Tommy that I'd carry on and live life to the fullest if he didn't make it back.'

She closed her eyes for a second and turned away.

'And I hate to admit this,' she opened her eyes again and looked at Helen, 'but there is a part of me that's accepted there's a good chance I won't ever see him again.'

Helen squeezed Polly's hand. Tears were pricking her own eyes.

'I knew I could keep that promise I made to him *if* I had a part of him with me.' She put her hand on her stomach and looked down. 'But if I'd lost this baby, and lost Tommy too, I really don't know if I could have.'

Helen put her other hand on top of Polly's and swallowed back her own emotions.

'Well, that's something that isn't going to happen,' she said, her voice strong and determined. 'What happens to Tommy is out of our hands, but we're going to do everything possible to make sure that this baby survives – and that it arrives in this world healthy and bawling its little lungs out.'

Chapter Forty-One

Two days later Helen called Rosie in to tell her that she had managed to get Polly a temporary position as the yard's timekeeper. It meant she could sit down whenever she wanted or needed to, and Alfie had been more than happy to head over to admin. He had been pestering the accounts manager for a while to be considered for any vacancies that might come up, and was taking to his new job like a fish to water.

Polly's move went some way to appeasing Agnes, but she still wasn't exactly over the moon. She had the sense, though, to realise that Polly was not prepared to be wrapped in cotton wool and would go stir-crazy if she had to stay at home – much as this would have been Agnes's preferred option.

Mother and daughter did agree on one thing, however, and that was telling Tommy what had happened, although their reasons for doing so were different.

Polly wanted her husband to know everything about their baby, even if Tommy was thousands of miles away. She had thought about Dr Billingham's words that the baby had been 'very, very lucky', and she wanted Tommy to know that their child was special and strong – a real survivor.

Agnes's thinking was more down to earth and practical. She wanted Tommy to know what had happened – how close Polly had been to losing their baby. She wanted him to know that nothing was certain and this pregnancy might not be all smooth sailing.

Polly had asked Bel to type a thank-you letter to Mr Havelock for the kind use of his car and chauffeur, and for paying the medical bills, but Bel kept forgetting – or putting it off. Polly couldn't decide which. When Polly reminded Bel – yet again – about the letter, she was taken aback when Pearl stuck her oar in, saying that the likes of the Havelocks didn't care about thank-you letters, and that from what she'd heard, it had been Helen who had organised everything – *not* the 'auld man'.

Every week Polly got the tram to the Royal to see Dr Billingham during her lunch break, then had a cuppa with Helen in her office afterwards.

Helen had been surprised that Polly genuinely liked Dr Billingham, and it was clear Dr Billingham had a soft spot for Polly, who, he'd said, reminded him of his own daughter presently serving in the Wrens.

Polly never asked how Helen knew Dr Billingham and Helen never volunteered an explanation.

She might have presumed that it was simply because of Helen's friendship with Dr Parker, but suspected there was more to it. When she was being prepped for theatre, she had overheard Dr Billingham asking Dr Parker how Helen was 'doing', and as the sedative had started to kick in, she was sure she'd heard Dr Billingham saying something about 'losing the baby'.

Polly remembered last year, when Helen had been rushed to hospital with a ruptured appendix and had been off work for a week recovering. Could that have been a cover story? Had Helen really been pregnant? She remembered Dorothy and Angie saying that Helen looked like she was putting on weight, and how she had then gone through a spell of looking rough. Throughout it all, Gloria had risen to Helen's defence.

Was that why? Because Gloria knew what Helen was really going through, but couldn't tell them all?

Was that why Helen had been so determined to save her baby – because she had lost her own?

Of course, Polly would never talk about her suspicions to anyone. She owed Helen her loyalty at the very least.

She had asked Helen about the costs, but her words had been shooed away with the wave of a hand. Helen had reminded her of Polly's own generosity in giving away her wedding money – Tommy's gratuity pay – to charity, adding that it was Mr Havelock's way of helping the wives left behind by the town's menfolk. 'It's the very least he can do,' Helen said.

Polly heard a hardness in Helen's tone, which puzzled her. She'd thought Helen and her grandfather were close.

The sound of church bells could now be heard summoning the townsfolk to church as the government had decided that the ban on bell-ringing could be lifted from Easter Sunday. The preaching on faith and hope was a message the whole country needed to hear.

Easter, however, had to be enjoyed without chocolate – or even paste eggs – although the Regal pushed the boat out and made a display of giant eggs and put day-old chicks in a glass case for the town's children. Gloria took Hope and was surprised when Dorothy and Toby, who had been given a twenty-four-hour pass, turned up and took them for a special tea at Meng's afterwards. Gloria thought they made a good match.

Hannah and Rina prayed that the tide might be turning when it came to what was being referred to as the 'plight of the Jews'. The situation was being discussed by Allied governments in Bermuda. Meanwhile, on the eve of Passover, the Warsaw ghetto uprising began in earnest, with the

Jewish community resisting German attempts at deportation. And in occupied Belgium, partisans attacked a railway convoy transporting Jews to Auschwitz. Over two hundred Jews were reported to have escaped from what was being labelled a 'Holocaust train'.

On Easter Monday the whole country celebrated the significant victory in Tunisia with the taking of Longstop Hill – a key position on the breakout road to Tunis. It followed the release of the Ministry of Information film *Desert Victory*, a documentary feature about the campaign in North Africa, which Joe and Bel went to see on a rare date together.

Easter meant school holidays, which in turn meant that Rosie had to work out how to keep Charlotte occupied – no mean feat. The problem was solved by Charlotte working part-time at Thompson's in the administrative department and taking over their 'current-affairs classes' in the canteen at lunchtime.

Rosie was particularly happy that not only was Charlotte being kept busy and out of mischief, but she was also getting to know the women who had saved them both from their uncle, for there had never been any doubt in her mind that if they hadn't come to her aid that day, her own life would have ended and Charlotte's would have been ruined.

Helen, meanwhile, decided to put her decision to live a life of no regrets on hold, arguing that doing what she had intended to do with John the evening of Polly's near miscarriage might have ended up being a huge mistake. She had a habit of plunging into life – and more so, love – head first, only to resurface and find herself surrounded by chaos.

She needed more time.

Besides, there was no rush, anyway, *was there?*

Instead, she resolved to simply continue the way they were.

When Gloria asked if she was going to try for a rerun of her 'date' with Dr Parker at Mrs Hoggart's café, Helen shook her head and told her, 'Not at the moment.'

Gloria didn't say anything, but Helen knew that she wasn't fooling the woman who had been more of a mother to her in the past year than her real mum had. What had happened to Polly had affected Helen more than she liked to let on. The wound, which she'd hoped had healed, had reopened. On top of which, her mother's words about being *sullied* and *tarnished goods* kept poking their way back into her consciousness.

Helen finally found the opportunity to take some time off to go and visit her father in Scotland, after which she went to spend a few days with her aunty Margaret and uncle Angus. When she'd told them about what had happened to Polly, her aunty had talked openly for the first time about her many miscarriages. It was only then that it occurred to Helen that her own inability to carry a child full term might well be a family problem.

Typically, it was while she was away that the King and Queen decided to pay a visit to the town and it was Thompson's they decided to visit – along with Laing's further up the river. They arrived at the station in the Royal Train and stayed for two and a half hours. Helen knew all of this because her mother rang her sister while Helen was there to relay every minute detail. She told Margaret to tell Helen she had saved the *Sunderland Echo*, so she could read all about it herself and see all the 'fabulous' photographs of the royal couple.

By the time Helen returned home, the furore over the visit had just about died down, but Helen could feel the shift in tempo and see the lift in the workers' spirits. King

George and his queen had succeeded in doing what they had gone there to do – raise morale.

On her return, Helen had been hoping to have another meeting with Georgina for an update, but the investigation into Bel's parentage had to be put on hold for a few weeks as Georgina's father had been unwell.

Now more than ever, Helen was convinced that Bel was a Havelock. Since Bel had perfected her shorthand skills, she was in Helen's office at least once a day, having letters dictated to her, or taking notes to be typed up into reports. Helen had noticed certain mannerisms that were identical to her mother's – the way she moved her hands when talking, and the way she walked . . . It was quite uncanny, especially as Bel and Miriam had barely ever spoken more than a few words to one another.

Throughout April the town's yards celebrated more launches – Laing's sent the *Empire Inventor* down the ways, Short Brothers the *Empire Manor*, Doxford's *Trevelyan*, Bartram's the *Empire Rock*, Austin's the *Empire Judy* and Thompson's *Denewood*.

Work was busy, but Helen made time to do something she had vowed to do on the evening she had clambered into the St John's ambulance.

She learnt to drive.

Chapter Forty-Two

Holme Café, Holmeside, Sunderland

Saturday 1 May

Georgina watched as Rosie said something to a young girl she presumed was her younger sister.

The girl rolled her eyes theatrically before disappearing into the boutique next door.

Sighing heavily, Rosie turned and walked the few yards to the café.

Georgina thought Rosie looked a little run ragged, but not unhappy.

'At last, we've finally found the time!' Rosie declared as she sat down at the little table Georgina had commandeered for them five minutes earlier.

Georgina laughed. 'I can't believe it's taken us so long to find the time to snatch a quick cuppa.' She tried not to show that she was a little nervous. She'd never been very good at socialising. It was probably why she didn't have many friends.

'I know,' Rosie said. 'There never seems to be a spare minute in the day, does there?'

She looked over at the waitress to show her that they were ready to order.

'I'm so sorry I've had to cancel – *twice* – you must think I'm incredibly rude,' Rosie said, returning her attention to Georgina.

'No, don't be daft. Of course I don't. I know you're work-ing more or less round the clock.' Georgina could have kicked herself. Rosie had not told her about her evening job. 'I mean,' she added quickly, 'at the yard, with all the overtime everyone's having to do.'

Rosie thought Georgina seemed a little flustered.

'There's that, but I've also got an evening job,' Rosie said.

She was suddenly aware of the waitress hovering over her shoulder. 'I'll have a cup of tea, please.'

'And I'll have a coffee, please. Black, no milk,' Georgina said.

Rosie smiled. She knew it was what her mam used to drink.

'Anything to eat?' the waitress asked.

They shook their heads and the skinny blonde girl hur-ried off.

'So, you've got another job?' Georgina said, trying her hardest to sound genuinely ignorant when nothing could be further from the truth.

'Yes, I do the bookkeeping for a woman in Ashbrooke,' Rosie said. Since Charlotte had burst back into her life, she'd realised she needed to be open – or at least relatively so – about her life and in particular her work at Lily's. It would seem odd – suspicious, even – if she didn't mention her evening job and further down the line Georgina was to find out.

'That's interesting.' Georgina was surprised by Rosie's honesty. 'A bit different to welding?'

'I know,' Rosie said. 'But at least it means I'm not on my feet all day and all night.'

Georgina felt herself blush. *She certainly wouldn't be. Not doing the kind of work she knew was being carried out at the place called Lily's.*

The waitress came over with a tray. They waited until she transferred their drinks onto the table and left.

'And what is it *you* do?' Rosie asked. 'Mam said you were a – what were her exact words? – a "right bright bairn". I remember her saying you always had your head in a book whenever she called round.'

Georgina blushed at the compliment.

'Well, funnily enough, I also do bookkeeping, accounts – that kind of thing.' *God, she hated lying. But she couldn't exactly tell her the truth, could she?*

'Is that why Helen had you in for an interview?' Rosie asked.

'Sort of,' Georgina stalled, recalling what she and Helen had agreed to tell Rosie. 'I'm helping with the annual audit and can work faster and more efficiently at home.'

'I suppose it also means you can be there for your dad. You said he had bad arthritis?'

Georgina nodded. 'He has his good days and his bad days.' She took a sip of her coffee. 'Was that your sister I saw you with just now – the young girl going into the boutique next door?'

'Yes,' Rosie sighed, 'and she's the other reason I've barely got a minute to spare these days.'

'She certainly looks full of life,' Georgina said with a smile.

'That's one way of putting it!' Rosie laughed.

'Just like your mam,' Georgina said.

Rosie laughed again.

'I wonder what our mams would say if they could see us now?' Georgina said.

'They're probably up there now. Your mam drinking her black coffee and mine her milky tea,' said Rosie.

Georgina thought they would have plenty to talk about – although she knew for certain that her own mother would not be happy with her daughter. Nor with the fact that just about every word she had spoken so far had been a lie. Honesty had been the virtue her mother had tried her hardest to instil in her. Georgina did *so* want to have a friend with whom she could be truthful. But she was kidding herself, wasn't she? She was setting herself up for a fall. If Rosie found out that not only was she a private investigator, but the person who had dug up all the dirt on her women welders, she'd hate her.

Georgina mightn't know how Mrs Crawford had used the information she had given her, but she was pretty sure her reasons had been far from altruistic.

'Just stand still,' Kate said. She was on her knees, pinning the hem of Charlotte's new skirt.

Charlotte didn't seem able to stay still for more than thirty seconds.

'There! All done.' Kate got to her feet and scrutinised the skirt.

'It looks lovely.' Charlotte twirled in front of the full-length mirror.

'No attempts at a pirouette, please,' said Kate, walking over to the curtain that divided the shop from the back snug. 'And don't fling the skirt about. Hand it to me as soon as you've taken it off.'

Charlotte tiptoed into the make-do-and-mend changing room as though pretending to wear high heels.

'Do you think you could do the hem while I wait?' Charlotte said from behind the curtain. Her hand appeared, holding the skirt.

'It depends how long I have the pleasure of your company, Charlie.' Kate smiled to herself. She loved Charlotte to pieces, but she wouldn't want to swap places with Rosie. She couldn't be getting a moment's peace.

'Rosie said she'd be an hour – at the most – with her new friend next door, but that you just had to come and get her if you'd had enough of me before then.'

Kate had to laugh.

'Come on then, I should be able to get this hem done in that time.'

A few minutes later Kate was sitting in front of her beloved Singer, carefully laying out Charlotte's new blue skirt. She'd love to be able to tell Charlotte that it had once been Helen's dress, but, of course, she couldn't. Kate afforded all her clients complete privacy.

'So,' Charlotte said, walking slowly around the boutique, inspecting whatever item of clothing, fabric or haberdashery fell into her vision. 'You know when there's an air raid?'

'Mmm,' Kate said, concentrating on threading the machine.

'Do you all go down to the basement?'

'No, Charlotte,' Kate laughed, 'we all go out and have a party in the backyard . . . Of course we go into the basement. Why are you asking?'

Charlotte ignored the question.

'And do you all go to bed straight afterwards?'

Kate chuckled.

'Lily's not a great believer in beauty sleep – she claims not to need it.'

'So,' Charlotte mused, 'if there's an air raid, she'd probably stay up afterwards.'

Kate pulled the thread through the needle.

'What's that expression you love so much – "Is the pope a Catholic?"'

Charlotte smiled and picked out a blue ribbon from a basket on the side, waving it around in the air.

'And does Lily have many visitors during the day?'

Kate stopped what she was doing and looked at Charlotte. 'Not really.'

'I didn't think so,' Charlotte said, putting the ribbon back and touching a roll of fabric that was leaning against the wall near the front door.

'Then why do you ask?' Kate tried to keep her voice casual as she started sewing the hem.

'Oh, no reason.'

A pause.

'It was just a while back, when Marjorie was visiting, we were going to call in on Lily on the way to the yard, but we didn't.'

Kate remembered the day. Rosie had been furious about it. She'd managed to keep a lid on it so as not to make Charlotte suspicious, but as soon as she'd been free to let rip, she hadn't held back.

'And?' Kate asked, manoeuvring the skirt around carefully, ensuring the hem was perfectly straight.

'And we saw some bloke come out the front door. He looked a little worse for wear. As if he'd just woken up, but it was nearly midday.'

'You never know with Lily,' Kate said, keeping her eyes on the fabric. 'She might have been helping someone out for the night. Someone down on their luck. For all her brash exterior, she can be a right softie at heart.' She stopped and looked up at Charlotte. 'Lily took me in when no one would even have spoken to me, never mind fed me or given me a bed. She's always taking in waifs and strays.'

Kate knew Charlotte felt comfortable with her. Connected. Perhaps because they came from the same village and were orphaned at around the same age. Thankfully, Charlotte had not found herself being looked after by the likes of Sister Bernadette and some of the other nuns who had made Kate's life so hellish that she had sought solace on the streets rather than within the four walls of Nazareth House.

'Did you know my uncle Raymond?' Charlotte suddenly asked.

'No.' Kate's reply was curt. 'He died before I met up with your sister again.'

'What? He's dead? Rosie didn't say.'

Kate cursed silently.

'Sorry to disturb you, Rosie.' Kate snuck round the door and into Rosie's office.

'Come in, Kate,' Rosie said, looking up from her ledger. 'I could do with a break. What's up? You look worried.'

Kate walked over to the chair and sat down. Clasping her hands together as though in prayer, she told Rosie about her conversation with Charlotte earlier that day.

'Oh dear,' Rosie sighed. 'I think I've been kidding myself that Charlotte would lose herself with new friends at her new school. Lose interest in me and Lily and our lives. But she hasn't. She just wants to be with me all the time. Or Lily. Or you.'

'I think she's trying to make up for lost time,' Kate mused.

Rosie furrowed her brow in a questioning look.

'For all those years she was on her own, with no family, no one to love and no one to love her back. Now she's got the sister she adores, an eccentric mother figure who is nothing like her own mam, so she doesn't have to feel guilty . . . And then there's me, her connection to her old, happier life. I probably fall into the role of the middle child. Not quite an older sister – more of an equal.'

Rosie felt like pouring herself a cognac but didn't. She never liked to drink in front of Kate when it was just the two of them.

'I think you're right.' She sighed and sat back in her chair. 'But can you imagine if she finds out the truth?'

Rosie stood up and walked over to the mantelpiece.

'Her whole world will be destroyed.'

'You really think so?' Kate turned to look at Rosie.

'I do,' Rosie said. 'She's so innocent. I've kept her so sheltered. She has no idea about places like this.' Rosie looked around. 'Can you imagine her shock if she found out what really goes on at Lily's? And worse still, that I didn't always *just* do the books here?'

'But,' Kate said, 'like all the women here, you did what you did for a reason. You did what you did to keep her safe. To keep her at Runcorn and away from certain people.' Kate never liked to say Raymond's name.

'But that's the point.' Rosie walked over to the chaise longue and sat down. 'If she finds out why – that *she* was the reason I did what I did – it would destroy her. I know Charlotte, and even though she tries to make out she's very hardy, she's far from it.' Rosie exhaled. 'Honestly, I don't know if she would ever be the same.'

Kate looked at her friend. The friend who had saved her life. She loved her so much. Her heart broke for her, for she knew that there was only one way this was going to end.

'Rosie, you've managed to keep Charlotte safe her whole life. You've protected her like a lion does her cubs. And here you are now, still trying to protect her. But I think you have to realise that Charlotte isn't a cub any more. She needs to be able to survive on her own.'

Kate looked at Rosie.

'I think it's time you stopped protecting her.'

Chapter Forty-Three

'Why didn't you tell me that our uncle had died?' Charlotte was sitting at the kitchen table while Rosie made the hot chocolate. 'Kate told me this afternoon.'

'I know she did.' Rosie turned around, her back to the stove. 'She told me she felt bad about it. She presumed I'd already told you.'

'So why *didn't* you tell me? I remember asking you about him after Arthur's funeral.' Charlotte was genuinely perplexed.

'Well, that was exactly why I didn't tell you then,' Rosie said. 'Because the day was sad enough already without me adding to it by telling you about someone else who had died.'

'Yes, but I wouldn't have been that sad,' Charlotte argued. 'I mean, I didn't even know him, did I?'

Rosie turned back to the stove. She took the pan off the hob and poured the milk into a mug.

'So, what happened to him? What did he die of?' Charlotte asked.

'He fell into the river and drowned after having one too many,' Rosie said.

'Really? Gosh, that's quite a dramatic way to go, isn't it?' Charlotte was intrigued.

'It is,' Rosie said, handing her the hot chocolate.

'So, was there a funeral or anything?' Charlotte asked, wanting to know more.

'The Borough buried him,' Rosie said; she was working hard to keep her voice steady.

'What? So, he had a pauper's funeral?'

Rosie nodded.

'Poor Uncle Raymond,' Charlotte said, taking a sip of her drink.

Rosie banged the pan into the sink and turned on the cold water full blast. 'Oh, I think he was old. He'd had his life.'

'Still,' Charlotte said, fascinated by such a bizarre death, 'it's a pretty grisly way to go, isn't it? Drowning in the middle of the night. In the Wear.'

Rosie forced herself not to say anything.

'Funny that Mam never mentioned him to us, isn't it? That we only got to know we had an uncle when he turned up for the funeral?'

'I don't think Mam and him got on,' Rosie said. She'd expected a grilling, but still, it was excruciating having to stop herself from telling Charlotte that their sick and perverted uncle did not deserve one iota of her kind thoughts or sympathy.

'Actually,' Rosie said, determined to change the subject, 'some good did come of it.'

Charlotte looked at her sister, surprised.

'How's that?' she asked.

'Well, it was Peter who came to tell me, as next of kin, that he'd died. Peter was the detective sergeant in charge of the case.'

'The officer in charge of the case?' Charlotte's eyes widened. 'Why was there a case?'

'Well, there's always a case if someone dies unnaturally,' Rosie explained.

'So, they didn't think anyone had *pushed* him in the river?' Charlotte's eyes widened even more. 'They didn't think he'd been murdered?'

'Honestly, Charlie.' Rosie forced out fake laughter. 'You have such a vivid imagination. Of course Peter didn't think anyone had killed him. It was just a process they have to go through. Legally.'

Charlotte sipped her hot chocolate, her mind churning over what she'd heard from Rosie this evening – and earlier on from Kate.

She suddenly perked up. 'It's a bit morbid though.'

'What is?' Rosie asked.

'Meeting your future husband when he comes to inform you someone's died.'

Rosie laughed.

This time it was genuine.

Charlotte looked at her sister and thought she had a strange sense of humour.

Half an hour later, after finishing off her homework and saying goodnight, Charlotte was up in her bedroom, looking through her wardrobe. She pulled out the hanger with her new skirt and looked at it. She couldn't wait to wear it next time she went out. Lily had promised to take her into town and give her a tour of the best places to shop.

She put it back on the rail and pushed some of her boring old clothes aside so she could look at her red dress. Her favourite dress. Now her only dress, after she'd convinced Rosie she'd grown out of all her old ones and foisted them off on Kate.

As she got ready for bed she kept thinking about her sister. Why did she keep feeling that Rosie was lying to her? Or at least keeping things from her. Like about their uncle Raymond. Why hadn't Rosie told her he'd died? And in such unusual circumstances.

It seemed odd she'd held back from telling her at Arthur's funeral. Did she really think she'd get upset about someone she didn't even know? Someone she'd met just the once? Someone she could barely recall.

Then there were the white lies about Lily. Rosie had told her that Lily went to bed early, yet it was clear from Kate's reaction that this was most definitely not the case. And knowing that Lily was a night owl, why had Rosie refused to seek sanctuary there that night of the air raid? It would have been much safer than running all the way back home.

Even the other night, when they'd gone to check Lily and everyone else was all right after the really bad air raid, Rosie wouldn't pop in for a quick cuppa. It was as though she was trying to hide something from her – something to do with Lily, or the house where Lily lived.

Jumping into her bed, Charlotte reached under the mattress and pulled out her diary. She turned to the back, where there was a page full of arithmetic. Lots of additions and subtractions. The final figure showed a big minus sign with an equally large number next to it. Thanks to Marjorie, or rather Marjorie's parents' openness about their personal finances and the cost of their daughter's private education, Charlotte had been able to work out roughly how much it cost Rosie to send her to the Sunderland Church High School. This included extras such as a new uniform, overalls and gym kit.

So much didn't add up.

There was her wage at the yard (she had seen Rosie's wage packet so knew exactly how much she got paid with and without overtime), plus the money she reckoned she got paid for doing Lily's books. (She had asked her teacher at school one day about jobs and what kinds of wages one could expect to get paid for certain jobs. Her teacher had commented on how impressed she was that Charlotte was thinking so sensibly about her future. She had even been inspired to dedicate a whole lesson to the subject.) The total of both jobs still fell short of the amount needed to pay for her schooling. Even if she had underestimated Rosie's earnings, it was still not enough to pay for her education and keep them both fed and watered.

The only way her sister could just about scrape by was if she was making money on the flat she owned. But it sounded as though that was more of an investment and any money she got for rent went straight to George to pay off the money he had loaned her.

Charlotte sat back and chewed the end of her pen.

She looked at her open wardrobe.

At her lovely red dress.

The red of the material was the same red she had seen at Lily's that day.

She had only managed to glimpse the room for a few seconds, but what she'd seen was unforgettable. Amazing. Red embossed wallpaper, a red and gold Persian rug, a huge gilt-framed mirror, and a massive brass four-poster bed piled high with plush red cushions. Charlotte had had to force herself not to run and jump on it.

The more she thought about that red room, the more she wondered whose bedroom it was. She knew Kate had the top attic room, which Lily often lamented was more a 'seamstress's sweatshop' than a bedroom, and that Lily's 'boudoir' was on the second floor – as were Vivian's and Maisie's.

So, whose bedroom was it?

Chapter Forty-Four

1940

At around the same time as the first bombs were dropped on British soil, Rosie was given the task of training up a mishmash group of women welders – half a dozen women, aged eighteen to forty, whose backgrounds ranged from selling china in the town's most high-class and exclusive department store to serving cakes at a seaside café. There had been opposition to the town's womenfolk working in the yards and doing such traditionally male jobs, but in the end concerns about gender had had to be pushed aside. Too many men had marched off to war, leaving too few to build the ships that were desperately needed to win it.

It was around this time that someone else made an appearance in Rosie's life. Someone she had hoped and prayed she would never have to set eyes on again.

Raymond Gallagher had just spent the last few years incarcerated in HMP Durham. His sentence, handed down to him after he'd been found guilty of raping several women in the town, had been cut short after he'd been given a 'ticket of leave' due to the outbreak of war.

Strangely enough, it had been Bel who had, unwittingly, been the first to make Raymond's acquaintance when she was working as a clippie on the number 66 Durham-to-Sunderland service. He'd made her skin crawl with his leering manner and sinister ram's-head walking stick.

Arriving back in his old hunting ground, Raymond had gone straight to Thompson's. He was unsure whether he would recognise his niece; after all, she had only been fifteen when he had seen her last. He needn't have worried, though, for the woman he spotted hurrying out of the gates at the end of the shift – haversack and gas mask slung over her shoulder, hair wrapped up in a patterned headscarf – was the spit of her mother, his sister Eloise.

Hidden from view, he'd followed Rosie back to her bedsit in Grange Terrace, and then a little later to the leafier suburb of Ashbrooke.

He'd watched her enter the house in West Lawn through the back door and his heart had lifted when he'd spotted the little red light shining through the partially drawn curtains.

On seeing Raymond standing in the drawing room at Lily's, Rosie had thought she was back in one of her nightmares. The ones that featured his face, his rancid smell, the wet of his spittle as he spat threats into her ear.

Thank God Charlie was miles away from this place. Safe in her all-girls school.

'Monsieur Gallagher, you didn't tell me you knew Rosie personally? Perhaps we should all retire to the kitchen so I can hear more about your former acquaintance.'

Rosie heard Lily's words, saw her look across at George, and felt her hand guiding her out of the reception room, where the other girls and clients were socialising.

Staring at him – unable to speak, her legs like jelly – she realised her instinct had been right. She had tried to run and hide from this man for years, but he had found her, as deep down she'd always known he would.

'What's all this about then?' Lily did nothing to hide her cockney roots as she placed both hands on the end of the large kitchen table and leant forward.

'Madame,' Raymond sneered, adjusting the lapels on the dapper three-piece suit he'd pilfered during a recent air raid, 'I've simply come to call in – how shall I put it? – an outstanding debt.'

'The debt being?' George asked.

'My dear, sadly departed sister, Eloise,' Raymond explained, a smile playing on his lips, 'may well have been tragically killed – mown down by some heartless hit-and-run driver – but the substantial amount of money she owed me is, well, still owed. An amount, I have to add, that has grown with interest over the past few years.'

His eyes fell on Rosie.

'An amount that has now fallen on my sister's daughter to pay.'

'She's no money to give you,' Lily said. Her words were met with another sneer from Raymond, the parting of his thin lips revealing yellow, nicotine-stained teeth.

'I doubt that very much, *Madame* Lily,' he said. 'In fact, I'd say the opposite is true. I'd wager that Rosie has plenty of money to give me. What with her work here.' He lifted his stick in the air. 'On top of the wage she gets from Thompson's, I'd say the girl's doing pretty well for herself.' Another smirk. 'Her mam and dad would be proud.'

Rosie eyed him with pure hatred.

Raymond laughed.

'Rosie, it's very simple – if you don't give me what I'm owed, I will make sure that every shipyard worker in the town knows exactly where yer gan every other evening. You'll never be able to show that pretty face of yers in any of the shipyards from here to kingdom come. And I'll also make sure that the headmistress of that posh school yer lovely little sister gans to knows exactly how yer managing to pay their fees . . . Oh, and I must say, Charlotte's looking like yer double these days, isn't she? My, isn't she growing up fast?'

Only then did Rosie find her tongue – and her fists – and physically go for him.

'I'll kill you with my own bare hands if you so much as look at my sister!' Now it was *her* spittle that was gracing *his* cheeks.

But Rosie's loss of control only seemed to please him more and he left the bordello a happy, satisfied man. He knew he had Rosie cornered. Not only was he going to get his money and wreak his revenge on the dead, but he was also going to enjoy playing with his prey.

Rosie knew her only option was to pay him. But still, she was determined to keep Charlotte safe – far away from the evil that had re-entered her life. And the only way of doing that was by continuing to pay her sister's school fees, which meant working every waking minute of every day.

For three months Rosie worked herself to the bone to make the weekly instalments to Raymond. The women welders started to voice their concerns about Rosie's physical and mental state quietly amongst themselves. Not only were her overalls now hanging off her as she'd lost so much weight, but she looked grey and gaunt.

Lily was also worried sick, frustrated that she too was powerless in the face of Raymond's threats. The situation would only be resolved if his poisonous life was to be snuffed out, but much as it had gone through both Lily's and Rosie's heads, doing it was a whole other ball game. Neither had the stomach for cold-blooded murder, even if it would have been totally justifiable.

The noose Raymond had put around Rosie's neck was tightened further when he wrote a letter to Charlotte's school requesting a visit, showing Rosie that he not only knew exactly where her sister was, but he was primed to see through his threat if need be.

And then, as if her life couldn't get any worse, Raymond broke into her bedsit and found her wage slips – evidence that she was holding back money she had earned doing overtime.

And it had made him angry.

Very angry.

Chapter Forty-Five

Saturday 8 May

'At the moment there are artificial legs available that have bending knee joints – a prosthetic knee socket – but the knee needs to be locked in place when the patient stands upright and then released with the press of a switch in order to bend it when sitting down.'

Dr Parker took a quick sip of his pint. He was sitting with Helen at their table in the Railway Inn. 'What's being developed at the moment – and what I'm really keen to be a part of – is a limb that mimics real movement.'

'And how would you be able to do that?' Helen asked. She knew prosthetics was what John really wanted to specialise in when the war was over. It was her belief that, having been forced to amputate so many limbs, he was driven by a need to redress the balance.

'That's the interesting part.' Dr Parker pushed back his hair; it had a tendency to flop forward, something Helen knew happened more frequently around the time he needed to go to the barbers. She'd have to remind him. 'There's been talk of a new "smart" knee that would only lock when the pressure from the heel of the artificial leg hits the ground. It would then bend when there was pressure on the toes, creating the feel of a natural walk.'

'Gosh, that sounds very clever,' Helen said. 'Very pioneering.'

'Well, it's about time there was some kind of advancement,' Dr Parker said, looking at Helen and silently reprimanding himself for feeling desire. Helen was a friend. That was all it was and ever would be. 'Most of the artificial limbs we have in use at the moment are made of wood and leather. It's prehistoric, really. They're too heavy, and too hard to keep clean, especially as they absorb perspiration.'

They were quiet for a moment.

'And talking about amputees, how's young Jacob?' Helen asked.

'Oh, he's getting a little better,' Dr Parker said.

'Just a little?' Helen took another sip of her vodka and lemon. She had not had much to eat during the day and she could feel it going to her head. They were sitting next to each other, their shoulders almost touching. Helen had been fighting the urge to lean into him all evening. It was as though the vodka was making her resolution to keep John at arm's length falter.

'Well, what is really good is that he's agreed to a transfer to the asylum, providing he stays under the care of Dr Eris.'

'That's good. Sounds like this Dr Eris has quite a way with patients.'

Dr Parker finished off his bitter and looked at the froth now languishing in the bottom of the glass. 'One for the road?'

'Why not?' Helen said. She looked at the clock. They had another forty minutes before she had to catch her train.

A few minutes later Dr Parker was back, a vodka and lemon in one hand and a beer in the other.

'And Polly's keeping all right?' he asked, putting their drinks down.

'Yes, she's really well,' Helen said. 'I saw her yesterday after she'd been to see Dr Billingham and he seems more than happy with how the pregnancy's going.'

'She must be what? About four – four and a half months gone now?' Dr Parker said. He looked at Helen, tried to read her face. She would be thinking of when she'd been at that stage of her own pregnancy.

'About that,' she said.

'And Tommy's all right?' he asked tentatively.

'Yes, he's writing lots, which is keeping Polly's anxieties at bay. Not that she would admit to having any,' Helen said.

'And how's everyone else at work?

'They're the same as always.' Helen smiled. 'Harold's spending his day shuffling paper, I'm doing his work for him, wishing *he* would shuffle off into an early retirement.'

Dr Parker laughed.

'And the women?'

'They're working flat out,' Helen said. 'Rosie's not got a replacement for Polly yet, but she seems happy to carry on the way they are for the moment. I don't think she wants Polly to feel like she's being pushed out if they get another woman welder. Plus, it means Rosie'll have to train the new girl up if we get one.'

They chatted on for a while longer.

'Dear me!' Dr Parker said during a lull in the conversation. 'I can't believe we've got through a whole evening without mentioning your Miss Marple.'

'No, neither can I,' Helen said. 'That's probably because there's not been much happening. Georgina's had to put the investigation on hold for a short while. Her father's not been too well.' Knowing that the next question off John's lips would be about the old man's medical ailment, she beat him to it. 'Arthritis by the sounds of it.'

She took a sip of her vodka.

'But we're due to meet up later on in the week for an update.'

'I will be intrigued to hear what – if anything – she has unearthed,' Dr Parker said.

Chapter Forty-Six

Five days later

Thursday 13 May

Walking from the tram stop down Bridge Street, Helen found herself glancing around, as though she were some character in a spy movie. She just needed to be wearing a mac with the collar pulled up and she would have looked the part.

Crossing the road, she glanced over at the Grand. Thankfully, it would be too early for her mother to be in there now, but still she hurried past, just in case.

Heading towards High Street West, Helen kept a beady eye out for anyone she might know, or who might know her. It was imperative no one saw where she was going.

When she reached the very innocuous-looking doorway at the corner where the two streets met, she had a quick look round to double-check she had not been spotted. Once through the main door, she started to breathe more freely, taking in the musty smell of the building's interior, which had seen better days.

She hurried along the hallway, still a little anxious that she might bump into someone she knew. Georgina had informed her that there was also a music teacher on the ground floor, as well as a solicitor who worked from home.

Seeing the brass plaque that read *Mr Pickering & Sons* to the side of the door, Helen rang the bell. She'd just taken her finger off the ringer when the door opened.

'Good afternoon, Miss Crawford.'

Helen looked at the old man welcoming her in. This had to be Georgina's father. He was exactly as her mother had described, grey-haired, dressed in a slightly shabby-looking three-piece suit and sporting a lopsided dicky bow. There was no evidence of a gravy stain, though.

'Mr Pickering, lovely to meet you,' Helen said, shaking his gnarled hand.

'Come in, come in, my dear.' He waved Helen through to the hallway before overtaking her and showing her into the main dining room.

'Georgina thought it might be better to conduct your meeting in this room rather than the office as it's so stuffy and hot today. This is by far the coolest room.'

'Of course, that sounds like a sensible option.' Helen stood and took in the large, high-ceilinged room that was not unlike her own dining room, only shabbier. But it was homely, and Helen could see that Georgina had already put a tea tray out on the long, oval-shaped table in anticipation of her arrival.

Turning her attention back to Mr Pickering, she thought she recognised him.

'You look familiar, Mr Pickering,' Helen said, putting her handbag and gas mask on the table. 'Do we know each other?'

Mr Pickering smiled.

'We don't know each other, but we have met once before. Very briefly,' he said.

He had braced himself for Helen asking him such a question; had resolved not to say anything unless she did.

'And where was that?' she asked, unsure what it was that had jogged her memory. Was it the gold-rimmed spectacles? Or his voice, soft and well spoken, with a hint of a northern accent?

'If my memory serves me right,' Mr Pickering said, 'it was one afternoon at the end of April last year. You were coming out of Mowbray Park.'

Helen felt her heart hammer. It had been the day she had thought Theodore was going to propose to her, but instead he'd dumped her. She had been devastated, had practically staggered out of the park, and had needed to rest against a wall to regain her composure.

'I remember,' Helen said, staring at Mr Pickering, her mind transported back to that humiliating day. 'You came and asked me if I was all right.' She smiled at Mr Pickering. At the time she had felt like collapsing into the old man's arms and sobbing her heart out.

'I think you'd had a bit of a dizzy spell,' Mr Pickering said.

'And you kindly offered to take me for a cup of "sugary tea".' Helen paused. 'Yes, it's all coming back to me now. You said you were meeting your daughter in a café up Holmeside.' She laughed. 'I'm guessing that was Georgina, unless you have other daughters?'

'No, one's enough, thank you very much,' he chuckled.

'What a strange coincidence,' Helen mused.

'Come and sit down.' Mr Pickering pulled a chair out. 'It's good to see you looking much improved today.' He had felt sorry for the young woman he had stopped to help that day.

'Thank you,' Helen said. 'And you, too, look well. Georgina said you have been poorly.'

Helen caught a flicker of confusion on the old man's face before he perked up. 'All good now. Old age gets us all in the end.'

Just then the door opened and Georgina came bustling in, a file under her arm.

'Oh, he's much better now,' she said, feeling herself blush and hoping it hadn't shown.

'Welcome to our home,' she said, walking over to the table. 'Are you happy here?' She glanced round the room. 'If you would feel more comfortable in the office, just say and I can take the tray in there.'

'No, this is fine,' Helen said. 'Preferable. Anything cooler is preferable.'

'And thank you for coming here,' Georgina said. 'I think it was wise. For the sake of confidentiality and privacy.' Georgina had actually not wanted to risk bumping into Rosie and have to tell more lies.

'Yes, I agree,' Helen said. A part of her had been intrigued to come here. To see where her Miss Marple lived. She couldn't wait to tell John.

Mr Pickering headed towards the door. 'Just shout if I can help in any way.' He looked at Helen. 'And lovely to meet you. Again.'

Georgina took her seat opposite Helen and put the file on top of the mahogany table.

'Again, apologies for the delay in seeing you.'

'Don't worry. Family comes first. Especially ill ones,' Helen said, as Georgina poured their tea and handed Helen her cup.

'I'm guessing that you have managed to make some headway,' Helen said, taking a sip of her tea.

'I have,' Georgina said, hoping her nerves weren't showing. This was not going to be the easiest of conversations.

She opened the file.

'I have typed up everything I have found out and researched, which you are more than welcome to have, although some clients prefer not to have any kind of documentation.'

Helen nodded but didn't say either way what she wanted. All of a sudden, she felt tense. She heard the squawking of a seagull and glanced out of the window at the building opposite.

'I have a feeling you have something definite to tell me,' she said, looking back at Georgina.

'I do – and I don't.' Georgina gave a nervous cough and took a sip of her tea.

'That sounds a little cryptic,' Helen said. She had picked up on Georgina's unease and had started to feel a little anxious herself.

'Well, to start with,' Georgina said, opening her notebook, not that she really needed it, everything she had learnt was pretty much imprinted in her head, 'I discovered that Bel is definitely *not* the daughter of your great-uncle Alexander.'

She looked up to see disappointment on Helen's face. This would have been by far the most preferable result.

'I managed to get hold of your uncle's death certificate and it would appear that you were right, he did indeed die of tuberculosis aged forty, in January 1913 – well before Bel would have been conceived.'

'Are you sure?' Helen asked.

'Yes, absolutely not possible.'

Helen sat back in her chair.

'With this in mind . . .' Georgina took a breath ' . . . I began to look more closely at the other men in the family. And found there *were* no other men that could possibly have fathered Bel.'

She paused.

'Apart from your grandfather.'

Helen felt a growing sense of trepidation that was reflected in Georgina's demeanour.

'This is where it all gets a little delicate,' Georgina says. 'And I think the best way forward would be for me to tell you all the facts and for you to decide for yourself how you think it is best to proceed.'

'Gosh, this all sounds very serious,' Helen said, suddenly having an overriding desire to have John by her side.

'These are the facts,' Georgina said, her voice flat and without emotion.

'First of all, I discovered that Pearl Hardwick is a former employee of the Havelock household.'

Helen's eyes widened. This was certainly a turn-up for the books. She couldn't imagine Bel's ma working anywhere but behind the bar in some east-end boozer.

'Yes, that surprised me as well,' Georgina said, seeing Helen's reaction. 'But two of your grandfather's staff, Eddy and Agatha, who, I'm sure you're aware, have worked at the house for a very long time, confirmed this.'

Helen nodded slowly. Eddy and Agatha were like part of the furniture. And almost as old.

'I managed to speak to them in confidence,' Georgina said, which was another way of saying that they had been paid for their information. 'And they remembered Pearl well. She was apparently very pretty when she was young.'

Georgina took a sip of her tea. Her throat felt dry.

'She turned up one night and your grandmother, who I think we have agreed was a little eccentric, took her in. Eddy said he had advised the mistress of the house against it, as they weren't in need of another maid, and also because the young girl on the doorstep had no experience from what he could gather – but Mrs Havelock had insisted. She had been convinced Pearl was,' Georgina glanced up at Helen, 'the character from the Hans Christian Andersen story "The Little Match Girl".'

'"*Den Lille Pige med Svovlstikkerne*".' Helen repeated the title in its original language.

Seeing the look of surprise on Georgina's face, she explained, 'For some reason my mother used to always refer to the story in Danish. The exact translation is actually "The Little Girl with the Matchsticks".'

'Interesting,' Georgina said, before continuing. 'Pearl apparently started in September 1913 – not long after she'd had her first daughter, Maisie, adopted. She worked mainly downstairs as a scullery maid, but did do a short stint as a housemaid the following Easter – and it was after this that she left.'

'Why did she leave?'

'Eddy had no idea. He said they simply got up one morning after Mrs Havelock had thrown a going-away party for your grandfather – as I'm sure you know he worked away a lot – and Pearl had gone. Disappeared.'

'How strange. Why didn't she tell anyone? Had she done something wrong? Did she steal anything?'

'No, from what I can gather she had been a good worker. Had fitted in well with the other staff there. And Eddy made a point of telling me that she didn't pilfer anything from the house before she did her midnight flit. Apparently, she even left her maid's uniform that your grandmother had bought her. Eddy said that it was Henrietta's gift to all her staff – their uniforms were theirs to keep. That was something that struck me as curious.'

'Why was that?' Helen asked.

Realising Helen had no idea what it was like not to have any money, or clothes, Georgina explained, 'Well, the uniform, which was really a dress with an apron over the top, was hers to take by right. She had earned it. But she didn't

311

take it, which I thought unusual because a young girl with barely two pennies to rub together would undoubtedly have taken it. If not to wear, then to sell.'

Helen sat back and looked at Georgina, who she thought was becoming a little flustered.

Georgina took a deep breath.

'Bel was born nine months later in the east end.'

She looked at Helen.

'And?'

'If you are certain that Bel looks and has the mannerisms of a Havelock, then the only person who could possibly be her father is Mr Havelock. Your grandfather.'

Helen shook her head.

'I don't understand,' she said. 'That can't be the case.' She did a quick calculation in her head. 'Grandfather must have been in his early fifties . . . and you say Pearl would have been, how old?'

'Fifteen.'

'Well, that's just not possible.'

Georgina didn't say anything.

They were both quiet for a while.

'Of course, there is the chance that Bel's similarity to the Havelock side of your family is simply a total fluke,' Georgina said. 'It could be that Pearl fell pregnant around that time to someone totally unrelated to the family.'

'Of course, that's always been a possibility,' Helen said, her mind whirring. She kept thinking of her grandfather.

Old.

And Pearl.

So young.

No. It just wasn't possible. Was it? *Could a fifteen-year-old girl and a man who was old enough to be her grandfather fall in love and have an affair?*

'My advice,' Georgina said, 'would be to approach both parties and ask them outright if this might have been the case.'

'What? Ask my grandfather if he got a fifteen-year-old girl pregnant when he was married to my grandmother?' There was no anger in Helen's voice, just simple incredulity.

'Or you approach Bel and her mother and ask them?' Georgina suggested.

Chapter Forty-Seven

Walking back onto High Street West, Helen was hit by a waft of hot air as one of the trams trundled past. She felt herself take in acrid air. Her chest felt tight. She hadn't felt this kind of shortness of breath for quite a while.

'Sorry,' she apologised as she accidentally bumped into a young woman and her little girl.

She turned left and started walking down Fawcett Street. It was busy and she felt overwhelmed by people. Shoppers. More women and children.

Turning left again into Athenaeum Street, she had an overwhelming urge to see John. He'd always been there for her. He was the only person she could talk to about what she had just found out. The only person she really wanted to talk to.

She and her grandfather might not have been as close as they once were, especially after her miscarriage, but he had always been a prominent presence in her life. Knowing what she did now had left her feeling blindsided. Deceived. Her grandfather had always portrayed himself as such a good and righteous man. She had always looked up to him. Just like most of the townsfolk did who had benefited from his philanthropy. But it was now clear that the picture he had painted of himself was a fake. And the reality more than a little disturbing.

Looking at her watch, she saw it had gone five. She turned right down Frederick Street. If she hurried, she might catch John before he started the evening shift.

She'd probably catch him in the cafeteria. He liked to be there for the relatives and loved ones of what he called his 'recruits'.

Turning left into Borough Road, Helen thought of Gloria. And Hope. Her sister. Her illegitimate sister. A sister who had to be kept a secret. For the sake of the family name.

She laughed aloud.

For the sake of the family name!

The bus took over half an hour to get to Ryhope.

Knowing she was going to see John had calmed her. Her breathing had returned to normal. She no longer felt as though she couldn't quite get enough air into her lungs.

As she walked down the long pathway that led to the hospital entrance, Helen looked beyond the new emergency hospital and saw a glimpse of the Borough Asylum. Its imposing Gothic towers and red brickwork just about visible.

The day was still hot, but there was now a cooling breeze coming in from the sea.

Hurrying up the main stone steps, Helen thanked a soldier on crutches who was gallantly holding the door open for her.

Hurrying along the main corridor towards the cafeteria, Helen crossed her fingers that John would be there, on his own, enjoying a cup of tea. As visiting time wasn't until seven, and afternoon visiting had ended well over an hour ago, there was a good chance he wouldn't be giving any informal consultations.

Walking through the main doors, Helen scanned the tables. It was still busy, but it was a covering of doctors' coats and nurses' uniforms that dominated the scenery rather than the streetwear of ordinary folk.

She stood for a moment, looking over the sea of white and blue. Her eyes searching for the man she realised – had realised for some time now – that she not only loved, but had fallen in love with.

'John!' she called out, overjoyed he was here and not in surgery or doing his rounds.

She saw him turn his head as he heard his name called.

She smiled.

On reaching him, she felt an urge to bend over and kiss him, so glad was she at finding him here.

'Helen,' he said, standing up and giving her a kiss on the cheek. 'This is a surprise.'

It took Helen a moment to realise that he wasn't being quite his normal self.

She followed his gaze to the other person sitting at the table.

A woman.

An attractive woman: tawny-coloured hair twisted into a French knot, high cheekbones, and full lips made even more sensual with a coating of natural lip gloss.

'Come, take a seat,' Dr Parker said, pulling a chair from one of the neighbouring tables.

'And meet Claire . . . Dr Claire Eris.'

Helen stood for a moment, staring at the woman sitting at the table with her legs crossed, wearing a smart brown tailored skirt and jacket.

'Dr Eris,' Helen said, forcing a smile and extending a hand.

'Please, call me Claire,' Dr Eris said, shaking hands. Her hold was firm. 'So lovely to meet you, Helen. I've heard so much about you.'

'Likewise,' Helen said, taking her seat. She was aware her tone was frosty. 'Forgive me if I appear a little taken aback, but when John told me about you,' she looked across at Dr Parker, 'well, I just presumed you were a man.'

Both women laughed.

'Sorry, that didn't come out right,' Helen said, again glancing over at Dr Parker. 'I had presumed, as you were a doctor – *a psychologist* – that you would be a man, which is terrible really, now that I hear myself saying it.' She shook her head. 'As if a woman can't be a doctor – or a psychologist . . .' Helen's voice trailed off.

'It's perfectly understandable,' Dr Eris said. 'I get it all the time – from both sexes. I'm used to it. I suppose there aren't that many doctors – or *head doctors* – who are women.'

Both women forced smiles.

'I suppose it must be the same for you?' Dr Eris continued. 'Being a yard manager. I'll bet most people assume yard managers are always men?'

Helen laughed; a little too loudly. 'And they'd be right in doing so. I think I'm the only woman yard manager I know of. Certainly in the north-east.'

'Quite a strike for the feminist movement then?' Dr Eris said, widening her almond-shaped hazel eyes.

Helen laughed. This time it was natural.

'Well, if it is, it wasn't intentional. I've spent most of my life in the shipyards. Thanks to my father.'

'Helen, let me get you a cup of tea,' Dr Parker butted in.

'And *I* must go,' Dr Eris said, looking at her watch. 'I have a session with a particularly challenging patient over at the asylum in fifteen minutes. Female. Borderline schizophrenic. Or at least that's what she's been diagnosed with. I'm not so sure myself.'

She stood up.

'Lovely to meet you, Helen,' she said as they shook hands once again.

Helen couldn't help glancing down to see her right hand was devoid of any kind of engagement or wedding ring.

'And you too, Dr Eris – sorry, I mean Claire.'

Dr Parker stood up again as Dr Eris said her goodbyes and left.

Helen watched as she walked out of the café. She noticed her departure caused a few heads to turn. Male heads.

'Won't be a moment,' Dr Parker said, weaving his way around tables to the counter and returning a few moments later with a clean cup and saucer.

'Well, that was a turn-up for the books,' Helen said. 'Why didn't you tell me Dr Eris was a woman?'

'I thought I had, to be honest,' he said, pouring Helen's tea from the pot in the middle of the table and adding milk.

'No, you didn't. I would have remembered,' Helen said.

'Well, if I didn't, it wasn't intentional,' Dr Parker said, his tone sincere.

He topped up his own cup.

'Anyway, come on, tell me why you've suddenly turned up out of the blue.' He took a quick sip of his tea. 'Am I right in thinking this has to do with the meeting you've had with your Miss Marple?'

Helen pushed back the feeling of irritation that Dr Eris had left in her wake.

She took a deep breath as her mind swung back to her meeting with Georgina.

'Oh, John,' Helen exhaled. 'It does . . . It does indeed.'

For the next few minutes, Dr Parker listened.

Nothing he heard surprised him. He had met Mr Havelock on a number of occasions and hadn't liked the man one bit. Not that he had let that show, or had ever voiced his opinion. Mr Havelock was a very important man. Especially when it came to the town's hospitals. He was, after all, one of the main benefactors. If not *the* main benefactor.

'I just can't comprehend my grandfather having an affair,' Helen said, 'let alone with a girl who was so young.' She blew out air. 'And then having a baby with her.'

'I'm wondering if he knows that Pearl had his baby?' Dr Parker said.

'I know, I've been wondering that ever since Georgina dropped her bombshell.'

Helen took a sip of her tea.

'Honestly, John, my head feels like it's spinning.'

They sat in silence. Both thinking.

'But, then again,' Helen said, 'you would have thought Pearl would have told Grandfather she was having his baby, wouldn't you?'

'If what Georgina says is true,' Dr Parker mused, 'it sounds as if she left under a bit of a cloud.' He'd thought it odd that Pearl hadn't taken her maid's dress. Sometimes it was the small details that painted the bigger picture.

'Yes, but even if they'd had a falling-out, you'd have thought that she would have gone and told him she was expecting. And that the baby was his. Even if it was simply to get some kind of maintenance?'

Dr Parker nodded.

'Unless he refused to accept the baby was his?' Helen said. 'Or he refused to pay for it.' She thought about her grandfather's attitude to the illegitimate baby she had been carrying. And to Hope. In his eyes they were 'bastards', and therefore less than insignificant.

Dr Parker looked at Helen. 'We have to consider that you might be barking up the wrong tree. That Pearl simply left your grandfather and your grandmother's employ for some reason we're not aware of – and that Bel's father is someone completely different.'

'I really, really wish that was the case,' Helen said, sounding anything but hopeful.

She pushed her cup of tea away.

'But something tells me it's not. To be honest, John, it makes me feel a little sick. Thinking of my granddad being so old and having an affair with someone so young.'

Dr Parker looked at Helen and realised that her discomfort was purely because of the age gap – that she perceived the relationship as being an affair, and not that Pearl and her grandfather's relationship could have been anything other than consensual.

Despite being quite worldly, Helen could still be very naïve.

Or perhaps it was *he* who was being too cynical? Perhaps Pearl and Mr Havelock had loved each other. Perhaps their love had transcended the *thirty-five years* that separated them.

'The question now is . . .' Dr Parker looked at Helen '. . . if your grandfather and Pearl *did* have an affair and Pearl had his baby – does Bel know that Mr Havelock is her father?'

'Oh, my goodness, I can't believe I never thought about that.' Helen's face dropped. 'Pearl must have told her. She won't have kept it from her, will she?'

'Well, there's only one way of finding out. You're going to have to ask her.'

When Dr Parker said his goodbyes to Helen and waved her off at the bus stop, he kept thinking about Mr Havelock. He'd seen him at charity dos and various events over the past few years and he'd noticed the way he looked at the younger nurses. He seemed to have a particular penchant for petite young girls with blonde hair. Similar to what Pearl must have looked like, judging by her purported similarity to the Little Match Girl.

Seeing one of the drivers on his way home, Dr Parker thought about the long evening ahead.

And he thought about Claire.

She too was working this evening over at the asylum.

As he made his way back to the hospital, his mind wandered to her reaction to meeting Helen.

And to Helen's reaction to meeting Claire.

There'd definitely been a slight edginess between the two women.

If he thought that Helen was secretly harbouring feelings for him, he might have perceived there to be a hint of jealousy.

He scratched his head.

Don't be stupid!

Helen had simply been surprised that Dr Eris was a woman.

God, why was he still such a dreamer?

He was pathetic – to even think there might be the remotest chance that Helen could possibly be jealous.

Of course, she wasn't jealous of Claire. Why should she be? Helen liked him – possibly even loved him – but as a friend.

He had to stop being such a martyr to love. Stop playing the pathetic knight of old – chasing a love that could never be.

As he walked back to the hospital he thought of Claire.

Now, he didn't believe he would be amiss in thinking that he *had* seen a little jealousy there.

He'd got to know Claire quite well during these past four months. She had suggested a few times that they should go out for a drink.

Perhaps it was time for him to move on? To leave his love for Helen behind.

They would always be friends. But, like he had told himself a million times before, Helen's heart belonged to another.

Chapter Forty-Eight

Two days later

Saturday 15 May

'So, tell me about this drumhead service you're so determined to see?' Rosie asked Charlotte as they made their snail-like ascent up Tunstall Vale. It was impossible to move forward with any kind of speed as it seemed as though every man, woman and child in the town had descended on Ashbrooke for the parade.

'Well, it's going to be massive,' Charlotte said.

'You're not joking,' Rosie mumbled.

She tutted as she was jostled from behind.

'Excuse me!' She glared at the woman and her husband as they pushed past.

'And it's to celebrate,' Charlotte continued, 'the third anniversary of the formation of the anti-aircraft battery.'

'Well, they've certainly had their work cut out of late,' Rosie groused. 'Come here,' she said, grabbing her sister's arm and tugging her onto the side of the road.

'That's better,' she said as they managed to walk with only a minimal amount of pushing and shoving. Others had followed suit since there was barely any traffic, other than the occasional army truck. She looked up at the clear blue sky. At least they weren't going to get wet.

'Where are we meeting everyone?' Rosie asked.

'At the far end of West Lawn, near the entrance to the cricket ground. I think we're all going to watch the parade and then go to the clubhouse afterwards to see the actual service.'

Rosie sighed. Charlotte was always so happy whenever she was going to meet up with Lily.

'It's going to be made up of hundreds of men from the DLI,' Charlotte said. 'That's the Durham Light Infantry.'

Rosie exhaled. 'I do know what DLI stands for, Charlie . . . I do know a little about life outside Thompson's.'

'There they are!' Charlotte waved her hand in the air.

Rosie looked over a smattering of heads to spot Lily's vibrant auburn hair, piled extravagantly high. Since Charlotte had blasted back into town, Rosie had never known Lily to leave the confines of the bordello as frequently as she did these days.

Next to Lily was George, who looked uncomfortable, but not as uncomfortable as if Lily had got her own way and had made him put on his regimental attire.

Standing next to Lily was Kate.

Next to her was Alfie. Rosie thought he looked very smart and very serious.

And, of course, there were Maisie and Vivian, pristine and incredibly glamorous, as always. She knew they wouldn't watch the whole parade as Vivian was in sole charge of the bordello today, and Maisie the Gentlemen's Club.

'*Mes chères!*' Lily's voice sung out over the swarm of spectators, causing a few curious looks to be thrown her way.

Rosie and Charlotte only just managed to squeeze through the crowd to what must have been the prime position, judging by how reluctant people were to budge even an inch.

Lily had her hands outstretched in anticipation of a hug for Charlotte and a kiss on both cheeks for Rosie.

'Hi everyone,' Charlotte said, smiling down the line at George, Kate, Alfie, Maisie and Vivian.

'Hi, doll.' Vivian's exaggerated American drawl caused a couple standing a few yards away to stare, which, in turn, caused Maisie to shoot her a warning look. Charlotte saw it. It added to her argument that there was more to the two of them than met the eye.

Suddenly there was the sound of drums in the distance, like the faint beginnings of thunder.

'Sounds like it's started!' Charlotte looked from Lily to Rosie.

'Try and get a good look at the actual drums.' George craned his neck to speak to Charlotte. 'The paintings on them are quite something.'

Charlotte nodded. She was going to do a project on the history of the Durham Light Infantry regiment, and George had agreed to help her.

Within minutes the air was filled not only with the sound of drums, but also trumpets, tubas, trombones and the occasional clashing of cymbals.

The crowds cheered.

Charlotte spotted a few small children on their father's shoulders and had a brief memory of her father doing the same as they had trooped along the beach, heading out to the best winkle-picking spots.

She pushed the thought away.

Out of the corner of her eye, she caught Maisie and Vivian talking to two soldiers. She looked back at the parade, thinking about her school project and how she needed to remember the various uniforms, the instruments, how the men all marched perfectly in tune, arms swinging in synchronicity with the rest of their battalion.

But there was something about the way Maisie and Vivian had been conversing with the two soldiers that compelled her to drag her attention away from the parade.

Maisie looked friendly but also quite serious. As did Vivian, who was now pointing down the street, as though giving directions. Was she telling them where they lived? Or perhaps she was telling them where the Gentlemen's Club was? Although, from what Charlotte gathered, the club was mainly for old fogeys, and didn't open until later.

Charlotte looked back at the parade. The soldiers from the anti-aircraft battery were now passing.

She looked at Lily and George.

Lily was leaning into George and whispering something into his ear. She saw him laugh.

Alfie was also saying something to Kate, who smiled, but kept her eyes glued to the parade. Charlotte knew she would be getting ideas for new designs.

Charlotte looked back again.

Maisie and Vivian were leaving.

With the two soldiers.

Odd.

They clearly didn't know them. And yet they were walking off with the pair.

Charlotte looked at Rosie, who seemed a million miles away.

When she turned her attention back to Maisie and Vivian, she was surprised to see them heading right, rather than back down West Lawn.

Seeing them turn left into Ashbrooke Crescent, Charlotte couldn't contain her curiosity. Taking a step back, she turned round and started making her way through the crowd.

She quickly looked to see if anyone had noticed her sudden absence, but they hadn't. A young girl around her height had stepped forward to get a better view and was now standing next to Rosie.

Charlotte argued to herself that she just wanted to see where Maisie and Vivian were going – then she'd get straight back. She'd only be a few minutes.

Hurrying around the corner, she was just in time to see Maisie and Vivian and the two soldiers turn left again and start walking down the back lane. She'd been right. They were clearly taking them to the Gentlemen's Club and were going the back way, presumably to avoid the crowds.

Rosie's right. You really are too nosy! Charlotte silently reprimanded herself.

She was about to return to the parade when she saw them walk past the Gentlemen's Club and stop at the rear entrance to Lily's.

Strange . . .

Why were they going to Lily's?

Charlotte stepped back into the shadows so as not to be seen and watched as all four disappeared through the wooden gate.

She continued down the lane, walking quickly and quietly.

She could hear Vivian's voice and laughter, followed by the jangle of keys.

Then she heard Maisie call out a girl's name she had not heard before.

Was there someone else at Lily's?

Charlotte inched nearer along the brick wall.

But why were they going in the back? It didn't make sense.

She heard the sound of boots being wiped on a wire mat.

Charlotte heard a young woman's voice that did not belong to either Vivian or Maisie.

Then the door closed.

Charlotte inched nearer to the gate and squinted through the wooden slats.

She couldn't see much, only the yard and the back of the house.

She was about to turn away when she suddenly saw movement across one of the rear windows.

The curtains, which had been drawn closed, opened slightly.

She could just make out what looked like a lamp peeping out from the velvet drapes.

Charlotte gave a start when it was suddenly switched on.

And then she stared.

The light now shining out of the little back window was red.

Chapter Forty-Nine

1940

Rosie had often wondered whether what happened on the first Saturday of November in 1940 had anything to do with her mam and dad.

Had they managed to manipulate the strings of fate so that the women welders finally gave in to Dorothy's pleas that they all have a night out?

Had they guided Gloria's vision to the inside of the timekeeper's cabin, allowing her to see the intricately carved cane that belonged to a rather sinister old man she'd seen?

Had they fanned the flames of the women's unease at Rosie's no-show at the pub, compelling them to go back to the yard to look for her?

Rosie's recall of that day was still vivid.

She remembered how bitterly cold it was as she'd gathered up her belongings, how she'd jumped out of her skin when he had appeared through the curtain of fog and told her he had found out she'd been holding back her overtime earnings.

She remembered how the weight of the bag on her shoulder had suddenly felt heavy and she'd let it drop to the ground.

'Hours and hours of overtime. I'm surprised you've had the time to write to that pretty little sister of yours.' Raymond's voice had dripped with venom as he'd waved her wage slips along with a couple of Charlotte's letters in front of her.

Even now, Rosie could remember the tidal wave of despair that had washed over her. For the first time in her life she'd felt powerless to protect her sister as he'd ranted on about the money he had found stashed away in her bedsit.

Was it, he'd asked, a stash for Charlotte in case something happened to her?

'Like what happened to yer mam 'n dad? God rest their souls,' he'd sneered.

There'd been something in his tone, something he'd wanted her to know.

And she was right.

They never did find the – what did the police call him? – the "hit-and-run driver" who killed yer mam 'n dad, did they?'

The sinister smile that had cut across his face would be forever embedded in her memory.

As would the moment the penny dropped.

It was him.

He had been the hit-and-run driver.

It had not been an accident.

Rosie had swung at him, but she was no fighter and Raymond had niftily sidestepped her, at the same time whacking his walking stick down on Rosie's arm with all his might.

She had crumpled over, clenching her arm in agony, before feeling another crack of the cane. This time, pain had seared through her skull and the fog around her was replaced by darkness.

When she'd come to, her head was being forced over a live weld. The light had been blinding, the heat unbearable, her head throbbing, and she'd felt the bite of metal on her skin. But it was the fragmented recall of what happened next

330

that always came back to haunt Rosie in the dark hours of the night. The feel of him as he pushed his body against her, his sinewy fingers pulling her hair, yanking her head back and forth over the fountain of sparks. Her feeling of powerlessness. His foul-smelling breath telling her she would never beat him. Her knowledge that she was drowning in a tidal wave of his anger and resentment. His words spewing forth, frustrated at having killed his sister and brother-in-law in the expectation of inheriting the money – and his fury in finding out that this too had been snatched from him.

But there had also been the sound of victory in his voice. It had taken more than five years, but he had finally scraped back the money he believed was his.

Rosie had known then that she was defeated.

She could still hear him now, telling her, 'I could take yer here. Now. Like I did before. But you've gotten too old, too used. Like a bit of tough old mutton, and yer know me, Rosie, don't you? I like a nice bit of lamb. Much more tender. Much more tasty.'

It was the memory of his final words, though, that always had Rosie breaking out into a sweat.

'I want you to breathe yer last with the image in yer head of me havin' my fill . . . feasting on some succulent tender meat. Just like I did with you all those years ago.'

She had screamed, but, just like in her dreams, she could not hear her own voice. All she could see was a dazzling fountain. And all she could feel was the stinging of burning flesh.

Her last desperate thought had been for Charlie.

She had closed her eyes and prayed.

Prayed for Charlotte to be saved . . .

Then, as if in answer to her prayers, she had heard a woman's voice booming out over the buzzing of the welding machine.

'Ger off her!'

It was Gloria.

With her were Polly, Dorothy, Martha and Hannah.

Raymond had tossed the rod holder aside and grabbed his walking stick, pulling Rosie in front of him as a human shield. She had felt like a rag doll. She heard Polly yelling, 'Let her alone!' And a sob that must have come from Hannah.

She had managed to lift her head and had seen the look of shock on Dorothy's face.

It wasn't until later, when she looked in the mirror, that she understood why.

Her cheeks and forehead were blackened and spotted with small circular welts where she had been burned. Part of her blonde hair was frazzled and singed to the roots. She looked more dead than alive.

'Give her here!' Dorothy had demanded, but her words had been met with laughter as the bottom part of Raymond's walking stick had fallen away, revealing a thick, glistening knife. He'd swiftly brought it up to Rosie's face, the sharp point of the blade just piercing the skin enough to draw blood.

'Are you really going to bother yourselves with this whore?'

And that was how they'd got to know her secret.

Rosie could hear him rant on, calling her a 'prostitute, a slag, a slut', then through her blurred vision she saw Martha charge forward.

For someone so tall and stocky she had moved fast, pushing Raymond away with such force she'd catapulted him backwards.

He'd staggered, still clutching his weapon.

Dorothy and Hannah had grabbed Rosie as she had gone down on her knees, no longer able to support her own weight.

She had heard Raymond snarling at them all, calling them 'stupid bitches', but he'd stepped back and onto a thick metal rod left lying on the ground, hidden by the low-lying mist. His footing had faltered, his arms flailing as he'd tried to stay upright, but he'd got too close to the edge of the quayside.

It happened in slow motion: Raymond's foot had lifted up into the air, and he'd desperately tried to catch hold of something to keep him upright.

But there was nothing.

Just wisps of fog.

He had let out a strangled cry before disappearing over the side of the dock, and a second later they'd heard the sound of his body as it hit the water's surface.

Everything had been a blur after that.

She had started retching.

But she had to know.

Leaning heavily into Polly, she'd pointed to the river.

They'd gone and peered over the edge of the quayside.

Dorothy had shone her torch down into the river's choppy black water, but there had been no sign of Raymond.

Martha had half carried, half dragged Rosie onto the ferry and then to Tatham Street.

It had been Agnes's face that she remembered throughout that entire night as she tended to her burns and the gash on the back of her head. She'd put Rosie's badly swollen wrist into a splint and nursed her through the most agonising case of arc eye Rosie had ever experienced in all her years as a welder.

Agnes had tried to comfort Rosie as she had thrashed about in agony. Tears silently spilled down Agnes's face as she'd watched this wreck of a girl cry out, her eyes and nose streaming constantly, all the while clutching her banging head in agony.

She had kept on calling out 'Charlie' and Agnes had kept reassuring her that 'Charlie will be fine,' even though she had no idea who Charlie was. Her gently spoken words seemed to do the trick, though, and in the early hours of the morning, Rosie's body had finally relaxed into the comfort of the bed.

Rosie knew she was alive because of the courage, love and care of her squad of women welders.

She also liked to think that her mam and dad had played their part.

A week later, while carrying out some underwater repairs to a damaged frigate, Tommy discovered Raymond's bloated body tangled up at the bottom of the Wear.

And, as fate would have it, on the same day, Rosie met the man who was to become her husband. DS Peter Miller had come knocking on the door of her bedsit to inform her, as next of kin, that her uncle had come a cropper and drowned accidentally in the Wear.

The theory was that he – like many before him – had had one too many and that drink had literally been the death of him.

Chapter Fifty

Saturday 15 May, 1943

Oh Peter, I'd give anything to have you here now. Rosie couldn't stop her wishful thinking.

Watching the drumhead parade for what felt like an age, her mind had begun to wander. As usual, it had gone to Peter and was regurgitating the same questions: *Was he all right? Was he in danger? Was he alive?* Not knowing was purgatory.

She had hoped that perhaps Toby might have brought another letter with him when he had come to visit Dorothy over Easter. But he hadn't. She'd felt like weeping, but knew nothing positive would come from crying. It certainly wouldn't help Peter. And the last thing her squad needed was to see her down and defeated. Especially Polly.

The clash of cymbals signalling the last of the soldiers snapped Rosie out of her reverie.

'Right, let's go, Charlie, off to the clubhouse—'

Looking to her right, Rosie suddenly realised that her sister had been replaced by another young girl who looked nothing like her, but who was roughly the same height.

'Sorry, I thought you were someone else,' Rosie apologised, looking round to see where her sister was.

'Have you seen Charlie?' Rosie turned to Lily and George. They looked at the place where Charlotte had been standing.

'I thought she was right there,' Lily said. Turning to her left, she saw Kate chatting to Alfie, but Vivian and Maisie were nowhere to be seen.

And neither was Charlotte.

She had a bad feeling.

'There she is!' George suddenly shouted out.

'Charlie! Where have you been?' Rosie looked at her sister. She had on her new blue skirt and a lovely short-sleeved blouse. She was looking so grown-up lately. She had to stop treating her like a child.

'I thought I saw one of my classmates,' Charlotte lied.

'And did you?' Lily asked.

'No . . . I mean, yes . . . but I lost her in the crowd,' Charlotte said, blushing slightly.

'Come on then,' Lily said. 'Let's get to the clubhouse before they run out of tea.'

Ten minutes later they had managed to get themselves a table, and although they weren't able to hear the open-air service from within the confines of the rather exclusive Ashbrooke members' club, they were able to see the pageantry of the proceedings taking place on the cricket ground.

Kate had wanted to hear the vicar speak and so Alfie had accompanied her to a spot in the spectator stands where she could catch what was being said. Lily had suggested the spot so as to keep an eye on them both. Or rather, on Alfie. There were only a handful of men that Lily trusted and as yet, Alfie was not one of them.

'So, the latest news from France is positive,' George said, taking a sip of tea.

'Really?' Rosie asked, her attention focused on George, unaware that Charlotte was being uncannily quiet and well behaved.

'The major strands of the Resistance movement have been pulled together to form the *Conseil Nationale de la Résistance*.'

Everyone automatically looked at Charlotte for a translation.

'What's that?' Charlotte asked, looking as though she had just been snapped out of a trance.

'The *Conseil Nationale de la Résistance*,' George said, glancing at Lily and seeing that she too clearly thought that something was awry.

'The *Conseil Nationale de la Résistance* means the National Council of the Resistance,' Charlotte said.

'Which means?' Rosie asked, looking at George.

'It means that finally the illusion that Pétain or another Vichy general might rise to challenge German domination has faded. Those heading up the Resistance have decided that it is only through de Gaulle and the help of the Allies that intelligence-gathering operations and paramilitary groups in France can be utilised more effectively if they are all working together.'

'In other words, the French have realised what side their bread is buttered and have put all their eggs into one basket to fight the Germans.' Lily got out her fan, snapped it open and started to fan herself. 'I do love the French, but, *mon Dieu*, they can be a little frustrating and slow off the mark. I mean, it's only taken them *three years* of occupation and abuse of their men, women and children to come to this conclusion.'

All of a sudden, Charlotte scraped back her chair and got up.

'You all right, *ma petite*?' Lily asked. 'You've lost all your colour.'

'I'm fine,' Charlotte said, not looking Lily, George or Rosie in the eye. 'I just need to use the loo.'

She hurried off.

'Rosie, go and see what ails the poor girl,' Lily commanded. 'Something's wrong. Very wrong.'

Rosie looked at Lily and George. Their faces showed their concern.

She got up quickly and followed her sister to the toilets.

Chapter Fifty-One

Helen went over and over in her head the best way to do this.

It would be pointless going to her grandfather as there was no guarantee that he would know the truth either. Pearl might not have told him. Or, if he *was* Bel's father and he knew that he was, there was a good chance he would deny it. After all, he wasn't going to be keen on admitting he had fathered an illegitimate child, especially when his wife had still been alive.

If he had nothing to do with Bel's paternity, Helen would have insulted her grandfather, but more than anything would have made herself look rather ludicrous.

John was right. The only way she would find out was by asking Pearl. She was the only one who had the answer.

God! She was going doolally thinking about all the possible actions and outcomes. She felt as though she was going round and round in circles, like the tiger that turned into butter. Her mind felt as though it too would melt if she thought much more about what to do.

She just had to *do it* and see what happened.

She had to speak to Pearl, and needed Bel to be there as well.

It was important to catch them unprepared – she'd know by their reactions if they were telling the truth.

Helen looked at her watch. It had gone six.

Picking up her bag, she got out her compact and checked herself in the mirror. She looked fine. Perhaps a little nervous. She shut her bag, picked up her gas mask and walked out of her office.

Twenty minutes later she was walking down Tatham Street, a road that had taken on great significance in her life this past year. She'd nearly died on this road, buried in a mound of rubble. She had helped save two lives, and in doing so had also gained the friendship of the women welders – or at least their forgiveness.

After waiting for a tram to trundle past, Helen hurried across the road. She saw a group of raggedy-looking children playing marbles outside one of the houses. The front door was open and Helen could smell what she guessed was some kind of stew.

Reaching the Tatham Arms, she stopped. Even this pub had become a part of her recent history. She'd been here for Arthur's wake, had said goodbye to the old man and a few hours later had welcomed in the New Year – and accepted that her feelings for John were far from chaste.

She pushed away thoughts of John.

They were for another time.

Today, this evening, was about family. Or not. Whatever the case might be.

Pushing open the door to the pub, Helen took a few steps into the main hallway. It had been her intention to simply pop her head around the door to see if Pearl was working. It would give her a heads-up on what to expect when she went round to number 34. She was about to open the inner door that led to the main bar when she heard Pearl's distinctive cackle of laughter, followed by a robust bout of coughing. She took her hand off the doorknob and turned to walk back down the hallway.

First step taken.

She had ascertained Pearl's whereabouts.

Now for Bel.

Two minutes later she'd crossed the road and was standing outside the Elliots' front door. Like most of the front doors in the street, it was open.

'Cooee! Hello! Anyone home?' Helen tried to sound casual yet confident. Not like the fish out of water she felt she was.

She saw Lucille appear at the bottom of the hallway and stare at Helen before quickly disappearing back into the kitchen.

'Who is it, pet?' Agnes's voice could be heard before she became visible.

Forcing a smile on her face, Helen gave a little wave.

'It's only me,' she said, a little self-consciously. 'Sorry to disturb.'

'Come in, Helen.' Agnes beckoned her into the hubbub of the Elliot household. 'We've just had our tea. You've missed Polly, though, she's nipped next door to see Beryl about an old Moses basket she's got stashed away somewhere.'

'Oh, don't worry, tell her I said hello,' Helen said, showing Agnes that it was not Polly their impromptu guest had come to see.

'*Helen!*' Bel stopped clearing the table of plates and cutlery. 'Is everything all right?'

'Yes, yes,' Helen reassured.

'Hope all right?' Agnes asked. She was now in the scullery, filling the sink ready to do the washing-up.

'Yes, she's fine,' Helen said, looking at Joe and Lucille. There was a look of slight concern on Joe's face.

She felt something tickle her calves and looked down to see that Tramp and Pup were at her feet.

'And Gloria?' Bel asked.

'Yes, she's fine too,' Helen said. She now felt awkward. Everyone was looking at her. She had only ever turned up unannounced at the house once before and that had been the day after the bombing to drop off Hope.

'Pol's just nipped next door,' Bel said.

'Actually, it's you I've come to see.' Helen tried to keep her voice light. 'I wondered if perhaps you might like to come for a drink with me?'

Everyone looked at Helen as though she had just grown two heads.

'Well, yes, that'd be nice. Let me just wash my hands,' Bel said, heading off into the scullery. Agnes moved out of the way so she could get to the sink. She gave Bel a quick, questioning look, which her daughter-in-law returned with an equally perplexed one.

As Bel scrubbed her hands clean, she could hear Joe asking Helen about the yard.

'Right, let's go,' she said, drying her hands as she came back into the kitchen. She put the towel down on the kitchen table and gave Joe a quick kiss on the lips before cupping her hands around her daughter's little cherub face and planting a kiss on her forehead. 'You be good for Daddy while Mammy's out?'

Lucille nodded her head vigorously.

Agnes followed them both down the hallway.

'Helen,' she said, as the two women stepped out onto the pavement, 'thank you for all yer help with Polly 'n the bab. That Dr Billingham has been an absolute godsend.'

Helen smiled. 'It's the least I could do. For Polly. And Tommy. And Arthur, of course.'

Agnes smiled at the mention of the old man. He still felt near.

'I hope you don't mind me just turning up like this,' Helen said while they both hurried across the road as an army truck headed into town.

'I wouldn't normally have come unannounced . . .' They reached the other side, and waited for a woman pushing a pram to pass. Helen looked at Bel and thought she caught a look of longing on her face. She knew that feeling. Had experienced it herself for a while after her miscarriage.

'I don't mind at all,' Bel said, her face brightening as she looked back at Helen. 'I'm partly intrigued,' she said, opening the door to the Tatham. 'And partly glad to be dragged out on a Saturday night.'

'Next time, I'll drag you somewhere a little more upmarket,' Helen said, checking herself and adding, 'Not that I'm saying there's anything wrong with *this* pub.'

They both walked down the hallway and went through into the main bar.

'I'll get the drinks in,' Helen said. 'Port and lemon?'

Bel nodded. 'Yes, please.'

Looking over to the bar, Bel saw her ma and Bill chatting away to Ronald and a few of the other locals. Geraldine, the other barmaid, was serving customers further down the bar.

Bel went to sit at one of the tables by the window. Her mind was working overtime. If Helen had wanted to chat to her about work, she would have done it at the yard. Perhaps it was something to do with Polly? The two had become quite pally of late. Or was it something else?

When she saw Helen talking to her ma, she knew it was 'something else'.

Her heart started to beat faster.

Did Helen know?

Bel watched as her ma took the glass she kept under the bar, poured herself a large whisky and lit herself a cigarette. She unhooked the wooden hatch and came round the other side of the bar.

Her face looked solemn.

As did Helen's.

Neither woman spoke as they made their way over to Bel.

Helen handed Bel her drink and put her own on the table.

Pearl pulled out the stool and sat down amidst a cloud of cigarette smoke. She looked at Bel but said nothing.

'First of all,' Helen said, 'I have to apologise for ambushing you both like this.'

She looked at Bel – and then at Pearl.

If she had been in any doubt that they were mother and daughter, it was instantly dismissed.

'I know I should have given you both some warning . . .' Her eyes were transfixed by Pearl. It was the first time she had noticed how similar she was to Helen's own mother. The two could have been long-lost sisters.

'But, you see, I didn't know quite what to do – or say – so I just decided to come here and see you both. On the spur of the moment.'

Neither Bel nor Pearl said a word.

'The thing is . . .' Helen began; their silence was disconcerting. She suddenly felt what it must be like to get stage fright.

'The thing is . . .' she began again.

'Aye,' Pearl said, 'yer've said that twice now. The thing is what? I can't sit here all night. I've got work to do.'

The harshness of Pearl's words seemed to shock Helen back on track.

Bel threw Pearl a look that said to rein it in.

'Go on, Helen, what is it you want to ask?' she said, her voice calm; she had never seen Helen so nervous and unsure.

'Gosh, this feels so strange now that I'm sat here with you both. Sometimes things seem to make so much sense when they're in your head, but as soon as you voice those

344

thoughts – those feelings – those *beliefs*, it seems a little insane.'

Pearl took a puff of her cigarette. 'Just spit it out, pet.' Her words were mixed with a swirl of grey smoke.

'All right,' Helen said. 'I really hope I don't cause you both any upset by saying what I'm about to say.' She looked at Pearl and saw the beginnings of anger now accompanying her impatience. 'And I hope you don't think I'm overstepping the mark, or putting my nose where it's not wanted, but you see, I think this concerns me as well. In a roundabout way.'

Helen looked at Bel.

'You see . . . Well . . . I think we might be related.'

There, she had said it!

She looked at Bel and then at Pearl.

And that's when she knew.

The looks on both their faces told her what she needed to know.

Bel was a Havelock.

'What makes you think that?' Bel asked Helen.

'It's a bit of a long story,' Helen began.

She looked at Bel. Was that relief she could see?

Then she looked at Pearl, but couldn't read her face.

'It started shortly after you began work at the yard,' Helen said to Bel. 'I kept looking at you and thinking you reminded me of someone. I kept saying to John – ' Helen looked at Pearl ' – Dr Parker – that it was really bugging me that I couldn't work it out. But that it would come to me eventually.'

She looked back at Bel.

'And then it did. Like a smack across the face.'

'When?' Bel asked. She had always known she was playing with fire when she had got the job in admin last year, being so close to the family of the man who had fathered her,

345

but she had done so because she had wanted to know more about her 'other family'. She had never thought it would even have crossed Helen's mind that they were related.

'It was at Polly and Tommy's wedding,' Helen said. 'I don't know if you can remember – but you came over to thank me for the floral arrangements and then my mother turned up.'

Helen looked at Pearl, who was lighting another cigarette off the one she had been smoking. 'Miriam. Miriam Crawford.'

'Aye, I knar who yer mam is,' Pearl said, taking a large gulp of her whisky. She looked at Bel. *Was this what Isabelle had always wanted? Why she'd taken the job at the yard?*

'So, you looked at 'em both 'n thought they looked alike.' Pearl took another drag. 'So what? Lots of people look alike.' Pearl knew, though, that she was fighting a losing battle. She should have denied it as soon as the words were out of Helen's mouth.

'But it wasn't just the similarities in looks.' Helen looked at Pearl and back at Bel. 'It was your mannerisms as well. You've not spent any time in my mother's company, yet you both do things the same way. Like the way you stand when you're talking to someone. The way you hold your hand. The way you walk. It's uncanny.'

Helen caught Bel looking at her mother.

'And then I found out,' Helen's attention was now focused on Pearl, 'that you had worked for my grandparents. That my grandmother, Henrietta, took you in and employed you as a scullery maid and you worked there for about eight months, but left all of a sudden the day after Easter Monday – and gave birth to Bel nine months later.'

Pearl looked at her daughter. Her beautiful, regal daughter. She had kept the secret of her paternity from her for so many years. More than two decades. If Isabelle wanted to

346

admit to the Havelock girl that she was right and the two were related, it was her decision. She sat back and gave her daughter a look that conveyed the ball was in her court.

Bel turned to Helen and nodded.

'So, it's true?' Helen looked at Pearl. 'You and my grandfather had an affair?'

'Pah!' Pearl erupted.

Helen felt herself flinch. The sudden burst of anger gave her a jolt.

'Affair my backside!' Pearl practically spat the words out.

Suddenly they all looked up to see Bill coming towards them.

'Everything all right?' He had been watching from the bar. Knew something wasn't right from the moment Helen had asked to 'borrow' his barmaid.

'We're fine.' Bel forced a smile up at Bill. He was like a big bear. Ready to swipe away anyone who might try and hurt Pearl.

'Aye, we're all right.' Pearl downed the rest of her whisky. 'My throat's a bit dry, though.' She held up her glass. Bill took it, returning a minute later with a refill.

'Ta,' Pearl said.

Bill looked at the three women and left them to it.

Pearl took another drink.

'If yer've done your sums,' Pearl stared at Helen, 'yer will have worked out that yer grandda was in his fifties.'

Pearl took another deep drag on her cigarette.

'I was fifteen, pet . . . fifteen years old. Do yer really think I would want to have an affair with someone who was old enough to be my da – if not my grandda?'

Helen's eyes were glued to Pearl. Deep down she had always known. It had been too hideous for her to accept, though, until now. Suddenly she felt so incredibly stupid.

So naïve. Who had she been kidding? *An affair?* She suddenly recalled John's face. He'd thought the same, but hadn't wanted to say, which was so like John – not wanting to hurt her.

'Yer darling grandda, pet, decided he wanted something,' Pearl said, her tone without emotion. 'And so he took it.'

Helen looked at Bel and then back at Pearl and knew every word this woman uttered was true.

She felt a wave of revulsion surge through her.

'He . . .' Helen hesitated. She had to say the words, had to know without a shadow of a doubt what Pearl was saying.

'He *raped* you?' She forced the words, scrutinising Pearl's worn-out face. She saw it change, as though her whole being was suddenly overcome with tiredness. A lifelong weariness.

'Aye,' Pearl said. 'He did.'

Helen saw her shoulders sag.

'Yer grandda forced himself on me.' Pearl spoke as much for her daughter's sake as for Helen's. She would tell them the hellish truth and be done with it. Perhaps then she could finally leave it all behind.

'There'd been a big party for his going back overseas,' she said, stubbing out her cigarette. 'He woke me in the middle of the night. Strangled me half to death. Did what he did.'

Bel moved her stool to be nearer her ma. She put an arm around her. This was the first time she had heard her mother say the words out loud. Almost a year had passed since the day of revelations outside Mr Havelock's house when she had learnt the truth about her own parentage. It was only now, though, that she felt as if she could have cried – not for herself, she had already done that – but for her ma.

Bel glanced up at Helen. She looked stunned. Horrified.

'I'm so sorry, Pearl,' Helen said, her eyes wet as she looked at this woman and her daughter.

She felt ashamed to be a Havelock.

Ashamed to be the granddaughter of such a vile, evil man.

Her heart bled for Pearl and for Bel, knowing that she had been conceived in such an abhorrent manner.

God, she'd been so desperate to take the top off Pandora's box and have a good look.

But now that she had, she wished she hadn't, for she knew she would never be able to forget what she'd seen. Nor close the lid.

Chapter Fifty-Two

Charlotte staggered back along the lane, her mind like a kaleidoscope flashing distorted images across her vision. *A red lamp . . . a red room . . . a brass bed . . . Maisie kissing a man in a white uniform . . . Vivian's serious face talking to the soldiers . . . Business.*

Reaching the end of the lane, Charlotte stopped. Took a deep breath. Random remembrances of the past six months careered to the fore.

The dishevelled man coming out of the front door of Lily's. A 'waif and stray' or a client? Had Kate lied too?

The sums in the back of her diary that didn't add up.

God, she had been so stupid!

Rosie was working in a *brothel*.

Her employer was a madam.

Lily was a madam! Of course she was. The orange hair. The clothes. The jewellery. The eccentricities.

And Maisie and Vivian were working girls.

It all made sense now. The way they both looked. Sounded. Behaved . . . Their 'dates' . . . the Admiralty . . . Christmas Eve . . . The wedding.

Oh my God! Did Bel know about her sister?

Charlotte walked to the corner of Ashbrooke Crescent and West Lawn.

Making her way through the jostling crowds, back over to Rosie, she caught her sister's profile as she turned to look for her. The sun caught her skin and she could see the scars.

At least her sister had not been a – *God, she could barely even think the word*.

At least Rosie hadn't been a *call girl*.

'Where have you been?' Rosie sounded worried.

Charlotte heard herself speak, telling her sister and Lily and George that she had seen a friend.

'Let's get to the clubhouse before they run out of tea,' Lily said.

Charlotte could tell Lily knew that she was lying. Of course she did. Lily knew her. Understood her. She *loved* Lily. But Lily had lied to her. She was a madam. She was running a *house of ill repute*.

Suddenly Charlotte was back in the kaleidoscope.

People were swirling around her.

She could hear the chinking of china teacups.

George was talking about France.

She looked at Lily, who was staring out of the window. She followed her line of vision and saw Kate and Alfie in the stands, watching the grand performance taking place on the green. A silent one. The vicar's mouth was moving, yet she heard no words.

He was there and she was here.

Or was it the other way round?

Was she the theatre and everyone else the spectators?

She felt as though she might be going mad.

'Conseil Nationale de la Résistance.'

Was she now hearing French?

It was George.

They were looking at her expectantly.

All these people she no longer knew.

'The *Conseil Nationale de la Résistance* means the National Council of the Resistance,' she said robotically.

She caught George glancing at Lily. They knew. They could read her mind.

'Illusion . . . Pétain . . . Resistance . . . working together . . . bread is buttered . . . eggs in one basket . . .' Lily and George's words seem to run into each other.

She couldn't sit here and pretend.

Their whole existence had been a lie.

She heard her chair scrape back.

Lies. All lies.

'You all right, *ma petite*?' Lily asked. 'You've lost all your colour.'

No! she wanted to scream.

You have all lied to me!

'I'm fine,' she said. 'I just need to use the loo.'

Everything had suddenly become topsy-turvy, back to front, inside out.

The reality from which she had been shielded was unreal. Fictional.

She felt like Alice after she'd followed the White Rabbit down the hole – only there was no returning to the real world.

This *was* the real world.

Chapter Fifty-Three

Rosie got to the toilets but not in time to catch up with Charlotte.

She waited outside, watching women go in and out.

After five minutes, Rosie went in.

'You all right, Charlie?'

'I'll be out in a minute,' Charlotte answered.

'I'll wait for you outside,' Rosie said.

Lily and George had been right to look concerned.

'Dear me.' Rosie tried to sound jocular when Charlotte came out. 'I know the Ladies here is nice – but not nice enough to take up residence here.'

Charlotte gave a wan smile.

'Come to the bar with me,' Rosie said. 'I'll get us both a glass of lemonade.'

Normally the offer of any kind of fizzy drink would have had Charlotte racing to the bar. Instead, she trooped behind.

'Two lemonades, please,' Rosie told the barmaid.

After paying, she handed one to Charlotte and took a sip from her own glass.

She started to feel a little unnerved by her sister's sudden change of mood.

What on earth had happened in the past hour?

'What's wrong, Charlie?' she asked tentatively.

'Nothing.' Charlotte was still unable to look her sister in the eye.

'You were fine on the way to the parade. Happy as Larry, I'd say. Then you disappear for a little while – you say you saw someone from your class but weren't able to speak to them – and then you come back miserable.'

Rosie looked at Charlotte, who was inspecting an invisible spot on the ground.

Seeing a free table by the side of the lounge bar, Rosie grabbed her drink.

'Come on, let's sit over there.'

Charlotte followed and the two sisters sat down.

Rosie noticed Charlotte had yet to take a drink of her lemonade.

She looked around; the room was just starting to fill up. The parade was now over and it was getting noisy.

'Right, you're beginning to worry me now, Charlie.'

Rosie looked at her sister. *Something wasn't right. Charlie was never this quiet.*

'What is it, Charlie? You know you can tell me anything, don't you?'

Charlotte didn't say a word. Nor did she nod or shake her head.

'*Did* you see one of your schoolmates? Were they horrible to you?'

Was Charlie being bullied again?

Charlotte shook her head.

'No, I'm not being bullied.'

Rosie thought she saw her sister's lower lip tremble. She was on the verge of tears. So unlike Charlotte. The last time she'd cried was when she'd told Rosie what had been going on at Runcorn.

'Everything's a lie,' Charlotte said finally. She still wouldn't look at Rosie. 'You've lied to me my whole life.'

Rosie had a sudden wave of nausea.

She didn't know, did she?

She took Charlotte's chin and tilted it so that her sister was forced to look at her.

354

'What do you mean, *everything's* a lie?'

Charlotte looked into her sister's eyes.

'I know,' she said simply.

The two sisters stared at one other as though seeing each other for the first time.

Suddenly Rosie was back in time. It was a year and a half ago. She was with Peter by the police cabin on the south docks. He was saying the same thing to her.

And now she was saying the same thing she'd said to him, but to Charlotte.

'What do you mean, "you know?"'

Her legs started to shake. Thank God she was sitting down. Again, the feeling of nausea. It had been dreadful when Peter had told her, but this was worse.

Much worse.

This was her sister.

Charlie was still a child. Charlie looked up to her.

'I know,' Charlotte said, her lower lip still trembling. 'I know about Lily's.'

Rosie felt breathless.

'What about Lily's?' She was stalling for time. Trying desperately to put off the inevitable.

'*I know.*' Charlotte dropped her voice. 'I saw the red light . . . Saw Maisie and Vivian take two soldiers back there. I saw one of the rooms,' Charlotte whispered. 'At Lily's. That day I went for tea. Didn't really understand.' She looked off into the distance. 'Until today.'

Neither spoke for a moment.

'Everything makes sense now,' she said. 'The school fees. The flat. Money for everything . . .' Her voice trailed off.

'And you've worked there for years. Lied to me *for years*,' Charlotte said.

Another moment's silence.

Rosie didn't know what to say. It was clear her sister knew. Her worst fears had come true.

Like she always knew they would.

She'd been kidding herself.

She was stupid for thinking Charlotte wouldn't find out. Of course she would.

And now she knew the truth, there was no point in lying.

'Yes,' Rosie said simply. 'I did work at Lily's.'

Charlotte looked at her sister and could read the mortification in Rosie's face. She wanted to tell her that she understood. *There was no real shame in just doing the books, was there?* Yes, it was a brothel, but it wasn't as if she had done what Maisie and Vivian did.

'I—' Charlotte was just about to speak but Rosie stopped her. Putting a finger on her sister's lips, she took hold of her hand.

'Charlie, I'm sorry. Sorry for lying.'

Charlotte tried to speak again, but Rosie continued.

'I didn't want you to know,' she said. 'Not until you were older, anyway.' Rosie squeezed Charlotte's hand.

'Lily told me I should have been honest with you from the start,' Rosie said. 'Told you the truth. She said you were old enough.'

Charlotte nodded. *Lily knew her so well.*

'But I guess I wanted to keep you innocent. Not a part of that world.'

Rosie looked at her sister.

'I didn't want you to know I'd worked there. What I did . . . I wish you hadn't found out this way,' Rosie said. 'I wanted to tell you myself.'

Charlotte felt her heart start to beat faster.

Something wasn't right.

'And I want you to know that I don't *work* there – as such – not now.'

356

She paused.

'Now I only do the books. All the accounts. That sort of thing.'

Charlotte felt her head explode.

Rosie.

Her Rosie.

Her sister.

Her beautiful, strong sister *had* been a working girl.

She had slept with men for money.

Rosie saw the change in Charlotte's face.

'So, you *worked* there?' Charlotte said incredulously. 'As in, *worked* there – as one of the girls?'

And it was at that moment that Rosie realised she had just made the biggest mistake in her life.

Charlotte had thought she was simply a bookkeeper. Albeit for a brothel. But only a bookkeeper.

She looked at Charlotte and saw the hurt. Then disgust. All mixed up with disbelief.

It was then and there that Rosie's heart broke.

Probably for the first time in her life.

For at that very moment she saw her little sister's loss of innocence.

It destroyed her to know that it was she – her older sister – who had been the cause.

She had tried so hard to shield Charlie, to protect her, and yet it was she who had dragged her into the world she had so desperately wanted her little sister to remain ignorant of.

If only she could have taken her words back.

But it was too late.

She watched as tears filled Charlie's pretty blue eyes. The eyes of their mother.

'You *slept* with men for money,' Charlotte said, tears running down her face.

Rosie watched as sorrow was replaced by anger.

'I used to,' she said, trying to lessen the blow. 'But not any more.' She tried to take Charlotte's hand, but her sister wrenched it away.

'Don't touch me!' Tears were now dribbling over her lips. 'Why?' Charlotte stood up. 'Why would you do that?'

But she didn't wait for an answer; instead she left, pushing her way through the throng now waiting to get served at the bar, needing to get out, to leave. To run away from this horrid reality.

Rosie jumped up and started to go after her. She needed to fix this, even though she knew that this could never truly be fixed. The clock could not be turned back, no matter how much she desperately wanted it to be.

She felt someone grab her arm and turned to see that it was Lily.

Rosie looked at her.

Lily flinched at the sight of the pain etched on Rosie's face.

'She knows.' It was all Rosie could say. The words seemed to stick in her throat. 'She knows.'

Lily looked around to see that Charlotte had just about made it to the exit.

'Stay here!' she told Rosie. 'Leave the girl to me.'

Rosie didn't argue.

All of a sudden, she felt exhausted.

Chapter Fifty-Four

After leaving the Tatham, Helen turned right and made her way towards Borough Road. It was still light enough to walk without the aid of her little electric torch. The marble-playing children had been called in for their suppers a good while ago and playtime for most of the street's youngsters had been replaced by bedtime.

Helen would have given anything to magically transport herself to the Ryhope to be with John. He was the person she yearned to be with. She would have given anything to be sitting next to him, feeling his body next to hers. The love she believed they had for each other replacing the feelings of horror and revulsion she had been left with after finally hearing the truth.

A truth she guessed John already knew.

John had been with her throughout this whole sorry saga, and it felt natural that she should be with him now. But of course she couldn't be. She knew he had a particularly difficult operation scheduled for this evening. She would have to wait until tomorrow to see him.

Walking down the stone steps to the little basement flat, Helen realised how lucky she was to have John – and, of course, Gloria. She didn't know what she would do without either of them.

Helen knocked. Not too loudly as she didn't want to wake Hope.

'Helen.' Gloria opened the door wide. 'What on earth are you doing here?' She ushered her in. 'Is everything all right?'

*

'Ah John!'

Dr Parker turned to see Dr Eris striding towards him down the corridor.

'Claire,' he said, smiling, 'you have such energy. Would you mind giving me a little if you have any to spare?'

'How looks can deceive!' She laughed and touched his arm gently as she reached him. 'Honestly, it's all a façade. Underneath this sprightly exterior is one worn-out, rather depleted woman.'

Dr Parker raised his eyebrows in disbelief. 'If you say so.'

'I'm guessing you've just been to see our young Jacob?' she asked, looking down at the thick, clearly labelled patient file he was holding.

'I have indeed. And I have to say again what a brilliant job you've done. I'm guessing he'll be going home soon?'

'I want to find him some kind of work placement or war work – office-bound, of course – before he goes,' Dr Eris said. 'He's an intelligent chap. He needs to have an aim. A purpose. Or he'll be back here before we know it.'

Dr Parker nodded. Psychologists like Claire got a bad press, but they too were quietly saving people's lives, just as he and his fellow surgeons were, only in a different way.

'So, where are you off to?' Dr Eris asked. 'I'm guessing you've not got the night off?'

'Well, actually I have. The op I was down to do has just been cancelled – or rather, put back.'

'Clinical or other?' Dr Eris asked.

'Clinical. His pre-op assessment has shown up a few concerns. Slight respiratory infection. The anaesthetist doesn't want to take the chance.'

Dr Eris thought for a moment.

'I'm off at seven this evening . . .' She moved a little closer to Dr Parker to make way for a porter pushing a patient on a stretcher. 'As we're both feeling like we need a little respite, why don't we escape for a few hours and go and refuel down at the Albion?'

'The Albion?' Dr Parker said. *Why was he stalling? Why shouldn't he go for a drink?*

'All right then.' He smiled. 'The Albion it is. For a few hours' R & R. Respite and refuelling.'

Dr Eris had to suppress her excitement. She had been trying to work out how to get John out for a drink on his own for a while now.

'That's a date then,' Dr Parker said. He was about to correct himself – explain that he didn't mean this was a *date* as such – but stopped himself. *Would it be so bad if it was?*

'See you there at eight then?' Dr Eris started to walk away. 'I look forward to it.'

Gloria pushed herself out of her chair and went over to Helen and gave her a big hug. 'This is awful, really awful. I'm so sorry.'

Helen allowed herself to be hugged; it still felt a little alien to her, but she was slowly getting used to it.

'It's poor Bel and Pearl I feel sorry for,' she said. 'I know Pearl's not the most likeable person, but I felt so sad for her. Her face when she told me . . .' Helen shivered. 'It was like a part of her was dead.'

Gloria picked up the pot of tea, which was now cold, and went into the kitchenette to put the kettle on.

'Pearl's got good people around her.' She walked back to the kitchen doorway and looked at Helen. 'Her life's probably better than it's ever been. She adores Bel. And Maisie. She's got a good home. Secure, with people who care. She'll never go cold or hungry. And she's got a job that suits her down to the ground. She can keep herself topped up with Scotch most of the day and get paid for it.'

Helen grimaced. 'I know. She likes her whisky, doesn't she? She was knocking them back when I was there.'

'I think that's always been Pearl's way of coping,' Gloria said, turning back and filling the pot with boiling water. 'Probably always will be.'

She walked back into the lounge with the tea.

'It's you I worry about,' she said, looking at Helen. 'This is a lot for you to take on board.'

Helen poured tea into their cups, added milk and stirred.

'It must be . . .' Gloria thought for a moment. 'It must be very disturbing for yer to know this about yer grandfather. Someone you've known 'n loved all of yer life.'

Helen took a sip of her tea. It felt warm and comforting. As it did being here with Gloria.

'To be honest, it's not really sunk in,' she said. 'When we were chatting in the pub, I was thinking how Grandfather's always had the glad eye for young blondes. He's never really tried to hide it. He makes jokes about it. Or at least I thought they were jokes. I never really took it seriously. Him being so old. It's that typical thing, isn't it? Old bloke looking at some pretty young filly and wishing he was a younger man.'

Helen shivered again as she thought of Pearl being a pretty young thing.

Gloria sat back on her little two-seater settee. She had been truly shocked by what Helen had told her this evening, although she had tried not to show it, or how angry she felt.

'And he's a widower,' Helen said. 'So it sort of made it all right if he was a bit lecherous.'

'When did yer nan die?' Gloria asked.

'I'm not entirely sure. I was only a baby, so a good twenty years or so ago.' Helen looked at Gloria. 'That's what makes this even worse, if that's at all possible. My grandmother was still alive when Grandfather did what he did to Pearl. Makes me feel sick.'

'Do you think *yer* mam knows? About Bel? About what yer grandda was like?' Gloria asked tentatively. Talking about Miriam to Helen was like dropping a spark into a tinderbox: guaranteed to make Helen's anger and resentment towards her mother ignite.

'Mother wouldn't know or care.' Helen's face hardened. 'If it doesn't concern her, she doesn't give two figs.'

She took a sip of her tea and was quiet for a moment.

'I don't think she knows about Bel, though. I would have seen it when the two of them met. I doubt she knew what Grandfather was really like. She and Aunty Margaret weren't at home that much when they were growing up. They only seemed to come back during the holidays – and even then they often stayed with friends.'

Gloria thought about what Helen had told her about her nana and wondered if perhaps she hadn't been as mad as she'd been made out to be. Keeping her pretty, young, blonde daughters away at boarding school – away from their father – might actually have been an incredibly sane and sensible move.

'You won't breathe a word of this to Dad, will you?'

'Not if you don't want me to,' Gloria agreed.

'Or anyone?' Helen looked embarrassed. 'I know you're about as far removed from a gossip as anyone can get, but I have to make sure, for Bel's sake – and Pearl's. They've said it's fine to tell you. Bel knows how close we are. But they've both begged me not to tell another living soul. At least for the time being. Bel hasn't even told Polly yet.'

'Really? That surprises me. I thought them two told each other everything.'

'I know, I was surprised as well.' Helen thought for a moment. 'Bel said that the time's never been right, but I think there's more to it.'

Gloria gave Helen a questioning look.

'I'm not sure, but there's a part of me wonders whether she feels shame,' Helen mused.

'But it's not her fault, is it?' Gloria said.

'I know, but I can understand *why* she might feel like that. I know it's not quite the same for me, but *I* feel ashamed.'

Another puzzled look from Gloria.

'For being related to someone like *that*,' Helen said. 'For being related to a monster. I have a monster as a grand-father. Bel has a monster for a father. And whether we like it or not, we both have that monster's blood coursing through our veins.'

Chapter Fifty-Five

'Charlotte!' Lily's voice sounded out down West Lawn. It was still quite busy, but not as packed as it had been earlier on. There was a small crowd waiting for the bus further along the street, and courting couples walking slowly, looking up at the big houses that could not fail but induce both awe and envy.

'Charlotte!' Lily's tone was now tinged with anger. It did the trick. Charlotte stopped in her tracks and turned around.

Lily could see that her pretty face was tear-stained. She'd also clearly pinched a little mascara from Rosie as there were dark smudges under her eyes. She looked bereft. Alone. Distraught. And so much more.

'Follow me!' Lily commanded as she stomped past.

She could hear Charlotte's slightly raised Mary-Jane heels on the pavement and breathed a sigh of relief that she was doing as she was told. When she reached the small gate at the bottom of the pathway, she turned to look at Charlotte.

'I'm not a believer in airing my dirty laundry in public, so we're going to have this conversation indoors, away from prying eyes.'

She swung open the gate. 'All right?'

Charlotte looked up at the house.

Lily saw her hesitation. 'There's nothing to be afraid of in my humble abode. It's probably the safest place you could ever be.'

Charlotte walked through the gate.

Lily gave another sigh of relief.

Two minutes later they were walking over the threshold and into the main hallway.

'Lily!' Vivian appeared from the kitchen and stopped in her tracks. She opened her mouth to say something, but nothing came out.

'Yes, my dear, it's me . . . And Charlotte.' She looked at her charge. 'Now, if you don't mind, Vivian, I would very much like a large Rémy, please, and I think Charlotte here could do with a hot chocolate with plenty of sugar.'

Vivian's eyes were like saucers.

The fact Charlotte was here – in the state she was in – while there was business being conducted upstairs meant only one thing.

Charlotte knew.

Boy, oh boy!

'We'll be in the office,' Lily said as she pushed open the oak door. She waited until Charlotte was in before pushing the door ajar and marching over to Rosie's desk to retrieve her packet of Gauloises.

'So you've worked it out?' Lily asked. 'You know that my home is also what many would call a brothel. I like to refer to it as a "bordello".'

Charlotte stood, not knowing what to do or even say any more.

'Why don't you sit down, *ma chère*.' Lily softened her tone. Charlotte did as she was told and sat on the chaise longue. 'And you can tell me what you know. And then we can go from there.'

Lily listened as Charlotte told her, haltingly, how, since she'd moved back, she'd started to wonder how Rosie had been able to afford the school fees, and everything else that went along with them. That she had seen 'the red room' when she'd come round for tea but not understood its true purpose. How she had seen Maisie and Vivian with two admirals on Christmas Eve and been puzzled when they had all ignored each other at Polly's wedding. And how this afternoon she had watched them both again as they had chatted to two soldiers before bringing them back to the house – which was when she'd seen the red light.

'Then everything suddenly just fell into place,' Charlotte said, her voice faint. 'Why Rosie hadn't told me about you, or her work here . . . Why she seemed determined to keep me away from here.' Charlotte looked around the room. 'Why she was telling me lies about stupid little things that it didn't make sense for her to lie about.'

'*Knock knock!*' Vivian drawled.

'Come in.' Lily had been leaning against the desk. She stood up to let Vivian put the tray down. Vivian handed Lily her brandy and took the mug of hot chocolate over to Charlotte.

'Here you are, hon.'

Charlotte glanced up at Vivian, forced a smile and mumbled, 'Thank you.'

'Nothing's ever as bad as it seems, honeybun, you remember that.' Vivian gave Charlotte a smile before throwing Lily a look and turning to make her way out of the room.

'Just holler if y'all need anything else,' she said, shutting the door behind her.

'You're shocked by everything you've found out.' Lily looked at Charlotte. Her face looked pale. 'Which is perfectly natural.'

'I just don't understand why Rosie had to do . . . *that*,' Charlotte said.

Lily heard the contempt and derision in Charlotte's voice. She bristled.

'Let's call a spade a spade,' Lily said. 'By *that*, you mean have sex with men for money?'

Charlotte nodded but didn't meet Lily's gaze.

Lily scrutinised Charlotte's face. The look of repugnance was still there.

'It's no different than a woman marrying a man for his money,' she said. 'And I'll bet you wouldn't give a woman who marries for money a look like the one I'm seeing on your face now, would you?'

Charlotte stared up at Lily. Now there was defiance. 'That's different.'

'Oh, *ma chère*, it all boils down to the same thing. It's a transaction. A business deal. You want something I have and I'm prepared to sell it to you. At least under this roof it's a safe place to conduct business, which is more than I can say for a lot of marriages.'

Lily looked at Charlotte. She was still young. She had a lot to learn – none of which she would be taught at that school of hers.

'Why?' Charlotte suddenly blurted out. 'Why did Rosie do it?'

'She did what she did for money,' Lily said simply.

'But why couldn't she just do the books – like she's doing now? Why did she have to . . . to sleep with men?'

Lily sighed.

She was glad Rosie was not here. She would not want her to see or hear Charlotte's judgement – or her disgust.

'Rosie could not have earned the kind of money she did by simply *doing the books*, Charlotte. Nor could she have earned that kind of money doing anything else. Not the kind of money she needed to do what she personally felt she had to do.'

Charlotte looked puzzled.

'What do you mean *to do what she personally felt she had to do*?'

She looked at her hot chocolate and put it on the coffee table.

'She didn't have to send me to boarding school. Which I *hated*, by the way. She didn't have to send me away full stop. I could have gone to school here. A normal school. Like every other normal person.'

Charlotte's anger was rising.

'We could have got by without her doing – ' she threw Lily a defiant look ' – *that*.'

Lily had to tell her. She knew Rosie wouldn't. Not in a million years.

Lily took a slug of her brandy, stubbed out her cigarette and went to sit next to Charlotte on the chaise longue. Charlotte mightn't be her blood, but Lily was as near to a mother as Charlotte was ever going to get – and she needed to know the whole truth. For her own sake.

'What I'm going to tell you is quite distressing, my dear.' She took Charlotte's hand. 'But you need to know why Rosie took you away from here. Why she put you in a school in the middle of nowhere, and why she did what she did to keep you at that school of yours.'

And that was when Lily told Charlotte the whole truth. How her uncle Raymond had forced Rosie to make a deal with the devil on the night of their parents' funeral. How he had forced her to be compliant while he raped her, to be quiet or else he would go and do the same to her little sister sleeping next door.

Lily looked at Charlotte and read the horror she was feeling.

It hurt to have to tell her.

But she went on.

She told Charlotte how Rosie had got her out of town as quickly as possible, leaving no trace as to where they had both gone, but particularly no trace of where Charlotte had been taken.

'The first few years after your mum and dad died, your sister was driven by fear. By a determination to keep you safe. Away from that sick, depraved man.' Lily shivered, remembering her brief meeting with him.

'Don't forget your sister was not much older than you are now.' Lily looked at Charlotte. There were the beginnings of tears. 'Rosie thought the best way to keep you safe and out of harm's way was to get you in a boarding school out in the country. A place where you would be educated and looked after. Most of all, a place where that monster would never find you, but if by some remote possibility he did, she knew the school wouldn't let him near you. Your sister had given them strict instructions that no one could contact you without her permission.'

Lily looked at Charlotte. The tears were now streaming down her face. She put her drink down on the floor and put her arm around her and gave her a hug.

The gesture seemed to make Charlotte cry even more.

'I know, my dear,' Lily tried to soothe her. 'What I have told you is quite appalling. It should not happen to anybody in life, but unfortunately it does. Your sister was dealt a pretty bad hand, but to her credit, she made the most of it.'

She leant back a little so that she could see Charlotte's face.

'So, you must never, ever judge your sister, you hear me?'

Charlotte nodded.

'I never, ever want to see that look of disgust on your face when you even think about what your sister did for money.'

Another nod.

'Because everything Rosie has done in her life has been for you, Charlotte.' Lily had to swallow. She felt tears pricking her own eyes. 'She kept you safe, got you the best education money could buy. She sold her body to buy you a future.'

Lily shook her head and smiled sadly.

'That girl would have given her own life for you if she'd had to. If it was *my* sister who had done all that for me, I'd feel like the luckiest girl on the planet.'

She smiled at Charlotte as one lone tear managed to escape.

'And the most loved.'

She gave her a hug.

'Rosie's not the only one who loves you, you know?'

Lily could feel Charlotte's body relax, her body gently juddering as she cried.

And cried.

After a while Charlotte sat up.

'If it wasn't for me, though, none of this would have happened . . . If it wasn't for me, Rosie could have stopped him doing what he did – or at least tried.'

There was a fresh burst of tears.

'This is all my fault. I've made all this happen!'

Lily cupped Charlotte's tear-stained face in her hand.

'Now, you listen here. None of this is your fault. *Do you hear me?'*

Charlotte wasn't convinced.

'You had no bearing on what that man did. He would have done what he did regardless. You were just a convenient pawn in his sick game.'

Lily sat up straight.

'You've got to listen to me, Charlotte, and listen properly. It's important you understand this otherwise what you know – what happened to your sister – will pull you down into the mire. It will infect your life. And I, for one, refuse to stand by and let one monstrous, malignant human being continue to destroy others from the grave.'

Charlotte sat up and wiped her eyes.

She looked at Lily.

'Good,' Lily said, taking her hand and clasping it in her own. 'Take it from someone who has been round the block more times than most people have had hot dinners.'

She squeezed Charlotte's hand and gave her a smile.

'You have to accept that you were in no way responsible for what happened to Rosie. You have to understand that here – ' Lily touched the side of her head with her free hand ' – and here.' She touched the top of her bosom. 'In your head and in your heart.

'There's only one person to blame for what happened to your big sister and that is that man. No one else. Not your parents. Not Rosie. Not God. Not anyone else. Only him.'

Lily took a deep breath.

'There's going to be times when you think *Why me? Why Rosie?* And I'm telling you now, when you do take a dip in the pool of self-pity, don't wallow in it for too long. What's happened has happened. It's in the past now and it's not going to spoil your future.'

Lily looked at Charlotte.

'Do you understand?'

Charlotte nodded.

Lily stood up and went over to the sideboard. She pulled out the top drawer and took out a lace hanky.

'Now, come on, dry those pretty eyes of yours.' She walked over and handed Charlotte the handkerchief. 'And let's go and see Rosie.'

Chapter Fifty-Six

Bill looked at Pearl.

He hadn't seen her this bad for a while.

'Go on, if yer must.' Pearl leant over the bar, her hand outstretched, shaking her empty glass. She was looking at Bill, although all she could really see was a fuzzy outline of a man who was taller than average, still had his hair, and whose rounded face seemed to match his rounded belly. He had one hand on top of the pump and the other was on his hip. She couldn't really make out his expression, but she sensed he was not a happy chap.

'Ahhm soo sorry, Bill,' she said, still waving her glass. 'I have jumped ship this fine evening . . . abandoned yer on yer own . . .' Her speech was slurred and had been for the past hour.

Geraldine, the barmaid, leant into Bill and spoke through the side of her mouth so that only her boss could catch what she was saying. 'She's been hammering the Scotch since that posh cow came in to see her.'

Seeing Pearl leaning her scrawny body over the bar in an effort to get to the bottle of whisky, Geraldine squashed past Bill.

'Here yer are!' Geraldine got to the bottle just before Pearl's hand nearly swiped it over. She poured Pearl a finger of whisky.

'Give it here!' Pearl made a grab for the bottle and missed, succeeding the second time round. 'That'll barely wet the back of my throat.' She sloshed Scotch into her glass and swivelled her body round.

'Here, Ronald, give us yer glass.' She raised the bottle in the air.

Everyone in the bar looked over at Pearl before going back to their own drinks and conversations.

'I think we need to get her home,' Bill said. 'I wonder if we should get Bel.'

'Good idea.' Geraldine undid the back of her pinny and walked to the end of the bar before ducking under the half-opened hatch.

'Come on, gorgeous.' Ronald's voice was gravelly and slurred. He was drunk, but not as inebriated as Pearl. 'I'm taking yer home.' He grabbed Pearl by the wrist and gently tugged her away from the bar. 'Bring yer bottle with yer as well.'

Pearl hugged the bottle to her as though she were a child and it her treasured teddy bear. She looked at Bill, although he could see she wasn't really able to focus on him.

'I think she might be better off in her own home tonight, mate,' said Bill.

'Nah! She wants to come back to mine.' Ronald slipped his arm around Pearl's waist.

Bill had to stop himself clambering over the bar and ripping Ronald's skinny, tattooed arm off Pearl.

'Ahhm all reet, Bill. Yer worry too much.' Pearl was now being led across the bar towards the exit. Ronald had hold of one hand. Pearl's other hand was gripping the neck of the bottle of Scotch.

Bill opened his mouth to object when one of the regulars shouted out, 'Poker?'

Ronald looked over to his drinking buddy and shook his head. 'Not tonight, mate.' He cocked his head towards Pearl. 'Bigger fish to fry.'

Bill watched as the door banged shut.

It took all his willpower not to go stomping after them.

A few minutes later, Bel came into the bar, followed by Polly, then Geraldine. The three women looked around.

'Where is she?' Bel mouthed the words over at Bill, who was busy pulling a pint but had noticed their arrival.

He put the frothy pint onto a beer mat, took the money for the drink and dropped it into the till. He motioned for them to come over, before going over and ringing the brass bell.

'Last orders at the bar!' he shouted out.

'Port and lemonade?' he said to Bel. 'Lemonade straight up?' to Polly.

Both women nodded and Bel opened up her handbag to get her purse to pay, but Bill waved a hand at her.

'On the house.' There was no arguing.

'Sorry to get yer both here this late on,' he said. 'But yer ma was in a bit of a state and I thought it best to get her home.'

Bel thought she saw hurt in Bill's eyes.

'But looks like Ronald beat you to it,' he said through gritted teeth.

'What? She's gone off with Ronald?' Bel was surprised. It had been a good while since her ma had been on a bender; even longer since she'd gone off with a bloke.

'Just with Ronald?' Bel asked, quickly scanning the room and seeing that the regulars who liked their after-hours card games were still there.

Bill didn't say anything, just nodded.

It was on the tip of Bel's tongue to say, 'Sorry, Bill,' but she didn't. Instead she thanked him for their drinks and went with Polly into the snug.

'What's happened?' Polly asked her sister-in-law.

Bel sat down with a heavy sigh. She was glad the snug was empty.

'Oh, Pol, where do I start?'

Chapter Fifty-Seven

'So, he's definitely dead?' asked Charlotte, entranced by the flickering orange and yellow flames in the hearth. It hadn't been cold enough to necessitate lighting the fire, but when they had got home it was as though they needed to dispel the chill left by all the talk of the past.

Rosie was also staring into the fire, her arm wrapped around Charlotte, who had changed into her nightie and dressing gown and was now nestled up on the sofa.

'Oh, yes, he's definitely dead,' Rosie said, thinking back to the sight of Raymond's inflated, putrid body as it was hauled out of the Wear.

'And was it true, what you said – before, when I asked you – about him being drunk and falling into the river?'

Rosie sighed. They had made a pact to be honest with each other from here on in. She had to honour that.

'Mmm . . . sort of,' she said. 'He'd certainly had a drink.' Rosie could still recall the rank smell of his breath.

'He came back,' Rosie began. 'Just turned up one day.'

'When?' Charlotte looked up at her sister.

'About two and a half years ago . . . September time.'

'Was that the first time you'd seen him . . .' Charlotte hesitated. 'Since Mam and Dad's funeral?'

'It was,' Rosie said.

'And what did he want?' Charlotte's voice was quiet.

'Money,' Rosie said simply. 'Money . . . and revenge for a perceived injustice.'

Charlotte looked up at her sister.

'What did *he* think had been done to *him*?' She was angry. *After what he had done to her sister?*

'He thought he'd been swindled out of his inheritance,' Rosie explained. 'He'd been cut out of the will by our grandparents. They left everything to Mam. So when Mam and Dad died, he thought he'd finally get what he believed was his due, but, of course, he didn't. It was all left to me – and you. So, he blackmailed me into paying him.'

'And did you?' Charlotte said.

'For a while, yes, I had to. He was threatening to tell the world about Lily's, and my working there – and, of course, you were his main bargaining chip.' Rosie kissed her sister on the top of her head. 'Not that he could have got to you.'

Charlotte thought about what Lily had said. Rosie's solitary aim in life had been to keep her safe.

'But then he found out I was holding back money from the overtime I was doing, and he came to the yard.' Rosie tensed at the memory.

'Was that when he went into the river?'

Rosie nodded.

'He attacked me.' Her hand automatically went to the small scars on her face. 'That's how I got these burns.'

Charlotte looked at her sister's face, now clear of make-up. 'So, it wasn't a weld gone wrong?' She remembered the day Rosie had come to visit her at the Rainers'. The scars had started to scab over. She'd been shocked but had believed what Rosie had told her.

'I had a lucky escape,' Rosie said. 'My squad came looking for me . . . Gloria, Polly, Martha, Dorothy and Hannah.' She smiled. They had been her knights in shining armour.

'Did they push him into the river?' Charlotte was now sitting up straight, entranced by what she was hearing.

'No,' Rosie said. 'I think it was a case of divine intervention.'

378

She looked at Charlotte.

'He tripped over a welding rod and went flying.'

'What? Into the river?'

Rosie nodded.

Charlotte exhaled loudly.

'Blimey, there really is a God!'

Chapter Fifty-Eight

Bill pulled on his coat and then his tweed flat cap.

The pub was empty, the beer trays had been swilled, the glasses all cleaned and polished, ready for another shift, chairs had been upended and stacked onto tables.

'You off?' Geraldine said as she tied her headscarf, then slung her gas mask over her shoulder.

'Aye,' Bill said, following her out of the main bar and down the hallway. 'The Welcome Tavern is having a lock-in tonight.'

Geraldine stepped out into the cool night. She looked up at the sky. It was cloudless. She never liked to see the stars. Her grandda always said it was an invitation to Jerry to come visiting.

'Night, then,' Geraldine said. 'Just give me a shout if I'm needed. I'm always up for an extra shift.' She'd bet money on her being called on tomorrow. There was no way Pearl would be in a state to work the afternoon shift.

'Aye, thanks, pet,' Bill said, forcing a smile.

He clashed the main door shut and turned the lock.

Tonight, he intended to get well and truly plastered.

It took Bill about a quarter of an hour to get to the lock-in, walking up Tatham Street, crossing the Borough Road, going left up Villiers Street, then turning right into High Street East, before finally arriving at the Welcome Tavern at the end of Barrack Street.

Within minutes he'd got himself settled at the bar with a pint and a whisky chaser.

Around the time Bill was ordering his second pint, the engines of sixty German bombers were turning over, getting ready to take off and head over the North Sea. Their target – the north-east of England.

It was a perfect night for flying. Fine and clear.

They flew fast and fairly low, but not low enough to evade the radar scanners.

At 1.44 a.m. the alarm went out, and the Sunderland sirens began to wail.

There was just enough time for people to get out of their beds, put on some clothes and get to a shelter before the drone of the bombers could be heard, vibrating the very air above them.

'Come on, Dor!'

Angie shoved her friend, who was lying fast asleep in bed.

'Blimey, it's like trying to wake the dead.'

'Noooo.' Dorothy finally surfaced from underneath the bedclothes. 'I hate Jerry! I hate air raids! I hate sirens! I hate this war!'

'Aye, 'n I'm guessing yer'd also hate being dead, so ger up!'

Within minutes they had pulled on their dressing gowns and slippers, grabbed a blanket each and had left their flat to make their way down the stairs. As soon as they reached the bottom, Angie stomped over to Mrs Lavender's front door.

'Mrs Lavender! Wakey-wakey!'

She put her ear to the front door.

Dorothy sighed.

Angie looked at her friend in disbelief. 'How can anyone sleep through this racket?'

She turned back to the door and started hammering again.

She bent down and opened the letter box.

'*Mrs Kwiatkowski!*' she shouted as loudly as she could.

Dorothy's mouth fell open.

'Since when did you learn how to speak Polish?'

Angie turned and looked at her friend.

'It's called *good manners*, learning how to say someone's proper name – even if it is in a foreign language.' Angie spoke like a teacher to her pupil.

Dorothy didn't have the chance to reply as the front door opened. Mrs Lavender was standing there, a blanket draped around her shoulders, looking more asleep than awake.

'Come on, let's get going.' Angie took her arm as Dorothy hurried ahead and opened the main door. The noise was deafening, but the street was relatively empty as most people along Foyle Street used their cellars and basements as shelters.

Once Angie and Mrs Lavender were outside, Dorothy let the door swing shut. Hurrying down the first lot of stone steps, she turned, taking more care as the second set of stone steps were much steeper. Having made it to Quentin's flat, she reached up to the ledge above the door and felt for metal. Grabbing the key, she quickly opened the door.

Seeing the bottom of Mrs Lavender's white broderie anglaise nightie, she looked up to see that Angie was having to take most of the old woman's weight as she struggled to get herself down the steps.

'Can you manage?' she shouted above the noise of the sirens, holding open the front door.

Angie nodded, finally making it to the bottom, manhandling Mrs Lavender over the threshold and into the flat.

Ever since the Tatham Street bombing, Angie had made sure it only took them a matter of minutes to get somewhere safe. They'd had a close call that night and she wasn't going to rely on Lady Luck helping them out again.

'I think it's going to be a bad one tonight,' Angie said, taking one last look as thick fingers of searchlights stabbed the open skies.

Shutting the door, Dorothy put on the light so they could see where they were going. The blinds were down and, as usual, Quentin had left his flat immaculate. He had also left them what he referred to as 'provisions' on a tray on top of the table.

Angie grabbed the tray and Dorothy lifted up the table-cloth and flung it over the top.

'Come on, in you go.' Dorothy gently helped Mrs Lavender to get under the large steel table that doubled up as an indoor air raid shelter. Quentin had made some adjustments to the Minister of Home Security Herbert Morrison's design, and had removed one side of the wire mesh and reinforced the top of the table with an extra layer of steel. He had also tied four gas masks to each leg, and for comfort's sake had added blankets, quilts and cushions to sit on.

Angie put the tray on a small wooden box in the middle of what could easily have been a child's den were they not at war.

'Come on,' Angie beckoned Dorothy, who dropped down on her knees and clambered inside.

They had just got themselves settled and had started to breathe normally when they felt the first tremor. It confirmed their fears. This was no false alarm.

Angie took off the cloth covering the tray. Quentin had left them a bottle of dandelion and burdock, some crackers and a packet of ginger nuts. Her favourites. She opened the packet and offered them to Mrs Lavender, who took one, and then Dorothy, who shook her head.

'I don't know how you two can eat at times like this,' Dorothy said.

'It's a survival instinct,' Mrs Lavender replied. 'Eat now because you don't know when you might eat again.'

Dorothy rolled her eyes. 'We're not in the middle of the desert, Mrs Lavender. The longest we'll have to go without food is the length of this blasted air raid.' All the same, she took a biscuit and forced it down.

They all jumped as they heard a loud whistling sound followed by a distant boom. There were a few more tremors. A few more explosions. Some distant. Some not so distant.

After a while Mrs Lavender's head started to droop forward. She was nodding off.

Angie and Dorothy shared the bottle of pop and ate more biscuits.

Suddenly, Mrs Lavender's eyes opened and she looked straight at Angie.

'Quentin's a good boy,' she said. 'Very kind. Thoughtful.'

Angie agreed. 'Aye, he is, isn't he?'

'And very rich,' Dorothy chipped in.

Mrs Lavender rested her eyes for a minute before opening them once again.

'He will make a very good husband.' Again, she looked straight at Angie.

'Aye, he would,' Angie said. She thought for a moment before adding, 'But he'll have to gan out more if he wants to ger himself a wife.'

She took another biscuit and bit into it.

Mrs Lavender and Dorothy looked at each other.

This time it was Mrs Lavender who raised her eyes to the ceiling – or rather the underside of the table.

'You all right?' Polly was sitting next to Bel.

They'd all had time to fling some clothes on and get round to Tavistock House before the first bombs had been dropped. But only just.

'I'm fine, honestly,' Bel said. 'It's me that should be asking if you're all right.' She looked down at Polly's tummy, which clearly looked very pregnant now. 'I swear you've got bigger these past few days.'

Polly rubbed her hand across her stomach. 'I do too. Dr Billingham reckons it's going to be a heavyweight.' She smiled. 'It's definitely a fighter. Just like its daddy.'

Bel laughed. 'I think you might find the baby's fighting spirit comes from its mammy.'

Polly smiled. 'Some might call it pig-headedness.' She nodded over at Agnes.

They both looked into the semi-darkness. The flickering of the candles they'd lit when they'd arrived gave them fleeting shots of those who were with them in the dank old basement.

Polly sat forward.

'You all right, Ma?'

Agnes nodded. Lucille was curled up next to her, sucking her thumb, her head resting in her nana's lap.

Joe was sitting next to her. He had brought today's *Daily Mirror*, which had a full report detailing the victory in North Africa: the capture of Tunis by the British First Army and the taking of Bizerte, forty miles north of the Tunisian capital by the Americans, had been followed by the final surrender of the remaining German Afrika Korps and Italian troops two days earlier. The Desert War had been won.

Bel knew Joe would keep that paper until it was yellow with age, for it was evidence that Teddy's death had not been in vain.

Seeing that Joe had his bad leg extended in front of him, and that he kept moving it every now and again, Bel knew it was paining him. Thank goodness he wasn't on duty with the Home Guard this evening, although there was no doubt that this would not stop him from hobbling off to do what he could as soon as the all-clear sounded out.

'You worried about your ma?' Polly asked Bel.

'No. If she's with Ronald, which she clearly is . . .' Bel felt a wave of disappointment ' . . . then she'll be fine.'

'He'll make sure she's all right? Sounds like she was totally blotto.'

'Yes. I don't particularly like Ronald, but he's not a bad egg. Certainly not as bad as most of the men Ma's had.'

Bel let out a sad laugh.

'He might well have had to carry her down to the basement, mind you. I know what Ma's like after she's had a skinful. Dead to the world. And it might seem like she's all skin and bone, but she's heavier than she looks.'

'And it's not as if Ronald's Mr Muscle either, is it?' Polly tried to keep the conversation light. She knew how much it hurt Bel when her ma went off on a bender. How much she worried about her. After what she'd told her this evening, she could understand that more now.

'I just feel it for Bill,' said Bel. 'He looked so gutted, didn't he?'

Polly nodded. 'Heartbroken.'

'Oh, don't,' Bel said, 'you're going to make me feel all depressed. Ma's such a train wreck when it comes to men.'

'Mmm,' Polly said. 'Perhaps that's because of what happened.'

'I think so too,' Bel said. 'I've thought that since she told me.'

Polly took hold of her friend's hand and squeezed it. She had no idea what it must feel like to know that your father, someone who was still living and breathing, had done something like that to your own ma.

She understood now why Bel had been so reticent about sending Mr Havelock a thank-you letter – and why Pearl's reaction had been so venomous.

'What do you think's going to happen now?' Polly asked.

'What, with my ma?' Bel asked.

'No, with Helen,' Polly said, trying to work out what her sister-in-law was really feeling. It still concerned her that Bel had kept this terrible secret to herself for so long, but what worried her more was that Helen's visit this evening would have repercussions. Perhaps not straight away. But it would. In time.

Of that she had no doubt.

When the sirens sounded, Helen dragged herself out of bed. It was almost a relief to be brought out of the dark, disturbing dreams she had been plunged into. Dreams of her grandfather's twisted, laughing face had plagued her for what seemed hours as he stomped around in a field that had been burned and charred. He was carrying a knife and occasionally stabbed at some invisible opponent. And there were rats everywhere. Big black rats scurrying around. It was as if her grandfather and the rats were one entity, as though he were their master and the fat, well-fed rodents his dutiful cohorts.

Pulling on her dressing gown and slippers, Helen grabbed her torch and made her way down to the first floor.

'Mother! Wake up!' She banged on her mother's bedroom door. No answer. The sirens seemed to be blotting out thought, never mind any other sound. *How on earth could her mother sleep through this?*

'Wake up, Mother!' Helen shouted, walking into her room and going over to her mother's bed. She was out for the count. Her bottle of sleeping pills was standing next to a crystal tumbler. Helen didn't need to smell it to know that the few drops of liquid left in there were the remnants of a G & T nightcap.

Her mother was lying on her back, her hands neatly clasped on her chest as though she was praying, an ivory-coloured silk mask over her eyes. Helen might have thought her mother dead were it not for the slight rise and fall of her chest.

'Mum, wake up!' Helen took hold of her mother's shoulders and shook her. Gently at first. Then more vigorously.

'*What's wrong!*' Miriam pulled off her mask and looked up at Helen. Her eyes were confused and bloodshot and for the first time, Helen thought her mother looked old.

'There's an air raid, Mother, and unless you fancy sleeping under a blanket of bricks tonight, I suggest you get yourself out of bed and down to the basement.'

Miriam sighed like a petulant child and hauled herself out of bed, pulling on her dressing gown and automatically sliding her feet into her slippers. She grabbed her glass tumbler and followed Helen out of the door and down the stairs.

'I'll meet you down there, darling.' Her words were slurred. 'Just need a little nightcap.' She staggered a little.

'For God's sake, Mum.' Helen grabbed the tumbler from her. 'Get into the basement and try not to fall down the steps.'

Helen hurried into the living room, sloshed gin and then some tonic into her mother's glass and hurried back out. As she headed down it occurred to her that Pearl and her mother were not dissimilar. They were both wrecks. Only her mother hid it better.

And, of course, they had something else in common.

Her grandfather.

As she reached the bottom step, she heard the first boom of an explosion.

After a few sips of her gin, Miriam curled up on the makeshift bed that had been put there at the very start of the war, and which lately had been getting plenty of use.

A few minutes later Helen could hear gentle snoring.

Normally she would have been glad that her mother had clapped out so quickly, but tonight she was particularly relieved. How could she have chatted to her mother after all she had just found out?

As she looked at her now, oblivious to the bombs going off, she wondered what her reaction might be, should she ever find out what her father was really like. Perhaps, deep down, she knew. Perhaps not. Helen didn't know any more.

Wrapping a blanket around herself and switching off her torch, Helen closed her eyes. She wondered what John was doing now. He wouldn't be sitting in some shelter, that was for sure. He'd probably be getting beds made up, ready for any casualties, going round the wards and checking on patients. That was assuming the Ryhope wasn't a target this evening.

God, she hoped not.

Rosie and Charlotte were on their own in the Jenkins' shelter. Their neighbours had decided they'd had enough of all the recent air raids and had gone to stay with an aged aunt not far from Lake Windermere.

Rosie was especially thankful, as the last thing she needed after the day that had just been was to deal with Mrs

Jenkins' incessant chatter. She had just spent most of the evening answering a stream of questions from Charlotte.

Rosie knew her sister's head must be full to bursting and it was for this reason that she had not told Charlotte about their uncle's incarceration for rape, or that he had been the hit-and-run driver who had killed their parents. That could wait.

'You all right?' Rosie asked. She was lying on the bottom bunk bed, a thick blanket covering her from top to toe.

'I'm fine,' Charlotte said.

Rosie could feel her shifting position, trying to get comfy.

'Rosie?'

'Yes?'

'Obviously, Peter knows everything?'

'Obviously.'

Silence.

'Do you miss him?'

'I do.'

'When he comes back . . .'

If he comes back.

'Mmm?'

'You don't think he'll mind me being here, will he?'

Rosie smiled. This was the easiest question Charlotte had asked so far.

'Far from it.'

'Far from it?'

'Charlie, there were two people fighting in your corner, arguing the case for me to allow you to come back to live here.'

Rosie felt Charlotte scoot round in her bed before her face appeared over the side of the bunk.

Rosie rolled her eyes. 'Lily, *of course* . . .

'And Peter.'

Rosie saw a big smile spread across her little sister's upside-down face.

'Now, can I *please* attempt to get some sleep?'

Charlotte's head disappeared.

More shifting about.

'Rosie?'

'*Yes.*'

'I love you.'

Rosie's eyes immediately clouded over.

'I love you too, Charlie. Very much.'

Chapter Fifty-Nine

The air raid lasted a total of one hour and twenty-five minutes. Not as long as most air raids, but long enough to do more damage than any bombing the town had suffered so far in the course of the war.

'What are you doing?' Mrs Perkins looked at her daughter as she came back down the stairs dressed in her air raid protection overalls and boots.

'I'm going to help.' Martha looked at her mother as though she was senile.

'But you're not meant to be on duty tonight?'

'I'm needed out there, Mam, you know that. You heard what the warden said on the way back from the shelter. It's pandemonium out there. They need all the help they can get.'

Mrs Perkins wanted to cry.

Didn't Martha understand? She just wanted her safe. Out of harm's way.

'Martha.' She grabbed hold of her daughter's arm. 'Just promise me you'll be careful. That you won't go and do anything daft.' She looked up at her strapping girl. 'Like walk into a collapsing building or anything like that?'

Martha saw the worry in her mother's eyes.

'Of course I won't, Mam,' she lied, bending down and wrapping her arms around her mother, giving her a bear hug.

'And just so you know,' Mrs Perkins said, 'I'm putting my foot down about you going to work in the morning.

When you come back here, you'll have a good feed and rest, you hear me?'

Martha smiled at her mam and at her dad.

'Agreed.'

She knew it would take her mother all of thirty seconds to realise that it was Sunday – and that she wasn't due to work anyway.

When Martha left, Mr Perkins walked over to his wife, still standing in the hallway, and held her in his arms.

She spoke into his chest. 'Do you think Martha wants to be a hero, to save people's lives, as a way of making up for what her real mother did?' It still horrified her that a mother, one who had given birth several times over – who had carried life in her belly for months on end – could then kill a child. Children. Poison them.

'I sometimes wish we'd never told her about her real mam.' Mrs Perkins rested her head on her husband's shoulder, not wanting to break free of his embrace.

'I don't know, my dear.' He stood and continued to hold the wife he loved. 'Perhaps she does think that – that she has to make amends for her mother's actions . . . Perhaps she doesn't.'

He thought.

'I really don't know. Perhaps she's simply a good person who knows she *can* help others, so that's what she does.'

When Martha stepped out into the street, she saw an army truck and waved it down.

It stopped just long enough for Martha to haul herself into the passenger seat.

'Where to?' she asked.

'Barrack Street,' came the reply.'

'How bad?' Martha asked.

'Two big ones,' the Home Guard soldier said, 'took out five houses and two pubs.'

'Any casualties?' asked Martha.

'Dozens injured . . . At least four dead.'

Chapter Sixty

Hundreds of air raid wardens, Home Guard soldiers, Civil Defence and emergency services worked through the early hours of the morning.

This time, the Luftwaffe had hit four out of the nine shipyards along the Wear. Greenwell's on the south dock, Austin's further upriver, Laing's, and Thompson's.

Martha returned home to find her mother was up, with breakfast on the go and a big mug of Ovaltine.

Her daughter had come back safe and sound and she had that to be thankful for. Like William kept telling her – she just had to take one day at a time. During times like this, there was no other way. She tried to heed his advice.

It was hard, though.

When dawn broke, Aunty Rina took Hannah a cup of tea in bed and told her to get herself ready for the day.

Half an hour later they had a kosher breakfast of cereal and toasted home-made bagels before leaving their house on Manila Street. Walking down Villette Road, they stopped off to collect Olly, and from there they walked the mile and a half to High Street East.

They would not have been able to take public transport even if they had wanted to as many of the main roads had been pockmarked with craters during the night.

They walked via Tatham Street and looked up Borough Road. The homes of those they knew and loved were still standing. *'Díky Bohu,'* Rina muttered, looking up at a sky that seemed so pure, so untainted, despite being contaminated by Hitler's harbingers of death just hours previously.

On seeing that Vera's café was still standing, Rina said a second '*Díky Bohu,*' and when Vera herself came to the door, griping about the ungodly hour she was being forced to leave the comfort of her bed, Rina smiled for the first time since the sirens had sounded out.

'Come on,' Rina told Vera in her sternest voice. 'Get your pinafore on. There's work to be done. Sandwiches to be made. Tea to be brewed.'

Vera huffed loudly, ushering Hannah and Olly into the café before poking her head out and looking down the street. It looked like a war zone. She could see rubble strewn about the road, shattered glass and a burst water main gushing everywhere.

An ambulance heading from Barrack Street further down the road trundled past slowly in an effort to avoid the mounds of bricks and mortar lying across its path.

If anyone had been scrutinising the old woman's face, they would have seen shock, then sadness – followed by defiance.

Flicking the sign on the front door of the cafe to 'Open', and kicking the wooden triangular door wedge into place, Vera turned round and marched back into the café.

Looking at Rina, Hannah and Olly, she waved her hand in the air impatiently.

'*Well, come on, what yer all waiting for?*'

When Helen woke up she looked at the time. It had gone nine o'clock. She'd slept surprisingly well. Probably because her mind was at rest knowing that those she loved were safe and sound. Once the all-clear had sounded out, she'd rung the Ryhope, and although she'd not been able to speak to John in person, she'd been reassured that he was all right. As expected, both the Ryhope and the Borough Asylum were expecting patients from town. John would be run off his feet.

She had also managed to find out from the operator that although both sides of the river had been badly hit, the Borough Road and Tatham Street had thankfully escaped unscathed.

Helen stretched and began to get herself ready for the day.

It was going to be a really important day. One, she realised, that had been a long time coming.

Now that the fog had lifted, she could finally see what was right in front of her.

Last night, while the town had been shaken to its core, her mind had gone to John. She'd realised how much he occupied her thoughts, her time, and, moreover, how much she actually *missed* him when she wasn't with him. *How crazy was that?*

Gloria was right. John felt the same. If he didn't, he wouldn't be spending every minute he had spare with her either.

As she'd sat in the cellar, she'd realised how stupid she had been to believe her mother's poisonous words. John didn't care about her past. She knew him better than anyone. Certainly better than her mother did.

Slipping on the dark green dress that brought out the emerald of her eyes, she looked at herself in the mirror. She went over and sat at her dressing table. Just a little make-up. Not too much. And she'd put her hair back in victory rolls. Attractive but casual.

Down in that dark basement, she had seen the light.

There was too much awfulness in the world and – thinking of her grandfather – too many awful people. So, when

397

something rather lovely came along – like what she had with John – you just had to grab it with both hands and make the most of it.

It was this realisation that had made her resolve to go and see John.

If he was in theatre, or conducting consultations, she would wait.

When she saw him, she would ask him to go for a walk with her around the grounds.

And then she would tell him what she really thought. How she felt.

Or perhaps she would simply show him.

When Pearl woke up she had the hangover from hell.

Not an uncommon feeling, though one she hadn't felt for a while now.

She sat up and looked around at her surroundings.

It took her a few moments to work out where she was.

Ronald's.

Then came a feeling she wasn't so used to. Guilt. And regret. Neither emotion usually succeeded in penetrating the layers of thick skin she had grown over the years, or the barrier of booze that shielded her from reality most of the time, but this morning they'd slipped through her defences and caught her off guard.

She flung off the blanket that was covering her.

She breathed a sigh of relief.

She still had her clothes on.

She vowed not to get so paralytic again.

Scrabbling around for her cigarettes, she found a squashed packet on the coffee table and lit one. Smoked. Coughed. Smoked some more. Then she stood up.

'See yer, Ronald,' she shouted up the stairs. She listened for a reply but heard only snoring.

She looked at the clock. Eleven. That gave her an hour to turn herself around and get to work.

The guilt returned.

She knew she had to apologise to Bill.

She didn't like saying sorry, but she needed this job.

Pah! Who was she kidding? This wasn't about her keeping her job.

She was sorry because she could remember the look on his face. It was about the only thing she could remember from last night.

Seeing her go off with Ronald, she knew what he'd think. What he would presume.

Normally, she didn't give two hoots what anyone thought, but loath though she was to admit it, she *did* care what Bill thought.

When Helen stepped out of her front gate on the corner of Side Cliff Road and Park Avenue, she was shocked to see just how near to her home the bombs had landed.

It was bedlam.

Firefighters, ambulances and army trucks were travelling in both directions along the main road that ran parallel to the park. She presumed they were taking the injured to either Southwick Hospital or Monkwearmouth. Spotting a warden walking down Roker Park Road, she hurried and caught up with him.

'Where's been hit?' she asked.

'More like where hasn't,' he said, shaking his head.

'That bad?' Helen asked, keeping abreast with him.

'They reckon a hundred and thirty bombs dropped,' he said, shaking his head. 'As usual this side's had it bad. The railway crossing's been hit up at Fulwell. There's been carnage up Atkinson Road way. Four houses totally obliterated. At least another hundred and fifty damaged.'

He exhaled.

Helen recognised the look.

'How many dead?'

'Eleven. Including a family of six.'

They exchanged looks. Neither needed to say anything. The warden tipped his tin helmet before hurrying across the road and disappearing into a crowd that had gathered outside the Wesleyan church. It too had taken a direct strike. Those who should have been worshipping and singing psalms this time on a Sunday morning were now salvaging furniture and books from their place of prayer.

A few minutes later Helen reached the corner of Roker Baths Road and stopped in her tracks. The Roker Park football stadium had been pummelled – and more than once by the looks of it. The car park, just twenty yards from the nearest turnstile, was wrecked, as was the old clubhouse.

Overhearing two old men in front of her, she learnt that the pitch was now a deep crater, but worst of all, a special constable who had been patrolling the area last night had been killed. He'd died just a few yards away from his home in Beatrice Street. Helen thought of the poor man's family. *Had they been the ones to find his body?*

Ten minutes later, Helen reached Thompson's to find it a hive of activity, and knew immediately that the yard had taken a hit.

'What's the damage?' She grabbed hold of one of the workers heading out of the yard.

'We've been lucky, Miss Crawford,' the man said. 'Just some minor damage over by the quayside.'

Heading over there, she bumped into Harold.

'*Denewood* took one. She's letting in water,' he said, puffing on his cigar.

'Will we lose her?' Helen said, her heart sinking. She knew the amounts of sweat and sheer hard graft that had gone into getting her down the ways.

One step forward and two steps back.

'We might be able to save her.' Harold sounded hopeful. 'The lads are on the case. They've got the pumps going. They should be able to keep her afloat long enough to get her patched up.'

Harold gestured over to the admin building and they both started walking.

'I think Jerry's managed to mark just about every district in the borough,' he said. 'They reckon about seventy dead and well over a thousand injured. And that's a conservative estimate.'

'Right, well, let's make sure we're up and running for start of shift tomorrow,' Helen said, reaching the main entrance to the admin building and pulling open the door.

It was the only way she knew how to fight back.

Chapter Sixty-One

It was twelve o'clock.

Half an hour before opening.

Pearl had managed to get herself cleaned up. She didn't look too bad, all things considered. Although behind the veneer of relative normality, her head was pounding, her mouth felt like cotton wool and she was filled with the familiar feeling of self-loathing that went hand in hand with the downer that inevitably followed a bender.

Pearl hurried across the road, thankful her journey to work took all of thirty seconds.

Looking up and down Tatham Street, you wouldn't have guessed that the town had been so badly bombed last night. Their street had escaped unharmed. Thank God.

Pearl banged on the pub door.

This was the first air raid she couldn't really remember. She could just about recall being half carried into the cellar by a blaspheming Ronald, but that was about it.

She'd heard Beryl's big gob going this morning as she'd been having a quiet fag in the backyard. She'd been yakking to one of her bairns, saying that Fenwick's Brewery in Low Row had been bombed; two Fire Guards had dodged death by the skin of their teeth when part of the building had collapsed; and that the nearby waste pipes had burst and there'd been sewerage everywhere. Pearl had almost gagged and ended up chucking her half-smoked cigarette and going back into the house, out of earshot.

Pearl banged on the door to the Tatham Arms again. Louder this time.

'Where's the bugger?' she mumbled.

She walked along the pavement, stood on her tiptoes, put her hands to the taped-up windowpane and looked into the bar. 'Place's dead as a bloody doornail.'

Turning around, she saw Geraldine crossing the road.

'Didn't think I'd see you here today?' She looked Pearl up and down.

'Aye, well, yer thought wrong, didn't yer?' Pearl snorted.

Geraldine reached the pub and tried the front door.

Pearl tutted loudly.

'I *have* tried the door, yer knar? I'm not just poking my nose through the bloody windows for the fun of it.'

Geraldine glowered at Pearl. She didn't know if she preferred her drunk or sober.

'Well, if he's not here, he's not here,' Geraldine said.

'Bill's always here,' Pearl snapped.

'He's probably sleeping it off at the Welcome.'

'What do yer mean? He didn't gan there last night, did he?' Pearl was taken aback.

'He said there was a lock-in,' Geraldine said.

'But he never gans to lock-ins. Not other people's anyway.'

Geraldine shrugged her shoulders.

'Well, if you see him,' she said, turning to cross the road, 'tell him just to shout if he wants me to do a shift.'

Pearl watched as the cocky young barmaid hurried back across the road and disappeared round the corner.

'*Ma!*'

Pearl shifted her vision to see Bel standing in the doorway of their home, her eyes squinting against the midday sun. Her face looked puzzled. She too was clearly wondering why Bill hadn't opened up.

'I dinnit knar where he is,' Pearl shouted out as she crossed the road. 'He always opens up,' she said as she reached Bel. 'That Geraldine girl says he went to the Welcome for a lock-in last night.'

Bel's face fell immediately.

'What's wrong?' Pearl demanded.

'Joe's just come back for a cuppa and he says it's bad down there.'

'What do yer mean, *it's bad down there*?'

'He said that he bumped into Martha and she told him Barrack Street was hit – badly. Two heavy bombs . . . Five houses and two pubs demolished.'

Bel motioned for her ma to come into the house. She was met with a vehement shake of the head.

'He didn't say which pubs, though,' Bel said.

'There's only two on that street. How many dead?' Pearl demanded.

'Four,' Bel said. 'And quite a few badly injured.'

Pearl turned on her heel.

'Ma, where're you going?'

'Where do you think?' Pearl was angry. Angry because she knew that if she hadn't got so hammered last night, Bill wouldn't have felt the need to go to some lock-in.

Pearl half walked, half jogged down Tatham Street. A few moments later she heard someone running up behind her.

Looking round, she saw it was Bel, juggling two gas masks and her handbag.

'Yer dinnit have to come with me, Isabelle. I'm auld 'n ugly enough to look after myself, yer knar.'

'I know you are, Ma,' Bel said, linking arms. 'I know you are.'

*

When Pearl and Bel arrived at what had once been Barrack Street they stopped in their tracks. It had been bad enough seeing the damage caused by last night's raid as they had walked the mile here – but this was catastrophic. Even worse than the Tatham Street bombing. Not only had five houses been razed to the ground, there were others that weren't far off and the two pubs were now just rubble.

Bel looked at her ma. Her heart went out to her. If Bill had been in the Welcome Tavern when the bombs landed, he would be lucky if he was amongst the injured.

'There!' Bel pointed.

'Where?' Pearl's voice rose.

'Sorry, Ma.' Bel realised her ma had thought she had spotted Bill. 'Follow me,' she said, 'there's a warden with a clipboard, which says to me that he knows what's what.'

Pearl followed, the pair clambering over plaster and bricks to get to the old man wearing a young man's uniform.

'Excuse me,' Bel said in her politest voice. 'We're trying to find a friend who was here last night.'

The old man turned to face them. He looked at Bel and then at Pearl.

'Yer not gonna find yer answer by gawping at us, are yer?' Pearl's voice was practically a growl.

Bel took her ma's arm and squeezed it.

'Sorry, we're just a bit worried,' she said.

'Aye, like half the town,' the old man said, giving Pearl a look like the summons. 'Name?'

'Hardwick,' Pearl said.

'Ma, he means Bill's name.' Bel saw the ravages of last night's binge on her mother's face.

'Lawson,' Pearl said. 'William David Lawson.'

Bel looked at her ma. She was surprised she knew his full name.

They both watched in silence as the old soldier put on his glasses and went through his list one by one. Pearl had to stop herself from snatching the clipboard off him. Instead, she held her breath.

'Here he is,' the Home Guard said, looking up and taking off his glasses.

'Is he dead?' Pearl spat the words out.

Mother and daughter seemed to be staring at the old man for ever before he opened his mouth.

'No,' he said. 'Your William David Lawson is still with us. Or at least he was when he left here.' He looked at the two women. The gobby one looked a pale shade of grey.

'But,' he added, 'he has been injured. I don't know how badly. All I've got down here,' he put on the glasses again, 'is that he's been taken to the Monkwearmouth Hospital.' He looked up at the two women. 'Which I'm sure you know is on the Newcastle Road.'

'Thank you, thank you so much.' Bel would have liked to have hugged the man, but he had already turned and was talking to another couple who looked as worried as they did.

'Bloody hell, Bill.' Pearl was grappling around in her handbag for her fags. 'Yer've just knocked ten years off my life.' She laughed as she sparked up her fag. 'Which, I'm sure yer'll agree, I can ill afford.'

Bel looked at her ma muttering to herself. Her relief was clear to see.

'Right then,' Pearl said, smoke swirling out of her mouth. 'Fancy a trip over the river?'

At one o'clock Helen and Harold had drawn up their battle lines.

'Right, I think our work here is done,' Harold said, scraping back his chair. 'See you tomorrow.'

As soon as Harold had left, Helen checked herself in the mirror before grabbing her handbag and gas mask and hurrying out of her office.

Ten minutes later she was walking along Dame Dorothy Street. Seeing a bus heading into town, she hailed it as if it were a taxi. Normally it probably wouldn't have pulled over as Helen was not waiting at a bus stop, but today was not a normal day.

'No charge today, miss,' the bus driver said.

Helen smiled her thanks and sat down on one of the front seats. There were only a few other passengers on the bus.

Ten minutes later, having picked up a few other stragglers who looked as though they had been up most of the night, the bus pulled into the main depot at Park Lane.

As soon as she got off, she saw that the once beautiful King's Theatre in Crowtree Road had been badly damaged by a load of incendiary bombs.

She thought of Theo.

They had met there on the afternoon he had told her he was ending their relationship.

Then John.

He had taken her there to see a movie she had wanted to see with Theo. They'd had a lovely evening. So much better than any she'd ever had with Theo.

It was another instance of how John brought light and laughter into her life. How the dark memories left by Theo had been replaced by happy new times she'd enjoyed with John.

Walking over to the stop for the Ryhope bus, she suddenly had a change of mind.

She was taking control of her life.
Taking hold of the reins.
She would drive herself.

*

Pearl and Bel were both thankful that the buses and trams had started running again, as neither had fancied walking the mile and a half over to Monkwearmouth Hospital.

'They reckon the death count's up to seventy-five,' the bus driver said over his shoulder, but keeping his eyes on the road.

Pearl felt that for once, fate had looked favourably on her. Thank God Bill was not one of the bodies lying in either of the makeshift mortuaries that had been set up to deal with the dead.

How badly injured he might be was a different matter, but he was alive. That was the main thing.

As they crossed over the Wear they saw a blanket of oil burning on the river, presumably from a damaged oil tank. It looked dangerously near the wooden gates to one of the main docks.

A few minutes later, the bus slowed down and stopped.

The driver had a short conversation with the Home Guard soldier.

Pearl and Bel could see the road ahead was in the process of being cordoned off.

'Sorry, folks,' the driver said, standing and hitching up his trousers. 'There's an unexploded bomb about two hundred yards up the road.' He took off his peaked cap and wiped his sweaty forehead with a large handkerchief.

'I'm afraid we've reached the end of the road,' he said, a resigned smile on his chubby round face.

There was a mumbling of discontent as everyone trooped off the bus.

Pearl and Bel looked at the crowd that was forming further up the street.

'Get yerself home, pet.' Pearl looked at Bel.

'You're joking, aren't you? I've come this far. You're not getting shot of me now.'

Bel took her mother's arm.

'Anyway, I know a little short cut.'

Walking out of the main bus depot, along Cowan Terrace and then along the main stretch of Ryhope Road, Helen saw yet more devastation caused by last night's raid.

Many of the buildings, which had been there for as long as she could remember, were now shadows of their former glory. Some were merely skeleton structures, others defaced, their innards on show to the public; a few had been obliterated, transformed in the blink of an eye into ugly, oversized scrap heaps of dust and debris.

Seeing it all made Helen realise just how fragile life was. How nothing was permanent. It made her think of those who had lost not only their homes and everything in them, but their loved ones.

She thought of John.

Entering the long stretch of road known as The Cedars, Helen immediately felt the cool in the air created by the natural canopy of large, overhanging trees; the cool changing to a chill as she turned into Glen Path and looked across at the walled-off Backhouse Park. She thought of Pearl and how she must have taken this route the night she had gone looking for work, knocking on the large oak doors of these grand houses with their sweeping drives and metal gates.

As she walked up the gravelled driveway to her grandfather's house, it was as though she was going there for the first time – knowing what had happened there made her see it with new eyes. Again she thought of Pearl, a fifteen-year-old girl who had just given her baby up for adoption, standing outside this very house. How she might have escaped the horror in store for her had her grandmother not answered the door. Had she not resembled the Little Match Girl.

Bizarre. The more she got to hear about her family, the more she felt as though she had only skimmed the surface. And that, like her mother had said to her, there was an excess of skeletons in the Havelock cupboards.

She rang the bell.

Within seconds, the door opened.

'Miss Crawford, how lovely to see you. Please, do come in.' Mr Havelock's manservant opened the door wide and gave Helen a genuine smile.

'Hi, Eddy, is Grandfather about?'

'I'm afraid he's having his afternoon lie-down, a bit earlier than normal due to the interruptions last night.'

Helen looked at Eddy. He was doing well for his age. Immaculately turned out, back ramrod straight. Thick grey Brylcreemed hair. His memory was also still evidently sharp as a pin.

'That's fine. Don't disturb him on my account,' Helen said, relieved that she would not have to see him. After what she had found out yesterday, she didn't feel she could look at the man, let alone speak to him.

'I've just come to borrow the car actually,' Helen said. She had been glad to see it parked in the driveway, although she'd guessed her grandfather wouldn't be going anywhere today.

'Ah, Miss Crawford.'

Helen jumped. *Why was it that Agatha always seemed to appear out of nowhere?*

'Did I hear that you wanted the use of Mr Havelock's car?'

'You did indeed, Agatha.'

'Well, I'm afraid Thomas is out helping with the clear-up. Alexandra Park's been badly hit.'

Helen walked over to the tallboy.

'That's all right, Agatha,' Helen said, seeing what she was looking for. 'I can drive myself.'

'Good afternoon,' Bel said to the receptionist at the hospital, who, judging by the dark circles under her eyes, had been up all night.

'Can I help?' the young girl asked.

'Are you all right?' Bel said. 'You look shattered.'

'Of course she's all reet,' Pearl said, nudging her daughter out the way. 'She's still breathing, isn't she?'

Pearl saw the look of disdain on Bel's face.

She looked back at the receptionist.

'Sorry, hinny, you go and get yerself a rest. But before yer dee, can yer tell us where a William David Lawson is?'

Bel glared at her mother.

'*Please*,' Pearl added.

The young girl smiled at Bel and looked down at an open ledger on her desk. She turned back the page and scrutinised a list of names.

'I'm afraid he's gone,' she said.

Pearl staggered back a little.

'He's dead?'

The young girl looked up and shook her head.

'No, no, I'm so sorry. He's not *gone* gone. He's just gone from here. They've had to ship a load of patients over to the Royal and out to the asylum.'

'Eee,' Pearl said, clasping her chest, 'yer nearly had *me* a goner there.'

The receptionist looked up at the two women. 'They're worried about an unexploded bomb. Your friend,' she said, looking back down at her ledger, 'has been taken to the asylum.' She looked back up. 'Which is probably a

411

good sign as the more seriously injured went straight to the Royal.'

Pearl let out a slightly deranged laugh.

'Trust Bill to gan 'n get himself put in the local loony bin.' She smacked her lips 'Probably end up staying there.'

'Come on, Ma,' Bel said, 'I think you need to sit down.' She looked back at the receptionist and mouthed, 'Thank you.'

Pearl allowed herself to be guided over to one of the chairs lined up along the wall of the foyer. She practically fell into it.

Bel looked at her ma. 'Looks like we're having ourselves a right day out.'

'Yer telling me,' Pearl huffed.

'I haven't been to Ryhope for ages,' Bel said.

Pearl patted her daughter's hand.

'Nah, me neither.'

Driving the Jaguar along the stretch of road that ran parallel to the North Sea, Helen felt a welling-up of nerves and excitement.

She looked up at the sky. It was bright and cheery. It mirrored her own lightness of being, her excitement about seeing John, and the thrill of driving herself for the first time since she'd had her lessons. Her mind danced around as she tried to keep her focus on changing gears and not going too fast.

Thank goodness she had come to her senses before it was too late.

She wound down the window and smelled the sea air.

She'd craved love – and all along it had been there. Waiting for her to see sense.

Standing right in front of her.

Well, the blinkers had been removed. Her vision was now twenty-twenty.

John was the one for her.

And she was the one for him.

Chapter Sixty-Two

Helen's heart began to thump in her chest as she reached the turn-off for the village.

Driving into the hospital grounds, she had to take some deep breaths.

Thinking about what she was going to do and actually *doing* it, she now realised, were two very different things. But she couldn't – wouldn't – back out.

As she pulled up and parked the Jaguar, heads turned. Those who continued to stare did a double-take on seeing it was a woman who was in sole charge of such a magnificent car.

Seeing the looks of appreciation as she walked up the main entrance to the Ryhope Emergency Hospital, Helen felt a surge of confidence. It was just the boost she needed.

As she trotted up the steps and walked into the main foyer, she was glad to see Denise sitting behind the reception desk.

'Miss Crawford, how are you today?'

Helen smiled.

'I'm fine, thank you, Denise.'

She looked around.

'I thought you'd be run off your feet today after last night's raid.'

'Ah, it was the asylum's turn last night. We're full to bursting, so "next door" has had to take in the poor souls that were hurt.'

'Ah.' Helen paused. She suddenly felt a little awkward. She didn't normally turn up unannounced. Especially during the day looking so done up. Even if her make-up and dress were subtle.

'I was hoping to catch Dr Parker.'

Now it was Denise's turn to hesitate.

'Oh, yes, of course . . . Let me just call the ward and see if he's there.'

Helen turned and looked about. The hospital was busy, but it wasn't frantic. Helen thought about the first time she had been here, looking for Theodore and instead finding John. She'd needed his help and he'd been there for her. And he'd been there for her ever since – through the bad and the good.

'Miss Crawford.'

Helen spun round.

'Yes, Denise, sorry, miles away.'

'Dr Parker is over at the asylum.'

'Oh, I suppose that makes sense,' Helen said, suddenly feeling the nerves. 'I'm guessing it'll be all hands on deck over there.'

'Mmm,' Denise said. 'They've had a few to take in, but not too many. I don't think it's terribly bad over there.'

Helen took a deep breath and straightened her dress.

'Good,' she said, smiling at Denise, 'hopefully that will mean I can borrow him for a while.'

Denise smiled back. Helen seemed a little different today. More stunning than normal. She thought she might struggle to 'borrow' the lovely Dr Parker, though.

By all accounts he'd had a busy night.

Helen got back in the car and turned over the engine. She still had to concentrate on what she had to do. Left foot down on the clutch, rev the engine, find the 'bite' and then slowly accelerate. She was pleased she hadn't managed to do her usual bunny hop, especially as there were people watching.

Driving out of the hospital grounds at a sedate pace, she squinted as she turned into bright sunlight and along the stretch of Waterworks Road. She briefly looked to her right to catch a glimpse of the rather magnificent Ryhope Pumping Station. It only took another few minutes before she had arrived outside the Sunderland County Borough Lunatic Asylum.

The asylum had been built forty-six years before the Ryhope Emergency Hospital, which had only come into being to cope with the huge numbers of injured soldiers after Dunkirk. The Ryhope might have been the younger and more modern of the two hospitals, but it was the ageing dame that caught your eye. She was beautiful, if a little foreboding, with her Gothic architecture. The architect George Hine had done an impressive job, as had those who had chosen the location. The surrounding countryside was picture-perfect, lush and green with views across to the North Sea.

Helen spotted a few military trucks and an ambulance as she parked. Denise had been right; it didn't look swamped with casualties from the air raid. If anything, it seemed relatively calm.

After quickly checking herself in the mirror, she got out of the car and walked over to the main entrance. She noticed her grandfather's name engraved on a brass plaque to the left of the door – he must have donated a substantial amount to this hospital, as well as to the Royal.

What was it about her grandfather and hospitals?

Thinking about her grandfather made Helen think of Bel and Pearl, and how she had yet to tell John the news.

Stepping over the threshold, Helen felt as though she was walking into a different world. It was imposing, but also surprisingly peaceful; almost serene.

'Good afternoon,' Helen said, walking over to the receptionist. The old woman appeared very stern and officious, but that changed when she smiled.

'Hello, my dear, how can I help you?' Her tone was welcoming and sincere.

'I'm looking for someone,' Helen said, suddenly overwhelmed by the high ceiling and slightly hushed atmosphere.

'Are you visiting?' the elderly receptionist asked.

'Sort of,' Helen said. 'Actually, I'm looking for a doctor. A friend of mine. He doesn't work here. He works over at the Ryhope.' Helen looked around on hearing the front door open. A nurse was coming through the main entrance, pushing a young girl in a wheelchair.

'And his name is?' the old woman asked, looking at Helen with curiosity. She thought she recognised her.

'Dr Parker,' Helen said, bringing her attention back to the receptionist. 'His name's Dr John Parker.'

'Ah, the surgeon,' the receptionist said. 'Tall, blond. Specialises in prosthetics?'

'That's the one,' Helen said, feeling another surge of nerves.

'I think you might find him over in the West Wing. I can get someone to fetch him for you, if you want?'

'No, honestly, there's no need,' Helen said. 'I want to surprise him.'

The receptionist hesitated.

'And you're a friend?'

Helen nodded.

'As you wish. But I have to warn you, it's easy to get lost here. If you keep following the signs to the West Wing,

417

you'll find your way. Once you're there, go to Lodge Cottage and ask for him at the desk.' Another slight hesitation. 'It's quite a walk. Are you sure I can't get one of the porters to fetch him for you?'

'No, honestly, I'll manage,' Helen smiled. 'Thank you for your help.'

The receptionist watched Helen walk down the main corridor, her heels clacking along the polished tiled flooring.

Getting off the train at Ryhope railway station, Pearl had spotted a couple of Home Guard soldiers climbing into a military truck and asked them if they'd drop them at the asylum. They'd agreed as it was only a quarter of a mile out of their way.

'Ta, lads,' Pearl said, climbing out of the truck. 'If yer ever in the east end, pop yer head into the Tatham and I'll buy yer both a drink.'

Bel looked at her ma in surprise. She didn't think she'd ever heard her offer to buy anyone a drink.

'Aye, we might take yer up on that,' the younger one said, smiling at Bel.

'As long as yer knar that's all yer'll be getting. This one's married.' She grabbed Bel's left hand and held it up as evidence. 'And her bloke's a war hero, so don't be getting any funny ideas.'

Now this really did surprise Bel. She had never heard her ma say anything remotely nice about Joe. Never mind boast of his bravery.

The younger man's face fell.

The older man chuckled. 'And good luck with *your* fella. Hope he got out in one piece.'

Bel looked at her ma, waiting for her to put the man right and tell him that Bill was not her 'fella'.

But she didn't.

They both walked towards the main entrance, craning their necks and looking up at the towering entrance.

'This place doesn't half give me the willies,' Pearl said.

Bel was inclined to agree – it felt overbearing and a little scary.

'Bloody hell.' Pearl spat the words out.

Bel looked at her ma. She was staring at a brass plaque.

'"Mr Charles Havelock, philanthropist and entrepreneur",' Pearl read. 'I could think of another name to add to that.'

As she started down what was to be the first of many corridors, Helen felt the return of nerves.

Nerves of excitement as well as apprehension.

Her plan to go for a walk with John around the grounds at Ryhope had now been scuppered, but she was sure they could walk around the grounds here.

She went over what she would do. She had decided actions would speak louder than words. A kiss would show him exactly how she felt.

Afterwards, she would tell him how she had always loved him, but that she had been too blind and stupid to realise it. That when she was pregnant she had only loved one being and that was the baby growing in her belly. Then when she had miscarried, there had only been sorrow in her heart. There had been no room for love.

But she had recovered and realised just how well they got on, how much they loved being in each other's company, and how they knew each other inside out. 'Warts and all', as he himself had said.

Helen stopped to check her bearings.

She'd passed a number of wards, a chapel and a large recreation hall, but she'd not seen any signs to the West Wing. *Honestly, the place was like a maze.*

As she walked towards a T-junction of corridors, she spotted a large map of the asylum mounted under glass on a wooden plinth. Going over to it, she studied the layout of the hospital. There was a farm and bakehouse, which she presumed provided food for the patients, an admissions hospital, convalescent villas and a nurses' home that appeared to be a part of the West Wing. The asylum certainly had everything it needed to be self-sufficient. It was like a castle minus a moat.

Continuing to walk, it took her another few minutes before she came to a sign for the West Wing. *At last.*

Walking through a set of double doors, she felt the sun on her face. *What a lovely place.*

It was like a small hamlet. A hundred yards away, she could see what looked like a little row of terraced cottages and further in the distance she saw a larger building that she knew from the map was the Isolation Hospital. John must be working there. Everywhere else looked like staff accommodation.

She started along the little pathway towards what looked like the lodge the receptionist had told her to report to.

As she did so, her attention was caught by a nurse coming out of one of the terraces. She was hurrying. Helen guessed she was late for her shift.

She continued walking, but seconds later she heard another door open.

She looked over at the row of cottages, expecting to see another nurse hurrying off to work, but on seeing the young woman coming out of the front door she stopped in her tracks.

Was that . . . ?

Yes, it definitely looked like her.

Helen continued staring.

It was.

It was Dr Eris.

She put her hand up to wave, but Dr Eris turned round. She was sure she had seen her, but she hadn't waved back.

Helen looked as someone else appeared through the front door.

Was it?

No.

Please, no!

But it *was* who she thought it was.

How could she be wrong? She knew him inside and out. *Or thought she did.*

Feeling sick to the pit of her stomach, Helen watched as Claire wrapped her arms around John's neck and pulled him close.

Unable to move a muscle, Helen watched them kiss.

When she finally came to her senses, she quickly turned and walked away – back, as quickly as she could, from where she'd come.

Chapter Sixty-Three

'Mr William David Lawson,' the receptionist repeated as she looked down her list of new patients.

'He was injured in last night's air raid,' Bel explained.

'Oh, I see,' the receptionist said, turning over a page and looking at another list.

'Here we are,' she said. 'Yes, your Mr Lawson is under our care for the day – and probably the night too.'

She stood up and pointed to the far corridor.

'If you go down that corridor, take the first left, then a right and just keep on walking. You'll find him in our new admissions ward, the Willows.'

'Thank you,' Bel said, smiling.

Pearl forced a smile but didn't speak as her daughter had told her to keep it zipped.

Helen staggered back along the corridors she had just walked down minutes earlier.

Had she not learnt anything?

Was she as delusional as the people in here?

Her love for John might not have been an illusion – but the love she'd thought he had for her clearly had been.

Her mother had been right. She was soiled goods. Sullied. No man like John would want to be serious with a woman like herself. Someone who had given her body to another man. Someone who had carried another man's baby.

Tears started to fall down Helen's face. Tears of anger. Resentment.

She thought she had moved on, grown older and wiser. But she hadn't.

She was exactly where she was before.

She must have been completely blind not to have seen it the other day in the cafeteria when she had learnt that Dr Eris was a woman. An educated, middle-class, *attractive* woman.

John had been spending time with her. He worked with her. Was often here at the asylum when she called.

She should have thought back to their past conversations and how John had gone on about Dr Eris and how brilliant she was – and what progress young Jacob had made because of her.

Of course John would want someone like Claire.

She was perfect.

Any fool could see that.

'Oh my goodness,' Bel said.

'Bloody hell,' said Pearl.

They both looked as Helen walked towards them. Or rather, staggered, occasionally touching the wall to steady herself.

And then Bel saw Helen's face.

The tears.

'Helen!' Bel hurried over to her. 'What's happened? What's the matter?'

Pearl stayed one step behind.

'Are you all right?' Bel took hold of her arm.

Helen stopped in her tracks and stared. It took her a while to focus on Bel.

'It's John,' she blurted out.

'Oh God, is he all right? Has he been hurt?' Bel asked.

'Committed?' Pearl mumbled under her breath. Bel heard and threw her ma a death stare.

423

'No, no, he's fine,' Helen said, trying to pull herself together. She wiped her eyes and straightened her back.

'*He's fine,*' she repeated. Now there was bitterness. 'Hunky-bloody-dory.'

Pearl nudged Bel.

'I'll gan 'n find Bill myself,' she said, rolling her eyes towards Helen. 'You sort this one out. I'll meet yer out the front when I'm done. Give us a little while, though, eh? I need to have a bit of a chat with him.'

Bel nodded.

Pearl turned to Helen. 'If it's about some bloke, pet, I'd say dinnit waste yer energy. They're not worth the hassle.'

Bel looked at her ma as she hurried off. She shook her head in disbelief. The irony that they had just spent the last few hours frantically trying to locate Bill seemed completely lost on her ma.

'You all right?' Bel asked Helen as they continued to walk along the corridor and into the main foyer.

'Not really,' Helen said, trying to force a smile.

'Do you want to chat about it?' Bel eyed Helen.

She nodded.

Took a deep breath.

Then laughed through the tears.

'What are aunties for, eh?'

The two young women looked at each other and both laughed loudly as they made their way out of the asylum and into the bright afternoon sun.

Chapter Sixty-Four

'Twice in the space of twenty-four bloody hours . . . like a bad bloody penny,' Pearl muttered to herself as she walked down the corridor.

'Not even a mention of a bleedin' Havelock in decades. Now they're every soddin' where I turn.'

Pearl took a right.

Even turning up in the local nuthouse – acting like one of the inmates.

Confused, she stopped in her tracks.

'Did the auld cow at reception say right or left?' Pearl spoke aloud to the empty corridor.

She stood, dithered for a moment, then turned left.

Ever since she'd told Isabelle the truth about who her father really was, there'd been a steady drip, drip, drip of Havelocks in her life – as though Bel's awareness had dragged the bastard back from the past and into the present. She'd spent her whole adult life successfully avoiding Charles and all the heinous memories that went with him, and now – like a bad rash – they had come back with a vengeance.

Pearl stopped again then turned right.

Isabelle had got herself a job at Thompson's and the drips had become a drizzle. A job Pearl was sure she'd applied for through curiosity about her 'other family' – at least that's what she *hoped* was the reason.

She prayed to God that Isabelle wasn't secretly after retribution.

If she was, she'd be swimming in shark-infested waters. You didn't go up against men like Charles. A man with too much money, too much power and no conscience to speak of. A dangerous combination.

Pearl reached the end of another corridor and stopped again.

She had a horrible feeling she was lost.

She took another right turn.

And now Charles's granddaughter seemed to be everywhere.

The drizzle had turned into a downpour.

Helen had ingratiated herself with the Elliot clan – as well as with Gloria and the bairn. She'd organised and paid for Pol's wedding flowers, and Isabelle's night classes. And she'd got her grandfather to pay for Arthur's funeral and Pol's posh doctor.

But worst of all, Helen had found out that Isabelle was blood.

Pearl stopped again and had a breather.

She was now officially lost.

This place was like a rabbit warren.

Hearing a voice further down, she decided to go and ask where on earth she was. Once she was pointed in the right direction, she would finally see Bill. Have her chat with him and get the hell out of there. This place was beginning to give her the creeps.

She started walking.

The voice became louder, clearer.

It was the voice of an elderly, well-spoken woman.

Her voice had a slightly melodic quality to it.

And was also familiar.

Pearl reached the room from where the voice was coming.

The door had been left wide open.

She knocked.

'Excuse me,' she said, looking into the room. The decor immediately took her breath away. The room was large, plush and filled with antiques. Beautiful. Almost majestic.

Not remotely like a hospital.

She took one step over the threshold and instantly felt as though she had taken a step back in time.

Her eyes fell on an ornate red-lacquered Chinese cabinet. *It looked so familiar . . .*

She looked at the woman who was sitting with her back to her, chatting away as though there was someone right opposite her. The woman was talking to her reflection in the mirror.

Despite her advancing years, the woman was wearing a huge crimson and purple skirt and tightly fitted bodice.

Those clothes.

Piled chaotically high, dyed a rich reddish brown, diamanté hairpins sticking out at random.

That hair.

'Sorry to bother yer,' Pearl said, her eyes fixed on the woman.

She looked so petite.

Pearl waited for her to turn around. It didn't take long – a few heartbeats – before the woman became aware of Pearl's presence in the mirror.

And when she did, her eyes scrutinised her, then widened.

Then the penny dropped for both of them.

The woman spun round.

Her small hands went to her heart-shaped face, covered in garish make-up – a thick layer of powder, rouged cheeks, generously applied cherry lipstick, and a dab of cobalt blue on her eyelids.

Just like a Russian doll, Pearl thought.

She was transported back to the distant past.

A past she had tried her whole life to escape.

'Oh my! What a surprise!' the woman said, a smile spreading across her face.

She stood up and walked over to Pearl.

'Den Lille Pige med Svovlstikkerne!'

Pearl was fifteen years old again – in her own mind, as well as in the mind of the woman now opening her arms in an embrace.

'It's my Little Match Girl!'

Welcome to

Penny Street

where your favourite authors and stories live.

Meet casts of characters you'll never forget,
create memories you'll treasure forever,
and discover places that will stay with
you long after the last page.

Turn the page to step into the home of

Nancy Revell

and discover more about

The Shipyard Girls...

Dear Reader,

So much of life, I believe, is about overcoming adversity. When I was a journalist, many of the stories I used to report on were known as TOT – Triumph Over Tragedy. They were always my favourite stories – the ones I really enjoyed writing, because I felt they gave hope to others who might be going through similar hardships.

My Shipyard Girls are such a diverse mix of women, but they all have something in common – they are all fighting their own battles, dealing with their own worries, and coping with their own difficulties. Just like most of us are today.

My belief is that triumph is in the trying.

And so, dear reader, I hope, if you are facing tough times yourself that you find the strength to keep trying. And to *keep on* trying.

With Love,

Nancy x

HISTORICAL NOTES

Local historian Meg Hartford came across this photograph of two real-life women welders who worked in the Sunderland shipyards. It was published in the *Sunderland Echo* during the Second World War with the caption: 'It was not only unskilled work the women undertook during the war. Here two women get to grips with a heavy metal welding job in a Sunderland shipyard.'

Image credit: *Sunderland Echo*

Turn the page for a sneak
peek into my new novel

A Christmas Wish for
the Shipyard Girls

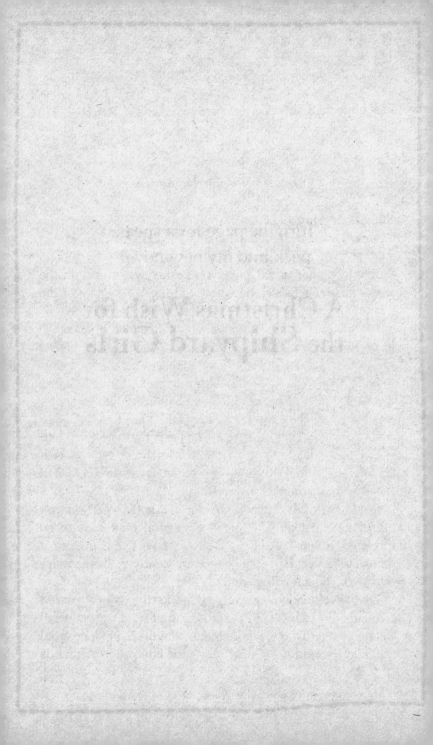

Prologue

Borough of Sunderland Lunatic Asylum

Sunday 16 May 1943
1.30pm

'Sorry to bother you, Claire.' Dr Parker was stood on the doorstep of Dr Eris' little cottage in the West Wing of the Borough of Sunderland Lunatic Asylum.

'Not at all, John. Come in. Come in.' Dr Eris opened the door wide. 'Seems like two minutes ago we were saying good night to each other.'

Dr Parker let out a bark of laughter and followed Dr Eris down the hallway. 'It does indeed. Although the intervening time has been somewhat eventful.'

'Very true. They're saying it's been the worst air raid yet.' Dr Eris lead the way into the kitchen. 'Sit yourself down. Let me make a quick cup of tea. It can be in place of the one you turned down last night.'

Dr Parker felt himself redden. 'I hope you weren't offended. I just didn't want the hospital grapevine to go into meltdown. I think the very fact we went out for a drink together had the effect of sending the gossip-mongers into a feeding frenzy.'

Dr Eris chuckled as she put the kettle on and placed two cups and saucers and a little jug of milk on the small kitchen table. 'That's the downside of working in a hospital that's in the middle of nowhere – the entertainment tends to be generated inhouse. You can't sneeze here without just about every member of staff and probably all the patients knowing about it too.'

Dr Eris poured boiling water into the tea pot and gave it a feisty stir. She had actually been the one to get the gossip going by casually dropping it into conversations with her colleagues that she and the eligible Dr Parker were going out for a drink and it was most definitely not for the purpose of talking shop. She'd also made a point of informing the receptionists at both the Ryhope and the asylum where she was going and with whom – *just in case there was an emergency, of course.*

'So, tell me, to what do I owe this pleasure?' Dr Eris put the pot on the table and sat down.

'I'm afraid I need to pick your brains about a patient who came in last night,' Dr Parker said.

Dr Eris tried to hide the disappointment; she'd hoped the visit was a social one.

'Tell me more,' she said.

'One old chap suffered a nasty bash on his head – fell over on his way to the shelter. He's quite elderly and a bit unsteady on his feet. He's been patched up, but he still seems very confused and I'm wondering whether or not his memory loss and lack of clarity are due to a possible concussion – or if it's dementia.

Dr Eris poured their tea and added milk.

'I can certainly take a look at him and give you my opinion,' she said, a smile playing on her lips.

Dr Parker narrowed his eyes. 'What is it you're *not* saying?'

Dr Eris crossed her legs and leant forward a little, her teacup in her hands. 'I was just thinking that – much as I'm sure you value my thoughts on the matter – it might be more enlightening if you got the office to track down his next of kin and find out if he seemed confused before the bombs dropped.'

'Dear me –' Dr Parker combed his hair back with his fingers '– I think it might be me with dementia. In fact, now that I'm thinking about it, I'm sure one of the nurses took a call from his son saying he'd be visiting later. I'll speak to him then. You must think I'm as thick as two short planks.'

'I think you're anything but, John. But I do think you've been working round the clock lately and are exhausted. You need a decent night's shut-eye. The effects of sleep deprivation, especially over the long-term, can mirror those of a dementia sufferer, you know?'

Dr Parker guffawed. 'Thanks for the reassurance.' He took a sip of his tea. 'So, tell me, how was last night for you?'

'At the pub or the air raid?' Dr Eris asked, deadpan.

Dr Parker laughed out loud. 'I meant the air raid, but I have to say that I personally had a thoroughly enjoyable evening at the Albion.'

Dr Eris smiled. 'Me too.'

As they drank their tea, the pair exchanged stories about the aftermath of the bombing. Dr Eris' time had been spent checking and medicating those inmates who had become distressed by the disruption, Dr Parker had spent until the early hours in the Isolation Hospital in the West Wing, which had been converted into a makeshift ward for the injured. All the staff had done their bit, and most had gone to bed when they'd normally be getting up.

Finishing off his tea, Dr Parker pushed back his chair and stood up.

'Well, I'd best get off.' He glanced at his watch. 'Rounds to do.' He looked at Dr Eris. 'And thank you for the belated tea.'

'You're more than welcome,' Dr Eris said, standing up and putting the teacups in the sink. 'And I'll take a look at your confused elderly gentlemen. You've got me curious.'

'Thank you,' Dr Parker said. As he made to go, he suddenly felt a little awkward. This would be the ideal opportunity to ask Claire out on another date. *So, why was he hesitating?*

'Let me see you out,' Claire said, turning and walking down the hallway.

As she opened the front door, she had to stop herself from slamming it shut again.

Helen was walking down the pathway to the Isolation Hospital.

Worse still, she'd spotted her, and was raising her arm to wave hello.

Dr Eris turned around to face Dr Parker.

'You know,' she said, 'it wasn't just the tea you passed up on last night.'

Dr Parker furrowed his brow in question as Dr Eris stepped forward, put her arms around his neck, and gently pulled him towards her.

Chapter One

Helen and Bel were sat on the wooden bench to the left of the entrance of the Borough of Sunderland Lunatic Asylum. The perfectly manicured lawns of the hospital grounds lay stretched out in front of them. Their faces turned heavenward and they basked momentarily in the solace of the afternoon sun. The beauty of their surroundings and balmy tranquility of this most idyllic of spring days was, however, in total antithesis of what had gone before.

Opening her eyes, Bel turned her head slightly. Helen still looked stunning despite the smudged mascara and slight puffiness around the eyes. 'Just because you saw him coming out of Dr Eris' accommodation, doesn't mean he spent the night there.'

Helen gave Bel a sideways glance. Within the space of a few days Bel had gone from being simply one of her staff to a family member. A blood relative. Her aunty. Her mother's sister. *Her grandfather's illegitimate daughter.*

'Oh, Bel, that's nice of you to say, but if you'd seen the way they kissed ...' Helen's voice trailed off.

'It mightn't have been what it looked like,' Bel argued. 'Dr Parker might have just popped in there for a cuppa. The kiss might have been chaste.' She glanced down at her watch. 'Anyway, it's late – a bit late for two people to be *getting up.*'

'This is *exactly* the time they would be getting up –' Helen felt the hurt in her heart as she spoke '– whenever there's an air raid, John – and all the rest of the doctors and nurses – work through the night, making sure any casualties are tended to, treated, operated on – ' She stared back up at the sun and closed her eyes. 'I feel such a fool.' She shook her head, annoyed at herself. 'To think that John would want me.'

Bel looked at Helen in surprise. 'I don't see why that would be such a foolish thing to think. I can't see any man *not* wanting you.'

'I don't mean *want* as in simply to desire.' Helen sighed heavily. 'I mean *want* as in want me as his sweetheart. His fiancée.' She turned her face away from the sun and looked at Bel. 'As the woman he wants to spend the rest of his life with.'

It was only then that Bel understood just how much Helen was not only in love with Dr Parker but how strong and deep her love for him was. This wasn't just about some other woman snaring the man she wanted for herself, but her losing the man she was desperate to be with – forever. And Bel knew better than most that love like that rarely came along twice. She had been one of the lucky ones.

'Well,' Bel said, looking back at Helen, 'I don't think you should give up until you know the whole story. All the facts. You don't know for certain he stayed over at her place. It might have looked like a kiss between two lovers, but that could have just been your imagination.'

'Mmm,' Helen mused. 'I'm not convinced.' She glanced at Bel and gave her a sad smile. 'But I think you're right in that I need to make sure I've got the correct end of the stick.' She sighed. Her mind fell back into the past traumatic twenty-four hours – the shocking bombshell about her grandfather, followed by the worst air raid to date. The pervasiveness of all the death and destruction meted out on the town had driven her determination to tell John that she loved him. That she didn't just want to be his friend, but his lover – his lifelong soulmate.

'Oh, there you are!'

Helen and Bel turned around simultaneously.

An attractive, smartly-dressed woman in a brown tailored skirt suit, with shiny, tawny-coloured hair twisted up into a French knot, was walking down the stone steps of the asylum. She had her eyes trained on Helen and a wide smile on her face.

'Oh, *no*,' Helen whispered under her breath.

Bel stared at the tall, slim woman now striding purposefully towards them. She reminded her a little of Katharine Hepburn. Amazing cheekbones, flawless skin with just a dusting of freckles.

Helen stood up and Bel followed suit.

'Helen, I'm so glad I caught you before you left.' She glanced at Bel and smiled before returning her attention to Helen. 'That *wa*s you I saw in the West Wing, wasn't it?'

Helen hesitated for a moment. She thought about denying it but realised there was no point.

'Yes, your eyes weren't playing tricks. That was indeed me,' Helen said, trying her hardest to sound upbeat, and hoping to God it wasn't obvious she'd been crying.

'Ah, that's good. Not going mad then.' Claire grimaced a little. 'I worry sometimes about making the crossover.' She cocked her head towards the Gothic red brick frontage of the asylum. 'They say it's never a good idea to live and work in a hospital of this kind. One might get confused. Doctor or patient? Patient or doctor?' She laughed lightly.

'I didn't see your friend with you though?' She looked at Bel.

'No, no, you didn't.' Helen didn't elaborate, but instead turned to Bel.

'Bel this is Claire – or rather *Dr Eris*.' Helen pulled her mouth into a mock grimace. 'That is, providing she doesn't "make the crossover".'

Dr Eris laughed and stretched her arm out. 'Pleased to meet you, Bel.'

Bel returned the handshake and gave a polite smile.

'I wonder,' Dr Eris said, focusing her attention back on Helen, 'if I could perhaps have a quick word with you?'

'Of course, fire away,' Helen said, showing the 'quick word' would have to be said in front of Bel.

Dr Eris hesitated before carrying on. 'I just wanted to say –' her eyes flicked to Bel before she fixed her gaze on Helen '– that, obviously, as you will have guessed, having seen John and I just now –'

Helen felt her heart race.

'– in a rather amorous embrace …'

No room for doubt now.

'– that as we are clearly more than colleagues, and because I know John and you are close friends, that just because we are "together" as such, well, that this doesn't mean you two can't continue to be friends.' Another smile. 'I'm not one of these women who demand their beaus aren't able to fraternize with any other person of the opposite sex.'

Helen continued to stand and listen. She had a feeling Dr Eris hadn't quite finished what she had come here to say. She was right.

'But you'll have to forgive him if he isn't able to see you as much as he has been.' Dr Eris gave a self-satisfied smile. 'You know what it's like at the start?' She didn't wait for an answer. 'You just want to be with each other every minute of every day, don't you?'

Helen laughed a little too loudly. 'I do indeed, Claire. I do indeed.' She looked into Dr Eris' hazel eyes. 'I guess the real teller is when you still want to be with each other every minute of every day once the shine's worn off.'

There was a moment's awkward silence.

'Anyway,' Dr Eris said, 'when I saw you back there, you seemed in rather a rush. Was there something you wanted? I'm guessing it was John you were looking for?' She forced a smile. 'I can't see any other reason you were here at the asylum?'

Helen gave an equally false smile. 'Yes, it was John I was after, but it's not important. It can wait.'

Dr Eris glanced down at her watch. 'Oh, my goodness, where does the time go?'

She looked directly at Bel.

'Well, lovely to meet you.' Dr Eris smiled.

Bel thought she had the most perfect teeth she'd ever seen.

'And,' Dr Eris turned to Helen, 'I'm glad we've managed to have this little chat. Anyway, best get a shimmy on. *Minds to mend* and all that.'

And with that Dr Eris turned and quickly walked back to the main entrance, hurried up the stone steps, and disappeared through the wooden swing doors.

Helen looked at Bel. 'Well, I guess that answers that question.'

Bel opened her mouth to offer words of reassurance, but none came out. If there had been any doubt that Helen might have misread the scene she'd happened upon, it had now been wiped clean away.

'I think that was called staking your claim,' Helen said.

Bel nodded but didn't say anything. She didn't know Helen well enough to offer her any words of comfort, not that she could think of any even if there were. Poor Helen, she looked bereft.

'Are you going to be all right?'

'Yes, of course,' Helen said as convincingly as possible. 'Best get back to work. *Denewood* took a battering last night.'

'Really?' Bel was shocked. She'd heard that Thompson's had been hit during last night's air raid but not any details.

'Badly?' Bel knew everyone would be gutted. The whole yard had worked flat out to get her down the ways on time.

'She was taking in water this morning, but they've managed to keep her afloat.' Helen straightened her shoulders. 'Honestly, here's me whining on about some bloke and the whole town's been bombed to smithereens.'

'That might be,' Bel said with a sad smile, 'but Dr Parker isn't just "some bloke" is he?'

'No,' Helen acquiesced, 'but he's going to have to be just "some bloke" from now on.'

They were quiet for a moment.

Helen looked at Bel and was again hit by the family resemblance: the same blonde hair, blue eyes, the same nose and lips.

'Gosh, you must think I'm so incredibly shallow. I haven't even mentioned the …' Helen stopped. '… the … God, I can't even think of a word to describe the abominable thing my grandfather did.' Helen's shoulders suddenly drooped. 'I'm so sorry Bel. I still don't know what to say. I don't think it's really sunk in, to be honest.'

'Don't worry about that now,' Bel said. 'A conversation for another time?'

'Yes, definitely,' Helen agreed.

'When everything's calmed down a little,' Bel suggested.

'Yes,' Helen said, 'yesterday and today have been quite tumultuous, to say the least.'

She looked over at the black Jaguar she'd borrowed from her grandfather. 'Are you sure I can't give you and your mother a lift home?'

'No, honestly, we'll be fine. Knowing my ma, she'll want the hair of the dog.' Bel rolled her eyes. 'She had a few too many last night. She mentioned nipping into the village after she'd seen Bill, which means an hour in the Railway Inn before we get on the train.'

Helen felt a sudden jolt of sadness. The Railway Inn had been her and John's favourite meeting place.

'Oh,' Helen let out a bitter laugh, 'tell her to have one for me.'

Bel's laughter was just as bitter.

'I will. Not that she'll need any encouragement.'

**WANT TO KNOW
WHAT HAPPENS NEXT?**

A Christmas Wish for the Shipyard Girls
Nancy Revell

PRE-ORDER YOUR COPY NOW

HAVE YOU READ

Join the Shipyard Girls